YE GODS!

Also by Tom Holt:

EXPECTING SOMEONE TALLER
WHO'S AFRAID OF BEOWULF?
FLYING DUTCH
GOAT SONG
THE WALLED ORCHARD

YE GODS!

Tom Holt

St. Martin's Press
New York

Library of Congress Cataloging-in-Publication Data

Holt, Tom.
Ye gods! / Tom Holt.
p.   cm.
"A Thomas Dunne book."
ISBN 0-312-08927-9
1. Mythology, Greek-Fiction.   2. Gods, Greek—Fiction.
I. Title.
PR6058.O474Y4   1993
823'.914—dc20   92-41803   CIP

First published in Great Britain by Orbit Books.

First U.S. Edition: April 1993
10 9 8 7 6 5 4 3 2 1

FOR KIM,
WHO, FOR ONCE,
LIKED ONE OF MY BOOKS

'Y ou mean God,' said the insurance man dubiously, 'singular.'

'That's not what the woman told me,' said the voice at the other end of the line. 'Gods, she said, plural. Quite definite about it. Even spelt it – G-O-D-S. Me, I just believe what I'm told. Anyway, does it make any difference?'

'Well ...' The insurance man hesitated. No reason why it should, in layman's terms, but when it comes to policies of insurance, one has to be careful. Insurance contracts, as any lawyer will tell you, are contracts of the utmost good faith, which probably explains the references to acts of God. God singular; not plural. If it was an act of gods, plural, would he need to send the claimant more than one claim form?

'You still there?' said the voice.

'Yes, still here,' said the insurance man, and he noticed that he had bitten halfway through the stem of his pencil. 'Could we just run this through one more time?'

The voice sighed. 'All right.'

'Your two pet rattlesnakes,' said the insurance man, 'somehow got out of their tank –'

'Which conforms,' emphasised the voice, 'to the strictest Ministry regulations. I've got receipts.'

'Yes, I'm sure. They somehow got out, anyway, crossed the main road, and crawled up the drainpipe of Number Seventeen, where they entered the bedroom of Mrs.

1

Derry's six-month-old baby. Who strangled them.'

'That's it, yes.'

'Mrs. Derry then told you about the incident, and claimed that it was an act of the gods.'

'Gods, yes.'

'I see.' The insurance man choked suddenly; he had swallowed the severed end of his pencil, rubber and all. 'Right, fine, well, I'll get a claim form off to you in tonight's post and we'll take it from there, shall we? Thank you so much.'

He put the phone down, and blinked about four times. Gods? Snakes? He hadn't heard such a load of old cod since the last lot of heavy storms ...

Inside his head, a sweet, extremely feminine but distinctly authoritative voice told him that he'd better believe it all the same.

The insurance man looked over his shoulder, but there was nobody there. He got up and opened the door; the next-door office was empty. In the end he even looked in the desk drawers and the waste-paper basket. Nothing. Inside his head the voice asked him what he thought he was doing. Then it giggled.

Two months later, Mrs. Derry's snake-fancying neighbour opened his post, looked at the cheque, whistled, and immediately phoned a pet shop to enquire about their special deal on anacondas.

In the back garden of his house, Mr. Derry was digging a very large hole. Every now and then he stopped and looked nervously over his shoulder. His wife stood by and said nothing.

'I mean,' said Mr. Derry, leaning on his spade and sighing, 'where did he *get* it from, that's what I want to know.'

Mrs. Derry mumbled something under her breath, and looked at the dead bear. Her best duvet cover concealed the upper parts, the massive head and enormous chest, but it wasn't big enough to reach down to the feet.

'And it's not,' said Mr. Derry, 'as if it's the first time.'

Mrs. Derry nodded uncomfortably. All over their small garden were the irregular shapes of small burial mounds; wolves, tigers, wild boar, and that very peculiar lizard thing. Soon there wouldn't be a single geranium left.

'Quite soon,' Mr. Derry said, wiping his forehead with a handkerchief, 'someone is going to notice something. Like, some zoo keeper somewhere is going to see all the empty cages.'

Mrs. Derry made a little whimpering noise. 'I've told him, Doug,' she said, 'I've said, it's naughty, don't do it. But he just doesn't listen. He's only three, for heaven's sake; he don't know right from wrong yet.'

'Don't give me that,' Mr. Derry replied. 'When I was his age I didn't go around thumping dangerous animals. If I so much as laid a finger on the cat, it was straight up to bed and no tea. Panthers ...'

Mrs. Derry bit her lip. Perhaps she should have told him right at the start, with the snakes. Or before that, even.

'Right,' said Mr. Derry, 'that should be deep enough. Now, you just get round that side and push.'

As he bent down, he became aware of something and stood up quickly. A small child was scampering happily down the path. In one hand it held a two-foot length of scaffolding pipe; in the other, the tip of the tail of an enormous crocodile.

'Oh for crying out loud,' said Mr. Derry. 'Not another one.' He looked around him wearily and sighed.

'Well,' he said, 'bang goes the rockery.'

It wasn't going terribly well, decided the games teacher.

Well, it never was the most brilliant of occasions; school sports days never were. But that was usually because all the contestants would far rather be at home watching the snooker, not because ...

He ducked. A javelin, travelling like a small cannon-shell, passed about an inch over his head, embedded itself in the pavilion door and quivered resentfully. At the other end of the field, a small seven-year-old was looking rather sheepish.

It had been the same, the games teacher remembered, with the discus and the shot-put. As for the egg-and-spoon race, that was best forgotten about. He passed his tongue across his dry lips and looked quickly at the programme. Four-hundred-and-forty-yard race. What could possibly go wrong with that?

The contestants were lined up, and the games teacher lifted his little flag.

'ON YOUR MARKS,' he said, 'GET SET, G . . .'

Something very fast started moving round the track. A few seconds later, it had completed four circuits and had wandered off into the bushes at the edge of the field, from which it emerged a little later trailing a large dead fox. Bigger than a fox, really, almost wolf-sized.

'Jason,' said the games teacher, 'put that down just a moment, would you?'

'Yes, sir.'

'Jason,' said the games teacher, 'do you know what . . . sportsmanship means?'

'Yes, sir.'

The games teacher swallowed hard. The boy was looking up at him with innocent, trusting eyes. Unfortunately, a large number of parents were also looking at him, and their body language was rather less appealing. He was going to have to ask the youngster to throw the next race.

'It means,' said the games teacher, 'sometimes letting somebody else win. Do you understand?'

'Yes, sir.'

'I know,' the games teacher went on, 'I know it's not really fair, but sometimes in this life, Jason, we have to cheat in order to be fair. Do you see what I'm . . .?'

'I know, sir,' said the boy. 'And I did try.'

The games teacher swallowed. 'What?'

'I keep trying, sir,' said the boy. 'But somehow ...' He looked down at his feet and blushed.

He was discovering that sometimes it isn't easy, being a Hero.

Mr. Derry parked the car, same as usual, got out and went to open the garage doors. He opened them. He stared.

After a few seconds, he rubbed his eyes. It was still there.

'That does it,' he said. 'It's got to stop.'

He closed the doors, pushing the tip of an outstretched trunk out of the way with his toe, and went into the house. There was a dead gorilla on the coatrack, so he put his anorak on the chair instead.

'Phyllis,' he called, 'there's a dead elephant in the garage. It's got to stop, do you hear me?'

The lounge door opened and a strange figure appeared in the doorway. Blue light burned around his shoulders, and his eyes burned deep scars on Mr. Derry's retinas. In his hand he held a slice of walnut cake.

'Doug,' said Mrs. Derry's voice from behind the apparition's shoulder, 'here's an old friend of mine I'd like you to meet.'

'Yes,' said Mr. Derry, 'I understand all that –' He closed his eyes, eased his brain carefully into first gear and opened them again. 'I think,' he went on. 'But why all the bears and wolves and tigers and ...?'

Outside, the garden was a blaze of colour, as the first marigolds turned their golden faces to the sun. In between them, the white tips of innumerable rib cages poked out through the earth.

'Well.'

The stranger took a deep breath. This wasn't going to be easy.

'You see, Mr. Derry,' he said. 'Douglas,' he added.

'Young Jason isn't like other boys his age.' Mr. Derry nodded vigorously. 'He has this sort of – well, you might say it's in the blood. You might say he – well, takes after his . . .'

Mr. Derry was about to protest, but then he remembered what he'd just heard. He wished, somehow, that he could feel angry about it, but that was apparently a luxury he wasn't to be allowed.

'You do a lot of that?' he asked. 'Clobbering wild beasts and so on?'

'No, no, not at all,' said the stranger, 'that's not what I'm trying to get at. It's more a sort of instinct, really, among Us.'

'You?'

'Us,' said the stranger, 'yes. Really, it's what we're here for.' He remembered something. '*Were* here for, that is. Were there for,' he experimented. 'Anyway, it's just a phase We all go through.'

'You mean he'll grow out of it?'

'Probably.'

'And how long will that take, do you think?'

The stranger wished he hadn't asked. Sure, all his other children *had* grown out of it, eventually, but it had taken rather a long time, if you were using a mortal timescale. And what with the erosion of the rain forests and the disappearance of natural habitats, it looked like the supply of large feral cats was going to run out long before young Jason had tired of braining them.

'Look at it another way,' said the stranger.

'Yes?'

Oh hell, thought the stranger, what's the point? You try being nice to them and where does it get you? 'Do you know who I am?' he said.

'Well,' Mr. Derry said, 'you told me just now you were Jason's real . . .'

'Yes,' said the stranger, 'but as well as that?'

'As well as that?' Mr. Derry said. 'No.'

The stranger told him. He didn't say anything; it would be impossible to communicate this particular piece of information verbally. Instead, he just relaxed his grip on his disguise very, very slightly.

Mr. Derry fell on his knees and started to bang his head on the carpet. He didn't know why; it just seemed the right thing to do. All around him, beams of blue and gold light leaped and sparkled. The air crackled with static electricity. In the kitchen, the silver plate started to peel off the canteen of cutlery that had belonged to Mr. Derry's grandmother's cousin. Just then, the back door opened, and Jason came in backwards. Behind him, he was towing the carcass of an enormous lion.

'Hi, Dad,' he said absently.

'Hi, son,' said the stranger.

Jason dumped the lion, kicked it scornfully, and put his school satchel on the table. He looked at the stranger.

'Is it all right if I go to the football with Stuart and Terry on Saturday?' he asked. 'Terry's dad said he'd take us.'

The stranger considered for a moment. 'I suppose so,' he said, 'so long as you get your homework done first. And mind you come straight back,' he added. 'You know how your mother worries.'

'Okay, Dad,' said Jason, and went upstairs.

The stranger grinned, and tiny flashes of lightning played round the light fittings. 'It's a shame they have to grow up, isn't it?' he said.

Mr. Derry looked up, his face a curious mix of fear, reverence and jealousy. 'You've met, then?' he said.

'Oh yes,' said the stranger, 'who do you think picks him up from school every day?'

Mr. Derry turned and glowered at his wife, who shrugged.

'Anyway,' said the stranger, 'if all the er ... animals and things are bothering you, just say the word and I'll send someone, all right? Mercury or ... well, someone,' he concluded. The thought of asking Mercury to go traipsing across the solar system with a huge dust-pan and brush every evening to sweep up his younger brother's mess wasn't exactly appealing. 'Don't give it another thought,' he added. He turned to Mrs. Derry. 'Nice seeing you again,' he said, shuddering slightly. 'We mustn't leave it so long next time, must we?'

He smiled weakly, snapped his fingers, and stepped into the great golden chariot which had suddenly materialised on the carpet. There was a peal of thunder and he was gone.

On his way back to the Palace of the Sun, Jupiter found himself feeling strangely guilty. Perhaps it was seeing how old and flabby the female mortal had become. It had only been – what, ten years? Twelve at the most, and already she was starting to look like a dried apricot. He shook his head sadly, whipped up the horses, and galloped through the fiery gases of the Sun's outer rays, hoping that his wife hadn't noticed he'd been out.

She had.

Apollo, sheltering under the rim of a huge bronze shield, looked at his watch.

'How long've they been at it now?' asked a voice from the corner of the ceiling.

'Six hours,' Apollo replied. 'And if you knew how silly you looked up there, you'd come down at once.'

The spider twitched nervously, slid quickly down its thread, and joined Apollo under the shield, where it changed back into Minerva, ex-Goddess of Wisdom.

'Push off,' Apollo said, 'there isn't enough room for two.'

A thunderbolt whizzed past his ear and crashed into the billows of burning helium that made up the conservatory floor. There was a shower of brilliant blue sparks, one of which landed on Minerva's nose.

'Ouch,' said Minerva. 'Move over, Pol, for pity's sake. It's not safe out there.'

Apollo shrugged. 'It's not exactly marvellous back here, either,' he said, and Minerva noticed that his eyebrows were singed. 'Just makes me feel better, that's all.'

Out in the blackness beyond the crystal windows, a comet suddenly appeared, blazed fervently for a few moments and burned itself out. Apollo relaxed slightly.

'I'll say this for Auntie Ju,' he said, 'her aim always was terrible.'

'You remember when Vulcan was born,' Minerva whispered, 'and He chucked him off the edge?'

'Vividly,' Apollo replied. 'Who do you think it was had to explain to the people of Lemnos why they suddenly had an extra valley where the mountains used to be?'

'I forgot.'

'Wasn't easy, Min,' Apollo went on. 'There's such a thing as prestige, you know. Can't go telling mortals their island's just been flattened by a falling God. There'd be grumbling. You know, why don't you look where you're putting your bloody great feet, that sort of thing. You can lose a lot of respect that way.'

Minerva nodded. 'Good job we don't have to worry about that any more,' she said. 'And it's always *Him*, isn't it?' she added in a whisper.

Apollo looked over his shoulder carefully, then nodded. 'It's just not fair,' he said. 'And it was always us got the blame. I suppose that was why we had to leave.'

Minerva sighed. 'You miss the old place, then?'

'Sometimes,' Apollo admitted. 'I mean, this is all very nice in its way, but ...'

They both ducked instinctively as a mass of burning magma whistled overhead and exploded. Far off, a voice like a female earthquake was saying that it wished it had listened to its mother.

'What I want to know is,' said Minerva, 'if they do split up, who'll get custody of the Fates?'

Suddenly, there was quiet. Dead silence.

'Come to that,' said a dreadful voice, 'who is it leaves her toenail clippings lying around the bedroom carpet every time she has a . . .?'

There was a blinding flash of red light, a dull thump that set the moons of Pluto wobbling on their axes, and a terrific hissing noise.

'She's thrown the kettle at him,' said Minerva.

'And missed,' Apollo added. 'Come on, let's make a run for it while we can.'

They jumped up and ran, crouching, towards the stables.

'We'll take mine,' Apollo said. 'It's faster.'

Minerva nodded. Her chariot was drawn by four silver owls; this was only proper for the ex-Goddess of Wisdom, but it didn't make for a smooth getaway.

It was only when they had passed the moons of Venus that they dared look back. Even from this distance, they could hear a voice like a shrill avalanche pointing out that at least she didn't leave wet footmarks all over the bathroom floor whenever she had a bath. Minerva winced.

'And people wonder,' she said, 'why I never married.'

Picture if you can (don't be ashamed if you can't) the highest point of the Caucasus mountains. Imagine the bare crags, the dizzying ravines, the blinding whiteness of the snow.

On the very highest peak, there is a human figure. The shape is human, but the scale is somehow wrong; this figure is huge. It covers the mountainside like a man-shaped town.

It is sprawled, face down, like a body that has just fallen from a high window. Its wrists and ankles are bound with adamantine chains (adamant is not the first choice of experienced chain-makers, but since what's keeping the prisoner there is the wrath of God, that is largely academic) to the surrounding peaks. Around the prisoner's body circles a great, red-beaked eagle. You are looking at Prometheus.*

You guessed? Well done.

The eagle lifts itself towards the eye of the Sun, banks and swoops down, extending its meat hook talons; it pitches on the prisoner's back and drives its beak into the half-healed flesh. Then, as it has done twice a day since the creation of the World, it starts to gorge itself on the prisoner's liver.

'Huh,' it says, again. 'No onions.'

Prometheus lifts his shaggy head from the rock. His teeth are clenched, his eyes screwed shut, his lips parted in a scowl of effort. He is trying not to giggle.

Thousands of millions of years ago, when the gods first created Man, Prometheus took pity on the wretched, naked mortals and stole fire (and something else) from heaven. He carried the fire down to Earth in a hollow stalk of fennel and gave it to Mankind, so that they would have warmth in winter, light in darkness, and something to boil the kettle over. The gods, as a matter of fact, didn't mind too much about the fire. It was the other thing that aggravated them.

'Morning,' said the eagle.

'Morning,' replied the good giant.

The eagle hesitated for a moment and stared at the clouds through its cruel, lidless eyes. 'Weather's on the turn again,' it said.

'Oh yes?' replied the giant politely.

'More snow,' said the eagle. 'Heavy frost, I shouldn't wonder. Anything I can do for you?'

'You could turn my page if you like,' said the giant.

'Hold on,' said the eagle, wiping its beak on its wing-feathers. Then it hopped over to the giant's head, flipped

---

* It's a *myth* that Prometheus was rescued by Hercules. That's what they want you to believe ...

over the leaf of the huge book spread out under the giant's nose, and weighted the pages down with small stones to stop them blowing over in the biting wind.

'Good, is it?' asked the eagle.

'It's okay,' said the giant. 'Not as good as his last one, though.'

'You can't win 'em all,' said the eagle.

Prometheus wiggled his ears – it was the only gesture he could make, what with the chains and everything – and sighed. 'A bit self-indulgent in places,' he continued. 'Slightly over the top, you know. Still, it'll do.'

'You got much more to read?' asked the eagle.

Prometheus considered. 'No, not really,' he replied. 'Could you just switch on the dictating machine before you go?'

'Sure,' said the eagle, scratching its ear with a meat hook talon. 'Oh, and by the way.'

'Yes?'

'Faldo was one up on the thirteenth,' said the eagle, 'with Ballesteros trailing by three and Langer nowhere. I thought you'd like to know.'

'That's right,' groaned Prometheus, 'cheer me up.'

The eagle shrugged its wings. 'I could bring you a radio,' it said. 'No trouble.'

Prometheus smiled. 'That's very kind of you,' he said, 'but how could I switch it off when it started playing music again? It's not exactly fun and games up here as it is without Vivaldi banging away at you as well.'

'Well, if you're sure ...'

The eagle spread its wings, pressed the record button on the dictating machine perched beside the giant's nose, thanked him for lunch and soared away. Soon it was nothing but a tiny speck among the distant peaks.

No, what really got up the noses of the immortal gods wasn't fire. Give human beings fire, they reasoned, and sooner or later they will use it to burn each other's houses down, which scores four any day of the week and six when the moon is in Scorpio. It was the other thing they could never forgive. Remembering, Prometheus chuckled. Then he lifted his head and started to roar with laughter.

'What time is it?' asked Apollo as they raced across the firmament towards the Earth.

'April,' Minerva replied. 'If we get a move on, we'll be there in time for Easter.'

They looked at each other for a moment. Then they started to snigger.

Among the gods, there is a dispute as to which one of them originally thought of Christianity; or, as they call it, the Great Leg Pull. Apollo has the best claim, but a size-able minority support Pluto, ex-God of the Dead, on the grounds that he has a really sick sense of humour.

How would it be, suggested the unidentified god, if first we tell them all to love their neighbour, pack in the killing and thieving, and be nice to each other. Then we let them start burning heretics.

It is therefore scarcely surprising that the Olympians find it hard to keep a straight face when they think of the religion that has effectively replaced them all over the world (except, of course, for parts of California). What they think of as the world, at any rate; the Olympians were always a touch on the xenophobic side and preferred to ignore the existence of the world beyond the frontiers of the Roman empire, probably because the inhabitants couldn't speak Greek or Latin and the gods could speak nothing else. They tried, of course; they tried speaking very loudly and slowly, but the mortals didn't understand, taking the peculiar noise for thunder.

The chariot of the Sun soared down over the Iberian peninsula, causing a flurry of frantic arguments amongst half the air traffic controllers in Europe, and landed on a hillside outside Delphi.

'Why are we stopping here?' Minerva asked.

'I just want to see if there are any messages,' replied

Apollo. He hopped out of the chariot, transformed himself into a small, elderly German with a video-camera, and made his way down towards the ruins of his temple.

Over the lintel of the door of the Treasury of the Athenians is an inscription. Time has ground it almost smooth, but that still doesn't excuse the generations of distinguished classical archaeologists who translated it as

KNOW THYSELF

when it actually says

WHILE YOU WERE OUT

and certainly doesn't explain why none of them has ever gone on to read the rest of it. This would, of course, be difficult, as the text of the inscription changes subtly every few years.

The German tourist paused and looked up at the faint lettering. As he did so, he became aware of a small, dumpy female figure beside him.

'Betty,' he said, 'I do believe your writing is getting worse.'

'Sorry,' said the female. 'It's my arthritis,' she explained.

'Ah.' Apollo made a mental note to do something about it. 'Anything important, was there?'

Betty-Lou Fisichelli, the eight-thousand-and-sixth Sibyl of Delphi, took a notebook from her bag and started to leaf through it. 'Napoleon called,' she said, 'please call back ... Bit late for that now, I suppose. A guy from Chicago wants to know how the Bears are going to do this season. There was a party of British guys with portable telephones who asked – I may have got this down wrong – they asked if it was the right time to sell Guilt.'

'Gilts,' corrected Apollo. Then he grinned wickedly. 'If they come back,' he said, 'tell them yes. Anything else?'

'No, I don't think so,' said the Sibyl. 'Oh yes, there was a woman asking about her kid. Seems he's been playing her up or something. Sounded like hyperactivity to me: you know, too much chocolate. Phyllis somebody.'

Apollo turned round and stared at her. 'Phyllis Derry?' he demanded.

'That's right,' said the Sybil. 'Was it important?'

Apollo ignored her. 'When was this?' he asked.

'About . . .' The Sibyl looked at her watch. It had two concentric dials: one for human and one for Divine time. 'About January,' she said. 'Sorry,' she added, 'you didn't say you were expecting . . .'

'That's all right,' said Apollo quietly, 'I wasn't. Look, did she leave a number?'

'I think so,' said the Sibyl, leafing through her book. 'Hold on a moment . . . No, that's the ·Delphi Pizza Express. Now, let me just . . .'

Apollo frowned. Something scuttled about nervously under the Earth's crust. Several large olive trees wilted on the hillside opposite. The Sibyl swallowed hard and found the right page. 'Got it,' she said. 'It's . . . Look, is that a five or a three?'

'I don't know, do I?' replied the god, and for a moment the EC olive oil lake seemed likely to dry up for a year or so.

'I think it's a five,' said the Sibyl nervously. She wrote the number out again, tore out the page and handed it to the god, who smiled grimly and thanked her. 'If she calls again,' he added, 'just let me know immediately, will you?'

The Sibyl trembled slightly. 'How?' she asked.

Apollo looked blank for a moment, and then snapped, 'Use your bloody imagination.' Then he turned himself into a swarm of bees and buzzed off.

'Have a nice day,' the Sybil whispered, and made a note in her book: *If Phyllis Derry calls back, tell A. at once.* Then she turned round and walked away slowly, reflecting (not for the first time) that she hadn't wanted the lousy job in the first place. Partly it was the industrial relations –

women through the ages who had offended Apollo suddenly found themselves transformed into flowering shrubs, and Ms. Fisichelli, who came from New York, where they don't hold with such things, shuddered at the very thought. She had a cousin called Myrtle, from Wisconsin, and that was bad enough. Mainly, though, it was the feeling that she hadn't spent ten years of her life at a selection of universities getting her Doctorate in Classical Philology just to be a glorified receptionist. Many was the time, she reminded herself, that she'd been on the point of giving in her notice and telling him what he could do with his gods-damned job. Then she would catch sight of a clematis or a wisteria and decide to put it off till tomorrow. But the worst part of it, if she was going to be honest, was the job description. For, of course, the senior priestess of the Delphi Oracle isn't called the Sibyl at all. The correct term is the Pythoness, and Ms. Fisichelli, who was only human – well, mostly human – could only take so much.

A small American lady tapped her gently on the arm, mistaking her for the tour guide. The Sibyl turned and glowered at her.

'Excuse me,' said the lady, 'do you think it's going to rain?'

Ms. Fisichelli grinned. The god had given her the gift of prophecy, but so what?

'No,' she said.

I n the beginning was the Word. Nobody knows what it
actually was, although it would be nice to think it was
'Sorry.'

After a while, the Word began to feel bored. It checked
its spelling, but that was all right. It tried rhyming with
itself, but it had an idea that that made you go blind. It
put itself into italics, but they hurt. There was nothing for
it but to create some other words and see what happened.

To begin with, the Words just bounced about, like a lot
of random particles; and when they bumped into each
other, small bits and corners were chipped off, fell through
space, acquired momentum and became Matter. Then,
most of the original Words decided to form a gang, dress
up in white sheets and beat the pulp out of the Adjectives,
who they felt were getting above themselves, and so
engrossed did they become in this that they failed to notice
that a rival group of sentient beings had materialised out
of nowhere. By the time they realised they were not alone,
the Words had been scooped up, parsed senseless and
imprisoned in the first ever word processor.

The newcomers were the gods. According to the oldest
versions of the story, there were three of them: Cronus,
Rhea and Thing.

Cronus created order out of chaos. Rhea separated
darkness from light and wallpapered the firmament with
stars. Then they coated the Words with molecules, until

each one had become the thing it stood for, and set them to work colonising the firmament. In all the excitement they forgot about Thing, who was no good at carpentry and tended to trip over the paste-bucket. When the work of creation was finished, the gods stepped back and looked at it, and saw that it was good; or, at least, that it could have been worse. They knocked off for the week-end.

When he was quite sure that they'd all gone, Thing crept out of the supernova in which he'd been hiding, brushed stardust off his trousers and scowled.

He'd show them.

Softly but persuasively, he announced himself to the Words as they clanked about awkwardly in their new shells. You don't like the gods, he said, I don't like them; let's teach those mothers a lesson they'll never forget.

The Words didn't say anything; they just nodded. Then Thing took a deep breath and dematerialised, turning his body into billions of tiny particles. The Words shrieked, as well they might – each one felt like an oyster who's just had a full-sized pearl inserted into it.

It was some time before the gods found out about this, and by then it was too late. All they could do was hope and pray (as it were) that none of the little bits of Thing ever got into the hands of the newly-created human race; because if they did, there'd be trouble. And, thanks to Prometheus, trouble there was ...

Jupiter put down the asteroid he had been about to throw and blushed.

'I'm sorry, too,' he said. 'And yes, you're still my fluffy little wifekin.' He transformed the asteroid into a huge bunch of flowers and handed it to Juno, who simpered slightly.

Far overhead, a comet with a large, jagged sliver of solidified helium sticking right through it expressed the wish that the great Sky-King could have found it in him to say that a few minutes earlier. He had been knocked some way off his trajectory, and if there's one thing that really upsets comets, it's being late. Messes things up for the princes, they say. Makes the beggars get uppity.

'I didn't mean to get so cross, Jo,' said Juno pacifically. 'I don't know what came over me.'

'That's all right.'

'But you did promise ...'

'I know,' said Jupiter. 'And I'm sorry.'

'It's not that I mind you ... well, turning into things. You're like that, and that's fine. It's just ...'

'What?'

'Jo,' said Juno, as winsomely as a great Sky-Queen can (which is not very), 'why do the little bastards always have to be Heroes?'

'I don't know,' Jupiter confessed. 'They just do, that's all.'

'They upset things, you see,' Juno continued. 'They get difficult. They go about righting wrongs and protecting the mortals.'

'I know,' Jupiter sighed. 'I don't like it either.'

'They rescue princesses,' Juno continued. 'They kill dragons. They retrieve golden fleeces. They bring back the Secret of Truth. You can't put something down for five minutes without some hero or other scuttling off with it. And you can't just tread on them or give them scarlet fever, that's the worst thing. They're all woven into the Skein of Destiny, and you know what that's like. Ladders as soon as look at it.'

'Yes,' said Jupiter, smiling like a doorknocker. 'I had noticed. Look ...'

'And now,' said Juno remorselessly, 'it looks like you've gone and sired another one of the little terrors. What's it called, by the way?'

'Jason.'

'Jason,' Juno repeated. 'Scarcely original.'

'True,' Jupiter replied, 'but inconspicuous. Look, it'll be different this time, promise. We aren't *involved* any more, remember. So what if the little toerag does succeed in banishing Discord from the Earth ...'

'If he does,' snapped Juno, 'she's not coming back here. Last time we had her to stay, she left grubby marks on all the towels.'

'Whatever,' said Jupiter firmly. 'Fulfilling his destiny, then. Even if he does succeed in fulfilling his destiny, who gives a toss anyway? Nobody believes in us any more, so what possible difference could it make? It'll just make the Game that bit more interesting,' he added, wickedly.

Juno gave him one of her looks. 'You are going to tell them?' she said.

'Eventually,' Jupiter replied.

'Eventually?'

'Yes,' said the Father of Gods and Men with a chuckle. 'Just as soon as I've had a chance to put a few side-bets on.'

Meanwhile, on another part of the sun, it was Mars's go.

Mars, ex-God of War, can easily be distinguished from his fellow gods by his twitch. Most things bring it on – the ticking of a clock, the sound of a speck of dust settling on a distant asteroid, even (especially) dead silence. Years of living with it had got on the nerves of the other eleven Olympians. That just made it worse.

The place of Mars, Feeder of Vultures, has traditionally been in the forefront of battle. This was originally no problem; in the good old days when the nastiest thing Mankind had thought up by way of settling disputes between neighbours was a poisoned arrow, golden armour, no worries. However, things had changed rather, what with armour-piercing ammunition, high explosives, napalm, chemical weapons, Exocets and Cruise missiles; in fact, the only thing that hasn't kept up with the times is Mars's defensive capability, which still consists of about three millimetres of gilded, low-tech bronze.

Theology is at best an imprecise science. The best

definition of an immortal is someone who hasn't died yet.

Hence the fact, not perhaps widely enough known, that on his shield Mars has painted probably the biggest CND symbol in the entire galaxy. Next time you go to one of those big demonstrations, look out for a tall, thin, gaunt chap with a serious nervous tic. That'll be Mars.

Sitting opposite him in the observation dome of the sun was his three-quarter-sister-once removed (divine relationships are rather complex), the ex-Goddess of the Moon, Diana. Unlike Mars, nobody ever shoots at her, and therefore she tends to be a trifle scornful of Mars's new-found pacifism. To her, as to the rest of Olympus, the way to a man's heart is through his ribcage.

'Seven,' said Diana. 'Hold on, here we go. One-two-three-four-five-six-seven and here we are. Now then.'

She took a golden tile from the neat stack that hovered in the air beside the bejewelled abacus and read it.

'You are assessed for street repairs,' she recited disgustedly. 'Pay one billion drachmas for each city . . .'

She peered down at the surface of the planet and counted. Then she reached for her trusty bow and arrow, drew careful aim and skewered a dense bank of cloud hovering over a major Western city. At once the cloud burst, sending furious torrents of water rushing through the streets. Mars turned his head away, hoping she wouldn't notice.

'There,' she said happily, 'that's saved me a few bob.'

Roofs floated by on their way to the sea. Mars opened his eyes and decided, for only the seventh time that day, that this was a truly horrid game.

'I'm not sure,' he said, in a high, strained voice, 'that you're allowed to do that.'

'You reckon?'

Mars's head twitched sharply a couple of times. Diana was giving him one of her looks.

'On the other hand,' he said, 'who cares? My turn, isn't it?'

He picked up the dice-shaker, threw hard and prayed. This is an unusual thing for a god to do, but he'd got into the habit during the Cuban missile crisis and it was hard to stop. The dice wobbled for a moment and landed.

'Lucky you,' Diana said. 'Double four.'

Another reason why Mars hadn't kicked the habit was that it seemed to work. Funny, that; when human beings used to pray to him, it had always been a complete washout.

'Let me see,' Mars said. 'That's nice, peace negotiations under way in Geneva, strategic arms limitation talks resumed, cease-fire in the Middle East conflict . . .'

Diana shook her head. She threw.

'Twelve,' she said. 'Go to . . . Oh, *nuts!*'

Thank you, said Mars under his breath, whoever you are. Three whole throws and not a shot fired in anger. Not even a shot fired in a spirit of reckless jollity, which can sometimes be a great deal worse. The Driver of the Spoil crossed his fingers, shook the dice-box gently, and spilt the dice.

Nine.

Mars twitched like a fisherman's float with a whale on the end of the line and turned towards the Earth. The wail of sirens was dimly audible across the emptiness of the solar system.

'Fire alarm?' he asked hopefully.

No chance. Pausing only for his head to stop moving long enough for him to put his helmet on it, Mars shouldered his shield and spear, whistled for his chariot, and trudged off to war.

Three small lumps of rock in the middle of a frozen sea.

The nearest land: the Argentine coast, approximately two hundred miles away. Natural resources: rock, ice and snow (in season). Strategic value: nil. Population: four.

Until recently, of course. Now, the population is fluctuating around the twelve thousand mark, as huge numbers of men hop out of big green aeroplanes on the ends of pieces of string tied to sheets. Down below, someone is staging an impromptu fireworks display.

In the middle of it all stands Mars, Destroyer of Men, holding a golden spear with the spearhead shot off and feeling a complete nana. Fortunately, he is invisible and his body, being composed of ichor and ambrosia, doesn't give off enough heat to attract the attention of the large number of heat-seeking missiles nosing about in the air like psychotic dolphins. Cautiously, his head bobbing up and down like one of those nodding dogs you see in the backs of cars, Mars starts to unwrap his sandwiches.

Cheese and gherkin, notes the Father of Battles with disgust. Cheese and gherkin, as if I didn't have enough to put up with as it is.

From the hill with the machine-gun on it came a succession of peculiar noises, which set Mars's head going like a beam-engine. First there was a terrible yelling noise, then a smart crackle of rifle-fire and some loud, deep thumps, then another yell and some screams of pure panic. Then loud cheering. Then silence.

Mars peered cautiously over the rim of the wrecked armoured personnel carrier, behind which he had taken prudent if inglorious shelter. The shooting appeared to have stopped. The only noise was the distant song of birds and the sound of the cheekpiece of Mars's helmet tapping against the mangled turret. What, asked the Widow-Maker, the hell is going on?

Gingerly, he took off his helmet, balanced it on the tip of his spear, and lifted it into the air. No bullet-holes or shrapnel-gashes appeared in it. Nobody seemed interested. It was probably some sort of diabolical trap.

On the other hand, Mars said to himself, maybe it isn't, and what the hell, you can only die once, if that. He rose unsteadily to his feet, put the helmet on, and whistled for his chariot. Odd, he reflected as he climbed up behind his four coal-black, red-eyed coursers, the way nothing ever seems to hit the bloody chariot. Sometimes I think they must do it on purpose. He gripped the reins, picked an unexploded mortar-shell out of the fold of his cloak, and shouted 'Giddyap!' in a voice like the crash of colliding battalions.

The battle was over. Even Mars, who had learned the hard way not to judge by appearances, was convinced of that. It was the way the soldiers were leaning thoughtfully on their rifles and looking out over the stricken field while the senior staff officers gave interviews to the *News at Ten* that convinced him. Mars tethered the chariot to a crashed helicopter, alighted, and crept over to where a slightly dishevelled man in a blue anorak was talking loudly to a television camera. Beside him, two technicians in leather jackets were operating a large portable electric fan, to give his hair the authentic wind-blown look.

'The Battle of Mallard Esplanade,' shouted the man above the whirr of the fan, 'is over. Shortly before three o'clock this afternoon, the entire enemy land forces surrendered to a man, it seems as the result of an unprecedented act of gallantry by a young private in the Catering Corps, Private Jason Derry, who apparently charged them single-handedly. This is Danny Bennett, *News at Ten*, Mallard Esplanade; George, you're standing on my hold-all.'

Mars rubbed his eyes with the heel of his hand, took off his shield and threw it in the back of the chariot. Great, he thought, marvellous; now let's get out of here quick before these lunatics change their minds. And a big thank you to Private Jason Derry, whoever the hell he is . . .

Jason Derry?

Mars twitched so violently that the chariot drew up suddenly in mid-air, executed a remarkable banking manoeuvre, and force-landed on a strip of wind-blasted grass in the valley below. Being stuffed full of land-mines, it blew up.

After a while, the tip of a charred and frantically

nodding plume appeared above the lip of the crater, and Mars slowly drew himself up by his fingertips. Having ostentatiously dusted himself off and thrown a collection of mangled sheets of metal and the ragged remains of a Cloak of Invisibility into a nearby ditch, he whistled for a rather badly dented chariot, swore at the horses, and departed sunwards, just as a camera crew looked up in the hope of filming incoming Harriers.

'Hey,' said the chief cameraman, pointing a trembling finger at the sky. 'Hey just look at that, will you?'

The reporter looked up, nodded and shrugged.

'If you ignore them,' he said, 'they just go away. Anyone got a pen?'

J ason got up, looked around him, and wondered where he was. It didn't take him long.

He was lost.

Pity, but never mind. When you're a Hero, being lost isn't exactly the end of the world, just a passing inconvenience between adventures. It happens to all of them, and they know how to deal with it.

For example; round about the end of the second reel, the Hero has usually been kidnapped and whisked away by helicopter to a secret location miles from anywhere where the villain tries to do away with him by some entertaining but hopelessly over-involved means. The Hero gets out of that, natch, and sprints out of the secret location just in time to clamber onto the wing of the villain's light aircraft, which is just taking off. Then there's a spectacular fight, the villain comes to a bad end, and the Hero has just enough time to leap out of the plane before it collides with the side of a mountain. We are, you realise, miles from anywhere by this point. No trains. No public transport of any kind.

Five seconds later, the Hero is strolling into the bar of the Casino, wearing a dinner-jacket, all ready for the final car/lorry/armoured personnel carrier chase sequence, which will end in a cloud of rolling flames out in the middle of the desert somewhere. Have you ever stopped to look at what these Heroes wear on their feet? No? Well, it certainly isn't walking shoes.

There is a perfectly simple explanation for all this. Behind every Hero travels a small semi-divine functionary driving something not unlike one of those motorised golf buggies. In the trunk there's three changes of clothes, assorted lethal weapons, a first aid kit and usually a thermos of hot soup. It's strange that so few people know about this handy and convenient service; perhaps it's something to do with Heroes being basically insecure. Or perhaps they all take it so much for granted that they forget to mention it.

Jason looked round, whistled irritably and tapped his foot. A moment later, the old familiar wheezing noise reached his ears as the buggy – a sort of deluxe version of the obese golfer's friend – bumped over the rocks towards him.

'What kept you?' he said.

'Sorry, boss,' said the driver, 'the power pack went flat just outside Kabul. You try getting two torch batteries in a fundamentalist Moslem country, you'll soon see whether you've got what it takes.'

'Where are we?' Jason asked, brushing a little dust off his immaculately-tailored battledress.

'Caucasus mountains,' said the driver. 'I think. Let's have a shufti at the map.' He pushed forward the passenger seat of the buggy to reveal a useful luggage area, which was crammed with the sort of old rubbish you and I keep in glove compartments, plus a few stun grenades and a copy of *War and Peace*. Heroes' drivers have to do a lot of waiting about.

'Here we are,' said the driver at last, and emerged with a well-thumbed atlas. 'Now, let the dog see the rabbit, if that's Tbilisi down over there ...'

Jason made an impatient noise. 'And anyway,' he said, 'what am I here for?'

The driver shrugged. 'Funny you should ask that,' he

said, 'the other day I was reading this book by Descartes, and he says ...'

'No, no,' said the Hero, irritably, 'what I mean is, why have I ended up here, when I thought I was going back to Aldershot?'

The driver wriggled uneasily in his seat. 'Now, boss,' he said, 'you know I'm not allowed to tell you things like that. Signed the Celestial Secrets Act, haven't I? It's not fair, asking me things like ...'

'All right, all right,' said Jason, 'just so long as this is where I'm meant to be, you know, right now.'

'Don't worry about that,' said the driver. 'Bang on.'

'Well,' confessed the Hero, 'sometimes I wonder, you know? I haven't really got the hang of all this, somehow. I mean, Daddy did say ...'

'What?'

'He said,' replied Jason, 'that I should do what I was told and keep my mouth shut. Fair enough, I suppose, but ...'

Heroes have these short intervals of what can only be described as Doubts, and the driver had heard it all before. Take Arjun, for example. Many was the time he'd had to give him a good talking-to on the eve of a big battle. 'Don't you worry about all that,' he said. 'The big fellas know what they're doing; you just carry on and enjoy yourself.'

Jason nodded, reassured. Ever since Daddy had told him, a few months ago now, just before his eighteenth birthday party, that he was a Hero and it was high time he stopped daydreaming about a career in hotel management and went out in search of his Destiny, he had done his best not to look back. And it had been fun, so far, hitting people, charging machine-gun nests, pulling the barrels off tanks with his bare hands, all that sort of stuff. Most of the boys he'd been to school with still thought smashing up space invader machines was a wild time.

'Anyway,' said the driver, 'far be it for me to drop any

heavy hints, but I think your destiny lies over there.' He pointed at a nearby hillside.

'What, the one with the trees?'

'No,' said the driver patiently, 'the one with the goats and the small shack. I think you'll find there's someone over there waiting for you.'

'Ah,' said Jason, 'right, then. In the shack?'

'Very probably,' sighed the driver. 'Why don't you go and find out?'

Overhead, a huge eagle hugged a thermal and scanned the surface below. When he saw the human figure plodding grimly up the hillside he let out a squawk you could have heard in Azerbaijan. Then he swooped suddenly to recover the copy of *Time* he'd been carrying in his beak, looped a swift loop, and sped away.

In the shack, Jason found an old woman. She was sitting by a fire stirring a big pot. A pair of black ravens perched on her shoulders, making her look like an old-fashioned bedstead.

'Hiya,' said Jason. 'Where to?'

The old woman scowled at him. This was her one big scene, and she wanted to make the most of it.

'Sit down, boy,' she said, and pointed with a gnarled finger at a low stool on the other side of the pot.

'No offence,' Jason said, 'but can we skip all that? I've had a hard day, what with having to parachute out of the Hercules when the rockets hit it, then landing in the tree, then getting the motorbike started and being chased for thirty miles over rocky terrain with helicopters shooting at me. Then,' he added, 'getting the flat tyre. So if we could just ...'

'You'll sit still,' said the old woman, 'and like it.'

'Bloody hell,' Jason whined rebelliously, but the old woman gave him a look which put the helicopter gunships firmly in context. He sat.

'Whither away, stranger?' said the old woman, after a gratuitously long pause. 'It is seldom we see strangers in these lonely parts,' she ad-libbed.

'I go to seek my Destiny,' said Jason woodenly. He'd say it, but he was damned if he was going to ham it up.

'Your Destiny?' said the old woman. She managed the capital D rather better than he did. 'And where will that lead you?' She cackled. Cackling is a dying art, so they say.

'Over ... Look, have I got to say all this shit?'

'Yes.'

'Oh, come on,' Jason pleaded. It made him feel so self-conscious. 'I mean,' he said, 'if we skip it no one'll ever know.'

'I will,' said the old woman. 'Say it.'

'No.'

'Very well, then,' she said grimly, and reached for her knitting.

About five minutes later, Jason cleared his throat and said, very quickly;

'I-go-in-search-of-the-source-of-the-mystic-Power-the-Power-of-the-Sun, all right?'

The old woman nodded. 'Know,' she said, 'that I am not what I seem.' She put down her knitting and grinned. Jason looked at her.

'Well?'

'Well what?'

'Get on with it,' Jason said.

'You're supposed,' said the old woman, 'to register surprise.'

Jason indicated that he would shortly be registering extreme annoyance, and the old woman put down her knitting quickly. 'Know,' she said, 'that I am none other than Hecate, Witch-Mother of the Mountains, and I shall grant you one wish ...'

'*One* wish?'

'You never heard of the cutbacks? *One* wish, to help you to achieve your heart's desire. But choose carefully; the gifts of the gods are very ...'

'Tell me,' said Jason firmly, 'what I'm supposed to do next. Or,' he added, 'I'll thump you one, okay?'

The old woman glowered at him. 'Over there,' she said, 'turn left at the second thorn bush, follow your nose till you come to a pillar of fire, left then left again through the Clashing Rocks, then straight on, you can't miss it.'

'Miss what?'

'It,' said the old woman. 'Now push off.'

Jason got up and headed for the door. 'Hang on,' he said, 'you've forgotten something.'

'Have I?'

'Yes.'

'Oh.' The old woman tutted loudly. 'That's what comes of rushing things,' she said. 'You lose your place.'

From under her chair she pulled out a long cloth bag. 'See,' she said, 'this is the Sword of ... Oh sod the thing, the cover's got caught on the pommel somewhere. Look, you hold this end and when I say "Pull" ...'

There was a tearing sound; then a metallic clang.

'Anyway,' said the old woman, leaning forward, 'this is the Sword of Glycerion, which may only be tamed by the pure in heart. To all others it brings Death. Wield it well, my son, for ... hey, didn't anyone ever tell you it's rude to snatch?'

'Right,' said Jason, looking at the Sword with mild disgust, 'about bloody time too.' He got up and strode towards the door.

'May the Power be with you,' the old woman called out after him.

'Oh, drop dead,' Jason replied. Then he clumped out to seek his Destiny.

'Your throw.'

'Right.'

Rattle rattle rattle. Clonk.

'Four and five, that's eight.'

'Actually, Pol, that's nine.'

'All right, it's bloody nine, then. One two three four five six seven eight oh, that's charming, that is.'

'Go back three spaces.'

'Yes, thank you, Vul, I can read, you know.'

Riffle riffle.

'GET OUT OF TROUBLE FREE. Oh well, that's worth having, isn't it? Your turn.'

Rattle rattle rattle rattle. Clunk.

Onetwothreefourfivesixseven *eight*.'

Pause.

'Oh.'

'Hello,' called Jason. 'Anyone at home?'

He leaned against the doorway of the curious stone building, rested the Sword of Thingummy against a pillar, and tied his shoelace. Heroism was all very well, he reckoned, but if he'd wanted to do a lot of walking he'd have become a postman.

Nothing happened. Jason put his newly-secured foot back on the ground and tapped it.

'Hello,' he repeated. 'Anybody there? I haven't got all day, you know.'

From somewhere inside the ruined temple there was the sound of someone dropping something, and the something breaking. 'All right,' said a sweet, enchanting female voice testily. 'Just wait a minute, will you?'

Then two women appeared in the doorway. Let us take the time to describe them.

First things first: they are a pair of absolute honeys. No mistake about that. You expect to see the title of a glossy fashion magazine floating above their heads in big block capitals.

One of them is tall, noble, austere. She is dressed in a simple, demure white robe, and on her head is a plain band of yellow gold. In the crook of one arm she carries what you instinctively know is a golden palm-branch symbolising something you can't quite remember. Her hair is the same colour as the band and the branch and her eyes are a sort of refrigerated blue. She doesn't happen to be wearing a sash right now, but if she was you could bet your life savings and next month's pay check that it would have VIRTUE embroidered on it.

The other one is dark, smouldering and has more curves than Le Mans and Indianapolis put together. In the crook of her arm she carries what used to be called a cornucopia – a sort of metallic cream horn with fruit in it – and what she's wearing is largely academic. She does, however, have a sash, but instead of LUXURY it has 'Miss Personality North-West Area 1992' on it, presumably in the vain hope of leaving something about the wearer's appearance to the imagination. In her mouth she has a couple of hairpins, and she doesn't look too pleased.

'Ready?' said Luxury, through the hairpins.

'Sorry?' Jason said.

'Oh come on,' said Luxury. 'I've got a lemon soufflé on the gas; let's not muck about.'

'Oh,' said Jason, blushing slightly, 'yes, right. I've got to choose, have I?'

'That's it,' said Luxury, 'and if you could see your way to getting a move on, we'd both be most terribly grateful, all right?'

'Er,' said Jason.

'Look,' said Luxury, 'if you're worried about hurting our feelings, don't be, okay? Just get on and choose, and then we can all carry on with what we're supposed to be doing.'

'I'm sorry,' said Jason, 'but shouldn't there be roads?'

The girls frowned and looked at each other. 'You what?' they said.

'A crossroads,' Jason explained. 'One road leading straight, narrow and uphill, towards a distant prospect of the battlements of the Shining City; the other winding, broad and downhill, leading to, you know, thing.'

The girls looked at him.

'Well,' said Virtue, 'yes, now you come to mention it, strictly speaking. But since you seem to know all that already, do you think we could possibly ...?'

'Ah,' said Jason. 'Yes, of course. Well ...'

Thirty seconds passed. Luxury looked at her watch. Considering where it was pinned, this was no mean achievement.

'I'm sorry,' said Jason, 'and I hate to be difficult, but I'm going to have to insist on the roads.'

There was a deep sigh. 'Please yourself, then,' said Luxury. 'Look, will you just hold on a minute while I turn down the gas? Vir, do the roads for me, there's a love.'

Virtue nodded.

Jason stared. There, in front of him, lay two roads, just as he'd imagined them. Except that the road of Luxury was paved with violets, not primroses, and the road of Virtue had a big sign saying NO SERVICES FOR 200 MILES beside the verge.

'Will that do?' said Virtue.

'Well ...' Jason replied. This should be easy, of course, but ...

Just then Luxury came back, removing a pinny with *The World's Best Cook* on it. 'Got it working, Vir?' she asked.

'Just about,' Virtue replied. 'Better get someone in to look at it tomorrow though, otherwise we won't ...'

The words dried on her lips. From out of the blue a large yellow placard had appeared and plonked itself down at a point just before the two roads diverged. On it was traced, in letters of synthesized fire, the word

DIVERSION

and a big white arrow pointing due west.

'Ah,' said Jason happily, and followed the arrow.

*

'Clever,' said Vulcan with grudging admiration. 'Lermontov's gambit on a double fluke score. Neat.'

Apollo gave him a worried look, such as William Tell might have given Isaac Newton. 'Actually ...'

H e had been walking along the Diversion for about
twenty minutes, whistling tunelessly and eating an
apple he'd found in the pocket of his battledress, when
Jason met the Erymanthian Hydra.

Since we took time out to describe Virtue and Luxury,
let us also paint a verbal picture of the Erymanthian
Hydra. You'll like this.*

Picture to yourself a bull, just an ordinary bull. Now
paint it gold. Now remove the head – this is one we
prepared before the programme – and add the head of a
lion. Using a pair of long tweezers, tease out the hairs of
the lion's mane and replace them with six-foot-long hissing
vipers. If you have any vipers left over, nip out the bull's
tail and pop them in there. Now remove the feet (do not
discard; these can be used to make a nourishing stock)
and substitute for them the talons of a gryphon. If you
have no gryphon, a hippocamp will do just as well.
Garnish with the wings of a dragon. Run away, terribly
fast.

The Erymanthian Hydra is a confounded nuisance. It
eats people. And cars. And railway shunting yards. It
makes disconcerting howling noises in the middle of the

*So to speak. If you do find yourself enjoying what follows, we
recommend that you seek professional help.

night and has been known to tear open dustbin bags with its chalcedony talons.

As it saw Jason approaching, the Erymanthian Hydra sniggered softly, lifted up its ghastly head, ran a comb through its vipers, and sprang out from behind its rock.

'Hello,' it said. 'I'm the Erymanthian *ouch!*'

Jason sheathed his sword, lifted the monster's severed head by its still-hissing locks, and looked around for a rubbish-bin.

Demeter, ex-Goddess of the Earth, sat down on the cushion recently vacated by Vulcan, blew her nose, and looked at the Earth.

'How's he doing?' she asked.

Apollo looked round, refused the offer of a freshly-baked upside-down cake and frowned.

'It's hard to say,' he replied, 'on account of, I don't know what he's supposed to be doing yet.'

Demeter raised an exquisitely plucked eyebrow and reached for the score-card. 'Easy,' she said. 'Visit to Kingdom of Colchis,' she read out, 'passing through Caucasus mountains. Meets Witch (2), gives Judgment of Jason (6), slays Erymanthian Hydra (10) ...'

'Yes, yes, all right,' said Apollo, 'but what's he do in the end?'

'I'm getting to that,' replied Demeter, running her finger down the envelope. 'Thessalian Centaurs ... Recovers Golden Fleece (2,000; replay). Where's he got to now?'

'That's just it,' Apollo said. 'You see, he's going the wrong way.'

'You what?' Demeter looked up sharply.

'He's going the wrong way,' Apollo repeated. 'Look.'

'He can't be.'

'He is,' Apollo assured her. 'There, see for yourself.'

The two gods focused their eyes and zoomed in on a rocky outcrop in the Caucasus. On a low crag stood a group of well-armed Thessalian Centaurs. Most of them had their arms folded. Some were tapping their hooves. Their leader had given up looking at his watch and was shaking it to see if it had stopped.

'He's late?' Demeter guessed. The intellectual requirements for making corn grow are not stringent.

'More than that,' Apollo replied. 'He's missed them out completely.'

The two deities looked at each other.

'Perhaps,' Demeter ventured, 'he's just chicken.'

Apollo looked down at the spot on the hillside where the blood of the Erymanthian Hydra had just burnt a crater in the living rock. 'No,' he said, 'I don't think it can be that. It's more as if he's ... well, going somewhere else.'

Demeter raised both eyebrows this time. 'But that's impossible,' she said.

'Well,' Apollo replied, 'it's very unprofessional.'

Demeter scratched her nose thoughtfully and, from sheer force of habit, produced half a million bushels of barley from behind her ear. 'Never heard of such a thing,' she said. 'Next thing, he'll be having a mind of his own. Can't have that.'

'What, he can't?'

'No, we can't.'

'Oh, I see.'

Apollo leaned forward and twiddled with a free-floating knob. The Earth seemed to grow larger.

'So where exactly is he headed?' Demeter asked.

'Good question,' Apollo replied. 'Now, let's see ...'

Apollo produced a pair of field glasses. 'We might know that,' he said, 'when we've worked out where he's going.'

'Clever,' Demeter said, impressed. 'Whose turn is it, by the way?'

Apollo looked up. 'Do you know,' he said, 'I'd completely forgotten about the Game. Let's see, now; my go's over, and so it's you and ...'

He fell silent, and his lips were pursed. 'I see,' he said.

'Or at least it's possible. I suppose.'

'Who is it?'

'Guess.'

Demeter's forehead wrinkled like a thrice-ploughed field. 'You know I'm no good at guessing,' she said. 'You'll have to tell me.'

Apollo said nothing, and handed her the Celestial Envelope.

'Oh,' said Demeter. 'Oh gosh!'

So what exactly was it, you are no doubt asking, that Prometheus stole from the gods and brought down to Earth, presumably not hidden in the hollow stalk of a piece of fennel?*

It is a dark night on the slopes of Mount Olympus. The Thirteen Olympians are sitting round the flickering light of Apollo's tripod, on the rim of which a number of tiny three-dimensional figures made out of coloured light are scurrying about in some sort of frantic dance. From the interior of the tripod comes the faint sound of music. The gods are watching *Life Wish III*.

Jupiter leans back in his chair and pulls the ring on a can of nectar. Demeter emerges from the kitchen with a tray of stars in batter and advises her fellow gods to eat them while they're hot. All is for the best in the best of all possible worlds.

Down below, however, on the surface of the Earth, things are not quite so jolly. Far from it. In their dark caves, our earliest forefathers huddle goose-pimpled in the smelly skins of mammoths and nibble listlessly at drumsticks of raw mouse. There is silence, except for occasional choking noises or the elder of the tribe saying how thoroughly unpleasant all this is. Then more silence, eventually broken by another elder saying that it is true that this

---

* Otherwise it'd have got burnt.

is unpleasant, but that being eaten by the sabre-toothed tiger is probably worse.

Back to Olympus. The thirteenth Olympian quietly gets up from his place on the sofa, puts his slippers on and creeps away into the kitchen. From the vegetable rack he selects a suitable fennel stalk, lights a match and pops it in. He waits for a moment, until he is satisfied that the small glow of fire is thoroughly concealed. Then he tiptoes off the edge of the mountain and sprints away towards Earth.

He stops outside a large cave and knocks on the rock. After a while, a man in an ill-fitting goatskin comes to the mouth of the cave and peers at the stranger.

'Oh,' he says. 'It's you again, is it?'

Prometheus peers anxiously at the sky. 'Yes,' he whispers. 'Look ...'

'Piss off,' says the mortal and makes a gesture with his arm. What he is trying to do is slam the door in the Titan's face; since there is no door, however, he has to rely on mime.

'Look ...' Prometheus hisses urgently.

'No,' says the mortal, 'you look. We've had enough of you, got it? After last time.'

'Ah.'

'Yeah,' snarls the mortal. 'Dunno how you've got the nerve to come back here after that.'

Prometheus winces slightly. 'I told her,' he said. 'Don't open it, I said.'

The mortal makes a contemptuous noise. 'You told her,' he repeated. 'Don't you know *anything* about women?'

Prometheus shakes his head. 'I did warn her,' he repeated. 'Pandora, I said, just leave it alone and ...'

'And you expected her not to open it?' said the mortal. 'Yes.'

'When it had *Open With Care, Free Gift Inside* written on it?'

'Well ...' Prometheus flushed slightly. 'All right,' he

conceded, 'so that was a bit of an error of judgment on my part. This time, though, I promise you, I'll make it up to you. Here.' He thrust the fennel-stalk into the mortal's hand. 'What d'you make of that, then?' he said eagerly.

'Fennel salad,' said the mortal. 'Thanks a lot.'

'No,' said Prometheus, 'just look inside it, will you?'

The mortal peered inside, then reared back, clutching his eyebrows. 'Ouch!' he explained.

'It's fire,' said Prometheus, proudly.

'So that's what you call it,' growled the mortal, rubbing the tip of his nose. 'And you know what you can do with that, my fine friend.'

'Wait a minute,' Prometheus said. He explained about fire.

He explained that with fire, you could see in the dark ('I thought that was carrots,' the mortal interrupted). How you could cook food. How you could smelt metal. How you could boil water, killing the germs, producing steam that could turn a turbine. How you could ...

The mortal wasn't listening. He was looking across the darkened valley to where a neighbouring tribe were tentatively building the first log cabin, and grinning mischievously.

'Right,' said the mortal, 'thanks, much obliged, don't let me keep you.' He turned to go back in the cave.

'Hold on,' said Prometheus, 'I haven't finished yet.'

The mortal stiffened. 'Oh yes?' he said warily. With his left hand he groped for the heavy flint axe he kept behind the door for just such occasions.

'Fire,' said Prometheus, 'is all very well in its way, but I've got something that's really going to change your lives.'

'Change?' enquired the mortal. 'Or just shorten?'

'Change,' Prometheus assured him, 'out of all recognition. From being wretched creatures of a day, dragging out a pointless existence in semi-bestial squalor ...'

'Here,' said the mortal's wife from inside the cave, 'I heard that.'

'Instead,' Prometheus said urgently, 'you will be the sons and daughters of light, peers of the blessed gods, basking in the glow of the Golden Age of the world. Promise,' he added.

'Oh yes?' said the mortal, his fingers tightening on the handle of his axe. 'That good, is it?'

'Yes,' Prometheus replied. 'Listen to this.'

He cleared his throat, drew himself up to his full height and said, 'When is a door not a door?'

The mortal frowned, puzzled. 'What's a door?' he asked.

Prometheus asked himself to give him strength. 'No,' he said, 'listen. When is a door not a door?'

The mortal shook his head. 'Dunno,' he replied. 'Maybe if I knew what a door was in the ...'

'When,' Prometheus howled desperately, 'it's a *jar*!'

The mortal was about to wield the axe when something strange, something that had never happened before, started to take place inside him. It was, he remembered later, a bit like a cough, except it seemed to start in the pit of the stomach, float up into your brain, slosh around for a moment and then come out of your mouth.

For the first time in the history of the human race, a mortal laughed.

Prometheus sagged exhausted against the wall of the cave while the mortal staggered about, his sides heaving with laughter. The rest of the tribe came sprinting up and stood staring at him in disbelief.

'That's a good one, that is,' said the mortal, wiping the tears from his eyes with the back of his hand. 'When it's a jar,' he repeated, and dissolved into a fresh torrent of hysterical laughter.

'Well,' said Prometheus, 'it's not *that* good. There's this other one about a chicken ...'

The mortal ignored him and turned to the rest of the tribe. 'Here,' he spluttered, 'you lot, listen to this. When is a *door* not a *door*?'

The tribe looked at each other. 'What's a ...?' one of them started to say.

'When it's a *JAR*!' roared the mortal, and quickly stuffed his hand in his mouth. There was a deadly silence.

'You've been chewing those funny leaves again,' said the mortal's wife at last. 'I told you, didn't I, they give you those turns ...'

Then, simultaneously, something clicked in the tribal consciousness. They all started to laugh. No studio audience ever found anything quite so funny.

'Well,' said Prometheus, backing away, 'I can see you've all got the hang of that quite nicely, so I'd better be getting back. Don't bother to see me out ...'

And that, of course, is why Prometheus was stripped of his divinity, hounded off Olympus, chained to a rock and condemned to everlasting punishment by his fellow gods, for the one crime that they could never forgive. But by then it was too late; the harm had been done. Even the Great Flood was powerless to eradicate the effects of Prometheus's treachery from the Earth; for when the waters finally rolled back, a small pun was found clinging to the side of Mount Ararat, and eventually became the ancestor of all the Polish jokes in the history of the world. At last, after aeons of enslavement and repression, Mankind had found a weapon with which to fight the gods. A mere thousand or so years later, in fact, the gods gave the whole thing up as a bad job, as we have already heard, and retreated to the sun; where the few indigenous life-forms, if asked what's black and white and red all over, will simply look at you and ask if you're feeling all right.

Actually, as you will have guessed, this triumph of Man over the gods was inevitable, ever since the Third Primordial, Thing, had made up his mind to get his own back on his uppity nephews. You will have worked out, without any assistance from the narrative staff, exactly what Thing was the God of and what it was that he inserted into each of the Words when Jupiter, Neptune and Pluto weren't looking.

What you may not have realised, however, is that deep down inside them, the gods still haven't given up the fight. Oh no. Not quite. Not yet.

J ason scrambled up the last few feet, regained his balance, and looked about him.

He wasn't certain whether or not he was enjoying this.

Up to a point, he said to himself, yes, fine. The belting large predators, charging machine-guns, beheading fabulous monsters, OK. The thinking, no. Nature had, after all, designed him as a superb natural fighting machine, equipping him with shoulders like boulders, arms like tree-trunks, sinews like ships' cables and thews (whatever they might be) of a similar high quality. He could lift articulated lorries, leap over crevasses, climb skyscrapers and shoot the eyebrows off a gnat at five hundred yards with anything from an assault rifle to a bow and arrow improvised from a TV aerial and a rubber band.

These accomplishments tended to give him a rather straightforward, positive view of life; any lip off you, he said to the world, and you'd better watch out. Or rather he didn't. You'd expect him to, of course; his father (the shiny one with the thunderbolts, not the one who grew dahlias) undoubtedly did. He didn't. He tended to see the world as a rather endearing mistake that someone would be bound to put right sooner or later. It fascinated him. He rather liked it. The urge to kick seven kinds of shit out of it on the rare occasions when it offered him any hesitant resistance didn't come easily to him.

He liked flowers, too.

Large predators, machine-guns and fabulous monsters had better look out when he was anywhere in the neighbourhood because he didn't hold with them; that was simple enough. They were big enough to look after themselves, they annoyed people and they had it coming. And insofar as Heroism consisted of putting that sort of thing in its place, he was definitely in favour of it, particularly as against, say, accountancy, as a vocation.

The problems were rather more subtle, but Jason wasn't one of those Heroes who define subtlety as not walking off the edges of high buildings. What worried him most of all was the feeling that somehow or other he wasn't in control. Not that he had any particular wish to control anything that wasn't organically attached to him; if someone were to offer him a throne, he would probably decline on the grounds that they didn't agree with him. But he did feel that it would be rather nice to be in control of his own body, actions and – above all – thoughts. And he had this nasty feeling that he wasn't.

Someone, somewhere, somehow was taking advantage of him to get things done which ought not to be done; and if only he were in full possession of the facts, he wouldn't have any part of it. It was as if there was this little voice in the back of his head which sometimes asked him, as he was washing off the blood or scoring another notch on the gun-stock, whether that had really felt *right*. If it did, said the voice, that's just great, I'm very happy for you. If not ...

The voice had this really aggravating habit of rounding off its remarks with three dots, and Jason was inclined to regard that as something of a cop-out. To which the voice replied that if that was how he felt, that was fine, really it was, but ... Sometimes, Jason considered, the little voice got right up his nose. However ...

Jason's brow furrowed, and he looked around for the Centaurs. No Centaurs. Funny. The Dream had implied that good, thoroughbred Centaurs were getting a bit scarce these days, and anybody who had any pretensions to being constellation material would be a fool to turn down the chance of kicking the shit out of the ten hand-picked guaranteed genuine specimens who would just happen to be passing through the Caucasus later on this afternoon. Chance of a lifetime. Go for it.

Perhaps, Jason said to himself, they saw me coming and ran for it. That, he knew, would be the sensible course, and the mortal part of him told him that if he was a Thessalian Centaur and got word that a semi-divine headbanger was in the area and would be along as soon as he'd finished lopping the head off an Erymanthian Hydra, he'd be off out of it as fast as his hooves could carry him. But Centaurs, of course, aren't like that. Probably explains why they're getting so rare.

Unless . . .

Not you again, said Jason to the back of his head. Look, either finish the bloody sentence or shut up, will you? Not for the first time, he felt that the back of his head was becoming a pain in the neck.

Perhaps, Jason said to himself, I'm lost. But if I were lost, there'd be George with the golf buggy; and George was nowhere to be seen. So I can't be lost; therefore I must be here. Funny.

Jason looked round once more, but he could see nothing except mountains, and from what he could remember of his Theory lessons, there weren't any merit points to be gained by getting heavy with the geography. He scratched his head, sat down on a rock and waited for something to happen.

He was hungry.

It had been a long time since he'd had that apple, and there was nothing more edible than a small oak-tree for as far as he could see. That puzzled him, too. Food, like transport, is generally laid on for Heroes by the Management – when was the last time you saw a Hero breaking off in mid-pursuit for a quarter-pounder and a chocolate shake? – and Jason had come to take it for granted. Actually, the food was pretty terrible but Jason's mother had been one of those women who think boiled potatoes are the staff of life and so he didn't know any better. Army catering had come as a pleasant surprise to him.

Time passed. The sun – when Apollo called it a day the contract for solar services had been put out to tender, and a consortium of Australian entrepreneurs had made the winning bid – rolled slowly across the sky. A mild breeze ruffled Jason's hair, reminding him that he'd left his hat behind when he'd parachuted out of the doomed Hercules. He was still hungry. If anything, hungrier.

He stood up, filled his lungs with air, and shouted.

'George!' he called. 'Where's my dinner?'

Nothing. Not so much as a fruit pastille. Jason's monumental jaw set in a firm line, and he gripped the Sword of Whatever-it-was with grim determination. Then he remembered something and drew a small, crumpled card from the top pocket of his battledress.

PIZZA TO GO, it read. WE DELIVER – ANYTIME, ANYWHERE.

That solved that, then. All he needed now was a call-box.

Jason stopped, swore and threw the Sword of Thingy on the ground. He had had enough. It was just as well for the Thessalian Centaurs that they were nowhere in sight, or they'd have been lunch.

After four hours of searching, Jason had failed to find a single phone booth in the Caucasus mountains. Well, there had been one; but it only took Phonecards.

Nor had he found any food. The few stringy tufts of grass that clung to the rock were inedible, the leather of his boots was stale and the stones were off. He was starving.

Pretty soon, he thought, I'm going to start seeing things. My brain will start playing tricks on me, and I'll have visions of huge cheeseburgers.

I said, he repeated to himself, I'll have visions of huge cheeseburgers.

Cheeseburgers ...?

Ah, so you're still there, are you? Yes, cheeseburgers with a large fries, banana shake and an apple fritter. Chop chop. Now.

Jason listened hard, but all he could hear was the distant sound of three dots laughing. He gave up, retrieved the sword, and plodded on towards the far summit of the mountain.

Then, from nowhere, a huge eagle appeared. It hung in the air just long enough for Jason to see the paper bag and styrofoam cup clutched in its talons, then launched itself into a thermal and whirled away before he had time to pick up a stone and let fly. He stood motionless and watched it recede, until it was barely discernible among the rocky crags.

Then it started to grow larger. It was circling. It was coming back.

Jason muttered under his breath, grabbed an aerodynamic stone and started to run. The force of wind-pressure had probably turned the chips stone cold by now, but that didn't seem to matter.

The eagle seemed to sense that it was almost in range, for it wheeled sharply, lifted and soared away. A single chip spilled out of the bag and floated, sycamore-seed like and mocking, down to the ground. Jason ate it. Then he sprinted away after the eagle.

Just when he'd given up all hope, the eagle turned a third time. This time, it dived. It came at Jason like a Rapier missile, low and exceedingly fast. He raised the stone and let fly, but his senses were weak from hunger and he missed, albeit by a fraction of an inch. As the eagle swept past him, Jason fancied that it gave him a filthy look. He ignored it and stooped for another stone, but too late. The eagle had gone again, this time for good.

'Hell!' Jason said. Then he licked his thumb, just in case there had been some vinegar on the chip.

And then it was back again; this time, hanging absolutely still in the air, just out of range, watching him coldly from round yellow eyes. It's waiting for me to give up, Jason thought. Bugger that. He lurched to his feet, wavered for a moment as his weary knees protested, and launched himself at the eagle.

The eagle waited for a moment, then changed position ever so slightly. A chip wafted down, and Jason sprang on it like a tiger.

Then the eagle moved again. Another chip descended. Then another movement, and another chip. Jason realised that he was being led, step by step, chip by agonisingly weary chip, towards the summit of the tallest mountain.

He didn't care. He didn't care that his body was no longer his own, that he was being manipulated by a large bird, just so long as there was salt and vinegar on the manipulations. The eagle seemed to sense its triumph, for a small slice of tomato and a sliver of lettuce drifted out of the sky and settled on the grey stone.

Jason did a quick calculation and worked out that at this rate he'd be in Istanbul before he got a square meal. But that didn't matter. All that mattered was the next chip. He gave in.

Then the eagle fluttered down, pitched beside him and dropped the paper bag and the milk shake onto the ground.

'Have a nice day,' said the eagle.

The explanation is as follows.

Every choice, every seemingly irrevocable act – the white shirt rather than the blue one, Jane rather than Paula, dying and so on – is not an end but a beginning.

The alternative is not sealed off; instead, reality is bifurcated and forks off at that particular point. At the critical moment, what was formerly one world becomes two, one a carbon copy of the other. In the one world, marmalade is spread on the slice of toast; in the other, honey.

Thus, although there is only one planet Earth, and it is the only one in the galaxy capable of sustaining life, there are innumerable Earths each with its own subtle variations. The variations are not, of course, infinite, as there have been a finite number of event horizons calling a new Earth into existence. There are, however, an awful lot of them, and to a greater or lesser extent, depending on how things work out, each Earth has all of us on it. Thus there is somewhere – or was, at any rate – an Earth on which there are still dinosaurs, an Earth on which Napoleon captured Moscow, an Earth where all the videos are Betamax.

There are, however, such things as the Laws of Possibility; and it is also universally acknowledged that everything in the world has an effect, direct or indirect, on everything else. On what we might call the Betamax worlds, therefore, the lesser or incorrect choice generally sets in motion a chain of causalities which eventually results in the Laws being infringed and the entire world slowly fading away into a tiny point of light, which then goes out.

Only one of the Betamax worlds has yet to fade away completely, and this is because some extremely powerful forces are being exerted to keep it in existence. This is the world on which Prometheus, on that fateful night, tried telling the caveman the one about the Englishman, the Pole and the Corcyraean, thereby completely failing to communicate the divine spark of humour to the human race.

Of course, the gods aren't consciously keeping it going, because they know that this would be impossible. Any interference by the gods in the alternative-world process is strictly forbidden by the Laws – in particular, Section 45(a)(ii) of the Possibility Act and Schedule 8, Article 57 of the Monkeying About With Time (Prohibition) Act, as amended – and the only thing the gods can truly be said to be afraid of is the Possibility Police; who, it is well known, have an innate bias against anyone who regularly flies without wings and walks on water, and have been waiting for a chance to catch the gods out of line ever since the Primeval Dawn. Subconsciously, however, the gods find it impossible to sever the final link between themselves and their counterparts in what they cannot help feeling were the Good Old Days; and some of them, who understand about such things, have recently taken to messing about with the thin dividing line between the conscious and the subconscious. They realise that, as things stand, it can only be a matter of time before affairs on the Betamax world get so completely out of synch that they will have to let go, and therefore if there is ever to be a chance of going back, undoing Prometheus's betrayal and snatching the Joke back from the human race, something will have to be done fairly quickly.

The eagle dropped the last chip, wheeled in a dizzying spiral, and dived. As Jason lunged forward and caught the descending chip, he saw that the eagle had pitched on something, folded its wings and was sitting there, looking at him sideways.

The thing looked remarkably like a telephone booth.

Forgetting that he'd just had a quarter-pounder with cheese, large fries and a banana shake (albeit by instalments) Jason summed up his last remaining dregs of strength, hauled open the door and fell inside.

He lifted the receiver to his ear. Against all his expectations, he heard the familiar bored-cat noise and searched in his pocket for some change. He had some. It fitted in the slot. He dialled the number on the crumpled card, and waited.

'Hello,' said a voice, 'this is Pizza To Go. Sorry there's no-one here to take your call right now, but if you'd like to leave a message after the tone ...'

Jason got no further than 'thoughtless, stupid bastards' before the pips went, taking with them his last coin. He slumped against the booth wall and replaced the receiver feebly.

Then the phone rang.

Odd, the way one can never resist the summons of a telephone ringing. There is, in fact, a reason for this. Purely by chance, the telephone engineers have chosen for the dialling tone the exact notes of the Last Summons, by which the Judges of the Dead will call up the souls of the departed to the final tribunal. Of course, the Last Summons will be considerably louder, since the dead are notoriously hard of hearing. However, some ghosts are sharper-eared than others, and the ringing of the telephone occasionally attracts them from the Asphodel Plains. This accounts for the phenomenon known to students of the paranormal as the Crossed Line.

Anyway, Jason picked up the receiver.

'Yes?' he said. 'What?'

There was a silence at the other end of the line, as if whoever it was wasn't used to being talked to like that. Jason, however, was past caring.

'Well?' he said.

'Well what?' It was an elderly, rather querulous voice, high and dry. That, at any rate, was all Jason could deduce from the small sample he had been given – not, frankly, that he was all that bothered.

'Well yourself,' he said. 'Who is this, anyway?'

Another thing about telephones is that every unknown voice on the end of a telephone line always wants to talk to Carol. Is Carol there, they ask. Could I speak to Carol, please? There is either some enormous conspiracy going on, or else Carol is getting a hell of a lot of calls from people wanting to leave an order with the Chinese Takeaway.

'Am I speaking to' – the voice hesitated, as if it was reading something off a piece of paper – 'to Jason Derry?'

'Yes,' said Jason.

'Then please replace the receiver – not yet, of course – and walk five hundred yards due west, turn through seventy-five degrees and walk a further two hundred yards due north. Then turn through ninety degrees. Please replace the receiver *now*.'

The line went dead, and Jason shrugged. Being a Hero, he didn't know the meaning of fear, just as the average person doesn't know the meaning of the word *foumart*.* The fact that there had been a voice giving him directions might well mean that if he followed the directions he would meet the owner of the voice. Tے owner of the voice might have some food. If the worst came to the worst, he could always eat him.

Jason sighed and opened the door of the phone booth. As he did so, the eagle spread its wings and soared away. Jason checked with his compass; the eagle was going due west.

He paced out five hundred yards – difficult, since the terrain was uneven – made a guess at seventy-five degrees and turned. The eagle banked and set off in the direction he had just decided on. Pretty shrewd guess, huh?

Hundred and ninety-seven, hundred and ninety-eight, hundredanninetinine, and *turn...*

Jason opened his eyes and blinked.

He was looking up at a hillside, far away in the distance. Chained – yes, they were chains – to the rocks was the body of a huge man, lying face downwards. There was a raw scab roughly the size of a steel works, on the small of his back, over which the eagle was standing. The eagle had

---

* polecat

got bigger too. Very much bigger. There was blood all over its beak, and its eyes were huge yellow globes. Jason may still not have known the meaning of fear, but he would have been prepared to hazard a guess.

'Punctuality,' said the giant, in a voice like the sea, 'is the politeness of princes. But not, apparently, Heroes. If you look under the small rock by your left foot, you will find a packet of sandwiches.'

Jason looked.

'Where?' he said.

'Under the small rock by your ...'

'What small rock?'

'The small rock by your ... Just a moment, please.'

The giant made an expressive gesture with his left ear, and the eagle hopped over and stood by his head. They whispered together for a moment.

'Did I say two hundred paces north?' said the giant. 'I'm sorry. Try going ten paces further.'

Jason uprooted his legs and advanced.

'Right,' he said, 'got the small rock. No sandwiches, though.'

'Ah.' The giant wiggled his ear again. The eagle hopped forward.

'Is it a squarish brown rock?' asked the giant.

'I don't know,' Jason replied. 'It's hard to say with rocks. They all look the ...'

'Try going back a bit.'

'Ah,' said Jason, 'got that. Small, squarish brown rock. Sandwiches. Yes.'

'Oh *good*,' said the giant. 'Now perhaps we can get down to business.'

'Fire away,' Jason said, with his mouth full.

'Allow me to introduce myself,' said the giant. 'My name is ...'

'There wouldn't be any mustard, would there?'

'No,' said the giant.

'Pity.'

'My name,' said the giant, 'is ...'

'Pickle?'

There was a long silence. Jason guessed that there probably wasn't any pickle.

'My name,' said the giant, and then paused, as if waiting for a further interruption. 'There is,' he said, 'no piccalilli. And my name is Prometheus.'

'Prometheus?'

'Prometheus, yes. Nor is there any salt.'

Jason chewed thoughtfully. 'I've heard of you,' he said. 'I think.'

'Have you really?' said the giant. 'I'm *so* thrilled. Now ...'

'My dad,' Jason said, 'says you're a traitor to your class and you sold us all down the river. My dad says ...'

'No doubt he does,' said the giant. 'That's just the sort of thing I would expect your father to say. What of it?'

'Nothing,' Jason replied. 'Which river?'

'I expect he was speaking metaphorically,' said the giant. 'I think he was simply trying to express his disapproval of me. You should be able to gather from what you can see that your father disapproves of me.'

'The chains and the eagle and everything?'

'Well,' said the giant, 'it could be that I'm sunbathing and the chains are here to prevent me getting blown away by a freak gust of wind, but that wouldn't really explain away the eagle, now would it? Yes, your father has a pretty low opinion of me, all things considered. And I,' added the giant proudly, 'have an even lower opinion of him. And what do you think of that?'

'How do you mean?' Jason said, chewing.

'Let me put it another way,' said the giant. 'On the one hand, you owe your father filial respect, love and obedience. On the other hand, I happen to know the whereabouts of a packet of chocolate biscuits and a can of diet Pepsi. The decision, of course, must rest with you. Only you can ...'

'Where?' said Jason quickly.

'Hidden,' replied the giant. 'Now, if you will do me a little favour, I'm sure the eagle will be happy to ...'

'Yes,' said Jason. 'Hurry up, will you, I'm starving.'

The giant raised his head petulantly. 'Not so fast, young man,' he said. 'First, you will have to listen to a certain amount of tedious explanation.'

'All right,' Jason said, 'but make it quick, because ...'

'In the beginning,' said the giant slowly, 'was the Word ...'

'What do you mean,' said Diana angrily, 'you've lost him?'

'Just that,' Apollo replied. 'One minute he was there, standing about looking hungry, the next minute he was gone.'

Diana made an exasperated noise and turned to Demeter.

'Dee,' she said, 'you tell me. It's no use trying to get any sense out of Pol when he's in one of his moods. What's been happening?'

Demeter shrugged. 'He's absolutely right,' she said. 'He just sort of walked out of sight. Bing,' she added.

Diana frowned and turned to Minerva, who was leaning on her spear-shaft looking sage. Pure habit.

'But that's impossible,' she said. 'Heroes can't just disappear. Perhaps he's gone down a hole or something.'

'I thought of that,' said Apollo, ignoring the fact that he was apparently too idiotic to be audible. 'So I tried the infra-red scanner. Nothing. Look.'

He flicked a free-floating switch and the Earth suddenly looked as if it was bathed in blood.

'Satisfied?' said Apollo. 'Nothing. Nor has he borrowed a Cloak of Invisibility, wandered into another dimension or disguised himself in a false beard and a raincoat. He's just gone. Phut!'

Diana set her lips in a thin line. Bing she could just about handle, but phut! was something else. 'Don't be so feeble, Pol,' she said. 'Send a messenger or something.'

Apollo grinned at her. 'I did,' he said. 'I've had Sleep, Death, Thought, Time and Indigestion flying backwards and forwards over the Caucasus for the last twenty minutes. Nothing. Except,' he added, 'a bloody great big chit for mileage allowance, which *someone* isn't going to be too pleased about ...'

Diana sagged slightly. 'Perhaps they didn't look *properly*,' she ventured. Minerva gave her a look.

'All right,' said Minerva, 'but he must be somewhere. Everyone always is. Have you spoken to his driver?'

'George,' said Apollo, 'is at this very moment trying to convince thirty-two very irritable Thessalian Centaurs that his master has just had to pop back for a pair of winged sandals and will be along in a minute. He's as baffled as the rest of us.'

Minerva bit her lip. On her right shoulder, her owl shifted from leg to leg nervously.

'Well,' she said, 'obviously he's out there somewhere, but ...'

'Look,' said Apollo, 'didn't I just ...?'

'Let me finish, will you? But,' Minerva went on, 'all reasonable and diligent enquiries ...'

'Thank you.'

' ...have failed to reveal exactly where,' Minerva said. 'We are gods, and nothing can be hidden from us. Except,' she went on, 'by other gods.'

There was a short pause.

'Oh,' Demeter said, 'I see what you're driving at. You think one of us ...'

Minerva breathed in in the manner she usually reserved for her male relatives. 'No, dear,' she said, 'Not one of us here now, because none of us, not even Pol, would be so very childish. One of us gods, on the other hand, as opposed to the mortals or the Tooth Fairy, yes. That, I would suggest, narrows the field down a bit, wouldn't you think?'

Demeter blinked. 'Does it?' she asked.

Minerva smiled terribly. 'Apollo, dear,' she said, 'why don't you take Demeter away and find her something to grow? I'm sure we needn't detain her further, and perhaps we'd all get on that bit faster if ...'

'Oh do shut up, Min,' Demeter said. 'And get to the point, if you've got one.'

'Very well, then,' Minerva said. 'What I'm trying to suggest to you is this. A Hero has disappeared. He must be out there somewhere. Therefore a god must have hidden him. Now, don't you think that points rather at Someone in Particular?'

Even Demeter couldn't fail to catch her drift. The poet Homer describes Jupiter as He Whose Delight Is In Thunder, but poets have to be polite. His fellow gods prefer to describe him as He Whose Delight Is In Being Bloody Difficult.

'He wouldn't,' Diana said, 'would he? I mean, why?'

Minerva smiled. 'Bonus points,' she said.

'Bonus points?'

'Precisely,' Minerva replied. 'Typical underhand cheating.'

Gods, it should be explained, have no objection to overhand cheating, which they prefer to call Fate. Overhand cheating consists of wiping out whole cities with the plague or flattening your opponent's best Hero with a thunderbolt. Anything that is devious, however, or smacks of low cunning, they regard with great distaste, largely because it's usually too clever for them to follow.

'What he's done,' Minerva went on, 'is to magic this Jason away for three or four moves, and then he'll pop him back in when we least expect it. Then one of us'll be left with a headless dragon or a defeated army and absolutely nothing at all we can do about it. Well, I for one ...'

'I'm not so sure,' said Apollo.

Minerva turned and looked at him. 'Well,' she said, 'if you have an alternative explanation, I'm sure we'd all be only too pleased ...'

'No,' Apollo confessed, 'I haven't. I just don't think ...'

'I know,' Minerva interrupted. 'You never have, either. Now then, I suggest that we send Mercury, with the Lamp of Truth and the Celestial Trufflehound. That ought to have him out of it in no time.'

Just then, a shining portal opened in the wall of the sun and all the gods rose instinctively to their feet. They always do. Partly this is because all gods, despite their incessant bickering and backbiting, have an innate respect for the Father of Gods and Men. The fact that He tends to throw those who don't off the battlements also has something to do with it.

'Right,' said Jupiter, taking his place on the golden throne that none but he ever dared sit in, 'who's the smartass?'

'Right,' said Jason, 'fine. Now, about those cakes ...'

Prometheus sighed. 'And so,' he said, 'what do *you* think?'

'Think?'

'Yes,' said Prometheus. 'About the morality of it?'

'*Morality?*' Jason's brow furrowed, and he considered long and hard. 'Dunno,' he said at last.

'You don't know,' Prometheus repeated. 'I see. I must say that I find that tremendously encouraging.'

'It's not something I think about a lot,' said Jason, 'morality.'

'Really?'

'Not,' he went on, 'in my line of work. I'm more, you know, blue-collar. Mine not to reason why, that sort of thing.'

'You're more,' said the Titan slowly, 'a sort of hired thug?'

'Exactly,' Jason said. 'The way I see it is, somebody somewhere knows what's going on, so who am I to make difficulties?'

'Well now,' said Prometheus, 'I know what's going on, and I'm prepared to pay in hard confectionery. What about it?'

Jason frowned. 'What,' he said, 'me take orders from you instead of him?'

'Very neatly put. Yes.'

'I don't think he'd like it,' Jason said. 'And, well, you know what happens to people who ...'

Prometheus laughed and rattled his chains until the mountains shook. 'Yes,' he said, 'I have a pretty shrewd idea. A pity. Well, I'm sorry to have troubled you. The biscuits are three paces east under the roots of a thorn-bush. The eagle will show you.'

Great, Jason said to himself as he tore open the packet and put tooth to chocolate. Great ...

Not *you* again. Go away.

Sure ...

I said go away, will you? I really don't need this right now.

Exactly ...

All right then, out with it. What are you getting at?

Nothing ...

Good, because if you haven't got anything to say, you can just push off and leave me in ...

In ...

Slowly, Jason got up, finished his mouthful, and turned to face the giant.

'Excuse me,' he said.

The giant turned his head – imagine Hounslow suddenly picking itself up and rolling over on one side – and stared at Jason, who saw the two round blue eyes for the first time. He swallowed and choked on a crumb.

'Yes?' he said softly.

'Well,' Jason said, 'I don't suppose there's anything I could do without him actually knowing, is there?'

Prometheus laughed. 'As it happens,' he said, 'there is.'

A lthough it was now over five years since Sergeant Smith had had his funny experience, he still hadn't recovered from it, and his superiors at the Axe Cross police station had long since decided that being a desk sergeant was all he was fit for now. As they saw it, when batty old ladies came in claiming to have seen flying saucers, they would at least be sure of a sympathetic audience.

Anyone less likely than the sergeant to be a dreamer of dreams it is hard to imagine. A long, hard youth spent watching fights outside chip shops and arresting the more seriously injured participants should have cauterised his powers of imagination many years ago; but the fact remained that he claimed to have seen Something, and ever since he had been as unshakable in his story as an interviewing officer telling the court that during interrogation the defendant had repeatedly got up and banged his head violently against the leg of the table.

It had happened, Sergeant Smith insisted, on a Thursday, about a quarter past eleven at night, bang in the middle of Pool Street, just opposite the bus shelter. This guy had appeared out of nowhere, wearing a sort of bronze body-warmer and a short skirt, screaming blue murder and carrying what the sergeant, a man of limited vocabulary, could only describe as a bloody great sword. Naturally, the sergeant had immediately taken up a position behind the bus shelter for the purposes of more efficient surveillance, and from there he had a clear view of the man running down Pool Street as far as the Co-op, stopping dead in his tracks and being confronted with some kind of very big reptile, which he proceeded to attack. During the course of the struggle, what the sergeant stubbornly maintained was a bloody great hand materialised out of thin air, grabbed the man and the strange beast, lifted them up in the air and deposited them both in the carpark of the Bunch of Grapes; whereupon the tarmac of the carpark turned bright pink and started to glow eerily. As the combatants touched down, big black letters appeared on the surface of the carpark, spelling out the legend TRIPLE DEED SCORE.

Then the man had cut off the reptile's head, and the sergeant fainted.

Subsequent investigation of the scene of the alleged incident revealed nothing but three sets of car keys and a half-eaten doner kebab, and the only other person who claimed to have seen anything unusual had been a regular customer of the Bunch of Grapes, who saw unusual things as a matter of course. The fact that when, a year or so later, a new landlord from up north somewhere took over the Grapes he changed the name of the place to the George and Dragon was dismissed as sheer coincidence.

It so happened that Sergeant Smith was for once not dwelling on this incident when a woman walked into the police station and asked to report a missing person.

'I wouldn't have troubled you,' she said, looking over her shoulder, 'but my, er, husband's a bit of a worrier.'

'Oh yes?' said the sergeant, and reached for the book. 'So who's gone missing, then?'

'My son,' said the woman.

'Name?'

The woman thought for a moment. 'Mine or his?' she asked.

'Let's start with yours, shall we?' said the sergeant.

'Derry,' said the woman. 'Phyllis Eva.'

*

'Right,' said a voice from the cloud of heat, 'let's all get our fingers out and clear up this mess, shall we?'

The other gods took his words as a sign that they could sit down now, and all began talking at once. Jupiter banged the altar in front of him with the butt end of his thunderbolt and cleared his throat with a sound like the Alps falling onto a drumskin.

'First,' – the word resounded in the utter silence – 'first,' said Jupiter, rather less loudly this time, 'let's find out who saw him last.'

Apollo stood up nervously, holding an envelope between shaking fingers. 'Well,' he said, 'I've been trying to re-construct his movements, and so far as I can make out, his driver took him up to the Witch's hut. There he collected the Sword of ... of ...' Apollo looked down at his notes. 'Glycerion, used it to slay the Erymanthian, er, Hydra, and then went to make the Judgment of Jason.' He paused self-consciously.

'And?' said Jupiter. 'Presumably he then followed the Road of Virtue. What next?'

'Actually,' mumbled Apollo, 'he didn't.'

Jupiter frowned, his eyebrows like mating rain-forests. 'Didn't he?'

'Strictly speaking, no,' said Apollo. 'Not as such.'

'You mean he followed the Road of Luxury?' Jupiter enquired. The Old Fool was keeping his temper remark-ably well in the circumstances, the other gods felt, but they couldn't help noticing that it had started raining quite heavily down below on the Earth. 'This is something to do with this new Free Will crap everyone's always on about, I suppose. Still ...'

'Actually,' Apollo interrupted, 'he followed the Road Marked *Diversion* ...'

'Sorry?'

'Diversion,' Apollo whispered.

There was a very long silence; so deep that the gods

could hear the rain lashing down on Earth, millions of miles away. Good, Demeter said to herself, for the crops.

'Diversion,' said Jupiter quietly. 'I see.'

'It was my go, you see,' Apollo went on, 'and there was a ten-point Killer Scorpion left over from the Wanderings of Odysseus in a cave just round the corner, and I thought, since he was there it'd be no trouble if he just ...'

'You diverted him?'

'More or less, yes, I suppose you could say that, really, though it was more a sort of short-cut, because it should have brought him out by the Thessalian Centaurs if only he'd followed the little yellow markers like he was supposed to, and the scorpion has been getting up the noses of the locals for ages now and it really did seem like a good idea at the ...' Apollo's jaw gradually stopped moving and he swallowed hard, smiled and speculated as to where he would be likely to land.

'And that,' Jupiter said, 'was the last anyone saw of him?'

Apollo nodded, rather more times than was necessary. Uncharacteristically, Jupiter managed to keep his feelings under control, admittedly only by blowing the stars known to astronomers as Orion's Belt into a million pieces.

'Ah well,' he growled, 'we all make mistakes, don't we? And it wasn't as if you did it on purpose, or could be expected to know what'd be likely to happen. I mean,' he added savagely, 'it's not as if you're bloody well omniscient, is it?'

'No, er ...'

'The main thing,' Jupiter went on, 'is to keep calm, and not go doing anything silly' – and as he spoke, a jagged fork of lightning crashed into a nuclear power station in the Urals – 'which we all might regret later. It's all too easy, in circumstances like these' – a long-dormant volcano in the Andaman Islands let out a horrifying burp that was felt in Melbourne – 'to go all to pieces and make matters very much worse, but if we all try and keep

absolutely ... WHAT THE HELL DID YOU THINK YOU WERE
PLAYING AT, YOU DICKHEAD?'

Out in the silence of deep space, the enormous masses of
flaming matter released by the explosion in the constellation of Orion were suddenly drawn together as by an
unseen hand to form new stars, thereby preserving the
equilibrium of the cosmos and forming a new star-pattern
known to future generations of astronomers as Orion's
Braces. A junior nuclear technician was declared a Hero of
the Soviet Union for having the foresight to nail an improvised lightning conductor to the side of his generator, and
as the seismic ripples in the Indian Ocean subsided, the
major powers issued simultaneous denials and postponed
all nuclear tests for a week. It even stopped raining.

'OF ALL THE ...' Jupiter checked himself, closed his
eyes and counted up to forty million. 'Do you realise, you
stupid little git, what you've done?'

Apollo shook his head.

'Then,' the Thunderer went on, 'perhaps it's time you
had a little geography lesson. Starting,' he added, 'with a
field trip.'

Observers at the new European Observatory in Switzer-
land later swore blind that a very large meteorite landed
heavily in the Caucasus Mountains. However, it all
happened so fast that nobody else saw it, and it was later
put down to a bit of fluff getting on the lens of the
telescope.

'Can you hear me down there?' Jupiter said.

Apollo picked himself up out of his crater, dusted
himself off and said 'Yes.'

'You are now,' Jupiter went on, 'in the Caucasus Mountains, not far from the scene of the Choice of Jason. You
have, in fact, been Diverted.' Jupiter chuckled. 'Anyway,'
he went on, 'just over there' – forked lightning helpfully
indicated the direction – 'is where a Certain Very Bad
Person is chained to a rock. Now do you see what I'm
getting at?'

Apollo nodded.

'Good,' said Jupiter. 'Now do you see what a silly billy you've been?'

The ex-God of the Sun said Yes, he saw perfectly and it went without saying that he'd never do anything so idiotic ever again and it was typical of Jupiter to take such a reasonable view of the whole episode and would it be too much trouble to send Aesculapius the Healer down when it was quite convenient because he thought that he'd clumsily managed to break his leg.

Jupiter sighed. 'That's all right, then,' he said. 'Go and fetch him, somebody. And fill in that hole,' he added, scowling at the crater. 'Mortals tend to notice things like that these days.'

Shortly afterwards, Apollo was restored to the Council of Heaven, smelling strongly of liniment but otherwise intact. Jupiter moved on to the next stage in the debate.

'Anyway,' he said, 'where were we? Oh yes, Jason. Well, we now know where he went, but we still don't know where he got to. Mercury!'

There was a sudden rush of air, and Mercury, messenger of the gods, was standing among them. On his feet were winged sandals, in his left hand the caduceus which is his badge of office, in his right hand three large, flat cardboard boxes.

'Right,' he said, 'a Deep-pan Seafood Special, extra tuna, a Pepperoni Feast with ... Oh.'

There was an awkward silence, broken only by the tapping of Jupiter's jackhammer fingers on the arm of his throne.

'Now look, Merc,' he said, not unkindly, 'sure, times are hard, but moonlighting ... no. Get rid of it, all right?'

Mercury nodded passively, and the boxes vanished. Oddly enough, the pizzas did get delivered in the end, but in a totally different dimension and without the garlic bread.

'Now,' said Jupiter. 'I want you to go to Earth, find

Jason, come straight back. Do you think you can remember that, or shall I burn it onto the back of your brain for you?'

Mercury smiled thinly. 'Thanks,' he said, 'I'll manage.'

'You sure?' Jupiter asked. 'It'd be no trouble.'

'Sure,' said Mercury. Paranoia, perhaps; but he had this feeling that Jupiter had never quite forgiven him for trying to get the other gods to form a union. 'I'll be right back,' he said.

A few minutes later, he was sitting cross-legged on a mountaintop in the Caucasus.

'Here you are,' he said cheerfully. 'You did say hold the onions, didn't you?'

Prometheus, his mouth full, nodded. 'How's business?' he asked.

Mercury shrugged. 'Could be worse,' he said. 'It's not that there isn't a demand; it's the damned overheads. You seen a Hero about here lately?'

Prometheus frowned and spat out an olive-stone. 'Hero?'

'Yeah.' Mercury scratched his ear. 'Six nine, maybe six ten, serious muscles, chin like a snowplough, very bad attitude towards large carnivores. Ring any bells?'

Prometheus thought for a moment, then shook his head. 'Mind you,' he said, 'maybe I'm not the person to ask. Try the eagle.'

'Oh yes,' Mercury said, 'where is the eagle today? Last time I saw it, it was coming out of a Burger King. You not feeding it properly or something?'

'Something like that,' Prometheus said. 'We had a quarrel. I said to it, "Look, just get off my back, okay?" and it took offence.'

'Sensitive creatures, eagles.'

'Very. Still, we've made it up since. In fact, we're having lunch again soon. On me.'

'Glad to hear it. Look,' said Mercury, 'love to stay, got to go. If you see that hero, just give me a shout, right?'

'Will do.' Prometheus stirred a little. 'Oh, Merc, one last thing.'

'Yes?'

'Can I have my book back? Only I've just got to the bit where Perry Mason's noticed the missing cake-tin, and ...'

Mercury, patron god of thieves, grinned apologetically. 'Sorry,' he said, 'force of habit. Cheers.'

Mercury departed, and Prometheus, having counted, lifted his head and whistled. From a cave in the nearest mountain, the eagle emerged.

'Sometimes,' it said, 'life can be a real bitch, can't it?'

Prometheus grinned. 'Forget it,' he said. 'I reckon it's a good sign. We've got them rattled.'

The eagle raised the area of its head-feathers most closely approximating to the human eyebrow. 'Trouble with rattling gods,' it remarked, 'they tend to get nasty. Might take it out on you. And I've got to watch my diet. The quack keeps saying, eat more green vegetables. Last thing I need is having to stuff myself with kidneys as well as ...'

Prometheus wiggled his ears reassuringly. 'Don't worry,' he said. 'Quite soon they'll have other things on their minds, believe you me. Anyway, I suppose we'd better let them find him, or else they'll do something to someone else and we can't have that. What did you do with him, by the way?'

The eagle grinned. 'I left him at Baisbekian's Diner,' it replied, 'eating honey cakes. Shall I fetch him?'

'Better had,' said Prometheus. 'Oh, and Eagle ...'

The eagle stopped in mid-launch and beat the air with its huge wings for a moment. 'Yes?' it said.

'Thanks.'

'Don't mention it,' said the Eagle, blushing under its feathers, and soared away.

*

Mercury, meanwhile, had completed a lightning-fast survey of the Caucasus and was starting to worry; so preoccupied was he, in fact, that he flew over the Kislovodsk People's Bank without lifting so much as a kopeck. If he returned to the sun without finding the mortal, he was going to be in trouble; and with his record, that might not be pleasant.

Just when he had almost given up hope, a blinding flash of blue light caught his eye. He looked down and saw the sunlight sparkling on the Sword of Damn It's On The Tip Of My Tongue, Begins With G. He dived.

Outside Baisbekian's Diner, Jason was pulling his seventh plate of honey cakes towards him and lifting his fork when he became aware of a very old woman leading a donkey across the town's dusty square. He noticed the glitter of gold* under the hem of her long black skirt, sighed, and put the spoon down. 'Over here,' he called.

Mercury tied the donkey to a tree and hobbled over. 'These look good,' he said, and ate one.

'I see,' Jason observed. 'You come all the way from the sun to help me eat my dinner. That's service.'

Mercury scowled. 'Leave it, all right?' he said through a mouthful of baklava. 'Things have been very tense round our way because of you, very tense indeed. Where have you been, anyway?'

Jason shrugged. 'Here,' he said, 'eating. You ask the waiter.'

'But why here?'

'I was hungry. I fancied eating Caucasian for a change. You can get bored with pizza.'

---

*Traditionally, when on Earth the gods adopt mortal guise. Because of the confusion this tends to cause, however, there is a convention that they leave one of their divine attributes visible to give at least some warning to reasonably perceptive mortals. Thus, if a large woman with an owl on her shoulder runs over your foot with her trolley in the supermarket, it is wise not to say anything you might later regret.

Mercury gave him a look. 'Fine,' he said. 'You're supposed to be out there mutilating centaurs, but instead you're having lunch. That's great, really.'

'Right,' Jason replied dangerously, 'glad you approve. Because today I've flown halfway across the world in a freezing cold Hercules air freighter with no buffet facilities, been shot down by surface-to-air missiles but not fed, chased by crack Soviet mountain troops who didn't offer me so much as a KitKat, told my destiny by a witch who had nothing in her larder except dried newts' tongues, attacked by an inedible giant lizard, and flirted with by two allegorical women on diets. I am now having breakfast. And lunch. And dinner. All right?'

Mercury shrugged. 'All that starch and carbohydrate is doing the most appalling things to your body, you realise. You keep it up, in five years you're going to have arteries like an underground railway.'

'Suits me.'

'Great.' Mercury shook his head sadly and liberated another slice of honey cake. 'Meanwhile,' he said, 'there's centaurs out there getting impatient.'

'Someone should try giving them something to eat,' Jason replied. 'Then perhaps they'd go away and stop bothering people. And give me back my magic sword before I brain you with it.'

Mercury sighed. 'Sorry,' he said. 'It's not as if it gives me any pleasure, either. I've got this lock-up garage, right, absolutely stuffed with non-stick frying pans, car radios, synthetic fur coats ... You couldn't give half of it away.' He smiled. 'Anyway,' he said, 'I can see you're busy, so I'll leave you to it. I'll buzz your driver, OK? I expect he's wondering where you've got to.'

'What I need,' Jason said, 'is one of those bleeper things, you know, radio pagers. When you see George, tell him to put some bread rolls in the toolbox.'

The old woman got up painfully, stretched her stiff back, surreptitiously pocketed a spoon and retrieved her donkey. A few seconds later, a small electric wagon rumbled into the empty village square and the hungry stranger got up, left some money on the table, and climbed into the cart. The village blacksmith paused, a glowing red horse-shoe, gripped in his pincers, and turned to his apprentice.

'You saw that?' he said. 'That's tourism, that is.'

The apprentice grinned, and the smith chucked the horseshoe into a bucket of water, where it fizzed angrily. Soon afterwards, the smith had smelted some more ore and was beating out a wrought-iron magazine-rack with 'A Present From Bolshoy Kavkaz' worked into it in flowing Cyrillic characters. Thirty years later, he managed to sell it for two roubles to the manager of the local farmers' co-operative, who needed something to keep his delivery notes in.

'Jason,' Mrs. Derry said. Sergeant Smith looked up.

'Here,' he said, 'I know that name from somewhere, don't I?'

Mrs. Derry looked down at her shoes. 'If it's about the tiger,' she said, 'we told the man, we'll pay for a new one. That's no problem ...'

Sergeant Smith gave her a startled look, and then thought better of it. 'Isn't he the one who's out in the Carwardine Islands?' he asked. 'You know, the war hero?'

'What?' said Mrs. Derry. 'Oh yes, that's right, that's Jason.'

'Charged a machine-gun nest or something, didn't he? Won the war and all that.'

'Yes,' sighed Mrs. Derry, 'that's our Jason.'

'Oh.' Sergeant Smith bit his lip, drawing blood from sheer force of habit. 'I see. Well, actually, Mrs. Derry ...'

'Yes?' she said hopefully. 'He didn't write, you see. He always writes, and I was worried ...'

The sergeant's face became grave. 'Actually, Mrs. Derry,' he said, and hesitated. 'Didn't you hear the radio this morning, then?'

'No. Was there something ...?'

'Mrs. Derry,' said the sergeant, 'I have to tell you that the plane he was on, coming home like, it sort of strayed over Soviet air space and got – well, shot down. Sort of.'

Mrs. Derry said nothing. The sergeant swallowed. How do you tell people?

'There wasn't anybody killed,' he said, 'like, no bodies or anything. Except, you see, they couldn't find your Jason. I mean, it was definite he was on the 'plane but when the rescue party got there and they called the roll he, well, wasn't there. If you follow me.'

'Wasn't there?'

'That's right.'

'Oh,' said Mrs. Derry, 'that's all right then, I expect his Dad fetched him home. You had me going there for a moment, you really did.'

'His Dad ...?'

'That's right,' she said. 'Maybe you should ring the Defence people,' she added, 'in case they're worried or anything. Well, thanks ever so much, sorry to have bothered you.' She smiled and turned to go.

'I ...' Sergeant Smith started to say something. It would have been tremendously helpful; about how it's no good lying to yourself, you have to face the fact that he's not coming home, I know, I know it's bloody hard, Mrs. Derry, but sooner or later you'll just have to come to terms with it, we all do, believe me, but that's the only way you're going to be able to pick up the pieces and start again ...

Mrs. Derry turned back and smiled. 'Was there something?' she said.

'Mind how you go,' said Sergeant Smith.

Megathoon, alias Crazy Horse, President of the Larissan Chapter of the Original Thessalian Centaurs, looked up and snarled.

'And what sort of time do you call ouch?' he said. Then he fell over.

The other Centaurs looked at each other for a moment; then, very sheepishly, they started backing away, taking off their leather jackets and crash helmets as they did so.

'And where do you think you're going?' Jason said.

'Who, us?'

'Yes,' he replied, drawing the Sword of Sounds Like Mice Weary On Or Something and tapping the blade with his fingers. 'You.'

'We're just innocent bystanders,' said a Centaur, trying to cover his more equine parts with his helmet, 'who just happened to be passing. Nothing to do with us, honestly.'

'Oh yes?' said Jason. 'Then how come you've all got the bodies and legs of horses?'

'Have we?' asked the Centaur. It looked down and feigned amazement. 'Well,' it said at last, 'as soon as I get back to Thessaly I'm going to sue that bloody pharmaceuticals company.'

'Come off it,' Jason said. 'I know perfectly well you're bloodthirsty, subhuman cannibal mutants, the result of the morbid nuptials of Chaos and Darkness. So the sooner we get started, the sooner I can have something to eat. Ready?'

'Mutants, yes,' said the Centaur. 'Yes, I think we're all prepared to hold our hands up to that one, you've got us there. But the rest of it, bloodthirsty and cannibalistic, I think that's being a bit extreme, don't you, lads?'

The other Centaurs grunted – or whinnied – their agreement. Jason raised an eyebrow.

'In fact,' said the Centaur quickly, 'I would say even mutants is a bit of a misnomer, really. More like disabled, I'd say. Like, if you could see your way to regarding these as a sort of rather more convenient substitute for a wheelchair, perhaps we could all understand each other a lot better. You know, raise your consciousness a bit, abandon your deeply-ingrained cultural stereotypes, that sort of thing. In fact, I'd go so far as to say you're being a bit, well, horsist, wouldn't you?'

'Horsist?'

'Yes.'

'I thought,' said Jason, 'he was a Saxon king who invaded Kent.'

'Hengist,' the Centaur corrected him. 'And Horsa. A Horsist is someone who has this outmoded bias against horses.'

'Horses I like,' said Jason, 'Centaurs I beat into pulp. Who's next?'

The Centaur went white under its fur. 'Toss you for it?' he suggested.

'No,' Jason replied.

'Best of three?'

'No.'

'Would it help if I also pointed out that we are an ethnic minority?'

'No.'

The Centaur gulped. 'Look,' he said, 'perhaps if we just talked it over, as between intelligent human ... well, subhuman ...'

'Nobody,' said Jason grimly, 'calls me prejudiced and gets away with it.'

The Centaur swore miserably, drew its sword and charged. The last thought that passed through its mind before it lost consciousness was that the real trouble with Heroes was that they always had to know best.

At approximately half-past eleven that night, a small electric cart whirred its way up Pool Street, past the Friendship House, past the George and Dragon, past the butcher's, and stopped at the Post Office. A tall man in a golden helmet and battledress jumped out and posted a letter. As he was about to get back in, a policeman came round the corner and stared at him.

'Bugger me,' said the policeman. 'You again!'

The man stopped and turned round slowly. His hand tightened on a canvas sack he was carrying, but since it was dark the policeman didn't see that. Instead he strode forward and stood between the tall man and the small electric cart, which he appeared not to have seen.

'I want a word with you,' said the policeman.

The tall man frowned. 'Can't it wait?' he said. 'My mum'll be worried and besides, my dinner'll be going cold.'

'Never mind about your bloody dinner, son,' said the policeman, 'what about my reputation in the force?'

'What about it?' said the tall man.

'Look,' said the policeman. 'I don't want none of your lip. You're coming straight down the station and you're going to tell me what you were doing outside the George and Dragon this time five years ago. And don't tell me you were . . .'

The policeman's words trailed away into a sort of gibbering murmur which three dots are really quite inadequate to express.

'You know what this is?' said the tall man.

'Erg,' replied the policeman.

'This,' said the tall man, 'is the Sword of . . . of . . . Anyway, if you don't take your hand off my sleeve in five seconds flat, I'll take it off for you. Got that?'

'Erg,' the policeman assured him.

'Thank you,' said the tall man. 'Now,' he said, 'for your information, five years ago I was still at school, and I didn't hang around pubs at half-eleven at night. Got that?'

'Erg.'

'Sure?'

'Erg.'

'Good.' He turned and put one foot in the golf cart. 'Oh,' he said, 'by the way.'

'Erg.'

'In case you were wondering, I'm a figment of your imagination. You've either been drinking or working too hard, and you didn't see me. Clear?'

'Erg.'

'Because,' the tall man said, 'I've had just about enough

of everything today, with the definite exception of food, and I really can't be bothered with the likes of you, so I suggest you go home and sleep it off. Right?'

'Ouch!'

About five minutes later, a small group of youths who had just been thrown out of the George and Dragon for extremely antisocial behaviour happened to trip over a recumbent police sergeant in the middle of Pool Street. Having tripped over him a few more times (for luck) they assisted him to his feet and enquired as to his health. They also stole his radio and his handcuffs, but the labourer is worthy of his hire.

'Fine,' said the policeman, wiping the blood absently from his chin. 'I'm fine, really. Now you go on home before I ...'

'Wassup, Smithy?' asked one of the youths. 'You been seeing things again or something?'

The police sergeant shook his head vigorously. 'I ain't seen nothing,' he said. 'I just walked into a lamppost, that's all.'

Jason Derry opened the front door, waved goodnight to his driver and walked in.

'Hiya, Mum, Dad,' he called, 'I'm home.'

'That you, Jason?' came his mother's voice from the kitchen.

'Yes,' Jason replied. 'Anything to eat? I'm starving.'

'There's some sandwiches,' Mrs. Derry replied. 'Jason.'

'Yes, Mum?'

'You haven't ... well, got anything with you? Anything that needs burying, or ...'

Jason quietly opened the door of the cupboard under the stairs and hid the Sword of Glycerion behind the ironing board. 'Course not,' he said.

The kitchen door opened. 'Your Dad's out,' she said. 'How was the war?'

'Oh,' said Jason, 'we won.'

'That's nice, dear.'

Jason remembered something. 'Sorry I forgot to write,' he said. 'You weren't worried, were you?'

'Of course not, dear,' said Mrs. Derry, looking away. 'Why should I be worried, when your dad ... your other dad, I mean, said he'd keep an eye on you?'

'Him!' Jason said contemptuously.

'Jason!' replied his mother. 'How many times have I told you not to speak disrespectfully of your father? You really ...'

Jason scowled. 'Sorry,' he said. 'Forget it, all right? I've had a hard day. What's in the sandwiches?'

His mother noticed a slight cut on the knuckles of his right hand. 'You've been fighting,' she said.

'That's right,' Jason replied. 'You remember, the war, all that stuff. Ham, is it?'

'Yes, dear,' said Mrs. Derry. 'You going to have a bath before you go to bed?'

'In the morning,' Jason said, yawning. 'Right now ...'

Mrs. Derry gave him a meaningful look and said, 'Sharon rang.'

Jason yawned again. 'Oh yes?' he replied and yawned again, this time artificially.

'Twice.'

'Wouldn't want her 'phone bill, then,' said Jason. 'Any Coke in the fridge?'

'Yes,' sighed Mrs. Derry. 'I think so. You could phone Sharon tomorrow. It's her day off.'

Jason winced. 'Look, Mum,' he said, 'that'd be really great, only I've got a lot on tomorrow. Maybe next week, all right?'

His mother sniffed and went up to bed. Jason stood in the hall for a few seconds longer, shrugged and went to look for the sandwiches.

It is the tradition, now well over three thousand years old, that the Sybil or Pythoness of Delphi trains her successor in her priestly duties. Betty-Lou Fisichelli, for example, had been trained by the Old Pythoness (confusingly named Sybil), who in turn had been initiated into the Mysteries by her predecessor, the great Madam Arcati.

In her small but well-appointed flat in the suburbs of Delphi, Ms. Fisichelli was on the point of explaining the Great Primordial to her apprentice.

'Have you got all that?' she said, 'or would you like me to run through it one more time?'

'No,' said the apprentice, helping herself to a handful of olives, 'that's fine. So then what happened?'

'Well,' said Betty-Lou, 'after Prometheus had told the Joke to the caveman, of course all the gods were furious. They just sort of flipped.'

'Really,' said the apprentice, removing a stone from her mouth with more grace than the act properly required. 'And?'

'And so,' said the Pythoness, 'once they'd gotten control of themselves again ...'

'Have an olive.'

Ms. Fisichelli hesitated. 'No thanks,' she said.

'They're good, really.'

'Well ...'

A moment later, the Pythoness spat out a stone into the ashtray and continued, 'When they'd gotten control of themselves, they all decided to see if they couldn't do something about it. So first they grabbed Prometheus and chained him to this rock up in the Caucasus somewhere, and they got this eagle ...'

'Go on,' said the apprentice, crossing the room to the drinks tray, 'I'm listening.'

'They got this eagle ...'

'Can I get you something?'

'No, thanks,' said the Pythoness. There was no doubt about it, Mary was a natural Pythoness, virtually, well, instinctive, but she sometimes wished she didn't find it all quite so easy. When she'd been doing basic training, she'd had to sit up nights learning this stuff by heart. 'They got this eagle,' she said, 'and every morning and every evening, it tears out Prometheus's liver with its beak.'

'Heavy!'

'And every afternoon,' Ms. Fisichelli went on, slightly shaken, 'and every night, the liver sort of, well, grows again. And that's how Prometheus was punished for his betrayal of the gods.'

Mary was sitting down again, cross-legged on the sofa, her mouth full of olives and retsina. 'Haven't you missed something?' she said.

'Have I?'

'About the Unbinding,' Mary said. 'You know, how one day ...'

'Oh yes,' the Pythoness said, 'right. One day, it is prophesied, a Hero will come who will cut the chains, slay the eagle, and release the god ...'

'You sure?'

The Pythoness frowned. 'About what?'

'About the eagle,' Mary said. 'That bit doesn't sound right.'

'Doesn't it?' Betty-Lou asked, puzzled. 'Why not?'

Mary shrugged and removed another olive-stone. 'Oh, I don't know,' she said. 'Don't mind me. Go on.'

Betty-Lou folded her hands in her lap. 'The next thing the gods did,' she continued, 'was try to devise a plan to remove Laughter from the world. Unfortunately, everything they did failed; whatever they inflicted on the mortals, the one thing they steadfastly refused to give up was Laughter. And so the Divine Plan has yet to be carried out, and Laughter lies hidden somewhere in the bowels of the earth, so deep that even winged Mercury, the messenger of the gods, cannot find him. One day, however, it is written that a young demi-god, son of Jupiter himself, will discover the hiding-place of the unseemly sprite and will carry him back to heaven where he belongs. Then the gods will return, mortals will once

again respect them and know their place, and the new
Golden Age will begin ...'

The Pythoness broke off her narrative. Her apprentice
was giving her one of those disconcerting looks of hers.
'Well?' she asked brusquely.

'A new Golden Age?'

'Yes,' said the Pythoness firmly, 'that's right.'

'Just like the first one, huh?'

'Yes,' said the Pythoness, firmly. Nobody could object
to *that*, surely?

'That would be,' the apprentice went on, 'the time when
we mortals lived in caves, dressed in skins and ate raw
meat, couldn't read or write, died young of horrible
diseases, got eaten by wild animals, were thoroughly
scared of the dark, and couldn't even take our minds off it
all by having a good laugh about something.'

'Yes,' said the Pythoness.

'And that was the Golden Age?'

'Yes.'

'Fine,' said the apprentice. 'I see. Sorry, you were
saying?'

'Yes,' said Ms. Fisichelli, 'well, I think that's about
enough for one evening, don't you? Anyhow, it's getting
late, and I've got essays to mark and ...'

'Okay,' Mary said, uncurling herself enchantingly from
the sofa, 'thanks a lot. See you tomorrow at the seminar.'

'Yes, yes indeed,' said the Pythoness, absently. 'Early
Classical epigraphy, isn't it?'

'The use of computers in modern archaeology,' Mary
corrected her. 'Or is that Friday?' she added kindly.

'No,' said the Pythoness, 'you're quite right. What
could I have been thinking of? See you then.'

'Goodnight, then.'

'Goodnight.'

The Pythoness listened for the soft click of the door
closing, and then sat down to do some nice, comfy
worrying. It was, she reminded herself, her duty to select a

suitable successor from the archaeology students who attended her classes at the American School, and by and large she was convinced that she'd made the right choice. Such aptitude. Such intuition. Such ability to learn. Greek, even, on her mother's side, though her father was a nicely prosaic mining engineer from Pennsylvania. It was almost, Betty-Lou told herself, as if she knew it all already. And yet there was something not quite exactly right about Mary Stamnos.

'It's no good, dammit,' she said to herself as she poured out two saucers of milk (one for her cat and one for the Sacred Serpent). 'He'll have to be told.'

'Well?' Minerva demanded, 'so where was he?'

'Eating,' Apollo replied.

Minerva frowned. 'I don't seem to remember asking you what he was doing,' she said. 'Where was he?'

'At some sort of village café in the Caucasus,' Apollo said, trying his best to be very sweet to his sister, 'eating.'

'All the time?'

'Yes,' Apollo confirmed. 'Mercury interviewed the waiter specially. It all tallies perfectly. He was there from when they opened right through to closing time. The waiter remembers him very well because he left a tip big enough to enable the waiter to open his own tractor factory, and he says ...'

Minerva gave him a look. 'No, you mark my words, something has been going on, and the only possible explanation is that You-Know-Who was involved.'

'I don't, actually.'

'What?'

'Know who.'

Minerva made an exasperated gesture and mimed someone laughing while carrying a stalk of fennel. 'Oh, *him*,' Apollo said quickly. 'No, apparently Merc questioned him very closely. And, of course, the Eagle. Nothing. Couldn't have been lying, he reckoned, or he'd

have known. Very shrewd, Merc is, sometimes, and lying
... well, it's a sort of hobby of his, so ...'

He could tell from the way she was looking at him and
the owl on her shoulder was sniggering into its wing-
feathers that his big sister wasn't convinced. So what,
Apollo thought, neither am I, particularly. I just want to
get Min off my back so I can look into it myself.

'Anyway,' he went on, 'one thing's for sure – there's no
harm done. Mission accomplished, ten Centaurs reduced
to quick-fry steak and the Golden Fleece safely recovered
and restored to the Sacred Grove at Blachernas,* so I
guess the best thing is just to pretend it never happened,
okay?'

'No it is not,' Minerva said. 'There's going to have to be
an enquiry.'

Apollo nodded vigorously. 'Oh yes,' he said, 'there'll
definitely have to be an *enquiry*, no doubt about that. In
fact, I'd say you'd better get it set up straight away.
Sooner the better, really, don't you think?'

Minerva nodded and stalked away, and Apollo grinned.
How Minerva had got to be Goddess of Wisdom, he said to
himself, was another story entirely but nothing to do with
her IQ.

Having satisfied himself that Minerva really had gone
away and wasn't hiding behind a helium flare eaves-
dropping, Apollo put down the lyre he'd been pretending
to restring and switched on the Commentary.

'*And now we're going over to the ringside where Derek is
just about to have a word with President George Jones, the
American premier, whose team the Yankees have just
succeeded in putting a manned space station into lunar
orbit. Well, George, I bet you're over the moon about this
one...*'

---

*Fortuitously now the Kavkad branch of the Standard Chartered
Bank.

A scowl flitted over Apollo's face and he clicked the switch off. There was more to all this, he felt, than met the All-Seeing Eye, even if the effects hadn't immediately made themselves noticeable. He went to find Mars.

He found the ex-God of War in the bar, pouring himself a large ambrosia and ginger ale with a shaking hand.

'Do you know,' Mars said, 'what those crazy bastards nearly did to me?'

'No,' Apollo said, 'Look ...'

'I mean,' Mars went on, 'they wanted to run their own show, so it stands to reason, they don't need me to fight their battles for them any more. How I see it, I'm just in the way. In fact,' he added bitterly, 'that's it exactly, except that what I'm usually in the way of is something made of lead and travelling fast. Look, Pol, see what those jerks in the Middle East did to my armour?' He held up what at first sight looked like a collander, but which turned out to be a helmet with holes in it. 'Well,' he said, 'this time I've had enough. First thing, I'm going to go to him and I'm going to lay my cards on the table. JOM, I'm going to say, either you let me have some decent protective clothing or else you can stick your lousy job up where the sun shines out of; and if he wants to chuck me off the Edge, that's all right by me, because right now ...'

Apollo gave him a soothing smile and the torrent of words subsided. Smiling was probably what Apollo was best at.

'While you were down there,' he said, 'you didn't happen to notice anything – well, *odd*, did you?'

Mars laughed miserably. 'Depends what you'd call odd, doesn't it?' he replied. 'I mean, if a whopping great SAM missile up the backside is odd, then yes, I did. Really, Pol, I ask you, I was just standing there minding my own business and wham! Be honest with me, chum, do I look like a bloody tank?'

'Possibly,' Apollo said. 'Maybe they were just nervous. Or bad shots. But apart from that, did you see anything which sort of caught your eye? Out of the ordinary, anything like that?'

Mars poured himself another drink, a lot of which ended up on the bar-top. 'Out of the ordinary?'

'That's it.'

'Let's see,' Mars said. 'The Sri Lankans beating up on the Tamils. The Ethiopians stomping on the Eritreans. The Chinese swapping missiles with the Vietnamese. The Irish shooting up the British. The British shooting up the Argentines. The Americans dropping bombs on the Libyans. The Libyans setting off bombs under everybody else. No, can't say that I did.'

'Right,' Apollo said, 'fine. Only while you were out, you see, we lost a Hero.'

Mars shook his head vigorously. 'Wasn't me,' he said. 'All the ones who copped it today were complete cowards, the lot of them.'

'No,' Apollo said, 'not lost in that sense. Mislaid. He sort of wandered off for a bit between choosing the Path of Virtue and duffing up some Centaurs.'

'I don't know, really,' said Mars, sloshing his drink round in his glass thoughtfully. 'Heroes, you know, they're a bloody funny lot, believe you me.'

'What are you getting at, exactly?' Apollo enquired patiently.

'Simple,' Mars said. 'It doesn't say this in any of the books, mind, but I've been watching the little creeps long enough to have twigged this one for myself. They don't belong in the human race. They aren't human. Mortal, maybe, but not human. Or not *exclusively* human. Do you see what I'm getting at?'

'No.'

'Ah.' Mars reached for the bottle again. 'Fancy one?'

'Not just now, thanks.'

'Suit yourself. Let me put it another way. You remember how there are all the different worlds, because of the bifurcation of thingy and all that stuff we had to learn when we were kids?'

'Some of it,' Apollo replied. 'Actually, I spent most of those lessons looking out of the window.'

'Me too,' Mars admitted, 'but I looked up my notes the other day. Now the way I think it works is that your Hero, being all sort of different, he can flip back and forward between the different possible worlds all at the same time. Like, suppose there's a choice ...'

'As it might be,' said Apollo, 'between conspiring with Prometheus and sitting under a tree eating shish kebabs?'

'Exactly,' said Mars, 'very imaginative example, that. Suppose there's a choice between your two courses of action, right? Your ordinary mortal makes the choice, and he splits off into two different mortals on two different worlds. One does the conspiring; one has the kebabs. All clear so far?'

'Give or take a bit, yes.'

'Well,' said Mars, wiping a drip off the rim of his glass and licking his finger, 'where I think Heroes are different, because of some sort of basic intrinsic weirdness in their molecular structure or some such crap, is that they can come up against one of these choices, bifurc-whatsits, and there's a sort of third choice that suddenly opens up for them out of nowhere, just for them, specially. Means they can have their cake and eat it, if you like; no, that's not actually what I mean. What I mean is, if they've got to make a choice between having the cake and eating it, then sometimes, because they're Heroes and not ordinary, they get the option of having a doughnut instead. Do you see what I mean or have I lost you completely?'

'Vaguely,' said Apollo, thinking of the Road Marked Diversion. 'But that's impossible, surely.'

'Let's leave what's possible and what's not possible out of it, shall we?' said Mars. 'Walls have ears, and all that. What I'm saying is that Heroes are ... well, I think "jammy bastards" puts it quite nicely, don't you?'

'Possibly,' Apollo replied. 'So what you're saying is, if a Hero had a choice between fighting some Centaurs and having lunch, he might find himself doing neither. He might sort of wander off into another dimension or ...'

'Dimension's the wrong word,' Mars interrupted firmly. 'That's all strictly theology-fiction, not theology-fact. But I think – and you've got to bear in mind this is just me speaking after I've had a nasty shock from a rocket – I think what you've just described is entirely possible. Well, not possible, in fact completely impossible; but I'd be willing to bet it could happen, with a Hero.' He drained his glass, wiped his mouth on his sleeve and stood up. 'Who knows?' he said. 'Come to that, who really cares, anyway? Who needs to understand the perishers when you can outlive them, that's what I always say.'

Apollo laughed politely. 'Very true,' he said. 'Still, if you could keep your eyes open for me ...'

'That depends,' said Mars, 'on what's visible through them at the time.'

A t approximately half-past five the next morning, the
door of Mr. and Mrs. Derry's house opened and
Jason Derry came out. He was carrying a long canvas sack
and a plastic carrier bag.

The sun rose in a confusion of pink seepage and
presented the first commercial break of the day. Unfortunately for the consortium of Antipodean tycoons who
manage it now, very few mortals have the necessary satellite dishes and decoding equipment to receive the signals it
broadcasts, but Australians are nothing if not patient. Just
as soon as the fossil fuels run out, they argue, and
everyone starts taking solar energy seriously, then we'll
have 'em.

By a curious accident probably connected with his
unique genetic makeup, Jason Derry was a natural
receiver of the sun's subliminal messages, albeit on a
subconscious level only, and he had often wondered why
looking directly into the sun made him want to change to
low-fat margarine and take out unnecessary life assur-
ance. He had eventually managed to come to terms with
the problem by telling himself not to be so bloody stupid.

A small electric buggy whined up to the front gate and
stopped.

'Morning, George,' Jason said.

'Morning, Boss,' the driver replied. 'Where to?'

Jason grinned. 'Glad you asked that, George,' he replied. 'Been a change of schedule.'

'Oh yes?' said George cautiously. 'Been rather a lot of those lately, haven't there?'

'Yes,' said Jason, undoing the top of the canvas sack, 'and there's going to be a lot more. You know what this is?'

George nodded. 'Sure,' he said. 'It's the Sword of Glycerion.'

'What was that last bit again?'

'Glycerion.'

'Oh,' Jason said, after a moment. 'That's what I thought the old bag said, but I reckoned I must have got it wrong. Anyway, the point is that it's very sharp, George, very sharp indeed.'

'I know,' George said. 'So?'

Jason frowned. 'Oh come on, George, don't be so damned thick. I'm threatening you.'

'Are you?' said George, mystified. 'Why?'

'Because I want to intimidate you into doing what I tell you,' Jason said irritably, 'that's why. Why else, for pity's sake?'

'But Boss,' George said, 'I always do what you tell me, don't I?'

'Yes, yes,' Jason said, 'but that's because I always tell you what I'm *supposed* to tell you. Look,' he went on, 'I'm not in the mood for deep metaphysical discussion so let's just get going, shall we, before anybody notices.'

George shrugged. 'Whatever you say, Boss. Next stop Thessaly.'

'No,' Jason said, 'Piccadilly Circus.'

'You sure?' said George. 'Look, it says here on the manifest: Larissa, ancient capital of Thessaly ...'

'That's what I've been trying to tell you, George,' said Jason wearily. 'We aren't going to Thessaly, we're going to Piccadilly Circus. Instead,' he explained.

'Why?'

'Shut up and drive the bloody car, will you?'

The little electric buggies supplied to Heroes are manufactured by Vulcan, ex-God of Fire and Craftsmen, and being of divine manufacture they can burn off Porsches without going into second gear. They also come with a twenty-million-year warranty and centralised locking as standard. It therefore took George less than thirty seconds to get to Piccadilly Circus; which was just as well, since it then took an hour and a bit to find a parking space.

'Will here do you?' George asked.

'Here'll do fine,' Jason replied. 'I shouldn't be more than a couple of hours.'

'I hope you know what you're doing.'

'So do I.'

George shrugged. 'Please yourself,' he said. 'What's in the carrier bag?'

'Sandwiches,' Jason said, 'and a thermos. If anyone wants me, tell them I died of cholera, OK?'

Jason climbed out, tied up the canvas bag carefully, and descended the stairs to the Underground station, where he stood in front of the ticket barrier and waited. After a few minutes, a very tall, thin man with a flower in his buttonhole walked up to him and coughed.

'The worship of Mithras,' he said slowly, 'has all but died out in Saxmundham.'

'You what?'

'The worship of ... Oh bugger, sorry,' said the tall man. 'Thursday is not a good day for peeling onions.'

'Friday,' Jason replied self-consciously, 'is even worse if you happen to be left-handed. So you're Virgil, are you?'

'Sh!' said the tall man, 'keep your ruddy voice down, will you? I'm not supposed to be here.'

'I know,' said Jason. 'Neither am I.'

'I told them at the office,' Virgil went on, ignoring him, 'I was going to a seminar on "Whither Hexameters Today?" at Spoleto, but I bet someone's going to phone through and find out I'm not there. I'm a fool to myself to be doing this.'

'You're dead,' Jason said; 'what's it to you?'

'Just because you're dead,' Virgil hissed darkly, 'doesn't mean they aren't still out to get you. Anyway, this is definitely the last time I get mixed up in anything like this.'

Jason tapped his foot ever so slightly. 'All right,' he said, 'you've made your point; now let's get on with it, shall we? And next time I need a guide to the Underground, I'll buy one of those little maps.'

Virgil gave him a poisonous look and produced a couple of tickets from his raincoat pocket. They weren't like ordinary subway tickets, being luminous and made of gold. 'Don't lose them,' he said. 'Right. Abandon Hope All Ye, and all that stuff. This way.'

They walked for a long time down gloomy winding passages which echoed with unearthly noises. All around them, Jason became aware of what looked suspiciously like souls in torment – murderers, parricides and people trying to find the westbound platforms. For all that he was a Hero, he shuddered slightly.

'It only goes to show,' Virgil was saying, 'the truth of the old saying that a friend in need is a pest. Just because I showed Dante the way through the Inferno when he got lost that time – you know, one poet helping another and all that stuff, though that's a myth if ever I heard one; you try asking a poet to help you mend a puncture in the rain and see how far you get – just because of that, they've got it into their heads I'm a sort of one-man package holiday company. Mind you,' he went on, 'I blame my agent, the damn fool. He encourages them. He's got me taking a party of schoolchildren round the Dutch bulb fields next month, which really isn't my idea of a good time. I'll never forget ...'

'Virgil,' Jason said.

The Mantuan turned his head. 'Yes?' he asked. 'What?'

'Are we going the right way?'

Virgil sniggered unpleasantly. 'Down here,' he said,

'there isn't a right way. The right way is to go by bus. We go left here, I think.'

'But we've been walking for ages,' Jason said.

'True,' Virgil replied, helpfully.

'So which line are we taking?'

'Ah,' said Virgil, 'that'd be telling.'

They turned a corner and came across a busker. He had a hat with no bottom and a guitar with no strings, and when he opened his mouth, no sound came out. A mouth organ hovered round his head like a large chrome hornet, buzzing ominously and occasionally swooping in and biting his ear. Virgil stopped and felt in his pocket.

'Oh good,' he said, 'I thought I had some somewhere.' He took out two pesetas, a corroded pfennig and a fruit-machine token and dropped them into the hat. They vanished.

'A sad case,' said Virgil. 'In life he was a great conductor but one Christmas he agreed to appear on one of those television comedy-variety programmes and after that it was downhill all the way. First it was chat shows, then double-glazing commercials, and when he died, it was straight down here. Diabolical, what they come up with sometimes.'

Jason stared. 'You mean he's *dead*?' he asked.

'Of course,' Virgil replied. 'You're in the Underground now, you know.'

Around the next corner they came across a woman. She was crouched on the ground, hard up against the tiled wall of the corridor, with her hands clenched over her ears, in which were the earphones of a Sony walkman. Although the music was plainly audible to Virgil and Jason as they passed by, it was clear that the woman couldn't hear a note of it.

'That one,' Virgil commented with a shudder, 'speaks for itself.'

For someone who didn't know the meaning of Fear, Jason was beginning to feel decidedly edgy; but since

Virgil seemed to be taking it all in his stride, he did his best to conceal it. Thus, when a haggard woman with staring eyes jumped out at them and demanded to know the way to Platform Seven, and Virgil told her, and she darted off in the opposite direction, Jason fought back the impulse to whip out the Sword of Sod It I've Forgotten Again and sweep her head off, and just stood back feeling embarrassed.

'Another hopeless case,' said the poet, as the woman's hysterical laughter died away in the distance. 'Her crime was forever to be nagging her husband to ask someone the way whenever they got lost. Serves her right, I suppose, but still ...'

It had been getting darker and darker the further they went, so that now they could only make out the walls of the corridor in front of them by the glow of the burning graffiti-artists conveniently nailed just above head height at regular intervals. The shadows in between contained strange, shuffling figures who made disturbing noises, which Jason did his best to ignore.

'Nearly there,' Virgil said. 'I'd better warn you, the next bit's not for the squeamish.'

'Oh *super*,' Jason murmured.

They turned yet another corner and came to a set of steps, which led down to a short passageway. Onto the walls of the passageway were glued a number of screaming, struggling people, on whose faces demoniac posters were drawing in moustaches. Then they came out onto a platform. It was empty.

'Here,' Jason said, 'this isn't too bad.'

'You wait,' Virgil chuckled grimly.

There was a clanking noise in the distance which gradually got closer, and a Tube train appeared. As it went past them, Jason could see it was filled with wan, spectral figures, all standing on one another's feet.

'Once a commuter,' said Virgil, 'always a commuter. Horrible, isn't it?'

The train slowed down and stopped, and the doors opened. Some of the people inside made a dash for it and tried to get out, but at once the doors slammed shut on them with sickening force. Jason noticed with a spurt of terror that the doors had teeth.

'Can't say they weren't warned,' Virgil said sadly. 'Do Not Obstruct The Doors, it says, plain as the nose on your face. Hang on, it'll stop soon.'

After what seemed to Jason a very long time, the doors finished chewing the people and a big red tongue appeared and drew them back inside. The doors closed, and when they opened again the carriages were empty. From somewhere near the driver's compartment came an unmistakable belch.

'Right,' said Virgil. 'I don't know about you, but I like having my back to the engine.'

Jason grabbed his sleeve. 'I'm not getting in *that*,' he said.

Virgil gave him a contemptuous look and got into the carriage. Behind him, Jason sensed that there were people coming down the steps onto the platform that he really didn't want to meet, and so he closed his eyes and stepped in. The doors closed.

When Jason opened his eyes, all he could see was a perfectly ordinary Underground carriage, and Virgil sitting on one of the seats, meditatively stirring a large pile of ash and charred bones. Jason winced.

'Let me guess,' he said, 'this is a No Smoking carriage.'

'On the contrary,' Virgil replied. 'Only here, the train smokes the people. Sit down and have a rest. It gets a bit hairy in a minute.'

'Not again!'

Apollo nodded.

'Honestly,' Minerva said. 'We're going to have to get him one of those collars with a little bell on it. Right, then, where did you see him last?'

'Piccadilly Circus,' Apollo said. Minerva raised both eyebrows.

'Really,' she said. 'Well, well, fancy that. No prizes for guessing where he's gone, then.'

'Let's not be too hasty about this,' Apollo said. 'Maybe he just wanted to catch a train or something.'

Minerva ignored him. 'You stay there,' she said. 'I'll go and see where Pluto's got to.'

After a long search she eventually found the ex-God of the Dead lying down, in a beautifully-tailored box, in the cupboard under the Stairs of the Dawn. She made an exasperated noise and tapped on the side of the box with her foot.

'Job for you,' she said. 'Up you get.'

'I've retired,' Pluto murmured sleepily. 'Go away.'

'If you're not up and dressed in five minutes,' warned Minerva, 'it's a wet sponge down the back of the neck for you, my lad. We'll be in the observation saloon.'

When she got back to the saloon, Apollo was studying the Earth through some kind of optical instrument, which he unsuccessfully tried to hide between his knees when he realised his sister was back in the room. Minerva made a familiar clicking noise with her tongue and held out her hand. Reluctantly, Apollo gave her the instrument.

'How does it work?' she asked.

'I'm not entirely sure,' Apollo replied. 'Apparently it sort of picks up waves of random particles activated by disturbances in the fabric of possibility.'

Minerva frowned. She was hopeless with gadgets but refused to admit it. 'Like a smoke detector, you mean?'

'Something like that, yes.'

'Got anything?'

Apollo shook his head. 'He left a trail of fused alternatives all the way down to somewhere under the Cafe Royal, but then the screen just went white and started bleeping at me, so I switched it off. My guess is that it means he's already entered, you know ...'

'Yes,' said Minerva hurriedly. Gods do not like to mention the place directly beneath the cellars of Hamley's by name if they can help it. Bad vibes.

'Which means,' Apollo went on, 'he's effectively given us the slip, doesn't it?'

'Nonsense,' Minerva said, and as she spoke Pluto walked in. He was wearing a black dressing-gown and slippers, and he was yawning. He hadn't had a haircut or trimmed his fingernails for a very long time.

'Well?' he asked sleepily. 'What's going on?'

'We need someone to go out to, er, Regent Street for us,' Minerva said.

Pluto scowled. 'Oh come on, Min,' he said. 'You know that place gives me the willies.'

Minerva gave him a look. 'Don't be such a baby,' she said.

'All right,' said Pluto, 'you go.'

'It's your kingdom.'

'Was,' Pluto reminded her. 'I sold out to an Anglo-French consortium, remember? They were going to try and link it up with the Paris metro. Bloody silly idea if you ask me, but ...'

'Yes,' Minerva interrupted, 'now, if you've quite finished, you can be getting along. We're looking for a Hero, tall, muscular, blond, the usual thing, answers to Jason Derry. I'll put him up on the screen for you.'

Minerva fiddled with the controls for a moment, and a thousand-mile-high hologram of General De Gaulle appeared in the night sky just below the Great Bear. 'Whoops,' said Minerva, 'sorry, wrong disc. Now, try that.'

General De Gaulle was sucked back into the heart of the Pole Star and was replaced by Jason Derry, standing with one foot on the severed head of a huge reptile and looking bored. 'That's him,' Minerva said. Jason vanished.

Pluto stood scowling at where the hologram had been for a few seconds and then tightened the cord of his dressing gown. 'Dangerous, is he?' he asked.

'Depends what you mean by dangerous,' Apollo said. 'In general terms, globally speaking, yes he very probably is. On the other hand, I don't imagine he'll try and bite you.'

'Sod it,' said Pluto, 'I think I'll take the dog.'

The train stopped.

Jason looked out of the window. There was nothing to see.

'Where are we?' he asked. Virgil looked at him gravely.

'You should know better than to ask questions like that, son of Jupiter,' he replied. 'Particularly here, of all places.'

'Why?' Jason asked. 'We haven't broken down or anything, have we?'

'No,' Virgil said, looking down at the floorboards, 'not exactly. This is where we were supposed to come to. It's what you told me you wanted to do.'

Jason nodded. 'So why aren't the doors opening?' he asked.

'They don't.'

'How do you mean?'

'This isn't a station,' Virgil told him. 'If anything, it's a state of mind. This is where the train stops, but you can't get out here.'

'Why not?'

'You're probably the first person in the history of Creation ever to ask that,' Virgil replied. 'The doors don't open here for pretty much the same reason as they don't open the windows on Concorde. The environment out there is somewhat hostile.'

'Is it?' Jason looked hard, but he couldn't see a trace of any sort of environment, hostile or not; there was just that sort of darkness that means that all you can see is your reflection in the window. He said as much to Virgil.

'That,' Virgil answered, 'is the whole point. There *is* nothing out there. It's probably the largest accumulation of nothing in the entire cosmos.'

'Oh,' Jason said. 'In that case,' he added, after a pause, 'someone's been pulling my leg.'

'Really?' Virgil studied his fingertips. 'And who might that have been?'

Jason felt a slight twitching under his scalp. 'Oh, just someone I met,' he said. 'And he told me that – well, something I was looking for was to be found at the Underground stop directly under Hamley's. And I said that as far as I knew there wasn't one, and he said I should ask you to take me there. So I did, and now you're telling me I can't get out here.'

'I said nothing of the kind,' Virgil replied. 'All I said was that if you're so incredibly fed up with life that you want to get out here, the doors aren't going to aid and abet you. That's all.'

Jason leaned back in his seat and sighed. That seemed to be that, he told himself. And yet ...

'Virgil,' he said, 'can I ask you something?'

'Be my guest,' said the Mantuan.

'If you had a little voice in the back of your head,' said Jason, 'that kept telling you to ... no, *suggesting* that you do things that you really don't want to do, because they're dangerous and you don't understand why they need doing anyway, how would you react?'

'I'd have a lobotomy,' Virgil replied unhesitatingly. 'Nothing worse than a chatty brain, I always say.'

'I see,' said Jason. 'Only I have this awful feeling that I ought to get off the train here and go and look for – well, the thing. It. I don't want to,' he added, 'not one little bit, but somehow I feel that I should. Do you understand?'

Virgil nodded. 'Indeed,' he replied sadly. 'I wouldn't worry about it, if I were you. Lots of people get that.'

'Oh,' said Jason, encouraged. 'Do they?'

'Yes, masses,' Virgil replied. 'Just before they get killed. A lot of people do get killed, you see, and ...'

'Will I get killed if I get out of this carriage?' Jason asked. 'For certain, I mean; no possibility of survival.'

'I wouldn't say that,' said Virgil.

'What are my chances, then?'

'I really couldn't guess,' said the poet. 'You see, no mortal has ever been where you're proposing to go. Or at least never gone and come back. Therefore, reliable data is a bit thin on the ground.'

'Ah, the hell with that,' Jason said, striving to sound cheerful. 'Nobody had been to America before Columbus.'

Virgil looked at him and leaned forward. 'Have you ever considered,' he asked, 'how many people before Columbus tried to get to America but failed because they fell off the edge of the world?'

'But that's ...'

'You can say that,' Virgil interrupted him, 'because you don't know what you're talking about. And,' he added, 'I'm buggered if I'm going to waste my time telling you, because very shortly you won't exist any more. Or at least, if I tell you, then you soon won't exist any more, because you'll leave the train. Whereas if I scare you shitless about what's out there instead of telling you the truth, then you won't leave the train and therefore you won't die. Clever, isn't it?'

'I don't know,' said Jason, 'you lost me quite early on, I'm afraid.'

'It's a bifurcation,' Virgil said. 'To be precise, it's an Impossibility Frontier. It's impossible for a mortal to know what's out there and live to tell the tale. You have to follow one of the two alternatives – know and die, stay ignorant and live. There is no third choice.'

'Isn't there?'

'No.'

Jason grinned disconcertingly and lashed out at the window with the Sword of Glycerion, still in its canvas bag. The glass smashed, and the train vanished. So did Virgil, the light, the Sword and – agonisingly – the sandwiches. The only thing that didn't vanish was Jason.

*

'Good dog,' Pluto lied.

Cerberus, the triple-headed Hellhound, ignored him and growled again. The guard went white but stood his ground.

'Sorry, mate,' he insisted, 'but unless it's a guide dog, you can't take it on the train. Rules is rules.'

Pluto shrugged. 'Do you contain bone marrow?' he asked.

The guard gave him a bewildered look. 'I suppose so,' he said. 'Why d'you ask?'

'It said on one of those commercials,' Pluto replied. 'It's good for dogs, apparently. How about calcium? They're supposed to need a lot of calcium.'

'Here . . .'

'I know,' Pluto said miserably, 'I don't enjoy it much either, all this threatening and menacing and so on. It's this damned dog that causes all the trouble. I'd leave him behind, but if he sees me going out and I don't take him with me, he grabs the lead in his mouths and jumps up at me and barks. I don't actually like dogs much, to tell you the truth.'

The guard swallowed hard and tried not to look at the six small, round red eyes that were fixed on him. 'Are you sure,' he said quietly, 'that it *isn't* a guide dog?'

'Positive,' Pluto said.

'Looks like a guide dog to me.'

'Does it? Oh I see. Yes, it's a guide dog all right.'

'Fine,' said the guard. 'Now go away, please.'

Pluto shook his head sadly and walked over to the escalator. There was a sign saying that dogs should be carried on the escalator, but it had clearly been put there by someone who hadn't considered all the possibilities.

'Next,' said Ms. Fisichelli, 'you take the patera in your right hand . . .'

'Like this?'

'No. I mean yes. Then you pick up the simpulum in your left hand, dip it in the sacred barley meal . . .'

'What sacred barley meal?'

'Drat,' said Ms. Fisichelli. 'Oh well, never mind. I usually use muesli anyway. It's not quite right, sure, but the worst that happens is the prophesy turns out ten minutes fast. Now place the simpulum on the patera and count to ten.'

Mary closed her eyes. 'One two three four ...'

There was a sudden roar, and a cold blue flame sprang out of the sacred tripod, much to the surprise of Ms. Fisichelli, who was leaning on it. There was no harm done, however, since the flame didn't seem to know that fire is supposed to burn. It simply played up and down her sleeve a couple of times and then subsided to something like Gas mark 4.

'However did you manage that?' said the Pythoness.

'I don't know,' Mary confessed, 'it just sort of happened. Why, isn't it supposed to?'

'Well, yes,' Ms. Fisichelli confessed. 'Only it never has when *I've* tried it. I usually end up having to use meths and a lighter.'

Mary smiled, slightly embarrassed, and murmured something about beginner's luck. Then, as directed, she placed the patera over the flame, sprinkled more of the sacred muesli, and poured a libation from the small silver-gilt cornucopia. The flame started to rise again, only this time it lifted the patera up with it.

'Zippy,' said Ms. Fisichelli, impressed. 'You've done this before, haven't you?'

'No,' Mary said, looking away. 'What now?'

'Strictly speaking,' said the Pythoness, 'we should now sacrifice a kid, a lamb and a white dove. However, I have the neighbours to think of, so I generally skip all that. Sometimes, though, I do pop in a casserole. Less blood and saves me having to cook an evening meal.'

Mary shrugged. 'Sounds reasonable to me,' she said.

'Usually, though,' said Ms. Fisichelli, 'I don't bother. I've never noticed it make a blind bit of difference. You know how sometimes you can't be bothered sacrificing just for one.'

'Fine,' Mary said. 'So what do we do now?'

'We wait,' said Ms. Fisichelli. 'Sooner or later the god will manifest himself, and then we can ... Oh hell!'

The flame flickered, rose up, crackled and went bright green. The patera bobbed on the crest of the flame and started to sink slowly down onto the tripod. There was a foul smell of sulphur.

'What's up?' Mary asked. 'Have we got something wrong?'

'No,' said Ms. Fisichelli, 'that's just the busy signal.'

'Oh.' Mary raised an eyebrow. 'Does that mean we have to start all over again?'

Ms. Fisichelli shook her head. 'Not any more,' she said. 'It used to, in the old days. But now there's a sort of Re-dial facility. Watch.'

She leaned forward and pressed an embossed lion's head on one of the legs of the tripod. The flame became blue again and the patera started to climb back.

'Look,' Ms. Fisichelli said, and pointed to the heart of the flame.

'Where?' Mary said. 'I can't see any ...'

The words died on her lips. In the very centre of the flame a man's face was slowly becoming visible; first just the eyes, then the lips, nose and chin. Then the fire seemed to mould itself into the shape of a head, the flames curling up from a fiery neck and flickering wildly to form the thick, curly hair. Mary gasped. The lips parted and the fire spoke.

'Hello,' it said, 'this is Apollo speaking. I'm sorry there's no-one here just now to take your call but if you'd care to leave a message I'll get back to you as soon as possible. Please speak clearly after you hear the tone. Thank you.'

Ms. Fisichelli scowled. There was a sudden blare of trumpets that seemed to shake all the brains up inside Mary's head.

'This is Betty-Lou Fisichelli calling,' the Pythoness said. 'Er ... Oh, dammit, I hate talking into these things ... Look, would you please very kindly sort of descend or send down a messenger or a dream or something, when it's convenient, of course, because we've had, well, it's rather hard to explain, some very funny things have been happening and perhaps you should know about them, so please do call back, thank you. Message ends,' she added.

The fiery head nodded three times and slowly became nothing more than a random pattern of flames. The patera sank back. The fire went out.

'Well,' said the Pythoness, 'that was a complete waste of time, wasn't it?'

'It was the most amazing thing,' Mary whispered, as much to herself as to the Pythoness. 'He was so ...'

'And if he does call back,' Ms. Fisichelli went on, 'you can bet your shirt it'll be while I'm in the bath or washing my hair or something. I really hate that, you know, having this great big burning face pop up at you while you've got your head over the washbasin. Still, there it is.' She started to clear away the sacred implements.

'Betty-Lou,' said Mary, after a while.

'Yes, dear?'

'What exactly is happening?' Mary asked. 'I mean, I know it must be important, because of what the entrails say, but ...'

'I'm not so sure,' Ms. Fisichelli replied. 'Maybe the entrails were wrong. I've never been entirely happy about divining with frozen chickens anyway, but I'm in enough trouble with the Residents' Association as it is without killing chickens all over the place. Probably all a storm in a teacup.'

'Yes, but ...'

'I think something funny happens to them when you defrost them in the microwave ... Sorry, dear, what were you saying?'

'I was thinking,' said Mary. 'Maybe we could work it

out for ourselves. What's happening, I mean.'

'I don't think so,' said the Pythoness stiffly. 'Best leave that to the experts, don't you think?'

'Yes,' Mary replied carefully, 'sure thing, but don't you think it's meant as an omen?'

'Absolutely,' said Betty-Lou. 'That's why he's got to be told.'

'But surely the whole point of an omen is that it's a sort of coded message,' said her apprentice. 'Which means that whoever sent it expected us to be able to understand it. So I thought . . .'

'Fine,' said the Pythoness with unwonted irony. 'So you just tell me what it means when a red plastic nose suddenly materialises on the sacred image of Apollo.'

'Well . . .'

'Or how a whoopee-cushion managed to find its way onto the Throne of Prophesy.'

'I thought maybe . . .'

'Or,' said the Pythoness, 'why the three heads of the Eikon Triceraunion are all suddenly wearing brightly-coloured paper hats. I mean,' she said, 'any fool can answer that, no point in bothering the god, is there?'

'I'm sorry,' said Mary, humbly. 'I was only trying to help.'

The Pythoness clicked her tongue in a not altogether unfriendly manner. 'I know, dear,' she said, 'and it shows initiative and all the rest of it. But it's not our place to go guessing at things; and besides, he'll have to know sooner or later. It might be important.'

'I suppose you're right,' Mary said. 'But the message . . .'

'That,' said the Pythoness, 'proves my point, surely. I mean, it could be highly significant, or it could just be kids climbing in through the ventilation shaft again. Really, we have to leave that sort of thing to the Chief. Now, give me a hand washing up these last few bits and pieces, and then I think we've earned ourselves a drink, don't you?'

Mary nodded and Ms. Fisichelli tried to dismiss the whole business from her mind, but as she dried the patera and put it back in the Holy Chest she couldn't help thinking that somewhere there was a simple explanation for it all, particularly when you considered the message which had appeared, cut into the rock of the lintel of the Treasury of the Athenians, that same morning. After all, it spoke for itself:

'WISEACRES OF THE WORLD UNITE,' it said. 'YOU HAVE NOTHING TO LOSE BUT YOUR CHAINS.'

About thirty thousand years ago, when telepathy was the only readily accessible form of mass entertainment, there was a popular game-show on the main brainwave channel called *Read My Mind.* A panel of guest celebrities had to guess what each of the contestants did for a living, and if they failed they were torn apart by wild dogs. It was good middlebrow family entertainment.

On the show in question, a panel consisting of two river-gods, a wood-nymph and the Queen of the Night were asked to guess the identity of a more than usually enigmatic character, who turned up wearing a loud check suit and a red nose, and answered all their questions by bursting into fits of laughter. The panel had got as far as the fact that the mystery guest was something to do with entertainment, but there they stuck. Time was running out. The mind-camera was playing lovingly on the slavering jaws of the dogs.

'He's a tax inspector,' guessed one of the river-gods wildly. The compere grinned, shook his head and made woof-woof noises. The Queen of the Night started to have hysterics.

'He's ...' said the wood-nymph desperately. 'Oh God, it's on the tip of my tongue. Whatsisname. Whatchamacallit ... Um, you know, er, thing ...'

The mystery guest looked up sharply and scowled.

'Someone told you,' he said.

Then time ran out and there was an advertisement for soap powder, and so the telepaths at home never discovered the whole truth; namely that the mystery guest (whose name was Gelos) was in fact the personification of Laughter, the sworn enemy of the race of gods; in his previous incarnation one of the original Three. Another point which didn't get out was the fact that Gelos is the only force in the cosmos who stands between the gods and total universal domination, because only laughter and a sense of the absurd makes it possible for human beings to dismiss the gods as a figment of the imagination; whereas if Gelos ever finds a hero brave and strong enough to protect him from the gods, he will be able to rule the whole of creation.

Pluto stopped, took a plastic bag from his pocket and opened it, revealing a sock.

'Here, boy,' he said nervously. 'Find!' He placed the sock in front of each of the dog's three noses in turn. The dog growled ominously, and two of its heads started snuffling at the ground. The third ate the sock and, shortly afterwards, was sick.

'C'mon, good dog,' Pluto muttered, and the ex-Hell-hound suddenly lurched forward, heads down, and dragged his master into the corridors that led to the Piccadilly Line platforms.

It is often held that two heads are better than one, and so Cerberus should have represented the optimum in scent-following efficiency. However, after five minutes of enthusiastic baying, tracking, tail-wagging and snapping at the ankles of women with small children, he stopped opposite a fire-bucket, pointed like a gun-dog and sat resolutely down. Having emptied the bucket and found no trace of the missing Hero, Pluto began to lose patience.

'Look, you bloody animal,' he said, 'far be it from me to get heavy with a dumb beast, but unless you pack in the clever stuff and get back to work, you'll be up the vet's so fast your paws won't touch. Got it?'

That, Pluto later admitted, had been a mistake. Cerberus gave him a foul look in triplicate, snarled very convincingly, and bit through the lead. Pluto toyed briefly with the idea of blowing gently up the dog's nostrils, as recommended by the lady at the obedience classes, thought better of it, and ran for his everlasting life.

Cerberus, however, didn't follow. Having satisfied itself that its master was out of sight, it grinned widely and trotted off down the corridor in the opposite direction. A wall against which it paused briefly to cock its leg collapsed shortly afterwards into a pile of fizzing lime.

Cautiously, Jason Derry lifted his left foot, moved it approximately a metre forwards, and tried to put it down.

He immediately regretted it. There was nothing there; his foot simply continued moving, finding nothing on which to rest. The thoroughly disconcerting thing was that his balance was not upset, and as soon as he stopped applying pressure with his leg muscles, his foot stopped. He wasn't standing on anything, he discovered; he was just standing. Floating. Whatever.

The important thing at times like these, he told himself, is to stay calm. This environment may be decidedly hooky, but as yet it has exhibited no overtly hostile symptoms. You could probably get to like it in time. Let's be terribly laid-back and cool about this, and just take it as it comes. Who needs gravity, anyway?

'Help!' Jason said.

He listened as the word he had just spoken flopped aimlessly about in the darkness, slowly growing fainter and fainter and finally dissolving into a clatter of disjointed consonants. He breathed in deeply (there was no air, but fortunately he didn't know that) and tried moving his right leg.

'Woof,' said a voice behind him.

He froze, and after a few moments his heart began to

beat again. He turned his head and stared; but there was no light.

'Woof.'

'Woof.'

Three different voices. Either I'm going potty or there are dogs down here. Given the choice, I'm going potty.

'Hello?' he ventured. 'Anybody there?'

'Woof.'

'Woof.'

'Woof.'

Three dogs. Jason muttered something under his breath and speculated about whether the person responsible for all this had got his priorities right, exactly. Dogs are all very fine and splendid in their way – absolutely nothing against dogs, either as pets or as part of an integrated sheep control system – but what we really need most of all right now is a floor.

'Here, boy,' he ventured. 'Who's a *good boy*, then?' he added.

'Woof,' said three voices, and there was just a hint of ennui in them; as if they knew from experience that when somebody addressed them as Good Boy, it would soon be time to start retrieving sticks from freezing cold ponds. Jason plucked up his courage and extended a hand into the darkness behind him. 'Heel,' he murmured.

Almost at once, he was aware of something large and hairy brushing up against his leg and a violent rasping sensation on the back of his hand, consistent with it being licked by three very sharp tongues at the same time. It wasn't pleasant; but compared to a number of alternatives that suggested themselves to Jason at that moment, it did very nicely, thank you very much.

'Now then, doggies,' Jason quavered, 'you and I are going to be friends, aren't we?'

Three voices said Woof in such a way as to suggest that a temporary alliance might well prove expedient at the present moment, but any more of this mushy anthropomorphic crap and the deal was off.

'OK,' Jason replied, 'suits me. Have you got the faintest idea where in hell we are?'

A trio of voices said Woof in such a way as to indicate that if Jason knew, he wouldn't like it terribly much, but if he insisted on a clue there was a pretty nifty one in his own last remark. Jason grinned nervously.

'I don't suppose you know how to get the hell ... to get out of here, do you?'

'Woof.'

'Thought not.'

'Woof.'

'Sorry.'

Jason wiped his hand carefully on his trousers; then, for the first time in his life, he listened hard in the back of his head for the sound of three dots. Nothing. Marvellous.

'.' said a canine voice beside him.

'.' said another.

'.' remarked a third.

'Oh come *on*,' said Jason despairingly. 'Let's all stop pissing about here, or I'm going to give the whole thing up on the grounds of complete incomprehensibility.'

There was a long silence. Then the dog spoke; all three voices, but speaking as one.

'We,' it (or they) said, 'are the dog.'

'Well yes,' Jason replied cautiously. 'I had gathered.'

'We,' the voice(s) went on, 'would like you to consider what you get if you spell our name backwards.'

'What, now?'

'Yes, now.'

'All right,' said Jason, after a short pause, 'you get god. So bloody what? If you spell moon backwards you get noom, but right now I'm more interested in getting back to Piccadilly Circus, if it's all the same to you.'

'Think,' said the dog.

'Oh no,' Jason replied. 'I tried that, and look where it got me. Look, thanks ever so much for dropping by, but perhaps we'd all get on much better if we went our separate ...'

'We,' said the dog, 'are merely Speakers.'

'Barkers.'

'Speakers,' said the dog coldly, 'for the Thought in your head. You called for us. We are here.'

Jason opened his mouth and then closed it again, waiting for some words to drip through from the filter-paper of his brain. Some time later he said, 'You're *what?*'

'We are saying out loud what the Thought in your head would be saying if it could speak out loud,' said the dog.

'Really?'

'Yes.'

'You mean to say,' Jason said, 'that I'm actually thinking all this garbage?'

'No,' said the dog.

Jason whimpered ever so slightly. 'Oh be fair, please,' he said. 'I can cope with gibberish just as long as it's *consistent.* I thought you just told me ...'

'The Thought is not you,' said the dog. 'The Thought is the god-turned-backwards. Previously I have spoken to you in the quiet of your mind. Here I am speaking to you through the dog.'

'Why?'

'Why not?'

There was another very long silence.

'Had you going there for a minute, didn't we?' said the dog.

Stuff it, Jason said to himself, enough is enough. He made a careful estimate of the position of the dog's rear end and kicked hard. There was a triune yelp and a sharp stabbing pain in the back of his head, but he really didn't mind about that. He felt better now.

'Ouch,' said the dog.

'Serves you right,' Jason replied. 'You had it coming.'

'Can't you take a joke or something?' growled the dog.

'No.'

The dog growled ominously; and was that a very faint breath of moving air Jason could feel on his cheek? 'Would you care to rephrase that?' ventured one of the dog's heads.

'Why should I?'

'Because,' said a different head, 'in the circumstances that wasn't the cleverest thing you've ever said, that's all.'

'So what?' Jason snarled. 'You can have too much of being clever if you ask me. Right now I fancy being mindlessly violent.'

'Keep your voice down, for dog's sake,' whispered all three voices (but not simultaneously). 'This is not the right time for aggressive posturing.'

Jason shook his head. 'I don't care,' he said. 'I've had enough and I want to go home. Failing that, I want an explanation. My final, fall-back option is a heavily-mangled dog, but perhaps we can sort something out if we work at it.'

'You want an explanation?' said the dog.

'Yes.'

'Then you shall have it.'

Jason suddenly became extremely still, as if someone had just unplugged him. 'Did you say something?' he asked.

'No,' whispered three very nervous dog-heads.

'Somebody said something.'

'We know.'

'Who?'

'Woof.'

'*Woof?*'

Then Jason felt something in the back of his head; not felt as in an emotional response; more like felt as in there being a large, heavy weight behind his ears which was swinging in a semicircle, taking the head with it.

'Come here,' commanded the darkness. But a tiny spark of courage flashed across the contacts of what remained of Jason's personality, and he stayed where he was. Fear of death, the unknown, darkness and the Devil were one thing, he decided; bad manners were something else.

'Only if you put the lights on,' he replied.

The darkness laughed. 'Sure?'

'Sure.'

And there was light.

O n his way back up, Virgil was stopped by a hairy old man with long fingernails whom he recognised at once. He shuddered and tried very hard to look like some-body else.

'Excuse me,' said Pluto, 'but have you seen a dog?'

'Frequently,' Virgil replied. 'So thank you all the same, but ...'

'No,' Pluto said, 'what I mean is, have you seen a dog *recently*?'

Virgil considered for a moment. 'Can't say I have,' he said. 'Not for ages. But I'm trying to give them up, actu-ally, so it's no skin off my nose. Good Lord, is that the ...'

Pluto looked at him carefully. 'Here,' he said, 'I know you, don't I?'

'Me?' Virgil shook his head vigorously. 'That's highly unlikely, isn't it?'

Pluto frowned. 'I do know you,' he said accusingly. 'You're dead.'

'Well yes,' Virgil said, 'If you want to be biologically exact I suppose I am, but I try not to dwell on it too much. Clearly where you come from, tact is held in roughly the same esteem as personal appearance. And now I must be ...'

'Then what are you doing here?'

'Where?'

'Here,' Pluto said, 'in the land of the living. You should be in ...'

'And the same to you too,' Virgil said quickly. 'Must rush. Bye.'

It was fortunate for the poet that Pluto had other things on his mind, for the ex-God of the Dead has never, despite his best efforts, completely retired, and he has extremely strong views on dead people who wander about topside, fiddling about with the Great Chain of Being and startling old ladies. Instead of taking the matter further, however, Pluto simply shrugged and carried on following the dog.

It wasn't difficult, actually; in many places, the tiles on the walls of the corridors were already starting to bubble, and the smell was unmistakable. He might be three-headed, immortal and capable of human speech, but Cerberus was very much a dog.

Down past the normal, everyday levels now, and Pluto began to feel that familiar feeling of uneasiness, together with a certain very faint nostalgia. It had been years since he last visited Hell (or, as he had always tried to think of it, the Autumn Leaves Rest Home); and – well, you can never completely let go, can you?

My God, Pluto said to himself as he wandered through the endless passageways, what *have* they done to the old place? All right, it had never exactly been what you'd call cosy – too many souls-in-torment for that – but at least he'd tried his best. You can do a lot with the odd pot plant here and framed print there, the occasional lick of paint and roll of woodchip when the budget could run to it; even just little things, like a table, a couple of chairs and a few old colour supplements, made a great deal of difference to the guests (Pluto always thought of them as guests). After all, a lot of people have to spend a lot of time here, and the least you can do is try to encourage them to think of it as their *home* ... He shook his head sadly and tried to remember where the laundry cupboard used to be.

He arrived on the platform just as the train was pulling in and jumped nimbly through the doors, stepping over the crushed bodies with the ease of long practice. The train was always pretty full at this time of day, he remembered, but he found one of those corner seats which have a little blue notice above it saying *Please give up this seat if an irrevocably damned person needs it*, put a damned expression on his face, and sat down. He was just starting to wonder where the dog could have got to when he became aware of someone standing over him.

'I said, Tickets please.'

Pluto looked up into what he took at first to be a pair of blue industrial lasers, and nearly jumped out of his skin.

'Look,' said the spectre, 'have you got a ticket or not?' Pluto twitched slightly and the spectre glowered at him, if yellow-fanged, goat-headed monsters can glower; the point has never been properly researched, understandably.

Pluto pulled himself together. 'Well, no,' he admitted. 'You're new here, aren't you?'

'If you haven't got a ticket,' said the spectre – how, Pluto asked himself, does he manage to avoid skewering his own upper lip every time he speaks? – 'you'll have to buy one now. That or I put you off at the next stop.'

Pluto, who knew what the next stop was, rummaged vigorously in his pocket for change. Being a god is all very well, but one doesn't like to push one's luck. Mercifully, he found some money.

'How much?' he asked, and the spectre told him. While it was writing out a ticket, Pluto laid the two coins across his own closed eyelids and waited.

'Here,' said the spectre, 'haven't you got anything smaller?'

Pluto apologised, took his ticket and his change, and started breathing again. Spectres were definitely new since last time, although he remembered that there had been demons. State-registered demons, naturally. They had been pretty horrible, true; but at least they were polite and had their watches pinned to their frontal scales.

The panic over, he leaned back in his seat and watched the stations go by – Lechery, Gluttony, Wrath (change

here for Murder, Parricide and Regicide), Sloth, Sloth
Circus, High Street Sloth, Sloth Central, Sloth Broadway,
Greed (escalator link to Simony), Pride and Being Found
Out ...

Being Found Out? Yes, thought Pluto, I guess I really
am out of touch. He shrugged and started reading the
advertisements.

'Ah,' Jason said, 'hello there.'

Me and my big mouth, he said to himself. Who was it
insisted on having the lights on, then? Old Mister Dickhead, that's who.

'Hello yourself.'

There was a long pause, and Jason took a cautious look
at his new companion.

Say what you like about Jason, he is not one of those
idiots who takes against people just because of the colour
of their skin. But he does like them to have skin, and this
chap palpably didn't. Instead, he seemed to have
masonry.

Description is the lifeblood of narrative, so let us start
with the furniture. The throne he sat in was made from
some sort of very shiny black metal, and its four feet,
carved in the shape of disconcertingly realistic dragons'
heads, rested on nothing at all. The little light that there
was seemed to be coming from the throne, but it wasn't as
if there were little bulbs hidden discreetly behind the
reliefs of writhing serpents and contorted bull-headed
shapes. The light just seemed to ooze out of the metal, like
acid from a very old battery. There were other things
oozing out of the throne apart from the light, of course, but
since they seemed to be turning into snakes and spiders
and other nasty things as soon as they got clear of the
throne Jason decided to do the sensible thing and pretend
he hadn't seen them.

So much for the furniture. Now for the clothes. He wore
a flowing black robe, heavy with glittering black

gemstones; jet and obsidian, that sort of thing, although ordinary gemstones don't hurt your eyes so much when you look at them. The cloth – Jason assumed for the sake of a quiet life that it was cloth – was simply the colour and texture of the absence of light. On his feet he wore shoes in the shape of huge hooked talons, except that they weren't shoes.

Which leaves us with himself. Well, he was big. Extremely big. Too big. You couldn't really think of anything roomy enough to accommodate him comfortably or at all. Nor was his appearance rendered any more cuddly and lovable by the fact that he was apparently sculpted from that very hard, slightly shiny black rock which the Egyptians used to use for their less cheerful efforts in portraiture.

We are pussyfooting, we know; but that is because, since the Great Adjective Shortage of 1976, we simply can't get the materials. We will therefore leave it at Very Horrible and hope that you will bear with us and use your imaginations. Carefully.

'Have a sausage roll,' he said.

Jason grinned weakly. 'No thanks,' he said. 'I had something before I came out, really. Er ...'

'Yes?'

'Well, it's ... I mean ... Like, don't let me keep you or anything, I ...'

'You're not.'

'Oh, I ...'

'I don't get many visitors. It's nice to speak to someone occasionally, even just a mortal.'

'Well, that's very kind of you to say so, but I'm sure you're very busy really, and ...'

'No I'm not.'

'Ah. Yes. Um ...'

'Are you,' he said, 'Jason Derry?'

That, Jason felt, was one of those trick questions, like *Was it you who broke the window?* He made a small, indecisive gesture. 'Er ...' he said.

'You are, aren't you?'

'Um ...'

'Your dog seems to think you are.'

'My dog?'

'I take it that's your dog? Who's a *good* boy, then?'

Jason looked round to see Cerberus nodding all three heads at once. Not for the first time, Jason remembered that he didn't much like dogs.

'Yes,' he said.

'Ah,' he said, 'that's all right, then.'

There was a blinding flash of multi-coloured light and the throne and its occupant vanished. The sheer force of so much light knocked Jason clean off his feet (not that he was exactly on them to begin with) and he fell headlong onto nothing at all.

Or, to be pedantically accurate, a carpet. Quite a nice carpet, in fact. Woolly, deep-pile, the colour of spilt tea.

'Sorry about that,' said a voice above his head. 'That was clumsy of me.'

Slowly, Jason looked up, and his eyes met the toes of a pair of slippers. Blue, slightly scuffed, comfortable-looking.

'Pleased to meet you, Jason,' said the voice. 'You don't mind if I call you Jason, do you?'

Jason managed to detach his eyes from the slippers and looked up further still. The throne and the living statue had gone; however, the floor had come back. Also the walls, the ceiling, the Sword of Whatsit (but not its name), and the bag of sandwiches. The latter two exhibits were on a coffee-table beside an armchair in which was seated a very nice, apparently quite friendly old gentleman in a dressing-gown and blue slippers. He had a plate of the most delicious-looking sausage rolls on his lap, and he offered one to Jason.

'Sorry about all the black stuff,' he said, 'but in my position you can't be too careful. It's supposed to scare the crap out of people. Of course, I've never actually seen it myself so I don't know if it works. Does it?'

'Yes,' said Jason with his mouth full. For some reason, which he couldn't quite fathom, he felt a strong urge to burst out laughing at this point; being possessed of semi-divine willpower, however, he managed to keep it to a discreet snurge.

'Oh good,' the nice man replied. 'Now, let me introduce myself, and then we can have a cup of tea and a chat. My name's Gelos. I gather you wanted to meet me.'

'Your economy,' said Diana carefully, 'and raise you fifty.'

Apollo nodded listlessly. Diana muttered something under her breath and rolled the dice.

'More fool you!' she crowed. 'We're welching on our National Debt, so sucks to you.'

Apollo hardly seemed to notice. 'That's nice,' he said distractedly. 'Look, tell me when it's my go, will you, I'm just watching something over here.'

Diana scowled. 'Pol,' she said, 'I've just wiped out three of your major clearing banks. Aren't you interested?'

'Sorry?'

'Pol!' Diana banged her goblet of ambrosia sharply on the table. 'Will you please pay attention to the Game!'

'Mmmm,' Apollo replied. 'Could you just bear with me a moment while I just nip down to Earth? Perhaps you could just ask Ma or someone to play my hand for me while I'm away.'

Diana was now seriously worried. Asking a fellow god to take your go for you was like offering the Big Bad Wolf a job in a crèche. 'Is it, er, important?' she asked.

'Quite,' Apollo answered, 'yes.'

'Shouldn't I call Min, then?'

'No,' Apollo said firmly, 'decidedly not.'

'Why?'

Apollo considered his choice of words carefully. 'For the same reason,' he said at last, 'why you shouldn't remove rings from coffee-tables with coarse grain sandpaper. Won't be long.'

Diana watched as he disappeared into the far darkness, shrugged, and tentatively moved the Chinese army into Nepal. As she did so, a single golden rose leaf drifted slowly down from above her head, twirled gracefully and settled on her knee. She picked it up and saw that there were tiny letters picked out on it in fire.

I saw that, they said.

'Ah nuts,' Diana said, and removed her army.

'What do you mean,' said Ms. Fisichelli, 'there aren't any?'

'I'm sorry,' Mary replied ruefully. 'The jar's empty.'

Ms. Fisichelli scratched her head. 'That's funny,' she said. 'There were plenty when I looked this morning.'

'I know,' said Mary.

'Pardon me?'

'I ate them,' Mary explained.

Ms. Fisichelli suddenly became very still and cold, like a mammoth in a glacier. 'You ate them,' she repeated.

'Well, er, yes.'

'Apollo's sacred olives.'

'Yes. I ...'

'I see,' said Ms. Fisichelli. 'Well,' she went on, 'that's fine. Thank you so much for letting me know. I suppose Mr. A is going to have to make do with tinned olives from the deli just this once but I'm sure he won't mind.'

'I ...'

'And now,' Ms. Fisichelli continued remorselessly, 'provided always that you haven't eaten the altar and the sacred tripod I think it's time we made a start. Pass me the simpulum, please.'

Mary bowed her head and handed the Pythoness the simpulum without comment. Nuts, said a voice at the back of her head. I was just hungry, that's all ...

Ms. Fisichelli, meanwhile, had turned on the Sacred Gas and was just trying to get the Sacred Lighter to work (guess who forgot to change the Holy Flint again) when the

Sacred Flame suddenly leapt up of its own accord, nearly taking her eyebrows off.

'Goddamnit, you clumsy ... Gee, I'm *sorry*.' In the presence of her god, Ms. Fisichelli's aggravation dissolved. 'I wasn't expecting.'

The divine head nodded on its neck of flame. 'Okay,' it said, 'my fault, sorry. Look, can we do without all this mumbo-jumbo for once? I've only popped out for a moment, and I don't want Min ... I mean, this can only be a brief audience. I've got to, well, see a man.'

'Master?'

'About a dog.'

'I see, Master.'

'So,' said the divine head, 'if it's all the same to you girls, I'm just going to slip into something more comfortable. Back in a tick.'

The sacred flame went suddenly out and the patera, deprived of its support, dropped like a stone and shattered on the rim of the tripod. Apollo materialised next to it just in time to be hit on the back of the hand by a flying potsherd.

'Ouch,' he said.

'Master!'

'Betty,' said Apollo irritably, 'let's just leave all that stuff, shall we? As a matter of fact, I'm perfectly capable of getting here on my own without having to be conjured up, dematerialised, transmuted into the Spirit, sucked up through eight yards of narrow copper pipe and set fire to, so in future I'll trouble you just to leave a message with Reception, all right?'

Mary giggled very slightly, thinking of the olives. Ms. Fisichelli, if she noticed her disciple's lapse, ignored it.

'I'm terribly sorry to have bothered you ...' she said.

Apollo sighed, removed a back issue of the *Journal of Byzantine Studies* from the armchair, and sat down. 'That's all right,' he said wearily. 'Can we get on now, please?'

Ms. Fisichelli flushed and sat down on the sofa. For her part, Mary folded her legs gracefully and kneeled on the floor. Apollo noticed, reflected that he was old enough to be her great - great-grandfather, and looked firmly at the Pythoness, who became suddenly flustered.

'It's nothing really,' she stammered. 'It's just, you did say to let you know if I came across anything unusual about the Derry boy, and there have been other things too, and you know how sometimes even things that don't seem important at the time ...'

The gods can be cruel, terrible, illogical and heartless, but sometimes they can be patient too. Apollo smiled reassuringly. 'I'm sure you're right,' he said. 'Please tell me all about it.'

Ms. Fisichelli swallowed the large clot of mud that had apparently formed in her throat and said 'Well ...'

'Yes?'

'It's like this. Er.'

Apollo smiled even more, until Ms. Fisichelli could feel little flakes of skin detaching themselves from the tip of her nose. 'Perhaps,' she said, 'you should see for yourself.'

Apollo frowned. 'How do you mean?'

The Pythoness twitched nervously. 'In the Sacred Bowl,' she said.

'The Sacred Bowl?' Apollo looked puzzled. 'You mean that thing still works?'

'Well ...'

'Well, I never,' Apollo went on. 'I thought it had packed up in the fifth century, when that clown Amaryllis IV used it for frying anchovies. Have you got it working again?'

'I cleaned it,' Ms. Fisichelli murmured, 'and it seemed OK. You don't mind, do you? Only it can be a great help sometimes and ... Well,' she said quickly, 'actually, I've been using it to watch the baseball. You can't get the

baseball on Greek TV, not even with a satellite dish, and
Chicago have got to the Rose Bowl this year, and ...'

'It works, then,' Apollo said.

'Seems to,' said Ms. Fisichelli. 'I'll fetch it.'

She jumped up and scurried off into the kitchen. While
she was gone, Apollo tried hard not to look at her new
disciple out of the corner of his eye. To the gods, Homer
was fond of saying, all things are possible. He was wrong.

'Er,' Apollo said.

'Sorry?' Mary smiled, warmly but respectfully. Apollo
suddenly felt a bit tongue-tied.

'Um – are you, well, doing anything tomorrow evening?'

Mary continued to smile.

'Only,' Apollo went on, 'I happen to have two tickets for
the open air Bad Vibes concert in Central Park, and I
thought ...'

'Sorry,' Mary said, 'only I'm washing my hair tomorrow
night.'

'Oh.'

Mary smiled again.

'Another time, then, maybe?'

Smile. And then Ms. Fisichelli came back with the
Sacred Bowl and Apollo wrenched his attention back to
far less important things. More important. *Damn.*

'I'm all out of holy water,' she said, 'so I used Perrier.
It's generally okay, I've found.'

She put the bowl down on the tripod, fumbled in her
pocket for her sistrum, and started to hum the incant-
ation. Apollo (who is also ex-God of music) winced,
thanked her, and hummed it for her.

At once, a pale golden glow filled the room, while the
electric light quietly went away and found something else
to do. There was also a strange, mysterious fragrance, but
that had more to do with the fact that Ms. Fisichelli's
lemon curd was boiling over on the gas-stove than
anything particularly divine. Apollo stood up and peered
into the depths of the bowl.

'Hey,' he said, 'this is good.' Ms. Fisichelli simpered.

On the meniscus of the still slightly effervescent water there was an image. There was a dog.

It was lying on a carpet gnawing three bones.

It was doing this at the feet of a man who was sitting in a very comfortable looking chair in an almost unbearably cosy looking room eating what appeared to be a slice of exquisitely yummy chocolate cake. Opposite him sat what could only be described as a very nice, friendly looking old gentleman who tended to wave his hands about a lot, making his companion laugh with his mouth full.

'Well,' said Apollo, 'I'll be a son of a thunderbolt. How do you turn the sound up on this thing?'

'Um,' said Ms. Fisichelli.

'Sorry?'

'You can't.'

'Oh,' said Apollo. 'No sound, then.'

'No.'

'Never mind ... Hey, now what's happening?'

Ms. Fisichelli flushed. 'It does that,' she said.

The picture of the nice room had vanished as suddenly as it had come, and in its place was the image of another man, a man with long hair and long fingernails. He appeared for all the world to be standing up in an Underground carriage. Now he was walking to the connecting door between the carriages. He was opening it, and getting out ...

There was a terrific hiss and all the water in the bowl suddenly became steam and flew upwards. The bowl overheated, cracked and shattered into splinters, one of which hit Apollo on the nose.

'*Ouch!*' he said.

Ms. Fisichelli looked as if she'd just gone into deep shock, and Apollo, as soon as he had recovered himself, helped her to a seat. 'Is she all right?' he asked, nervously.

'I think so,' Mary replied. 'She's a bit highly-strung, you know.'

Apollo nodded. 'I wonder what made it suddenly do that?' he said, to himself but aloud.

'Too much current,' Mary replied.

Apollo nodded and then turned round quickly. 'Sorry?' he said, and stared at her.

'I'm just guessing,' said Mary modestly, 'but maybe you put too much strain on it, making it look down into the Forbidden Regions.'

Apollo's divine brain told his divine heart and divine body to stay cool and let it handle this. 'Just out of interest,' he said, as casually as he could, 'how did you know that was the Forbidden Regions?'

Mary caught her breath, gave Apollo a look of pure poison, turned into a huge eagle, and left the room.

In the dry heat of a Betamax sun, a column of Roman soldiers stopped in the market square of Tiberiopolis, until recently known as Jerusalem. A young man was led forward and made to take up a large wooden cross. As he did so, he instinctively examined the workmanship.

'Huh,' he said. 'Call that a mortice and tenon joint, 'cos I don't.'

The centurion snapped an impatient command to his troops, but they refused to budge. On his enquiring as to why this might be, they told him that Good Friday was a Bank holiday, and if they were expected to go around crucifying people, it was going to have to be time and a half.

The centurion fumed for a moment, said, 'Oh, bugger this for a game of soldiers,' and stalked off to the wine-shop on the corner. After a long silence, the three condemned prisoners edged quietly away and went home, the soldiers lifting not a finger to stop them.

That was why it was a Betamax world, after all.

Unlike most Betamax worlds, however, this one survived the inevitable ensuing possibility crisis and remained extant. This was because of what can only be described as a spatio-temporal cock-up, involving the arrival of a team of interplanetary missionaries from the neighbouring Betamax world, where interstellar travel had been developed before the discovery of printing.* Soon after the mass conversion of the Betamax-human race to Methodism, however, the severe possibility problems caused thereby were all solved at a stroke by the timely intervention of a huge meteor, which smashed the planet into rubble.

The reason why possibility errors are treated so seriously by the authorities, however, is because once they start they tend to continue. It therefore came as no surprise to the Incident Room staff at Possibility Police HQ when particles of incandescent matter released by the destruction of Betamax 9567432 burst into the atmosphere of the world which originally sent out the missionaries, landed on the roofs of all the churches and burned them all down. The embarrassing result of this was that the majority of the population at once abandoned Christianity (thus cancelling the projected nuclear religious war against the Eastern Heretics which should have ended the planet) and set about persuading the remaining faithful of the error of their ways, inventing printing as a necessary method of information dissemination. The world thus created was so perilously close to the Absolutely Possible that the police were compelled to intervene, in the interests of Possibility Preservation, by planting a few absolute impossibilities in rarely-visited areas of the planet and then coming back next day and atomising the entire planetary system under Article 47(1) of the Sirius Convention.

Even then, however, their problems were far from over, since the force of the explosion of Betamax 5609765 was so violent that Planet VHS – our planet – was temporarily

---

*Which meant they could send probes to the moon but the astronauts were unable to sell their stories to the tabloids afterwards.

rocked on its axis, with the result that at a crucial moment a buckshee Thursday was suddenly introduced into the week; the Thursday, in fact, when Jason Derry went down to the Underground to find Gelos. More important, it meant that an extra day had been introduced which had not been foreseen when the Order of Play was drawn up at the very start of the Game. As a result, at the vital point of the story which follows, it was nobody's go at all.

'You mean to tell me,' Jupiter said, 'that all this time we've had a mole?'

Apollo wondered whether it was worth pointing out that it had been an eagle rather than a mole, but decided no, probably not.

'Yes,' he said.

'I see.' Jupiter had this knack of asking questions he already knew the answers to; a common mannerism among the omniscient, but aggravating nevertheless. 'And this mole has been collaborating with . . . with That Person all this time?'

'Yes.' Why is it, Apollo asked himself, that just because I'm the one who tells him, it's suddenly all my fault? There, I'm doing it now; I know exactly why. Because I'm a mug, that's why.

'And nobody noticed, is that it?'

'Yes.'

'And you lot,' Jupiter went on, 'call yourself gods, do you?'

'Yes.'

Jupiter laughed, and black clouds scurried guiltily across the skies of Earth to the positions they should have been in ten minutes ago. It can be tough, being a cloud.

'And now,' Jupiter said, 'that you have at last found out, may I ask what you're proposing to do about it?'

Apollo recognised that this was a question that couldn't be answered with Yes, and searched his divine mind for an answer. 'I don't know,' he said.

'The old brain a bit slow today, is it?'

'Well ...'

'GET IT SORTED OUT,' said Jupiter – when you're the Great Sky God it's no problem at all to shout in capital letters. In fact, when he was really upset, he could shout in bold face, italics and pitch ten.

'Yes,' said Apollo, 'we ...'

'NOW.'

'Yes indeed,' Apollo said, 'But ...'

For all his omniscience, Jupiter didn't seem to understand the implications of But. He just frowned, with the result that race meetings on four continents were washed out. Apollo backed away, tripped over a self-propelled footstool (which apologised in Latin) and ran.

Not long after leaving the presence of the Father of Gods and Men, he bumped into Mars. To be exact, he trod on his foot.

'Watch it,' said the ex-God of War, 'I've had enough of it today with Claymore mines without you as well.'

Apollo apologised – he had often reflected on the aptness of his name – and stopped running. Mars looked at him.

'What's up, Pol?' he asked. 'You seem a bit flustered.'

'Flustered.' Apollo turned the adjective over in his mind. A bit on the weak side perhaps, but it was in the right ball park, so to speak. 'Yes,' he added, from sheer habit.

'Why?'

'There's been a bit of a cock-up,' said Apollo – everyone else was having a go at understatement, he said to himself, why not me too? – 'and I've got to sort it out, apparently.'

'Hard luck,' Mars said sympathetically. 'Now what's happened?'

'You know Prometheus's eagle?'

Mars nodded, making the shrapnel-shredded plume of his helmet nod.

'Well,' Apollo went on, 'apparently it turns out that that

bloody fowl's gone and changed sides on us. It's been working for You-Know-Who all along.'

'Really?'

'Yes.'

Mars thought for a moment. 'I wouldn't call ripping someone's liver out for him every morning and evening working for him exactly,' he said. 'Cheaper than a dialysis machine, I suppose, but ...'

'It's not that,' said Apollo. 'It seems that that dratted eagle's been running errands for him. Subverting Heroes. Spying on us.'

'Spying?'

'That's right,' Apollo grunted. 'Been dressing up as a human and passing itself off as the apprentice Pythoness of Delphi.' Apollo reflected briefly on his brief infatuation with the feathered temptress, and shuddered. 'Which means that the Big P has known every move we make. Vexing, isn't it?'

Mars rubbed his chin, 'You mean like a sort of mole?' he asked. Apollo smiled. He could say it now.

'No, Ma,' he said, 'an eagle can't be a mole. Biologically impossible.'

Mars frowned impatiently. 'You know what I mean,' he said. 'Bit of a problem, that. You have my sympathy.'

'Also,' Apollo went on, 'though I'm pleased to say the Old Sod hasn't found out yet, he's also got Cerberus on his side.'

'Cerberus?'

'That's right. Bit poor, isn't it? Pluto's going to be in for a nasty shock any minute now, I can tell you.'

'He's down there?'

'At this very minute,' said Apollo, with just a hint of less than charitable feeling, 'looking for Jason Derry. He's the Hero who's been subverted ...'

Just then, Minerva came in. She was somewhat red in the face and not in the best of moods. This was understandable, since she'd just had to tell Jupiter about a certain dog.

'There you are,' she said. 'You are a pair of idiots, aren't you?'

Mars opened his mouth to protest but Minerva ignored him. 'Anyway,' she went on, 'here's your orders from the Boss. Pol, you get down to Earth and deal with Prometheus. Nail that eagle and get a replacement, right?'

'All right,' Apollo sighed.

'And you, Ma,' Minerva said, 'you'd better pop down and see that Pluto's all right. And deal with the Derry boy while you're at it. He's getting out of hand and ...'

'You're joking,' Mars said. 'I was listening to the Commentary just now, and it said he's armed with the Sword of ...'

'Don't be such a baby,' Minerva replied. 'You are supposed to be the Driver of the Spoil, Ma, or had you forgotten?'

'Driving the Spoil I can handle,' Mars said rebelliously. 'Driving the Spoil is what I'm good at. Getting snipped up into tagliatelli by muscular youths with magic swords doesn't feature in my job description. Sorry, but ...'

'Mars.' Minerva looked at him sternly. 'You don't want me to tell Pa about your trip to Greenham Common, do you?'

Mars sagged like a tent with no pole. 'You wouldn't,' he said weakly.

'He wouldn't like it, would he?' she said. 'A son of his climbing over the wire and daubing *No Nukes Here* in green paint on the missile silos. I think you'd better do as you're told for once, don't you?'

Mars inflated his lungs to speak.

'Language,' said Minerva pre-emptively.

'Anyway,' said the ex-God of War, 'what does he mean by Deal With? You might at least tell me ...'

'Jupiter thinks,' said Minerva with an iceberg smile, 'that the constellation of Cassiopeia looks a bit lop-sided. Could do with an extra star somewhere in the middle. See to it, will you?'

Minerva turned, adjusted her owl, and walked serenely out. Mars drew in a deep breath, sighed and jerked his head at the space Minerva had just occupied.

'Daddy's girl,' he said.

'So,' said Gelos, 'that's more or less it, I think. Is there anything you'd like to ask me?'

Jason leaned forward in his chair until his elbows touched his knees and struggled for breath. When he had got some semblance of control over his body back, he removed the handkerchief from his mouth and gasped greedily for air. He hadn't laughed so much since the time the Nine-Headed Serpent of the Sun had tried to bite him.

Not, it should be stated, that Gelos had been in any way outstandingly witty, amusing or novel; it was, as far as Jason could make out, all in the way he told them. Otherwise, why had he nearly had a cerebral haemorrhage when the old gentleman had asked him if he wanted a scone?

'No,' he croaked, 'thank you, I think I've got all that.'

'The thing to remember ...' Gelos paused politely while Jason rolled on the floor kicking his legs helplessly and making little wheezing noises. 'The thing to remember is that ... Look, are you feeling quite all right? Would you like a glass of water or something?'

'No,' Jason shrieked, 'I'm fine, really.' He dabbed ineffectually at the tears in his eyes and rose unsteadily to his knees. 'Please do go on ... I'm sorry, I'm not usually like this ... I ...' He collapsed into a private hell of giggles. Cerberus gave him a look. Three looks.

'This really only goes to prove,' said the old man equably, 'what I was saying. There's nothing in the world stronger than laughter. If it can have this sort of effect on someone like you, a Hero, son of Jupiter himself, just think what it could do to the ordinary man in the street, if only he came into contact with a strong enough dose. I could take over the world and be the One True God with no trouble at all. But I wouldn't want that.'

He paused while Jason ironed out the spasmodic convulsions in his chest and dragged air into his lungs. Sometimes, the old man was thinking, I don't seem to know my own strength. 'Look,' he said, 'perhaps it would be better if I changed back into the other shape – you know, the threatening statue stuff. Would that help?'

Jason managed to find just enough strength to nod his head, and immediately the cosy little room vanished and Jason found himself lying on nothing again, looking at a pair of talons.

'Better?'

'Much,' Jason said. 'Go on with what you were saying.'

'I can cut out the hissing snakes if you like.'

'No,' said Jason, 'that's fine. Just so long as you lay off the jokes, that's all.'

'I don't make jokes, actually,' said Gelos wistfully. 'In fact, sometimes I wonder what a sense of humour is like. I'm disqualified from having one, you see.'

Jason nodded weakly. The risk of internal combustion, he supposed. Nasty.

'I wouldn't want to rule the world exactly,' Gelos was saying, 'not the world the way it is, you see. It's too – well, completely and utterly and irrevocably fucked up for my liking. All I could do would be take people's minds off it all, and I suppose that's better than nothing. It's what I do now, more or less. But that wouldn't be right, would it?'

'Wouldn't it?'

'No,' Gelos said. 'You see, I'd be making people forget about all the horrible things in the world, and that would mean they'd never do anything about them. And then, of course, something terrible would happen – a plague or a disaster at a power station, that sort of thing – and everybody would be so busy laughing about it that they wouldn't get around to actually doing anything to put it right, and then where would we be? In fact,' he added, 'that's exactly the possibility curve that I've calculated. You know about possibility physics and all that, do you?'

'A bit,' Jason said. 'But let's not get bogged down in all that theory stuff. What you're saying is that you want the world set right before you take over.'

'More or less.'

'And in the meanwhile, you just want to stay where you are and not be bothered by anyone?'

'That's it, yes,' said Gelos. 'People think I came down here, where it doesn't actually exist – you know, not as *such* – to hide from old Jupiter. Not a bit of it.'

'Really?'

'Really. You see, I'm a bit like radiation. I leak. If I was anywhere else in the world but down here, where it isn't actually possible to be, then great excess doses of laughter would sort of seep up through the ground and get into everything, and that would cause absolute chaos. As it is, enough of the stuff gets out to keep the world ticking over more or less, but it never reaches a critical level. And I think that's how it should stay, for now.'

'I see,' said Jason, nodding. 'So where's the problem?'

'Jupiter,' said Gelos. 'And all those other idiots too, of course. They want to kidnap me. Now they don't scare me, not one bit; if they were to come down here and try throwing their weight about, I could make them laugh so much they'd bust their heavenly guts. The trouble is, I'd have to release so much laughter it'd be bound to get out into the Topside and mess things up for people. That's why it's essential that things are kept under control, do you see?'

'I think so,' Jason said. 'You need someone to keep the gods off your back for the time being.'

'That's it,' said Gelos, nodding. 'Really, it's a case of making sure they don't get to me. That would have been all right, except that they've been looking for me a lot lately – I think the Betamax world where I don't exist is reaching critical level – and it was only a matter of time before they did their calculations and found out I was here. That's why I got Prometheus to bring you here.'

Jason raised his eyebrows. 'What can I do?' he said.

'Diversion,' said Gelos. 'You can fight the gods for me.'

Jason stared. '*Me?*' he said. 'You must be kidding.'

'I'm deadly serious,' said Gelos, 'if that's not a contradiction in terms. I want them to think you've rescued me or abducted me, and you've somehow got hold of me and want to take over the universe. Then they attack you, and you give them a good hiding, and ...'

'Excuse me,' said Jason, 'but is that certain? Likely, even?'

'Absolute certainty,' said Gelos. 'You see, I shall give you a secret weapon.'

'Oh good,' said Jason. 'I was hoping you'd say that.'

'Well,' Gelos added, 'more sort of lend, really. I was thinking of lending you one of the Three Jokes.'

'Three Jokes?' Jason's face must have fallen slightly, as if he had been expecting something a bit more tangible, like a tank. Gelos smiled.

'Let me explain,' he said. 'As any comedian will tell you, there are only Three Jokes. All other jokes are minor variants on the Three; they have to be diluted right down before people can take them, otherwise – well, they'd be fatal.'

'That funny, huh?'

'Oh yes. Now the first Joke, the strongest of them all, is called the Great Primordial. If you were to tell the first Joke, you would make the sun laugh so much it would trip and fall onto the Earth, which would be so cracked up with laughing it would fall into the sea.'

Jason nodded. 'Would that be the one about the three Scotsmen and the reel of cotton?' he asked.

'No,' said Gelos, 'though I know the one you mean. That's actually one of the Lesser Arcana of the Triple-Bodied Zephyr, and if properly told it can crumple up sheet steel like paper. The Great Primordial is rather better.'

'Wow,' Jason said.

'The second Joke,' said Gelos, 'is called the Celestial

Labarum and involves an Englishman, a Pole, and a Goth.
You've heard of the eruption of Krakatoa?'

'Yes.'

'My fault,' confessed Gelos. 'I have this habit of talking
in my sleep sometimes, and one night the punch line – just
the punch line, you understand – must just have slipped
out. By the time it got out past all this nothingness and
found its way through the magma layer to the South Seas
there wasn't much left of it, I can tell you, but ...'

Jason shuddered. 'Hot stuff, eh?'

'You could say that,' said Gelos. 'The third Joke,' he
went on, 'is the weakest of the three. It's known as the
Mighty Cloud Spirit Joke, and it's more of an anti-
personnel joke, really. Knocks out people, leaves buildings
standing, that sort of thing. And that's the one I'm going to
lend you.'

'Um ...'

'I know what you're going to say,' said Gelos. 'Too risky,
you were going to say. You're quite right. That's why we
needed the dog.'

Jason looked blank. 'The dog?'

'Quite so,' said Gelos. 'You see, what I propose to do is
tell half the joke to you, and then send you out of the
room. I shall then put two of the dog's brains to sleep while
I tell one-sixth of the Joke to the remaining brain. And so
on, until each of the dog's brains knows one sixth, and you
know all the rest. It's a sort of failsafe system, really.'

'Well ...'

'I know,' said Gelos, 'it's still a hell of a lot to ask, but I
wouldn't take the risk unless I thought it was absolutely
necessary. Trust me.'

'All right,' said Jason.

'Thanks,' said Gelos. 'You remind me a lot of me when I
was younger,' he added.

Jason blinked. 'I do?' he said.

'Not surprising, really,' said Gelos, smiling. 'We are
related, after all.'

'Are we?'

'Oh yes,' Gelos said. 'You see, although I am Gelos, spirit of Laughter, I wasn't always what I am now. Before I was Gelos, I was ... well, never mind that. Here, doggie.'

Cerberus jumped forward, wagging his tail. Gelos made a slight gesture with his right hand and the dog was suddenly fast asleep.

'I put a long joke in his minds,' Gelos explained. 'Good as an anaesthetic, I always find.'

'A long joke?'

'Shaggy dog story, I think they're called. Now, are you ready to receive your half of the Joke?'

Jason nodded and braced himself. Although he was very frightened and not a little confused, he knew that the three dots in his mind had become words now, and the sentence was complete at last.

'Right,' said Gelos. 'There was this guy who went into this bar ...'

P luto reached out. Eventually, to his initial relief, his hand connected with something. It was wet.

'Yuk,' Pluto said, and reached for his handkerchief.

After a further period of exploration, however, he arrived at the conclusion that beggars can't be choosers, and set out to follow the series of damp, smelly patches on the walls of Nothingness to their eventual conclusion. If the dog came this way, he reasoned, Derry can't be far behind.

He had been feeling his way in this manner for perhaps ten minutes when he felt something that wasn't wet and smelly. If anything, it was rather worse.

'Don't mind my asking,' said a voice, 'but why are you holding on to my ankle?'

Pluto considered the cold, scaly surface he had just made contact with and shuddered. 'Beg pardon?' he said.

'My ankle,' said the voice. 'You appear to be holding on to it. Why?'

'Because it's there?' Pluto suggested. 'Whoever you are, might I trouble you for some light, by any chance?'

'Light,' the voice said thoughtfully. 'I may be able to manage that. Just bear with me for a moment, will you?'

A moment later there was indeed light.

'You've just missed him,' said the voice.

Pluto blinked. The same could not be said for the piercing eyes of the colossal obsidian statue, which seemed to be trying to see through the back of Pluto's head.

'Have I?' Pluto asked.

'I imagine so,' said the statue. 'He went that way.'

'Did he have a dog with him?'

Gelos made a show of thinking about this, and then replied, 'I believe he did, yes. And a man, too.'

Pluto drew his brows together in a frown. 'Did he indeed?' he mused. 'What sort of a ...'

'Ah,' said Gelos, 'there you have me. Let's see.'

'Late middle-aged,' Pluto suggested, 'friendly looking, big smile, probably in dressing gown and slippers.'

'Now you come to mention it,' Gelos said, 'I think you could be right.'

'Thanks,' said Pluto. 'Er, how about the light? Do you think you could fix it to stay on for a bit, only I get a bit jumpy in the dark. You know how it is.'

The statue nodded its head. 'I'll do my best,' he said.

Pluto turned to go and then looked back. 'We've met before, haven't we?'

'No,' Gelos lied, 'I don't think so.'

'Ah well,' Pluto said, 'I've got a rotten memory for faces. Occupational hazard, I suppose. Thanks anyway.'

'My pleasure,' said Gelos. 'Go carefully, now.'

Pluto waved and soon was lost to sight among the shadows. For his part, Gelos sighed and shook his head. Of his three nephews, he considered, Pluto was probably (though only by a short head) the dimmest. He reflected for a moment on the fact that these same three nephews, idiots all, had castrated his brother Cronus, imprisoned his sister Rhea and made him, Thing, the greatest of the three, hide out at the end of a sleazy underground railway line for most of the history of Creation. Fool's luck, he said to himself; or something like that.

There is an old accountant's proverb that it's no good the meek inheriting the earth if they end up having to pay tax on it at 40p in the pound. For his part, Thing (as Gelos should properly be called) didn't really mind being cheated of his inheritance just so long as none of the other members of his family got their grubby paws on it. Having reassumed his true shape, therefore, he reached out his mind into the World and made contact with his oldest and best ally, presently suspended from a number of mountaintops in the Caucasus.

'Pro?'

'Is that you, Gel?'

'How are things your end?'

A flicker of a shadow passed across Prometheus's thought-waves. 'I don't know,' Prometheus replied. 'I have a feeling something's going to happen.'

'You're right. Apollo is coming to get you.'

'I know *that*,' Prometheus thought back. 'The eagle told me. I've told it to lie low for a bit. Any suggestions?'

'None that spring immediately to mind, Pro. I'd send you the boy, but I need him here. Mars is on his way, and Pluto's just come through. I need the dog, too. Sorry.'

'That's fine. I'll think of something.'

'Look, Pro, if things get out of hand, call me, will you? I might be able to help out, you never know.'

'What was that? It's a very bad line.'

'I said I might be able to help,' Thing replied.

'Don't worry about me,' Prometheus assured him. 'But send the boy when you can spare him; I'll stall them till then, all right?'

'That's the spirit.'

Thing let the mental link subside and made himself a cup of Ovaltine; but his mind still moved on his comrade's dilemma. It was a pity he couldn't send the boy.

Of course, he said to himself, I could always send the next best thing.

At the very end of the corridor there was a door.

Like most doors in the Underground it had a very silly notice above it. It said *No Exit*.

Extremely silly. After all, if you couldn't go out of it,

what was the point in it being there? Jason shrugged and tried the handle. It was locked.

'What do you think, dog?' Jason asked. It was a rhetorical question really, as he knew that the reply would be Woof, but asking gave him time to weigh up the pros and cons of the move he had in mind.

'Woof.'

'That's settled, then,' Jason said happily. 'What *is* the point, after all?'

He lifted his leg and gave the door an almighty kick. A door is just a door. It flew open, and a moment later Jason realised that the notice hadn't been so silly after all.

'Jason Derry.'

For someone who had led an adventurous life, frequently paddling in the backwaters of the paranormal and semi-divine, Jason hadn't quite managed to develop the proper attitude to apparitions. Contrast his reaction to Gelos in his statue persona, for example, with Pluto's, recounted above. Pluto, you noticed, just took a colossal talking statue in his stride. Pluto, after all, knows that something that looks like that can only be something else dressed up, since colossal talking statues are not, of course, possible.

'Er,' was all that Jason could find to say. Curiously enough, the apparition somehow managed to find it intimidating, because it crouched further down behind its shield and trembled slightly.

'Don't count on it, mortal,' said the apparition.

Jason took another look at the monstrous figure in front of him. Was it possible that this apparently divine and heavily armoured person was afraid of him?

'Don't count on what?' he asked.

'Look,' replied the apparition, 'I'm only doing my job, okay? I didn't ask to be sent. I just got volunteered.'

Time, Jason thought, to do a little essential spadework. 'Who are you?' he asked.

'Mars.'

'Pardon?'

'Mars.'

Jason didn't relax, but the quality of his tension improved. 'Really?' he said.

'It's not the sort of thing you'd lie about,' replied the ex-God of War. 'But if you don't believe me, I've got one of those little cards with my photograph on it. Hang on.'

The Widow-Maker leaned his spear against the door-frame, slipped off his shield and rummaged around in the inside pocket of his breastplate until he found a creased plastic folder. He opened it and Jason's eyes grew round.

'Wow,' he said.

'You what?'

'I mean,' Jason said, 'I've heard so much about you.'

Mars was so surprised he dropped his spear, which fell with a clang on the ground. At once Jason leaned forward and picked it up for him.

'Are you trying to say,' Mars asked, 'that you're actually pleased to meet me?'

'Of course,' Jason said. 'Hell, when I was at school I had posters of you all round the walls of my bedroom.'

'I ...'

'You were my favourite,' Jason went on enthusiastically. 'I read all about you in the mythology books. I even had a tee-shirt printed with ...'

Mars dropped the spear again. 'You're sure you're not thinking of someone else?' he asked. Jason shook his head, then blushed and produced a scrap of paper from his pocket.

'I wonder,' he said. 'I know this must be really boring for you, but could you just write ... I don't know, *Best Wishes from Mars*, something like that. It's not for me, it's for my ...'

'You do know,' Mars said, 'why I'm here?'

'Well, no,' Jason said. 'Is there anything I can help you with?' he added hopefully.

Mars swallowed hard. 'In a manner of speaking,' he said, 'yes.'

'What?'

Mars closed his eyes. Was this, he asked himself, yet another manifestation of his usual filthy luck? The boy's eyes were shining at him with the golden light of hero-worship; for the first time ever, he told himself, somebody is actually glad to see me. Oh nuts ...

'You see,' Mars said, as gently as he could, 'I've been sent ...'

'Yes?'

'I've been sent by Jupiter ...'

'Yes? How is Dad, by the way?'

'... to kill you,' Mars grinned feebly. 'As it were.'

Physiognomists would have you believe that it is impossible for the human face to have no expression whatsoever; and if that is the case, then Jason was more divine than human. Mars bit his lip.

'When I say kill,' he went on, 'it's not as bad as it sounds. More translate you to the stars. Immortality. Apotheosis. Haven't you ever wanted to be a star?'

Jason said nothing.

'And,' Mars continued hopelessly, 'the apotheosis framework is designed for maximum flexibility, to cater for a wide range of individual aspirations. Red dwarf, blue giant, supernova, you name it. Just so long as you're not ... well, alive, really.'

Jason said nothing.

'They tell me,' Mars whimpered, 'that it doesn't hurt a bit. It's not really death, you see, though of course death does come into it, peripherally. But really it's more a sort of *ouch*!'

Jason woke suddenly from his reverie and kicked the dog savagely on the rump.

'Cerberus!' he shouted, 'let go!'

Two of the dog's heads obeyed; the third needed a clip round the ears to convince it. Mars rubbed his ankle and then looked up.

'Thanks,' he muttered wretchedly.

'*Bad* dog,' said Jason. 'Mars, I'm so sorry, this bloody dog ...'

'Look,' Mars said, 'don't worry about it, right? I mean, if someone should be apologising, it ought to be me. Except,' he added without conviction, 'really, it's more of a career move than anything else. And you don't actually have any choice, of course.'

'Sorry?'

'So am I,' Mars sighed, 'believe me. But when the Big J says that's the way it's got to be, then that's the way it's got to be. And ...'

Jason looked at him. 'No,' he said.

'Sorry,' said Mars, 'but I'm afraid ...'

'No,' Jason said again. 'Just because Dad says something doesn't mean anything of the sort. I thought *you* would have realised that.'

Oh, for crying out loud, Mars thought. 'Listen, son,' he said. 'I wish it didn't have to be like this ...'

'It doesn't.'

'Yes it does.'

'No it doesn't.'

'Yes it does.'

'No it doesn't.'

In the very back end of his mind, Mars's memory nudged his consciousness and reminded him that in the old days, when he used to be the God of War, he didn't have to take this sort of shit from anybody, let alone a snot-nosed kid who thought the Widow-Maker was a more suitable candidate for a role model than, say, Mother Teresa. Enough of this, it said.

'Now you listen to me,' Mars said. 'I'm saying it does, and I'm the one who *ouch*!'

About ten seconds later, Jason helped Mars up again, handed him his spear, bent the chin-guard of his helmet back into shape, dusted off his cloak for him and apologised.

'Now get lost,' he added.

Mars, his divine head still swimming, tried one last protest. 'Look,' he started to say.

'. . . or I'll have to hit you again.'

'Right,' said Mars. 'Nice to have met you. Classy left hook you've got there, if you don't mind me saying so.'

Jason's face lit up. 'You really think so?'

Mars humped his throbbing jaw into a grin. 'You bet,' he said.

By a strange coincidence that would have had the Possibility Police round in ten minutes flat with a forged warrant had they known about it, Mrs. Derry was at that very moment removing Jason's Mars posters from the walls of his bedroom.

Part of being a mother is realising that one of these days, the fledgling is going to leave the nest for good. The sensible mother realises that this is perfectly natural, and also a heaven sent opportunity to give parts of the nest their first thorough cleaning for eighteen years.

She was just wiping away a tear while trying to scrape off a chunk of petrified Blue-Tack with the handle of a spoon when the doorbell rang. She muttered something, climbed down off the chair and went to see who it was.

'Hello, Phyllis.'

Mrs. Derry gave Jupiter that particular look that only female mortals can manage. It is a masterpiece of non-verbal communication, and says (*inter alia*) that you are not welcome to come into my house because of what has happened between us in the past, because you never even sent flowers or a postcard, and most of all because the kitchen floor hasn't been cleaned for a week. It is to Jupiter's credit that he managed to field it without falling over; but the gods, as Homer reminds us, are stronger by far than bread-eating mortals.

'It's about Jason,' Jupiter said. 'Can I come in?'

Mrs. Derry hesitated, even then. Because of Jupiter, her married life had been a cross between a Feydeau farce and one of Landseer's more exuberant productions; there was also the matter of the unwashed breakfast things. But in the end she nodded, and Jupiter walked past her into the house. As he did so, small clumps of incredibly sweet-smelling flowers sprang up where his divine feet left their print in the soft pile of the carpet. This is a common manifestation of a divine presence and Mrs. Derry could hardly fail to notice it.

'Oh for heaven's sake!' she said. 'Wait there.'

She darted off and returned with a bundle of old newspapers, which she arranged by way of a footpath leading from the hallway to the lounge. Having placed the final page on the seat of the sofa, she sniffed, sat down in the armchair, and folded her arms disapprovingly.

'Well?' she said.

'Yetch,' said Pluto, in fact. He had been reduced to drying his hands on his handkerchief, an operation which always made him feel seedy. Having put the now damp hanky away, he looked in the mirror, adjusted his tie and set out once again to find Jason Derry.

This time, he was successful, probably because Jason was now looking for him.

'Hold it right there!' said the son of Jupiter, 'or you'll taste the edge of my sword. You got that?'

Pluto turned round slowly and drew himself up to his full height.

'I'll trouble you,' he said, 'not to take that tone with me. After all, I am your uncle, so let's have a little respect, if you please.'

Jason's brows knotted. 'Respect?' he queried.

'Respect. And for pity's sake put that sword down, before you break something.'

Without quite knowing why, Jason did as he was told. Pluto nodded severely.

'That's better,' he said. 'And take your hands out of your pockets.'

The explanation is, of course, simple for non-Heroes to grasp. Having throughout his career been confronted with a succession of opponents who were bigger, stronger, faster, nastier or better equipped with limbs than he was, Jason had never developed the necessary techniques for dealing with people who were smaller, weaker or better mannered than himself. He had killed dragons, but he'd never had to jump a queue of pensioners in a post office.

'You *are* Pluto,' he asked.

'Certainly,' said the god stiffly. 'And I presume you're the Derry boy.'

'Well, yes.'

Pluto gave him a look, and Jason suddenly became painfully aware that his fingernails weren't as clean as they might be.

'In that case,' Pluto continued, 'I really must insist that you return my dog and stop making a nuisance of yourself.'

Jason shifted guiltily. 'Have I been?' he mumbled.

'Indeed you have,' said Pluto. 'Wandering off, encouraging the dissidents, disturbing the guests, not to mention being extremely rude to a god you haven't even been introduced to. You ought to be thoroughly ashamed of yourself.'

Suddenly and for the first time, Jason was; and it was a distinctly unpleasant feeling. Not only do Heroes not know the meaning of fear, they are also generally immune to embarrassment; otherwise, they simply couldn't do their job. You can't be expected to rush in where angels fear to tread if the opposition can make you feel six inches tall simply by reminding you to wipe your feet.

'The dog, please,' Pluto demanded. Cerberus looked up at Jason with six worried eyes, which Jason couldn't meet. Instead he made a vague Good-Dog-Go-To-Master movement with his head and then looked away.

The dog bit him.

Jason's first reaction was to retaliate. Although somewhat unfashionable these days, retaliation is a tried and tested human reaction to threatening and inconvenient events; and deep down, Jason Derry was a traditionalist. He had therefore raised his foot to give the dog a kick that would have propelled it back topside when it occurred to him that the dog might be trying to tell him something. Not that there aren't more civilised means of data communication these days than a full set of teeth in the calf of the leg; but when the audience is likely to be unresponsive, subtlety is likely to be counter-productive. Jason lowered his boot, confused.

'I said,' said Pluto, 'give me the dog.'

'No,' said Jason. (What he actually said was 'No ...', but the three dots were silent, like the W in 'shipwright'.)

'I beg your pardon?'

'No,' Jason repeated. 'I don't think he wants to go with you.'

Pluto frowned magisterially. 'That's hardly the point,' he said. 'Now, if you don't mind, my time is not without value.'

This remark had an effect on Jason. 'Mine too,' he said. 'Push off.'

'How dare you speak ...?'

Jason grinned. For the first time in his life, he was beginning to wonder whether there might not be just as much fun in beating up small, weak, defenceless people as in beating up mighty demons. Probably not, but he would never know if he didn't try. 'I said push off,' he growled. The dog nodded his heads, wagged his tail and even managed to scratch one of his ears at the same time. Dogs have powers of balance that defy orthodox scientific explanation.

Pluto, for his part, remembered that he was a god, and a high-rolling, time-served god at that. He drew himself up to his false height* and folded his arms grimly.

---

*About fifteen feet six inches. Pluto's main fear was that one day he'd stick like it.

'Impudent mortal ...' he began to say. Then he became aware of an agonising pain in his left big toe, and looked down.

'Ouch!' he said, and hopped up into the air. Jason pulled the sword clear of the deep incision he had just made, and laughed unkindly. A drop of ichor – god's blood – sparkled on the blade.

'Now clear off out of it," he said, 'or else you'll get this up your ...'

Pluto, now withdrawn to a relatively safe distance, scowled horribly and called on the Legions of the Damned to assist him. There are perks to being a god, and instant access to a large number of semi-divine heavies is one of them. 'Arrest that mortal!' Pluto cried melodramatically. From the shadows behind him, about ten or twelve muscular, well-armed figures stepped forward and advanced towards Jason, truncheons out.

At the risk of spoiling the impact of what follows and interrupting the narrative curve, a word of explanation would seem called for. Although at one time service in the divine cohorts was regarded as a supreme honour, ever since the evacuation of Olympus the gods have found themselves with a serious recruiting problem on their hands. The sad fact is that the pay is so much better in the private sector, and the prestige of being an instrument of divine justice comes a poor second to flexible working hours, a company chariot and a free uniform, usually with a dragon logo on it. As a result, the gods have lately taken to recruiting from those inhabitants of Betamax 76249708 who have inadvertently sailed off the edge of the world in the course of an ill-fated attempt to find a shorter sea-route from Leningrad to Kiev. This has resulted in an overall lowering of staff quality. In fact it is rumoured that the entire divine army could only extract itself from the proverbial paper bag with the aid of massed air support and covering fire from offshore naval batteries.

There was a blur, and not long afterwards a contingent

of celestial men-at-arms picked themselves painfully off the ground, gathered up their severed limbs and limped away in search of something to stick them back on with.

Jason lowered his sword. 'Push off,' he said.

'You won't get away with this,' Pluto muttered. 'The mills of the gods grind slow but they grind exceeding small.'

'And cracked pitchers,' said Jason, 'have big ears. Hop it.'

Pluto is unusual among the gods in that he knows when he's beaten. But he had one last weapon in his armoury; and although he usually despised it as mere shallow mummery, there was nothing to be lost by using it. He shouted an arcane word, made a magic pass and snapped his fingers. At once he vanished, and was replaced by an apparition that Jason didn't manage to forget for a long time. Pluto changed himself into a skeleton.

No ordinary skeleton, at that, but a grotesquely large, gaudily decorated and extremely animated skeleton. The general effect was designed to convey an impression of extreme and irreversible death, coupled with an urgent desire to impose a similar condition on anything in the near vicinity, and it worked. There wasn't the smallest scrap of flesh anywhere to be seen, and the bones looked like malevolent ivory; ivory that has never really got over being separated from a perfectly good, comfortable elephant. As for the eyes, you could have defrosted pizzas with them.

Jason, as has already been more than adequately recorded, didn't know the meaning of fear; but it is arguable that you don't need to know precisely what the word *Fischhändler* on a street sign means if directly under it you can see a shop with a slabful of dead cod in the window. He winced with his whole body and covered his eyes.

Not so the dog. He took one look at the biggest collection of jumbo-sized, yummy-looking bones ever gathered in one place, uttered a threefold yelp of pure pleasure, and broke for lunch.

*

In the newly-restored quiet of his study, Gelos was communicating with Prometheus. As usual, it wasn't easy – the thoughtwaves are horribly congested these days, and if you aren't careful you can end up getting a stray fax right between the ears – but despite interruptions they were in the middle of a highly serious discussion.

'And what about the boy?' thought Gelos.

'Don't worry about it,' replied Prometheus. 'It'll be the old, old story; boy meets eagle, boy loses eagle, boy finally gets eagle ...'

'Supposing he isn't interested?' Gelos objected. 'I mean, he may think there's more to life and being a Hero than just ...'

'Pulling a bird?'

'Well ...'

'Leave that to me,' thought Prometheus. 'Back to business. Has he got rid of those two clowns for you?'

Gelos laughed, something he tried not to do if he could help it. 'Yes indeed,' he thought. 'Young Jason has learned quite a lot today, I fancy. About life, and disappointment, and coming to terms with the way things really are; and, of course, that when all is said and done the only really effective way to deal with people is to hit them. Oh yes, he's coming along nicely, for a youngster.'

'Actually,' thought Prometheus, 'I didn't want to worry you with this, but Eagle says that a Certain Person has been to see a Certain Person, and ...'

Gelos frowned. Telepathy is hard enough to understand as it is without archness as well. 'What?'

'J-U-P-I-T-E-R,' Prometheus spelt out in a mental whisper, 'has gone to see P-H-Y-L-L ...'

'All right, I think I see what you're getting at. Problems?'

'Possibly,' Prometheus replied. 'You see, we've been concentrating so much on the fact that Jupit ... that You

Know Who is the boy's father that we may have neglected the other side of the equation.'

'You think so?' queried Gelos. 'I'm sure she's a very nice lady, but ...'

'All I'm saying is,' thought Prometheus, 'oh hell, someone's coming. I'd better think you back later. Ciao.'

A long shadow fell across Prometheus's face and a voice spoke somewhere above him.

'Traitor,' said the voice.

Prometheus twisted his neck round until he could see a pair of golden sandals with a PA monogram on them, which he knew stood for Phoebus Apollo. They were the relic of an ill-fated sponsorship deal between a major multi-national sportswear company and the most photogenic of the male Olympians – ill-fated because Jupiter doesn't hold with his family appearing in full-page colour on the backs of the Sunday supplements and took his wrath out on the company in question by turning them all into lizards.

'Hello, Pol,' Prometheus replied. 'I'd offer you a drink or something but I'm a bit tied up at the moment. Could you call back later?'

'Traitor,' Apollo repeated; not from any great depth of feeling in the matter but because he was embarrassed and couldn't think of anything else to say. Strictly unofficially, and then only outside the range of Jupiter's mental radar net, he had always considered the treatment meted out to Prometheus to be not only unjust but injudicious. The Titan, unlike the rest of the gods, was clever – wise, even – and it was surely only a matter of time before he pulled a stroke that would deal the divine prestige of the Olympians such a blow that thereafter they would be hard put to it getting work doing conjuring tricks for children's parties.

'You think so?' enquired Prometheus, mildly.

'Yes.'

'Oh.' The Titan shrugged. 'I'm sorry about that, Pol.

One does what one thinks is right, you know.'

'I don't.'

'Sorry,' said Prometheus, 'I forgot. You're a god; you don't have to worry about that sort of thing.'

'Are you implying ...?'

Prometheus chuckled. 'I never imply,' he said. 'Not any more. I occasionally implied a bit when I was younger, but at my age it takes me all my time to insinuate, let alone imply. Usually I just say things.'

'Are you saying ...?'

'I'm saying,' said Prometheus, 'that since you're a god and effectively beyond any form of retribution, you can do what you damn well like. Absolute power; is that right?'

Apollo tried to look stern. 'Correct,' he said, and his eyes sparkled with pale blue fire. 'Absolute power.'

'Then how come,' said Prometheus quietly, 'you can't afford a new chariot?'

This took Apollo by surprise, as if he had sliced into a hard-boiled egg to find a baby chicken sitting in there looking at him. 'What?' he said.

'You heard me,' Prometheus replied. 'I could hear the wheel-bearings squeaking from here. Also, from the sound of it, your suspension is completely shot, your axle is about as straight as a bent corkscrew, there's enough body putty in your wings to fill in the Cheddar Gorge and if your offside front shaft makes it through another five thousand miles you have my permission to use my head as a basketball. So?'

'Well,' said Apollo, weakly, 'You can't get the parts these days.'

'So why not get a new one?' Prometheus answered. 'They tell me Vulcan does a very nice little two-seater, four-winged horsepower, ABS brakes, adjustable scythes on the wheels as standard, four thousand gold staters plus interest free credit.'

Apollo frowned. 'Where am I likely to get that sort of money?' he said. 'With no worshippers and no sacrifices?'

Prometheus made a mighty effort and nodded his head. 'Exactly,' he said. 'And whenever you try any little side-line, just for a bit of pin-money, the Old Fool puts a stop to it. You'll notice, by the way, that he never drives the same chariot two years running; and how many temples has he still got? Or Minerva? The last recorded sacrifice to Minerva took place in AD 512, but she isn't driving round in a Gamma reg Vulcan Popular with knackered brake-linings.'

'Look . . .'

'Or Venus,' Prometheus went on pitilessly. 'What's it she's got now? Vulcan XR7 GTS with front-dove drive, isn't it? Or Neptune, with that big new Valhalla Donnerschlag – *Vorsprung durch Zauber* and all that. Trust Nep to be the one to have a flash foreign chariot. Or Mercury – zippy little Vulcan Elite Turbo with a sticker saying *My Other Chariot's a Vulcan 696* on the rear sunguard. Or Diana . . .'

'All right,' said Apollo, 'you've made your point.'

'Maybe,' said Prometheus, 'and obviously you really don't care about such demeaning things as status. I'm impressed, honestly. If I was in your position and had to suffer the indignity of being burnt off at traffic lights by part-time river-gods in souped-up Vulcan Firebirds . . .'

'All *right*,' said Apollo. 'Look . . .'

' . . .with furry dice hanging from their rear mirrors . . .'

'*Look* . . .'

'Yes?'

'I . . .' Apollo had forgotten what he was going to say. He scowled ferociously and scratched the back of his neck.

'All I was trying to suggest,' Prometheus went on, 'is that you must be in it for the job satisfaction, not the material rewards. I'm right, aren't I?'

'Well . . .'

'I can understand that,' said Prometheus. 'You're a god's god, Pol, if you don't mind my saying so. Or you were, at any rate, before Jupiter decided to pack it all in and retire. Nice, is it, up there in the sun?'

'Very.'

'Playing the Game all day, so I hear. That must be very ...' The Titan paused, as if mulling over his choice of word ' ... fulfilling, mustn't it?'

'Well ...'

'Admittedly,' said Prometheus, 'there's not as much averting plagues and redressing wrongs as there used to be, but at least you can lie in of a morning. Now you couldn't do *that* when you were driving the chariot of the sun, could you?'

'I ...'

'That must have been fun, I bet,' Prometheus said with a chuckle. 'Out of interest, what could the old bus do? On the flat, with the wind behind it?'

'Oh, a million and five, million and ten,' Apollo said dreamily. 'Nought to two hundred and fifty thousand in four point seven two, I once got out of her.' He stopped and made an impatient noise. '*Look* ...' he said angrily.

'Whereas now,' Prometheus murmured, 'there isn't really any reason to get out of bed at all, is there? You could sleep in all day and nobody would either know or care. Still, if that's what you want out of everlasting life ...'

'Prometheus ...'

'But I was forgetting,' said the Titan. 'You may not get to drive the sun or answer the prayers of cities, but you do get to run little errands for the Big J. And Minerva, of course; I expect she keeps you pretty busy, doesn't she?'

'It's ...'

'Odd that,' Prometheus mused, 'the way she bosses you about, when strictly speaking ... But that's none of my business. Forgive me, please; I don't get many people to talk to these days, except the eagle. You've met the eagle, haven't you? Nice girl – it's a she, you know. In fact, more she than eagle.'

Apollo couldn't help asking what Prometheus meant by that, exactly.

'Didn't you know?' replied the Titan. 'I thought they'd have told you – how strange. No, Eagle isn't really an eagle at all.'

'Isn't it?'

'She,' Prometheus corrected him. 'She's actually a wood-nymph, name of Charionessa. Nice name, don't you think? Jupiter turned her into an eagle as a punishment.'

'What for?'

'Unfriendliness,' Prometheus replied. 'Jupiter likes his wood-nymphs friendly, you see. Unlike Juno; she likes Jupiter's wood-nymphs decidedly hostile. In fact,' Prometheus went on blandly, 'that's why there are so few of them about these days, what with Jupiter turning them into things if they *don't* and Juno turning them into things if they do. Still, it's not for me to pass comments on the morals of my betters. Now, what's the little errand they've sent you on this time?'

Apollo struggled for some words and found a phrase that Minerva had supplied him with. 'I've been sent,' he said, 'to punish a traitor.'

'Really?'

'Yes.'

'Anyone I know?'

'Yes.'

'Are you going to tell me,' said Prometheus, 'or is it a secret?'

Apollo ground his teeth wretchedly. 'I think you can guess,' he said.

'Not me,' Prometheus replied. 'Always was hopeless at guessing. Do you remember all those games of Twenty Questions we used to play when you were a boy?'

Apollo remembered very well; he had had the misfortune to be a plump, querulous child with a tendency to burst into tears when rebuked, and the Titan was the only grown-up who could ever be bothered with him. 'No,' he said.

'Don't you? Ah well,' said Prometheus, 'never mind.

Like they say, just because you're omniscient doesn't mean you don't forget the occasional birthday.'

Apollo suddenly recollected that today was Prometheus's birthday; his five-million-and-fifth. Now gods are very sensitive about such things, and the phenomenon that mortals know as the Milky Way is in fact the reflection in the Space-Time continuum of the seven million candles on Jupiter's birthday cake. It was therefore not unnatural that Apollo's somewhat soft heart should have been affected by this, particularly when he noticed, out of the corner of his all-seeing eye, a milk bottle with a single dandelion in it standing on an adjacent rock, and next to it a piece of plain card with *Hapy Birthday Pormeethius From Eegle* scrawled on it in crayon. In fact, a tiny tear lurched out of the corner of one sky-blue eye, until the heat of His gaze evaporated it into a tiny saline deposit.

'All right,' said Apollo with a badly muffled sob, 'if you must know, I've been sent to punish you.'

'Oh yes?' said Prometheus mildly. 'Why's that?'

'For subverting Heroes,' Apollo snuffled.

'Subverting Heroes,' Prometheus repeated. 'I see. And what are you going to do to me?'

'First,' Apollo sobbed, 'I'm supposed to flay you alive with a lash made of vipers; then I've got to hang you by your ankles from the Firmament and have vultures gnaw at your ... Oh, Uncle Pro, I'm so unhappy!'

Apollo sank to his knees and subsided into a small, whimpering heap. Just like when he was a boy, Prometheus reflected, and Minerva and Diana used to take his golden bow away from him and put comets down his back. For a moment, he felt ashamed of taking advantage of the boy's kind heart (it was hard to think of Little Pol as anything but a boy); then he thought of the vultures and hardened his mind. It's a nasty world, he told himself; god eat god is the rule, and the one thing a superhuman being can't afford to have is humanity.

'It's all right,' said the Titan softly. 'Now then, what's the matter with you?'

Jupiter paused for a moment, searching for the right word, and looked out of the window.

'It's not as if,' he said, 'he's done anything wrong ...'

'But you just said ...'

'Well,' Jupiter replied, 'that's not quite true. He's been very naughty. Conspiring with prohibited persons. Duffing up gods. Can't be allowed to do that sort of thing. But nothing *serious*; nothing we can't deal with ...' Jupiter's words tailed off and he squinted at something sticking up out of the ground between the rose bushes and the Arum lily. 'Excuse my asking,' he enquired, 'but is that the skeleton of a tyrannosaurus I can see out there?'

'Where?'

'There.'

Mrs. Derry looked closely. 'Oh that,' she said. 'Yes.'

'Where did he get that from?'

'I don't know,' said Mrs. Derry. 'I don't want to know, either. Hopefully, he's given up doing that.'

'Has he?'

'Well,' replied the Hero's mother, 'last month there were a couple of Rottweilers and a big sort of lizard thing, but apart from that there hasn't been anything since the mammoth. Just as well, if you ask me; it's a small garden and it was getting so bad we were having to double-bank them in places. And it only takes a shower of rain or something like that ...'

'Yes,' said Jupiter, shuddering, 'yes, quite. Well, as I was saying, I really don't want to have to come the heavy father with the lad. It's really not my style at all. So if you could see your way to having a word with him ...'

'I'll try,' said Mrs. Derry doubtfully. 'But you know what they're like at that age.'

'Not Jason,' said Jupiter. 'And I always knew that if

you told him not to do it, then he'd stop. You know he always listens to you.'

'Well ...'

Jupiter managed to restrain his grin of triumph. 'Just tell him,' he said, 'that you've heard he's been getting into trouble and how worried you've been and ask him to stop it; that'll do the trick, I promise you. He looks up to you, you know.'

'Well,' said Mrs. Derry again. 'If you think it's for the best ...'

'Stands to reason, doesn't it?' Jupiter said. 'Not that I'd ever willingly let him come to any harm, you understand, but even I can't be in more than four places at once, and these people he's been seeing – Prometheus and Gelos and that crowd – really, they're no good. I mean that. Sooner or later they'll get him into real trouble, and it may well be that I won't be able to do anything for him. It's for his own good,' Jupiter added, recalling the phrase from the back of his mind. 'You'll see.'

'All right, then,' Mrs. Derry said. 'I'll see what I can do.'

Jupiter smiled. 'That's splendid, then,' he said. 'Right, well, it's been great seeing you again, Phyl, but it's time I wasn't here. Give my regards to ... er, you know, your husband.'

'Douglas.'

'Quite so, yes, Douglas. How are things in the – what is it he does?'

'He repairs television sets.'

'Does he *really*? How very clever of him. Not that I watch much television myself, actually, but ... well, do give him my regards, anyway.'

'I will.'

Jupiter's smile became slightly more glassy, if anything. 'And you take care of yourself too, of course. How's the back?'

'Painful.'

'Still? I *am* sorry. I must remember to get Aesculapius to fix you something for it.'

Mrs. Derry's eyes said *You promised me that the last time*, but she said nothing. She had a thin, crimped look on her face, and Jupiter felt very strongly that he wanted to go now. He went.

Halfway down the street, on his way to his rendezvous with his driver, he met a policeman on his beat. Being omniscient, he knew that the officer's name was Sergeant Smith and that he had acquired a wholly unjustified reputation for seeing things. Being possessed of a rather anti-social sense of humour, he transformed himself into a twelve-foot-high djinn with ten arms and three heads, stepped deliberately into the policeman's path, raised his three hats, nodded affably, and vanished in a cloud of opalescent light.

Jason stepped back, whipped the Sword of Glycerion from its scabbard, shouted his battle cry, and sprang forward.

The Hoplites of Hell grinned at him, clashed their swords on their shields, and advanced to meet him. There was a crunch, like a huge crab being run over by a lorry, and a number of thin screams.

'Next!' Jason demanded.

The Hell-Captain looked at his twelve decapitated warriors, shrugged disinterestedly, and felt in the pouch that hung from his belt. It contained dragon's teeth which, when scattered on the ground, turned into hideous and well-armed warriors. Warriors with no mercy. Warriors who knew no fear. Warriors who were insensible to pain. Warriors who didn't need to be paid. The Hell-Captain broadcast a handful of teeth, stepped back, and folded his arms.

Perhaps because he was getting a little bit tired, and this time there had been fifteen of them rather than twelve, it took Jason all of twenty seconds to reduce this contingent of draconian by-products to rubble. On the other hand, one of them had contrived, in his death-throes, to tread on Jason's foot, thereby kindling his fury.

For the first time, the Hell-Captain felt a trifle uneasy. He
felt in the bag and found there were only another fifty or so
teeth left. Being prudent rather than chivalrous, he sowed
the lot.

'That's more like it,' Jason yelled. 'If there's one thing I
can't stand, it's all this hanging about.' He flourished the
Sword like a tennis player practising flowing backhand
smashes.

A spectral warrior, taller by a skull than its fellow-
demons, grounded its shield and scimitar with a clang.

'Right,' it said, 'that does it.'

Jason and the Hell-Captain both stared at it. It folded
its arms defiantly.

'It's all right for you,' it said. 'You just look at it from
our point of view for a second, will you?'

'Can we please get on now?' Jason interrupted. 'I
haven't got all day, you know.'

'Stuff you,' said the spectral warrior. 'And don't you
start, either,' it went on, turning and giving the Hell-
Captain a filthy look through the eyeslits of its coal-black
helm. 'We've had it up to here with the both of you,
haven't we, lads?'

The other spectral warriors nodded their inky plumes in
agreement. There was a small autumn of falling shields.

'I mean,' the spectral warrior spokesthing went on, 'just
think about it, will you? We start off life in the mouth of a
bloody great dragon, right? Now that's not exactly fun and
games, what with the bad breath and the fireworks display
sloshing round you every time the sodding thing sneezes.
You wouldn't think it could get worse, would you? Only it
does, because some nerd whips us out of it with a pair of
rusty pliers, dunks us in a vat of magic potion, and the
next thing we know we're a phalanx of doomed psycho-
paths getting smashed to buggery by some eight-foot jerk
with a sword. Somebody tell me, for crying out loud, what
is the point?'

The other spectral warriors clapped their fleshless

hands and cheered. Jason frowned ominously. The Hell-Captain tried hiding behind his shield. This sort of thing wasn't supposed to happen, was it?

'All right,' he said. 'So what am I supposed to do about it? Explain it all away to Management while you lot all puddle off and become hairdressers?'

His words were drowned out by the clamour of furious serpentine dentistry. He closed his eyes and banged on the ground with his shield for quiet. Eventually, he got it.

'Look,' he said, 'believe me, I'm not unsympathetic. I know how you feel. It can't be easy, I know. But you've got to accept that in this life ...'

The spokesthing made a rude noise. 'But we're not in this life, are we?' it pointed out. 'We aren't even human, that's the bloody galling part of it. We're just a job lot of recycled bridgework, and we aren't going to stand for it. You want this job done, you get some of your precious fellow-humans to do it. Right?'

The Hell-Captain went as red as a tomato. 'Who are you calling human?' he demanded.

'Oh yeah?' replied the spokesthing. 'Want to make something of it, do you?'

There was another crunch like a huge crab being run over by a lorry, and a number of thin screams. Jason leaned on the hilt of the Sword, scratching his head and wondering, as he did from time to time, exactly why he bothered. There was a quiet cough at his elbow.

He swivelled round, Sword uplifted, to find a small fiend with a pitchfork in one hand and a cellular telephone in the other looking up at him.

'Jason Derry?' it asked.

'Yes.'

'Call for you,' said the fiend and offered him the telephone. Jason took it, nodded and thanked him. The fiend didn't move, except to extend its hand meaningfully. Jason sighed, felt in his pocket and produced a fifty pence and two tens, the sum of his monetary wealth at that moment. Heroes rarely carry money around with them, as it spoils the line of their clothes. The fiend gave him a contemptuous look and withdrew.

'Hello?' Jason said into the phone.

'Jason?' said a female voice, 'is that you?'

'Hi, Mum!' Jason replied. 'How did you get my number?' he asked suspiciously.

There was a brief pause. 'I ... I got it from your Dad,' said Mrs. Derry.

'Dad?' Jason asked. 'Which one?'

'Big Dad.'

'Oh,' Jason said. 'I might have known. What did he want?'

'Jason,' said his mother, 'I want you to come home right now, do you hear me? I'm very worried about you.'

'But Mum ...' He ducked to avoid a severed arm. 'I can't come now, I'm busy.'

'Don't give me that, Jason,' said Mrs. Derry severely. 'You're to come home *right now*, or I'll be seriously angry. Do you hear?'

'But Mum ...'

'And no buts,' said Mrs. Derry. 'I'll expect you back for tea.'

The line went dead, and Jason handed the phone to the dwarf. While he had been otherwise occupied, the Hell-Captain had reduced his fifty remaining myrmidons to a mound of battered and dismembered calcium, and his martial ardour was beginning to ebb slightly. That, he realised, only left him.

'Now, then,' Jason said, hefting the Sword and wafting a graceful square cut through the clammy air. 'Let's make this as quick as possible, because I really do have to go soon.'

'Suits me,' said the Hell-Captain. 'In fact, why not let's just leave it at that, shall we? Call it a draw or something.'

'A draw?'

'Why not?' replied the Hell-Captain. 'I make it fifty spectral warriors each. A tie.'

Jason shook his head and advanced crabwise, whirling the Sword above his head like an enchanted rotor-blade.

'Actually,' remarked the Hell-Captain, backing away, 'on reflection I find that you win, on higher scoring-rate. Congratulations. You played a fair match, hard but fair, and the best man won.'

'Will win,' Jason corrected him. 'As soon as you stop moving about.'

'Did I happen to mention,' said the Hell-Captain, 'that I've done my shoulder? You can't expect me to fight you with a dicky shoulder, now can you?'

'Shut up and fight.'

'Shan't.' The Hell-Captain sheathed his sword, dropped his shield and jumped on it. 'I yield,' he said. 'Got you there, haven't I?'

Jason considered this for a moment; then he sheathed the Sword and hit him.

'Nobody loves a smartass,' he remarked; then he marched off up the tunnel towards the distant crack of daylight.

About five minutes later, the Hell-Captain stopped shamming dead, picked himself up, and looked cautiously round. As far as he could tell, there was nothing there except the butchered components of a hundred spectral warriors, but he wasn't taking any chances.

'I,' he said, 'am dead. I was killed in the fight. This is just my astral body talking. Since I am dead, I am excused further duty. If you want any other Heroes catching, you can bloody well catch them yourself.'

He stripped off his dented helm, tossed it aside and limped off towards the topside, Piccadilly and a new life. For the record, he later became a successful and highly respected chiropodist. Further details have been suppressed at his own request.

'I dunno,' Vulcan said doubtfully. 'Tricky.'

'But you can do it?'

Vulcan scratched his head, walked three times round the vehicle, kicked the offside front wheel and said, 'Maybe.'

'That's great,' Apollo said. 'How soon can you start?'

'It'll cost you, though.'

'Never mind that.'

'It's all right your saying never mind that,' Vulcan replied seriously. 'First there's your parts, that's ...' he made a few rough calculations on the back of an envelope. 'Plus your labour, at a hundred staters an hour, let's call that ...'

'Just forget all that,' said Apollo impatiently. 'Expense is no object. Just get started, will you? We can discuss the rest of it later.'

Vulcan shook his head. 'Beats me why you can't be satisfied with something simpler,' he said. 'Look, I can do you a Vulcan Mustang Sports Turbo, alloy wheels, hot cams, hydraulic suspension, one careful owner, still in warranty, yours for ...'

'Forget it,' Apollo snapped. 'It's this or nothing, OK? If you can't handle it,' he added menacingly, 'I know dwarves who can.'

Vulcan scowled at him. 'You please yourself,' he said. 'It's your money.'

'Exactly,' Apollo said. 'I'll need it by the weekend, so get busy.' Then he left, thereby neatly guillotining the debate.

After he had gone, Vulcan spent about twenty minutes scribbling little sketches on the envelope. Then he looked at it, turned it upside down, shrugged, tore it up and summoned his assistants. His assistants are the Cyclopes, the monstrous one-eyed cannibalistic thunder-giants of Sicily. At that particular moment, they were sitting round the tyre-changing press with the transistor radio turned up to full volume, playing poker and ogling the Pirelli calendar (not easy if you're one-eyed).

'Brontes!' Vulcan called. 'Sthenos! Bias! Kratos! Gather round, we've got work to do.'

Grumbling, the Cyclopes abandoned their game and trooped through into the main bodyshop, their knuckles ploughing furrows in the dust as they came.

'Yeah, boss?' said Brontes.

Vulcan pointed to the thing on the hydraulic ramp. 'You see that?' he demanded.

'Yeah, boss.'

'What is it?'

Brontes scratched his head. Thinking, as opposed to overtightening bolts and hitting things with a mole wrench, was not his forte. 'Looks like a Volkswagen to me, boss.'

'Well done,' said Vulcan. 'Now listen to this ...'

'Thanks, George,' Jason said. 'Call back at about half past nine tomorrow, okay?'

George scowled. 'You said that the last time, remember?'

'All right, all right ...'

'Meet you here in about half an hour, you said.'

'George ...'

'Fourteen hours,' George said.

'I lost track of time a bit,' Jason snapped. 'I said I'm sorry, okay?'

George made no reply. Instead he shook his head resentfully, put the golf cart into gear and drove away.

Jason fumbled for his key, opened the door and walked in. 'Hi, Mum,' he called out, 'I'm home.'

'Is that you, Jason?' came a voice from the kitchen.

Jason, as usual, mumbled 'No, it's the Pope' to himself under his breath and went through.

Mrs. Derry was making biscuits. There had not been a time, as far as Jason could remember, when his mother hadn't been making biscuits. And that was the funny thing; he was fond of biscuits and had eaten a great many. So was his father fond of biscuits. So was his mother. But the three of them, eating in shifts round the clock, couldn't possibly have stuffed away the infinity of Melting Moments, gingernuts, Maryland cookies and Viennese fingers that had poured out of this kitchen in the last fifteen years or so. Which meant that most of them must still be here, somewhere. In the cupboard under the stairs, the greenhouse, the tool-shed, wherever; one of these days, he would open a door and they'd all come pouring out . . .

'Sorry I'm late,' he said, 'I got held up. Spectral warriors.'

'That's nice, dear. Your father came round.'

'I know,' said Jason, 'Big Dad, you said. What did he want?'

Mrs. Derry stopped kneading and dusted her hands off purposefully. 'He's very angry with you, Jason,' she said.

'So?' Jason said wearily. It had been a long day, his head was buzzing and his knuckles were sore. He wanted a cup of tea, a nice warm bath, and bed.

'Jason,' his mother said.

Now some names, as we know, have meanings. Dorothy means Gift of God, Winifred means White Wave and Stephen means Crown. Jason, to the best of our knowledge, doesn't mean anything. Except, of course, when said in a significant tone by somebody's mother.

'Mum,' Jason complained, 'I'm tired. Can't it wait?'

'Your father,' said Mrs. Derry, 'is very angry with you.'

'Tough,' Jason replied. 'But I really couldn't care less. I've had it up to here with him, and ...'

'Jason,' Mrs. Derry said, 'you mustn't disobey your father. It's not right.'

'Mum ...' Jason was on the point of pleading.

'Now you promise me you won't do it again,' said Mrs. Derry, 'and we'll say no more about it, all right?'

'Mum,' Jason said – it took a lot of strength of will to say it, too – 'I can't do what Dad says. It's wrong.'

'Jason,' said Mrs. Derry sternly. 'That's nonsense and you know it. He's your father.'

Jason wanted to object. He wanted to say that Attila the Hun had had a son, and so had Genghis Khan; that there was a flaw in the logic of her argument you could drive a very large vehicle through without even clipping your wing mirrors; that what Jupiter wanted him to do was as gross a betrayal of his mortality as it was possible to get; that Jupiter had sent a god – his own half-brother – to kill him today, and if that hadn't dissolved the filial contract, he wanted to know what would. What he actually said was 'Mum ...'

'He's your father,' Mrs. Derry said again. 'And he's worried about you.'

That was almost too much – almost – for Jason. He was about to say that if he was worried about his son's safety, why was he sending divine assassins to have him forcibly stellified, but somehow he didn't. Instead, he said 'Look ...' Which was a change from 'Mum ...' but not an improvement on it.

When the gods first designed Heroes, they intended them to be a special reserve category of super-mortals, with all the good mortal features souped up to competition standard and all the bad mortal features either sublimated or omitted. The design team assigned to the job had obviously enjoyed it, because they took a pride in their work that was notably absent from the standard production mortal. The everyday hatchback model, on leaving the showroom, has inbuilt design flaws: cowardice, greed, spite, frailty, appalling power-to-weight ratio and fuel consumption, and a tendency to measles. Not so Heroes; they are godlike in their strength and prowess, but most ungodlike in that they exhibit nobility, courage and altruism; seek to alleviate the sufferings of mankind instead of scoring five points (ten for a double Woe Score) for them; right wrongs; succour rather than sucker the weak; generally speaking, don't bicker like tired, spoilt children at every opportunity. In fact, Heroes are such a successful design concept that not long after the first batch were released, the gods realised that they'd cocked it up again and recalled the whole issue with almost indecent haste. Something had to be done.

What was done was this. Into each Hero, a tragic flaw was introduced, individually tailored to self-destruct the Hero just as soon as he began to show signs of getting too big for his seven-league boots. Achilles his pride; Oedipus his curiosity; Hamlet his indecision; David Gower his tendency to flap at deliveries aimed at his leg stump – each Hero has been deliberately sabotaged to prevent him making that final leap across the terminals of the spark-plug from imperfect to perfect. Jason, of course, was no exception.

'Mum ...' he said.

'Jason,' said his mother, 'what is that dog doing in my kitchen?'

The words 'what dog?' froze on Jason's lips. 'Oh,' he said, 'yes. That's Cerberus.'

'Outside.'

'But Mum ...'

'Outside.'

'But Mum ...'

'Outside.'

Miserably, Jason grabbed hold of Cerberus by one ear and led him out to the garage.

'Good dog,' Jason said guiltily. 'Stay.'

Cerberus gave him a threefold look that reflected perfectly what Jason was himself thinking at precisely that moment, right down to the three dots. But Jason could only shrug his shoulders and look extremely silly.

'I *know*,' he said. 'But what can I do?'

He closed the door, locked it and went back into the house, trying to ignore the stereophonic whimpering and scratching noises coming from the garage.

'I don't mind your bringing them back dead,' said his mother. 'Alive is another matter. First thing in the morning you're taking him up the kennels.'

Jason could have said 'But Mum' again, but he felt it was beginning to lose its impact. So he tried sulking instead. Eighteen years of experience told him that it didn't work, but so what? They'd said the same thing about Eddison and the light bulb.

'Now, then,' said Mrs. Derry cheerfully, 'now that we've got that sorted out, you can have a biscuit. I made some Melting Moments. You know how you like Melting Moments.'

Jason nodded resignedly. Yes, he liked Melting Moments and would do what he was told. Pity about the human race, but whoever said life was fair?

'Another thing,' said Mrs. Derry as she made more biscuits. 'Sharon's coming round for her tea tomorrow, so don't be late home.'

'*Mum...*'

Mothers since the creation of mankind have learned that the best way to stifle objections from their offspring is to stuff biscuits in their mouths. Nobody, not even Lenin, can preach rebellion effectively with a mouth full of Melting Moment. 'Six-thirty sharp,' she said. 'I'm doing lamb with pearl barley. You like lamb with pearl barley,' she reminded him.

'Yes, Mum.' In a sudden access of memory, Jason seemed to recall himself breaking into the Underground, conspiring to overthrow Jupiter, duffing up two gods and rounding it all off by pulverising fifty crack Hell-troopers. Or did he? All of a sudden he became aware that the memory can play strange tricks. Very probably he'd imagined it all.

'Goodnight, Mum,' he said.

'Mind you brush your teeth.'

'Yes, Mum.'

'Goodnight, Jason.'

''Night, Mum.'

When he got to his room, he noticed that all his Mars posters had disappeared and that someone, probably the Revenue, had been and impounded all his personal records. He found some of them later in a large cardboard box on top of the wardrobe, and the rest of them the next morning neatly packaged up in black dustbin bags outside the back door.

It wouldn't have been much of a consolation to Jason even if he'd known, but Hercules had had more or less the same trouble with his wife. The most notable occasion was on his return after the completion of the Twelve Labours, to find that in his absence Megara of the Fair Ankles had given half his clothes to a jumble sale, put a further quarter in the loft and washed and ironed the remaining quarter, thereby destroying at a stroke the carefully-compiled ambience of thirty years of blood, toil, tears and sweat. Mythology records that, at this point, Hercules lost his rag good and proper and settled his family's hash once and for all with several hearty blows of his club. This is all, of course, pure nonsense. Mythology, it should be remembered, is composed largely by men. What actually happened, apart from a few unheeded protests, was nothing at all, and the reason why Megara fades out of the Hercules legend at this point is that while Hercules was away killing monsters and averting evils, Megara had happened to meet a rather nice insurance broker who, although shorter, punier and incapable of dealing with any form of hostile wildlife bigger than a money-spider, was at least there at weekends and public holidays.

As Jason slept, a number of very insistent dreams came and stood beside him. He swatted them with a back issue of *Model Railway Enthusiast* and went back to sleep.

'Gel.'

 'Here, Pro. Fire away.'

 'Trouble.'

 'What?'

 'Big trouble.'

 'All right, so it's big trouble. What?'

Telepathic communication is actually much faster than this. It belts through the air at a simply alarming rate, just like the new information technology that so nearly reproduces it, and so we can legitimately omit Prometheus's resumé of the scene between Jason and Mrs. Derry, logging back in at the point when Gelos says 'Oh *shit!*', without having abridged more than three seconds of actual time.

 'Oh *shit!*'

 'Exactly,' agreed Prometheus. 'Now what do we do?'

 'Nothing for it, is there?'

 'You mean ...?'

 'That's right,' thought Gelos gravely. 'The eagle has landed.'

In the sick-bay of the sun, Aesculapius was doing more business in one afternoon than he had done for the last fifty years.

 'Right,' he said briskly, 'this may hurt a little.'

Nobody knows exactly why doctors say that. It can't be to set the patient at his ease, because anybody above the age of three knows from bitter experience that the words are the invariable prologue to agony, just as 'You may feel a little bit woozy for the next twenty-four hours' means that you're going to spend the next three days bumping into things and feeling like an LSD addict after a particularly bad trip, and 'It's just for a few routine tests' means that it's now too late to see about some life insurance. Perhaps they do it on purpose, just in case you weren't actually scared rigid to start with.

Mars shut his eyes and braced his few remaining rigid components. There was a click, a flare of therapeutic orange flame, and the noise of a god complaining.

'You can put your clothes back on now,' said Aesculapius.

'Want to bet?' Mars replied.

'That will do,' said Aesculapius. 'Next, please.'

Mars dragged himself off the couch and Pluto took his place.

'Now then,' said the heavenly physician, 'what seems to be the trouble?'

Pluto scowled at him. 'Did you do anatomy at medical school?' he asked. Aesculapius nodded.

'Very well then,' Pluto replied. 'Look at my skeleton and start counting the gaps.'

Aesculapius ignored him and started prodding him about. 'Hm,' he said at last, 'we've got a few bones missing here and there, I see. And what have we been getting up to to get ourselves in this state, then?'

'I'd rather not discuss it,' Pluto said. 'A dog was involved.'

Aesculapius, being a doctor, is at perfect liberty to ignore anything anyone says to him. 'We'll have to see what we can do about that,' he said briskly. 'Wait there.'

He went to the bone cupboard, picked out a number of bones from the stock, and tried them for size. They more or less fitted, roughly as an 11/16 inch bolt will fit a 15 mm thread if you ease it into place with a lump hammer. He fitted them quickly and fairly accurately and told Pluto to stand up.

'Ow,' said Pluto. Aesculapius helped him to his feet, told him to practise, and advised him that he might possibly experience some slight discomfort for the next forty-eight hours. Then he shooed him out and sat down for a quiet half-hour with a cup of Bovril and a gynaecological journal.

Outside his surgery, Mars and Pluto compared notes.

'It's not good, is it?' Mars said.

'Distinctly worrying,' Pluto agreed. 'What I want to know is how that confounded Derry boy managed it.'

'Well,' said Mars, 'in my case he sort of drew back his left hand like this ...'

'No, no,' said Pluto, wincing slightly, 'that's not what I meant. How did he get the power to fight with gods? Mortals can't fight with gods, not usually; it's just not possible, like wrestling with the wind. We're in a different dimension to them – unless, of course, they have help.'

'Help,' said Mars bitterly, 'isn't usually hard to find, is it? I have scars to prove it.'

'Oh, I agree with you,' Pluto said. 'In the past, one of us has always been only too glad to give his or her pet champion a helping hand against the rest of us. But not in this case, surely. We're all united; nobody has anything at all to gain from enabling Derry to fight with us. So, either he has the ability himself, without the need for any assistance – which means that he's a bigger god than any of us – or else someone very big indeed is helping him out. And the only Person that big is ...'

'Exactly,' said Mars. 'And Jupiter may be ...' He looked anxiously around him, 'but he's not as crazy as all that. He's more worried by all this than any of us. That can only mean that the boy did manage to get through and make contact with ...'

'Yes,' said Pluto hurriedly. 'It really isn't looking terribly good, is it?'

'Quite right,' said a third voice. 'And while we're on the subject, you both think I'm crazy, do you?'

The two gods looked round and saw Jupiter standing behind them. He hadn't been there five seconds ago, but really, that is neither here nor there. When you're dealing with an omnipresent supreme being, even looking behind the sofa and turning on all the taps is a complete waste of time.

'Anyway,' said Jupiter briskly, 'I've solved everything, with no help from any of you clowns, as usual. All our troubles are over; you can get back to loafing about and looking decorative. Put your collar straight, Ma. You look like you've just been let out of prison.'

And Jupiter vanished. Mars turned to Pluto and shrugged.

'What we need right now,' he said, 'is a drink.'

Pluto nodded.

'Or two drinks.'

'Quite right.'

Having come to this eminently reasonable conclusion, they left the sick-bay and were crossing over the road to the bar when they were knocked down by Phoebus Apollo, who was test-driving a 1960s Volkswagen Beetle converted into a chariot drawn by four winged dragons.

Jason was woken from deep sleep by a sound uncannily like a large bird tapping on his window with its beak.

Being half-divine, Jason could sleep through most things, but not this. After a period of semi-consciousness, during which he was troubled with dreams involving huge thrushes knocking snails out of brightly-coloured shells, he pulled himself out of bed, groped hazily for the Sword of Who The Hell Cares, Anyway, and tottered to the window. He pulled aside the curtain and saw a large bird tapping on the glass.

'Shoo,' he said.

The bird refused to shoo. He noticed that it was in fact an eagle, and although one eagle looked pretty much like another to him, he made an intuitive assumption and opened the window six inches.

'What do you want?' he asked.

The eagle replied by thrusting a talon in the crack and

shrieking. With a sigh, Jason opened the window fully and the eagle hopped in, shook the rain out of its feathers and turned into an extremely beautiful young woman.

'Hello,' she said. 'Sorry if I woke you. Have you got a moment?'

Jason nodded and waved vaguely at a chair. It had rather a lot of socks on it, some of them of considerable maturity, but the girl affected not to notice them.

'I'm Eagle,' she said, 'but you can call me Mary.'

Jason nodded again. He was fresh out of words.

'I'm a friend of Prometheus,' the girl went on. 'And Gelos. Gelos isn't actually called Gelos, by the way; or at least he is, but it's not his real name. Really he's called Thing.'

Jason nodded a third time, as if this was the most logical thing he had ever heard. The girl smiled at him, crossed her legs and went on.

'What they want to know is, would you do them a small favour? It's to do with what Thing – that's Gelos – was telling you about earlier on; you know, Jupiter and the diversionary tactics? I'm sorry to bother you with it now, but there have been gods watching the house most of the night, and I've only just managed to get rid of them.'

Jason's befuddled expression must have seemed to the girl like a request for an explanation of how she had managed that, because she coloured slightly. 'Oh, it was easy,' she said. 'I just told each of them in turn that I'd meet them in ten minutes behind the ...'

'Ah.'

'So,' said the girl, 'what they'd like you to do is ...'

'No,' Jason said. 'Sorry.'

The girl stared at him. 'Sorry?'

'Yes.'

'No,' said the girl, 'I meant sorry meaning what was that you said.'

'I said sorry.'

'Before that.'

'No.'

'Oh.' the girl frowned. 'Why?'

'I'm busy tomorrow,' Jason replied. 'Another time, maybe.'

This seemed to have a strange effect on the girl. First she peered closely at her arms and then her legs; then she got up and looked at herself in the mirror. Having apparently satisfied herself that all was well, she came and sat down again.

'No, but seriously,' she said, 'what we'd like you to do is ...'

'Really, no,' Jason answered. 'No can do. Out of the question.'

'But ...'

'In fact,' Jason went on, 'I hate to do this, but I'm afraid the whole thing's off. I've thought it over, and the fact is that I'm not going through with it. After all, Jupiter *is* my father, and it really isn't ...'

'He tried to kill you.'

'Well yes, there is that,' Jason admitted. 'In a sense there's something in what you say, but ...'

'He sent Mars, and Pluto, and a hundred Hell-troopers.'

'The Hell-troopers were just for fun, surely,' Jason said. 'I mean, you can't be expected to take an opponent seriously when he pops up out of the ground at you like one of those fast-motion films of a tree growing.'

The girl put her head on one side and nibbled absently at her shoulder-blade. 'You really expect me to believe you've had a change of heart?' she asked. 'Seriously?'

'Yes,' said Jason.

'No, you haven't.'

Jason felt a tiny green shoot of irritability thrusting its head up through the surface of his general bewilderment. 'What are you,' he demanded, 'a mind-reader or something?'

'Yes.'

Jason took that one in his stride. 'In that case,' he said, 'you can see that my mind is made up. Now, if you don't mind ...'

The girl recrossed her legs petulantly. 'Are you throwing me out?' she said.

'In a manner of speaking, yes.' Jason said. 'And you can tell your friends that if I've got to be bossed about by one side or the other, I might as well be bossed about by Jupiter. After all, he is my Dad and he is winning.'

'Bossed about?'

'Yes,' said Jason, with a sudden access of feeling, 'bloody well bossed about. Do this. Do that. Fulfil your Destiny. Chop the head off that serpent over there. Steal those golden apples. The hell with the lot of you. I'm sick and tired of being ordered around by people, and if you think I'm going to betray my own father just to be ordered around by you lot ...'

'But Jason ...'

'Don't Jason me,' Jason said. 'I've had all the Jasoning I can handle tonight already. Now put your feathers back on and sling your hook, all right?'

'Jason ...'

'And it's no good you saying you're a protected species, because in this house the Wildlife and Countryside Act has no jurisdiction. Clear off before I stuff a cushion with you.'

'Jason ...'

'I mean, you can say that Jupiter and his mob leave a lot to be desired, but what sort of a world would it be if there was a bunch of comedians in charge? Everybody would be so busy telling each other jokes, sooner or later someone would forget to plant any crops and then where would we be?'

'Jason ...'

Jason Derry made an exasperated noise, grabbed the Sword and whirled it round his head, neatly but unintentionally slicing through the electric light flex. The girl squawked, grew feathers, and hopped onto the windowsill.

'Out!' Jason said. The eagle gave him a filthy look, spread its wings and vanished.

Trembling slightly, Jason closed the window, put the Sword away and climbed back into bed; and not long afterwards, he was asleep again. That, he realised in retrospect, was a mistake.

He had been sleeping quite happily for upwards of a quarter of an hour when a dream came to him. Since the window was shut, the dream had to squeeze in via the mains through the severed electric flex, and it stood at the head of Jason's bed for thirty seconds or so, getting its breath back. Then it gingerly inserted itself into his mind and got down to business.

It seemed to Jason as if he was standing in a queue. It was a long queue, and he couldn't see the end, and he didn't know what it was for. The people in front of him and behind him had no faces; the fronts of their heads were blank and polished, with no openings on them.

The queue shuffled forwards and, because it was a dream, the whole sequence was able to fast-forward a bit, so that Jason was aware that he had been in the queue for an intolerably long time without that part of the dream taking more than a sixtieth of a second. Then quite suddenly he was at the front of the queue, and he saw Jupiter; and standing beside him, Mars and Pluto. They had big felt-tip marker pens in their hands, and as the people in the queue shuffled past them they drew in faces on the blank surfaces of their heads. Or at least they put in two blobs for eyes and an upside-down semicircle for the mouth; a sad face. Then they pushed each person over the edge of a cliff.

Well yes, said Jason's subconscious mind. Fair comment, I suppose. Allegory is all about value-judgments anyway and maybe I shouldn't have had that cheese sandwich before turning in.

Then he looked round and saw another queue, parallel

to the one he was in. It was exactly the same, except that
Gelos and Prometheus were at the head of it, and the faces
they drew in had upright semicircles for mouths; smiling
faces. And when these people were pushed over the cliff,
they didn't fall. Instead, they drifted up into the air like
spacewalking astronauts, hovered for a few moments,
touched down again and walked round to the back of the
queue.

Heavy, said Jason's subconscious. If Sigmund Freud
could see what was going on here, he'd have me in a
padded cell so quick my feet wouldn't touch.

Then he suddenly found himself at the front of Jupiter's
queue, and Jupiter – Dad – was drawing a face on him. A
sad face. Then he felt a large hand in the small of his back
and he was flying through the air over the edge of the cliff. He
opened his mouth to scream and could feel the ink smudging.

And then, as he fell (but slowly, since it was a dream),
he saw three dots in the sky, very far away. The further he
fell, the larger the dots became, until they turned into
three eagles. Two of them flew straight past, but the third
swooped down, caught hold of him in one talon and carried
him back up. The other talon held a bag of chips, which it
offered to him.

Then he was back on the cliff top again, and feeling
extremely angry. He had a duster in his hand now, and he
walked up to Jupiter, wiped his face off, and drew in a
very sad face indeed. Then he picked the god up and
tossed him over the edge. His subconscious mind started
kicking up no end of a fuss but he ignored it. It felt good.

The dream grinned and stood up. The bit with the
duster had been its own idea, and although it knew that
Thing didn't really approve of ad-libbing, it felt that it was
probably the duster which had turned the scales. Pausing
only to blow deep sleep into Jason's eyes, the dream
trickled back up into the light flex and vanished.

Half an hour or so later, Jason woke up, sweating. He
could hear something.

He listened carefully. Nothing. He swore drowsily and tried to go back to sleep. Then he heard it again. It was the sound of a dog, or three dogs, or one dog with three heads, barking.

Indigestion woke up suddenly, gurgled, realised what was going on and made a grab for the alarm clock.

At the fourth attempt he made contact and prevailed upon it to stop ringing. That made things better. Slightly.

The various personifications of abstract concepts who form the non-commissioned ranks of the divine hierarchy – Greed, Fear, Spring, Hope, Pennsylvania, Wealth and Appendicitis, to name but a few; Plato refers to them as the Forms, and why not? – have an arduous time of it. As their great spokesman Discontent put it on the occasion of the January Rising of 1979,* the Forms do all the work but the gods get all the gravy. This dichotomy between work done and status accorded was marked enough before the gods left Olympus; after the move, however, the gods delegated the entire management of their various portfolios to their respective teams of Forms – Mars handing over the conduct of war to Death, Fear and Victory; Minerva appointing as her attorneys Philosophy, Prudence and (curiously enough) Needlepoint; and so on – but neglected to raise their salaries, grant them the right to receive the worship of mortals or even let them use the Management Cloakrooms. Each Form remains answerable to his Head of Department for any errors or omissions, but receives little or no practical assistance with anything but the broadest and most far-reaching policy decisions. A certain degree of resentment was inevitable; and the final straw is believed by many to have been the so-called Form-busting measures introduced by Jupiter in

---

*The direct result of the gods' refusal to allow the Forms to attend the Celestial Christmas Outing to Weymouth; now better known as the Winter of Discontent.

the early 1980s. As a result of these, all Forms are now ultimately under the jurisdiction of the Great Sky-God himself.

As a Form Grade D in the College of Humours, Indigestion generally had little to do with Jupiter, and he was heartily glad of it. The work was bad enough as it was without having the Lord of Tempests to contend with. Only the previous evening, for example, Indigestion had been ordered to attend a reception for the Australian Ambassador in Moscow, with instructions to afflict no fewer than three hundred and twenty-seven guests. What with one thing and another, and in particular the Australian trade attaché's wager that he could drink the Secretary of State for Production under the table, it was well after half past three in the morning before Indigestion had finally got to bed, and now he found that he had woken up with something of a headache.

Having dealt ruthlessly with his clock-radio, Indigestion tried turning over and going back to sleep, but somehow the knack had left him. After a little fruitless cursing, therefore, the wretched Form got out of bed, put on his dressing-gown inside-out and went in search of orange juice.

Fortuitously, he found some in the fridge and drank it quickly. He was just starting to feel that he might, with the assistance of the best medical attention, eventually recover when the telephone rang.

It was a loud telephone at the best of times. Indigestion located the receiver and put it as close to his head as he dared.

'Lo?' he mumbled.

'Morning, Ind,' said a cheerful voice at the other end. 'How's tricks?'

Indigestion winced. 'Could you please speak a little more quietly, please?' he whispered. 'I have a slight ...'

'My God, Ind,' said the voice, 'you aren't hung over *again*, are you? Beats me how you manage it.'

Indigestion scowled at the receiver until he discovered that contracting his brows made the rest of his head hurt. It was in the nature of Health, his immediate superior, to be rude; but just now he wasn't in the mood to make allowances.

'I was working late last night,' he replied coldly. 'And it is my day off ...'

'Sorry, Ind,' Health said, 'all leave cancelled, by order. Be at the departure bay by nine sharp.'

'Hel ...'

'Sorry, mate,' said his boss, 'that's how it is. All maladies and infirmities to report immediately; no excuses accepted.'

'Oh come on, Hel ...'

'No buts, chum,' said Health. 'Oh yes, and you'll be in charge. You'll like that, won't you? Try not to cock it all up, there's a good lad.'

'Bloody hell, Hel ...'

Health laughed. 'I know, I know,' he said. 'But I can't make it. Off sick,' he explained. 'Actually, I promised faithfully to take the old bag round the shops this morning, and if I don't she'll kill me. But that's just between you and me, right?'

Despite his annoyance, Indigestion could feel a slight flicker of sympathy for his superior. Health was, after all, married to Efficiency. Ruthless Efficiency, the lads in Vouchers called her.

'So what's so important that I've got to work on my day off?' Indigestion said resignedly. 'If it's just another 'flu epidemic ...'

'If only it was,' Health replied. 'No, my son, there's something extremely mega happening upstairs. No idea what it is. But the order is that we've got to go and afflict Prometheus. ASAP.'

'I'm sorry,' Indigestion said, 'I thought you just ...'

'Prometheus,' Health repeated. 'The coach leaves at 09.12, and remember to call the register. All absentees to be reported to me personally. Have a good time.'

The line went dead, and Indigestion knew how it felt. He climbed into his work clothes, retrieved his toolkit from behind the sofa, where it had fallen last night, and staggered off towards the bus depot.

He got there just in time to see a flight of winged chariots howling off overhead, packed full of heavily-armed Spectral Warriors. If there was a single dragon anywhere in the cosmos with a tooth left in its head, he reckoned, it would be something of a miracle.

Thanks to Mrs. Health's determination to do her shopping instead of her work, someone had made one almighty mess of the transport arrangements; and when Indigestion arrived at Bay 340, he was informed that the coaches intended to convey the Maladies to the Caucasus mountains had been commandeered by Vulcan and the Cyclopes to transport themselves and their mobile workshop. All the other coaches were spoken for, of course; and with all the winged chariots taken by the military, it looked as if Prometheus, whatever he was going to have to endure today, would be doing so in virtually perfect health. After ten minutes or so of running round arguing with irritable Forms with clipboards, Indigestion happened to bump into Venezuela, who was standing in a long queue behind the only telephone box on the concourse that didn't take phonecards.

'What are you doing here?' Indigestion asked.

'Standing in for Violence,' Venezuela explained. 'He'd got tickets for some poetry reading or other, so I said I'd help out. If I'd known what was going on, I wouldn't have bothered.

'What is going on?' Indigestion asked.

Venezuela grinned. 'Balloon's finally gone up,' she said. 'The word is that the Old Fool has finally flipped and put a contract out on You Know Who.'

Such is the level of paranoia in heaven that periphrases such as You Know Who are practically meaningless.

Indigestion sighed and asked her to be more specific.

'You know,' Venezuela hissed. 'Laughing Boy.'

'Indigestion stared at her. 'You can't be serious,' he said.

'On the contrary,' Venezuela replied, 'if the Big J's to be believed, this is your last opportunity to be anything but serious. Twenty-four hours from now is to be VG Day, and the password is Killing Joke, if you're interested.'

'Look,' said Indigestion, 'what on earth is going on? What have I missed?'

'Well,' Venezuela replied, looking round carefully, 'I was talking to Rumour, and he reckons that that Hero who went off the rails and we all had to look for; you know, the Derry kid ...'

'Yes,' said Indigestion, 'I know him.'

'Do you?'

'He's been eating a lot recently,' Indigestion explained. 'Go on.'

'Apparently,' said Venezuela, 'the Derry boy was subverted by You Know Who ...'

'Look ...'

'All right,' said Venezuela, 'by the person we don't talk about whose name begins with G and who makes people laugh. You know that old prophesy thing.'

Indigestion nodded; a mistake on his part.

'And then,' Venezuela continued, 'when the two of them – Derry and the Person in question – had broken out of wherever he's been holed up all this while – beating up Ma and Plu on the way, I might add – the Big J very cleverly managed to nobble Derry and make him change sides.'

'I thought he'd already done that.'

'Yes,' said Venezuela. 'I mean no. Look, he was on our side, right? Then he defects to them. Now Jupiter's got him to come back to us. Quite the human tennis ball, in fact.'

'Quite.'

'Apparently,' Venezuela went on, 'Jupiter fixed it by getting at Derry through his mother. Anyway, that's what

Bliss told me a moment ago; but you know Bliss, dead ignorant. And so what that means is that the enemy's come out into the open but without a Hero. In dead shtuck, in other words. And so it's all hands to the pump time, to see if we can nail him before he gets back to his place of safety. Fun, isn't it?'

Indigestion breathed in deeply and sighed. Venezuela wasn't the sort of person one would choose to talk to when one has a poorly head, but he had caught the gist of it. 'Hang on, though,' he said. 'If we're supposed to be going after Gel ...'

'*Shh!*'

'All right, after You Know Who, why did Hel say we were all being sent to afflict Prometh ...'

'*Shhhh!*'

'... Whatsit?' said Indigestion. 'Surely we should all ...'

Venezuela grinned. 'And who do you think the Great Smartass will go running to once he's realised his pet Hero's ditched him?'

'Oh,' said Indigestion, 'I see.'

'Particularly,' Venezuela added, 'when he hears that his old buddy and fellow traitor is being beset by maladies and Spectral Warriors and so forth. Be round there like a shot, don't you worry, and then we'll have him. Smart thinking, no?'

Indigestion nodded – slowly this time – and pulled a wry face. 'Oh well,' he said. 'I suppose it had to happen. Look, do you know where I can get hold of at least four large coaches? We should have been on the road about fifteen minutes ago.'

'Coaches are a bit tricky,' Venezuela replied, 'but if a winged chariot or so'd be any use to you ...'

'Fine.'

'You could try OFT,' Venezuela said. 'Oh marvellous, the call-box is free. You got change for a twenty?'

Indigestion finally tracked Old Father Time down in the bar drinking Guinness, and talked him into a loan of his old but reliable Vulcan V12 Camaro. It would be rather a tight squeeze getting all the Maladies on it, he reckoned, but it was worth a try; and in the circumstances, if the worst came to the worst, it probably wouldn't be the end of the world if they left Tennis Elbow behind.

Once he'd found the vehicle, put the horses in the shafts, put the harness on the horses, checked the tyre pressures and wound back the in-flight movie it was nearly half-past ten. Fortunately, Old Father Time's chariot can cope with that sort of problem, and by a quarter to eleven Indigestion was coming in to land on the peak of one of the Caucasus mountains. Not that he was the first to arrive; not by a long way.

I t was raining.

'Aren't you going to take a coat?' said Mrs. Derry.

'No,' Jason replied, thinking of something else.

'Don't be silly, Jason,' Mrs. Derry said. 'Here, I'll get you one.' She disappeared and returned with one of Mr. Derry's anoraks. 'And you aren't going out in *those* shoes.'

Through the window, Jason could see George in the golf cart, looking at his watch. Was today the Serpent-Haired Gorgon of Sphacteria or the Hundred-Headed Hell-Dragon? Not that it mattered terribly much. Once you've slain one, you've slain them all. 'Look,' he said, 'I might be a bit late tonight, don't ...'

'You aren't leaving this house till you change those shoes.'

Jason winced. 'Mum,' he said.

'This instant.'

There was a brief silence, charged with strong emotion. Then Jason let out a plangent sigh, leaned the Sword of Glycerion in its canvas case against the door-frame and sprinted up the stairs. When he came back he was wearing a different pair of shoes.

'Right,' he said. 'Now, if you don't mind ...' He picked up the sword-case and reached for the door-handle.

'Hanky?'

'Yes,' Jason growled.

'Show me.'

'You what?'

'Show me that you've got a clean hanky.'

Jason turned slowly round and gave his mother a look that would have turned the Gorgon to stone and had the Hell-Dragon running in search of the nearest battered dragons' hostel. On his mother it had absolutely no effect.

'Hanky,' she said.

'I'm going beheading monsters,' Jason said, 'I don't think I'm actually going to need ...'

'Hanky.'

My mother, Jason said to himself, a woman of iron will and limited vocabulary. 'Look,' he said, 'I'm late already, so ...'

This time, Mrs. Derry didn't even say Hanky; she just looked it. That was somehow infinitely worse.

'All right,' Jason snapped. 'All right.' He hurried back up the stairs again. A moment later, his voice floated down over the bannisters.

'Mum ...'

'Yes, dear?'

'Where are my handkerchiefs, Mum?'

'In the airing cupboard, dear, second shelf down at the back, where they usually are.'

'Oh. Right.'

'And don't run up and down stairs like that, Jason. It's not good for them.'

'Yes, Mum.'

Having proffered a spotless handkerchief for inspection and picked up the Sword, Jason lunged for the door-handle and rotated it. Even if it turned out that Jupiter had lined up the entire race of Titans for him today, he felt things could only get easier from now on.

'Jason.'

He froze. 'Yes, Mum?'

'Don't forget Sharon's coming over today.'

'Mum ...'

'So make sure you're back by quarter to six at the

latest, because you'll need to have a bath and wash your hair.'

'Mum ...'

'Have a nice day, dear. Go carefully, now.'

'Yes, Mum.' And so saying, the Seed of Jove crawled out of the door and slumped across to the golf cart.

'Morning, boss.'

'What?' Jason hurled the sword-case onto the back seat and sat down.

'I said Morning.'

'Be that as it may,' Jason replied. 'What's the old git want me to do today?'

'Shh!' George was cringing. 'Keep your voice down, boss.'

Jason shook his head. 'If I want to call the Old Git an old git,' he said loudly, so that a passing milkman nearly dropped a crate of gold-top, 'then I shall call the Old Git an old git, and if the Old Git doesn't like it, then the Old Git knows what he can do. All right?'

George nodded. Since he was hunkered down almost under his seat, all Jason could see was the top of his head, but from its movements he could extrapolate a nod.

'Fine,' said Jason. 'So what has the ...'

'Nemean Lion,' George whispered quickly, 'followed by Storm-giants, then half an hour for lunch, followed by wrestling with Time and ending up with stealing the Golden Pear of Truth from the Temple of the Nine Winds which is guarded by ...'

'I know,' Jason said. 'Right, let's get on with it. And if I faint from boredom halfway through, don't forget to wake me.'

George put the cart in gear. 'Right you are, boss. Oh, and boss ...'

'Yes?'

''Scuse me saying this, but it's good to see you back to normal, boss, after you went over all funny. I said to myself ...'

'George.'

'Yes, boss?'

'Drive the cart.'

George shrugged and released the brake. 'Still,' he added, 'Glad to see you've put all that defecting crap behind you, boss. I could have told you no good would come of it.'

'George ...'

'The lads were saying,' George went on, and Jason wondered why saying someone's name quietly didn't seem to work when *he* did it, 'he won't be able to keep it up, they said. Not once his mum's sorted him out. Right old battleaxe ...'

'George!'

'Boss?'

'For crying out loud, George,' Jason hissed, glancing over his shoulder at the front door of the house, 'keep your voice down!'

The eagle banked sharply and dived, slicing through the cold air like a worried knife. Behind her, ten winged chariots full of Spectral Warriors pulled up, wobbled in thin air, and changed tack. A flash of lightning narrowly missed the eagle's wingtip.

Nothing left for it, the eagle realised, but to climb. Try and outmanoeuvre them. G-forces, gravitational pull, power-to-weight ratios, Sopwith Camels, all that sort of stuff. It wasn't exactly her forte, but there it was. As the careers officer at theological college had told her, it is extremely ill-advised to overspecialise too early. She rose as sharply as she could, nearly pulling her own wings off in doing so, and soared.

'After her!' shouted the Captain of Spectral Warriors.

'But ...' said his charioteer.

'No buts,' snapped the Captain. 'Follow her!'

'OK, boss,' said the charioteer.

Not long afterwards, ten empty winged chariots drifted

away towards the ground, their crews having all fallen out when they tried to follow an eagle who was looping the loop. For a moment the eagle slowed down, exhausted, and rested on the crest of a strong thermal. Then she saw another ten winged chariots emerge from behind a bank of cloud, and jinked just in time to avoid a burst of lightning bolts.

Grimly, she started to climb; but the chariots didn't try following her this time. Instead they split up and spread out, rising in slow circles around her. Obviously, she decided, these were the teeth of one smart dragon. Wisdom teeth.

She reset her wings and dived, sending rabbits on the far-distant surface scurrying for cover in all directions. When it looked as if she was certain to hit the deck with extreme force, she pulled up as hard as she could – was that a bone in her left wing breaking, or just a few tendons? – and skimmed parallel to the ground. When she cocked her head over her shoulder, she could see that the chariots were following. Good. In a manner of speaking, of course; really good would have been if they had stopped following her and gone away, but this would have to do for the time being.

As well as making good starters for a dinner party, the eagle recalled, larks are good teachers. She slowed down slightly and zagged about, exaggerating the slight malfunction in her left wing. The chariots were gaining on her. They were coming up very fast now, the charioteers lashing the winged horses up to maximum effort. In fact, they were going so fast now that in less than twenty seconds they would have overtaken their quarry easily, if only they hadn't flown into a railway bridge first.

The eagle spread her aching wings and glided for a moment before looking round and seeing one winged chariot come out from under the railway bridge. With a squawk of furious despair the eagle flapped her pinions and rose up into the air; and the chariot, manned by fifteen Spectral Warriors, all minus their helmets, followed.

It didn't take long for the eagle to come to the conclusion that this bunch, unlike the others, had rather more intelligence than the average ex-molar. They declined to crash into the branches of trees when she led the way, and when she pitched on a low branch and sat tight, they hovered overhead for a while and then set the entire forest alight with thunderbolts, making it imperative for the eagle to leave. She had managed that, purely by dint of hiding between two large, slow-moving crows, and had been quietly sneaking off back the way she had just come when they'd spotted her and resumed their pursuit. Nothing flashy, you see, nothing clever; just plain, textbook stuff. Her wings hurt like hell and her head was dizzy from too much climbing and swooping.

Meanwhile, the chariot was closing in; showing, it was true, a certain amount of circumspection, but nevertheless shortening the distance between them to an alarming extent. She'd tried looping a loop again, but they hadn't followed. They'd just waited till she came back straight and level again and resumed where they'd left off. When she'd hitched a ride in the undercarriage of a passing helicopter they had simply flown alongside throwing lightningbolts, until the helicopter pilot had bailed out and his craft had gone spiralling away out of control. There really wasn't a lot left she could do, except maybe try smiling at them; and that probably wouldn't work, either.

'No,' said the Gorgon, 'not with a G, with a D.'

Jason frowned. 'You what?' he said.

'My name's Gor*don*, not Gor*gon*,' said the serpent-haired monster through the letter-box. 'You must have got the wrong address. Gor*gon* with a G lives – oh, a long way from here. Over the other side of those mountains over there, I think.'

'I don't believe you,' Jason said.

'Don't you?' The flap of the letter-box quivered slightly. 'Whyever not?'

Jason looked around at the large number of extremely lifelike stone statues that lined the drive of the house. Statues of postmen. Statues of milkmen. Statues of Jehovah's Witnesses. 'I just don't, that's all,' he said. 'Now are you coming out, or do I have to kick the door down?'

The flap snapped shut and Jason could hear a sound like a heavy stone statue being dragged against the door. Probably, he reflected, a double-glazing salesman. He shrugged, strolled round to the back door, and kicked it in.

It was a curiously furnished house, to say the least, what with everything in it being made of stone and there being no mirrors or reflective surfaces; but Jason had a cousin who lived in one of those new developments in Docklands, so it didn't come as too much of a surprise to him. He made his way through the kitchen – there was a cup of coffee, literally stone cold, on the worktop; however did the poor creature ever manage to eat anything, he wondered; or did it live on nothing but gravel? – and arrived at the living-room door only to find it locked. He sighed and knocked politely.

'Hello?' he said.

'Go away.'

'I can't,' Jason said. 'Sorry.'

'No you're not,' replied the voice. Jason fingered the edge of the Sword and gave the surface of his brightly-polished shield a final rub.

'What I mean is,' he said. 'I'm not doing this for fun, you know. Left to myself, I couldn't care less. If you insist on turning people to stone, that's really a matter between you and your conscience. But I've got my job to do and I'm going to do it, so we can either do this the hard way or the easy way.'

There was a long silence. Then the voice said, 'So what's the easy way?'

'You come out,' Jason said, 'I cut your head off with this sword, that's it.'

'I see,' replied the voice. 'Let's give the hard way a shot, shall we?'

'I don't know what you're making all this fuss about,' Jason said. 'After all, I'm the one who should be scared. All you have to do is look me in the eye and I turn to stone, right? Me, now, I've got to smash my way in, avoiding looking at you, of course, then fight with you, somehow keep myself from getting bitten by your hairstyle, cut your head off and wrap the bits up in a black velvet bag. Just ask yourself, where's the smart money going to be on this one?'

There was no reply. Jason considered this for a moment, then dashed quickly out through the kitchen and back to the front door. It was open.

'Oh bugger!' Jason said.

He lifted the shield and examined the reflection of his surroundings in it. There was a statue just by the door which hadn't been there before. He considered his next move carefully, while whistling.

'*Ouch!*' said the Gorgon, shortly afterwards.

'Don't blame me,' Jason replied. 'I gave you the choice, remember. Now, this may hurt a little.'

'You cheated.'

Jason drew his brows together, offended. 'I did not cheat,' he said. 'I just used my intelligence, that's all.'

'You cheated.'

'Rubbish.'

'If you don't call pretending to wander away and then rushing back and jamming a flowerpot over my head cheating,' said the Gorgon, 'then I do. A real Hero wouldn't have done that.'

Jason drew the Gorgon's attention to the fact that there were quite a few very realistic statues of real Heroes lining the drive, most of them with birds nesting in highly improbable places.

'Cheat.'

'You brought it on yourself, you know,' Jason said. 'Anybody else would have been satisfied with a couple of gnomes pushing wheelbarrows or fishing in the water-butt; but no, you had to be different.'

'So what's wrong with being different?'

'Nothing,' Jason said, 'so long as you don't leave large flowerpots lying about the place as well. You can do one or the other, but not both. Now, the next bit is rather tricky, so if you'll just hold still ...'

A single snake's head pushed its way up through the hole in the bottom of the pot and hissed spitefully at Jason. 'Bully,' said the Gorgon.

'Sticks and stones,' said Jason. 'Now, then ...' He pressed his foot firmly into the small of the Gorgon's back, swung the Sword up above his head, and made ready to strike. Then he saw something.

'Hey,' said the Gorgon. 'Just get on with it, will you?'

'Yes, all right,' Jason said. 'Just give me a minute, will you?' He was staring at the sky; or, to be more precise, at an eagle.

Not, let it be stressed immediately, that Jason was or ever had been a bird-watcher; whatever else he may or may not have done, his conscience was clean on that score. In the normal run of events, if a bird wasn't sitting on a plate with roast potatoes on one side and runner beans on the other, then he didn't want to know. But this bird was unusual in that it was being chased by a chariotful of Spectral Warriors, who were throwing bits of lightning at it. He lowered the Sword and stood watching.

'What,' said a resentful voice, slightly but not unduly muffled by a five-millimetre thickness of terracotta, 'the hell do you think you're doing?'

'Shut up,' said Jason, preoccupied. All eagles looked the same to him, but he could have sworn he'd seen that one before. Twice.

'Look,' he said, 'just wait there a minute, will you? I won't be two shakes.' Then he took his foot off the Gorgon's back and darted away.

For at least ten seconds the Gorgon simply lay there, too bewildered to move. Then it leapt to its feet, dashed its head against the flank of a life-sized marble effigy of an Avon lady, shook the fragments of flowerpot out of its snakes, and bolted. Compilers of dictionaries of mythology might like to note that the orthodox view that it was never seen or heard of again is not strictly true; it was, in fact, shortly afterwards offered a job by Fabergé staring at eggs and became a useful and productive member of society.

It was definitely the same eagle, and as he stood watching it struggling through the air Jason remembered that he owed it a hamburger. He sheathed the Sword, cupped his hands round his mouth and shouted, 'Hey!'

Aboard the winged chariot, the Captain of Spectral Warriors looked down at the figure on the ground below him.

'Hold it,' he said. 'That's the Derry kid.'

The charioteer turned his head and glanced quickly. 'So what?' he said. 'We're way out of range up here. Let's just keep going and ...'

'What's he doing with that lump of *ouch*!'

Jason swivelled round, broke the other arm off the fossilised political canvasser who had at last proved useful to somebody, and let fly. The winged chariot banked violently and hurtled away across the sky like a frightened comet. The eagle fluttered for a few seconds, flopped to the ground and turned into a girl. Jason hurried across.

'Hiya, Mary,' he called out. Then he stepped back, looking puzzled. 'Or rather,' he said, 'Sharon.'

Betty-Lou Fisichelli polished her spectacles on her handkerchief, parked them on her nose and drew in a deep breath. She had never done this before.

Nobody now living – nobody now living and capable of death – had ever done this before. Partly because it was the most sacred of sacred mysteries; mostly because there just hadn't been any call for it. With a slightly moistened J-cloth she wiped away a thousand years of dust from the imperishable bronze of the statue's face, opened the manual on her knee, and looked for the place.

She was nervous. Apart from the perfectly understandable apprehension that anyone would feel about attempting the most sacred of sacred mysteries, there was also the fact that she was inside the vaults of the Delphi Archaeological Museum at half-past one in the morning without a pass. If she got caught, what with the Greek police being as they are, she doubted if even Apollo himself could save her.

CHAPTER ONE, she read, SETTING UP.

With trembling fingers, she took the two small, shining chips of metal from the matchbox in her handbag and pressed them carefully into the statue's empty eye-sockets. They fitted easily, and there was a faint click. At once, the broad bronze shield on the statue's arm began to glow, the verdigris giving off a bright green light. Then, suddenly, it went black, and a row of green lines materialised from nowhere. Once she had got her breath back, the Pythoness glanced down at the manual again.

Operating the Keyboard, it read.

The shield had stopped flashing green lines at her. Instead it displayed a message in sparkling green letters. It said: © *Copyright Olympian Software dlc. Unauthorised use of program material shall render the user liable to civil and criminal penalties.*

Then it went black again, and the statue said bleep, though without moving its lips. And then there were more letters on the screen, which read: *Hi!*

Ms. Fisichelli hopped that *Hi!* would disappear and be replaced by something rather less disconcertingly jovial, but it didn't. She dragged her attention back to the manual. Operating the keyboard.

Oh, very clever. Each of the fingertips of the statue's outstretched hands was a key, and to operate the upper case you stood on its toes. Tentatively she touched the left index finger. The shield flickered, and then read: *Error!!!*

Marvellous. She looked back at the manual and pressed the left middle finger. At once, a whole shieldful of words appeared, and a little green dot of light flashed on and off underneath them. That, the manual explained, was the Cursor. Ms. Fisichelli wondered idly what the Curse might turn out to be, and studied what the manual had to say about selecting a functions menu.

After a few minutes of bewildered concentration, she decided that what she wanted was Feedback Input Scan, and pressed the appropriate finger. The shield responded immediately. It now read: *Hiya!!!!*

Wouldn't it be easier, Ms. Fisichelli asked herself, to try and muddle through with a card index and a notched stick? Probably not. The manual now advised her to press the right ring fingertip and the left big toe simultaneously. She did.

Ouch!

Ms. Fisichelli apologised instinctively and looked down. No, she'd done it right. She glanced back at the screen, which now said: *Only kidding!!!*

Oh-for-crying-out-loud. If this was the state of the art in Olympian micro-electronics, perhaps now was the time to consider converting to Zen Buddhism.

Fun, this, isn't it!?

Painstakingly, Ms. Fisichelli selected the necessary fingertips to type in *No.*

The shield gave her a puzzled look and read *Error!!!* but she ignored it and went back to the right ring fingertip and the left big toe stage. She then remained aloof while the thing went through its tired little joke. Clearly you had to be something of a micro-electronics wizard if you wanted to input humour of your own into this gadget.

By this stage the shield read *Ready!!* which was apparently what it should do. Unfortunately, the next page of
the manual was missing.

'Oh nuts!' said Ms. Fisichelli, uncharacteristically. She
tried reading on, but it was hopeless. There was only one
thing to do. Feeling slightly self-conscious, she stood on
both the statue's feet and grabbed both its hands.

The result was incomprehensible but gratifyingly large-
scale. The shield shimmered with a brilliant coruscation of
messages in all the known languages and alphabets, alive,
dead and intermediate. The statue said bleep, not once
but many times. Its left ear began printing out.

After a while, things appeared to settle down, until there
were only four words left on the shield. They were: *All
right, you win.*

Ms. Fisichelli beamed, and then wondered what to do
next. Fortunately, the shield told her.

Vocal input acceptable, it said. *Speak now.*

'Er,' she said.

The statue's lips quivered, then parted.

'Hi!', said the statue.

Ms. Fisichelli's jaw swung open and she forgot what she
was going to say next. Probably just as well.

'C in a circle Copyright,' the statue went on, in a clear,
high monotone, like a Dalek newsreader. 'Olympian
Software dlc. Unauthorised use of programme material
shall render the user liable to civil and criminal penalties.'

'I ...'

'Error!!'

'But ...'

'Error!!'

'Scumbag!!'

'Ready!!'

'Oh.' Ms. Fisichelli wondered about that for a moment,
and then decided that maybe you were supposed to lose
your temper with the doggone thing. 'Look ...'

'Input mode selected,' said the statue. 'Receiving,' it

added helpfully. Ms. Fisichelli took a deep breath and
started to talk, on the grounds that if the blasted thing
said 'Ready!!' just one more time she would quite
probably scream.

'Well,' she said, 'I'm terribly sorry to bother you like
this, but none of the other divining instruments seemed to
work, and I tried conjuring but of course you need an
assistant for that really, and mine just turned into an eagle
and left, so I wasn't able to get through that way and I was
at my wits' end and then I suddenly thought, Wait a
minute, I thought, there's always the Holy Icon, why don't
I try that, and if you say "Error!!" at me I shall melt you
down and have you recast as a bedstead, so be very
careful.'

'Processing data,' said the statue, 'please wait.'

'Sure.'

The statue bleeped a couple of times, coughed and
sighed. 'Input request command,' it said. 'Receiving.'

'Sorry?'

'What seems to be the problem?' said the statue.

Ms. Fisichelli relaxed and smiled. 'Right, then,' she
said. 'It's sort of like this. You know I do prophesies,
right?'

'Receiving,' said the statue. 'Oh, *sorry*, forgot. Yes?'

'Well, usually the prophecies come from Apollo,
because, well, that's his job, OK? But the last couple of
days I've been getting these prophecies, well, more sort of
prophetic utterances, and I'm sure they can't be from him,
because – well, I just sort of *know* they're not, OK? Don't
ask me how I know, I just do. And of course, they're all
like sort of riddles and I can't make head or tail of them,
and I thought perhaps, well, you might ...'

'Input,' said the statue. 'Or rather, shoot, oh stuff this,
input.'

'You're sure it's no trouble?'

'That's what I'm here for, receiving, continues, please
wait, ready.'

'The first one,' said Ms. Fisichelli, 'came to me in my bath last night. I was just sort of, you know, sitting there, when suddenly I could hear myself saying this, well, *thing.*'

'Gee.'

'Sorry?'

'Error,' said the statue. 'Mine, not yours. Apology. Input. Open fire. Shit. *Shoot.* Sorry.'

'Er,' said Ms. Fisichelli. 'Oh yes. Well, what I must have said was ...'

'Input?'

'Sorry,' replied Ms. Fisichelli. 'It's just a bit embarrassing saying it out loud. I mean, it all sounds so funny, if you see what I ...'

'Correlates,' said the statue, sympathetically. 'Ignore error and continue.'

'Thanks. It went something like:

When that the Seed of the Pig conspires with the Door-Half-Open,
Then shall the Ducks'-Foe-Dwellers despair of their humourless purpose,
As Zippo, loosed from his bonds, devours a bacon sandwich.

That's what it said, anyway,' Ms. Fisichelli added. 'Really.'

The statue bleeped thrice and burped. 'Computing,' it muttered. 'Data input up tree. Memory circuits active. Proceeding to foot of our stairs. Ready.'

'You mean you can understand all that stuff?'

'Confirming. Comparative values follow. Please wait.' The lights in the statue's eyes went out and then came on again. 'For Door-Half-Open, read When is a door not a door, when it's a jar, search, find First Joke, equivalents search to read, output equivalent Gelos Prometheus. For Ducks'-Foe-Dwellers, read Nice weather for ducks, find sun is foe of ducks, correlate sun-dwellers, output gods. For Zippo, read Fire-Producer, find Prometheus, correlates.

For Seed of Pig read Jupiter is a Pig, find Jason Derry, correlates, bleep. Bacon sandwich does not copy, suggested correlation Prometheus is hungry, eats bacon sandwich, search completed, ready for new input.

'Gosh,' said Ms. Fisichelli, 'aren't you clever. Well, the other one went:

Remember that Mother knows best how to deal with the Smiter of Centaurs;
That swords cannot cut what is stronger than steel that is tempered in cocoa;
Tough though the whites may be, the boil-wash may now be dispensed with.'

The statue made no noise of any description for a very long time. Then it sniggered, and said 'Computing. Offspring of canine female. Ready.'

'Yes. but ...'

'Comparative values found,' the statue continued. 'For Smiter of Centaurs read Jason Derry, for difficulty rating read falling from chopped-down tree. For unit comparative value, read Jason Derry may be a right little tearaway but he's afraid of his mother, programme ends, exit.'

The lights in the statue's eyes went out, the shield ceased to shine, the little pieces of metal fell from the eye-sockets and landed with a soft tinkle on the ground. Ms. Fisichelli stooped and put them back in their matchbox. That, it seemed, was that for this evening. She could take a hint. She put the matchbox and the manual back in her bag, switched off the lights and crept back up to the main gallery. Then she rummaged in her coat pocket for her skeleton key, unlocked the staff canteen door, and (ultimately) left the building.

A useful night's work, she said to herself, and just as soon as I can get hold of Apollo I'd better tell him all about it. Pity, though, she thought, that the statue hadn't waited to hear the third prophecy.

*

'Ungrateful little sod.'

'I am not an ungrateful little sod. Anyway, what the hell have you ever done that I should be grateful for?'

Sharon made a rude noise. 'Oh yes?' she said. 'All right, who was it warned you about the snakes in your pram, then? If it wasn't ...

'Nobody *warned* me,' Jason replied angrily. 'I just knew ...'

'Bullshit,' said Sharon, who was not very ladylike, even for an eagle. 'If I hadn't swooped down and made shrieking noises at you, you'd have been fast asleep. As it was, you nearly swallowed your sucker and I had to get it out of your throat with my claw. You bit me.'

'Good.'

Sharon raised one foot and made a sort of pawing movement with it before putting it back on the ground. 'And what about that time when you were three and you got stuck halfway up that big fir tree looking for phoenix nests ...'

'I wasn't stuck,' Jason interrupted, 'just resting, that was ... Hang on,' he said, as an unpleasant thought struck him, 'Are you trying to tell me you've been sort of watching over me or something ever since I was a kid?'

'Since before you were born, more like. Nasty little brat you were then, too.'

'I ...'

'Talk about a messy little brute,' Sharon remembered. 'When you weren't up to your elbows in lion's blood you were all smeared with melted chocolate. Always stuffing yourself, even then.'

'Look ...'

'When I remember the fuss you used to make whenever you had to have a bath! We could hear you in the next street; it was like someone killing a pig.'

Jason growled dangerously. 'Now look ...' he said.

'And I'll never forget,' Sharon continued, either oblivious

or unconcerned, 'that time when your mother left you in your pram outside the post office with the shopping bag, and when she got back ...'

A true Hero, they say, will never strike a woman; so it was fortunate for Jason's blood pressure that Sharon was, at least to a certain extent, an eagle. If challenged, he reckoned, he could always say that he'd been aiming for the aquiline bits.

'*Ouch!*'

Jason lowered his hand, feeling that sort of furiously angry guilt that is usually reserved to small children. 'It's your fault,' he half-snarled, half-whimpered. 'You started it.'

'Didn't,' Sharon snuffled.

'Did.'

'Didn't.'

'Did.'

'Didn't didn't *didn't.*'

Jason was just about to rebut this line of argument when he caught sight of himself in the brightly-polished shield he'd used to fight the Gorgon with. What he saw, he recognised immediately as an idiot.

'Look,' he said gently.

'*Didn't!*'

'All right,' Jason shouted, 'you didn't bloody well start it, whatever it was. Only for pity's sake stop that bloody whimpering and tell me what's going on.'

'Shan't.'

Gods give me strength, Jason muttered under his breath, and then revoked the request at once. They'd already done that, and look where it had landed him. 'I'm sorry,' he said, 'all right?'

'You hurt me,' Sharon whined, and rubbed her ear vigorously. It would have been more effective if it had been the right ear, of course; but pain is an extremely transient condition for supernaturals, and in some areas they have extremely short memories. This can, in fact, be very inconvenient sometimes; for example, when they break a leg.

'Well, well,' Jason said. 'Something attempted, something done has earned a night's repose. Now, will you please tell me ...?'

'All right,' Sharon said sullenly. And she told him.

She told him about the great plan to restore Gelos and thereby dislodge the gods for ever, and how he was an integral part of it, and how it was so important that he develop in the right way to fulfil his destiny that Prometheus had sent his own eagle to be born and grow up as the objectionable girl next door, where she could keep an eye on him, nudge him in the right direction, drop heavy hints about hostile snakes in prams and so forth; how ...

'I knew it!' Jason was furiously angry now, more so than he could ever remember being. 'Isn't that just bloody typical! That's my whole life, that is.' He toyed with the idea of drawing the Sword and splitting the Earth's crust with it, laying the Nether Kingdom open to the sunlight, out of pure pique. 'I mean, that's just bloody marvellous, isn't it? On the one hand, I've got Mum and Dad pushing me around, making me be a Hero and kill monsters and steal golden apples and all that crap; and now I find that Prometheus and your bloody lot have been doing exactly the same all along, only different. Why can't the whole bloody lot of you just bugger off and leave me in peace?' He jumped on the Gorgon-reflecting shield, denting it beyond economic repair, and kicked it away, Sharon folded her arms and looked at him, reminding him very much of his mother.

'All my life,' he went on, 'it's been nothing but do this, do that, and nobody gives a flying fuck what I want or what I think about anything. Well, that does it, I've had enough.' He looked around for something else to break, and eventually lit upon a life-size marble statue of a plumber, which he decapitated. 'At least that explains why Mum's been trying to push me off on you for as long as I can ...'

Through the red cloud of rage that was fogging up his mind shone a tiny little ray of confusion. Did it?

'Does it?' said Sharon.

'Of course it does.' Doesn't it ...?

Of course it does ...

Oh no, not you again ...

But ...

Sharon seemed to melt suddenly. Her dumpy and exceptionally unerogenous figure blurred in front of his eyes, and grew taller and less broad. And then she wasn't there, but Mary was; and you could tell that Sharon had never really existed at all, just as a suit of clothes ceases to have any real meaning once the wearer has been removed from inside it.

'That's the spirit,' said Mary.

'Don't be so bloody patronising,' Jason managed to grumble; but his heart wasn't in it, being otherwise occupied.

'Sorry,' Mary said, 'I didn't mean to be. Look, Sharon's gone now, gone for good. She's served her purpose, you see. There's just me now.'

Just me, coming from her, was a contradiction in terms. Even so, that tiny little ray of confusion still glowed in his mind, like a distant lighthouse seen through dense mists.

'The reason for Sharon' Mary was saying, 'was to get you nice and angry, just like you are now. That's what you had to do. Your mum doesn't have the faintest idea who Sharon was; neither did Jupiter. No, the whole point about Sharon was that one day you'd get so sick of the sight of her and her nasty, whining voice and her incessant fault-finding that you'd finally have the guts to break free from the power in heaven and earth capable of controlling you.'

Jason frowned. 'You mean Jupiter?'

'No.'

'Prometheus? Gelos?'

Mary shook her head. 'Your mother,' she said.

Jason thought about that. 'I see what you mean,' he said. 'Odd, I'd never seen it like that myself.'

'Well you wouldn't,' Mary said, 'now would you?'

'I suppose not.'

'That's the secret,' Mary went on. 'That's how Jupiter controls you. So, if you were ever to snap out of it and become a free agent, then you'd have to defy her, tell her to go boil her head; and the only thing we could think of that would make you do that was ... well, a Sharon. And it's worked, hasn't it? Actually,' Mary admitted, 'it's gone and cocked itself up, because of course you found out about it before it could happen – before the final show-down, I mean – but the effect's been the same. Am I right?'

Jason considered. 'Yes,' he said slowly, 'I think you probably are. But,' – there was that little speck of light again; not three specks or dots of light, just one – 'there's something wrong with all this.'

'Is there?'

Jason scratched his head. 'Yes,' he replied. 'Most definitely. You see, I'm not a free agent, not a bit of it. I was right the first time. You are pushing me around, just as much as Jupiter's lot. And,' – Jason stood up straight, looked the girl of his dreams in the eye and saw nothing there that interested him – 'I'm having no part of it. Where's the point?'

'I'm sorry?'

'I said,' Jason replied, 'where's the bloody point? You aren't Mary, any more than you were Sharon. You designed Sharon expressly to get up my nose, and you've designed Mary to be the ... the ... well, anyway. What you are, when you get right down to it, is a damn great eagle. And I'm very sorry, but I'm not selling my soul for something in feathers with a six-foot wingspan and little round yellow eyes. My profound apologies, but the deal's off.'

'Off?'

'Off,' said Jason. 'Go look for another Hero, because I'm retiring. Got that?'

'But Jason ...'

'Don't anybody Jason me,' the Hero shouted, 'ever again. From now on, nobody tells me what to do. Nobody.'

He instinctively took a step back and put his hand on his sword-hilt. He was suddenly aware that he was big enough and ugly enough to do what the hell he liked, and the realisation was incredibly wonderful.

Mary smiled. 'You see?' she said.

Jason deflated like one of those balloons that people blow up at parties and then let go. 'You ...'

'Exactly,' Mary said. 'It's worked. You've defied us, too.'

'Oh.' With what remained of his mental strength, Jason wrestled with the idea. 'Have I?'

'Looked like it from here.'

'Really?'

'Absolutely.' Mary came towards him and put her hands gently on his shoulders. 'We all knew you had it in you,' she said.

'So,' Jason said, 'I could tell you all to go and get stuffed, right now, if I wanted to.'

'If you wanted to,' Mary said, 'yes.'

'And nobody can tell me what to do?'

'Nobody can tell you,' Mary said softly, her lips close to his ear. 'But that doesn't stop them asking, does it?'

'No,' Jason said. 'I suppose not.'

Had Jason attended Professor Haagedorn's course at Wounded Elbow University, Wyoming, on predestination theory, he would have known that free will is perfectly possible, in the same way as a free lunch is perfectly possible. Just not very likely, that's all.

'And you wouldn't,' Mary whispered, 'want the gods to abolish laughter, now would you?'

'Well,' Jason said, 'no, I suppose not.'

'And you don't really think that Jupiter and Mars and

Minerva and all that lot ought to be allowed to take the Universe over again, do you?'

'I ...'

'Just think what a mess they made of it all last time.'

'Er ...'

'So you will help, won't you?' Mary said. 'Please?'

'That's six and two makes eight, doubled for a free go, plus six penalty points because you revoked on the bidding, plus six above the line for a straight flush, plus fifteen for a clear round in Mercury, plus three bonus points for breaking service, makes ...' Demeter had run out of fingers. 'Damn,' she said. 'Right, that's six and two makes eight ...'

'Forty-six,' said Minerva coldly. 'Can we get on now, please?'

'Oh yes,' Demeter added, 'and another two for passing Novgorod. Forty-eight.'

Minerva gave her a look that would have kept milk fresh in the Sahara. 'Forty-eight, then,' she said. Now ...'

'And,' Demeter said, 'another one for having two options in play during the same contract. Forty-nine.'

'Fancy!' Minerva replied. 'Now, if you've quite finished with the dice, perhaps I might have a ...'

She threw, and the dice clattered on the marble floor of the sun.

'Oh hard luck, Min,' Demeter commiserated. 'That's the third time you've done that.'

'Yes,' Minerva said. 'I had noticed, thank you.'

'Not your day today, is it?'

'Indeed.'

'Now then.' Demeter scooped up the dice, blew on them

211

(where did she get into that dreadfully common habit, Minerva wondered) and threw them, not omitting to shout 'Ha!' at the approved moment. 'Oh look,' she said, 'Double nine again. I am having a good day, aren't I?'

'If you throw double nine one more time in this turn,' Minerva said distantly, 'you go to Hades for three moves.'

'Well,' Demeter replied, 'that's hardly likely, is it?'

'It was hardly likely you'd throw it the last three times.'

'Fool's luck,' Demeter replied cheerfully. 'Well well, isn't that fortunate. You were just about to invade me and now I can invade you instead. Jolly hard luck, Min.'

Minerva closed her eyes for a moment, just long enough for a goddess to count to ten. 'Well, never mind,' she said, 'it's only a Game after all.'

The very thought of Minerva regarding it as only a Game was too much for Demeter. She sniggered. Then she invaded.

'It really isn't your day, is it?' she said. 'Look, all your armies have run out of petrol on the other side of the desert. Now if that isn't just the rottenest possible ...'

Minerva stood up. 'How you can sit there wasting your time with this frivolous nonsense when there's important work to be done completely amazes me,' she said, and sniffed. Demeter looked up.

'Want to give it a rest for a bit, do you?' she said.

'I do think that in the circumstances ...'

'You losing, you mean?'

'I am not losing.'

'Yes you are,' Demeter replied. 'But since it's only a Game, what do you care? Actually, I wouldn't mind a few minutes' break myself. Cheerio.'

And, having ostentatiously noted the positions of the pieces on the board, Demeter wandered away in the direction of the kitchen. As she sat and stared at her stranded army in the flowing, trackless sands, Minerva found herself thinking, not for the first time, that it was a pity that Demeter had come into being several million years before Australia did. Otherwise, she felt, they would have been made for each other.

Frivolous nonsense, Minerva reminded herself. Instead, she would go and find out what was happening and do something about it.

Better to observe the passage of events, she climbed the spiral staircase to the Observation Saloon and sat in the Viewing Chair. From there, thanks to a freak refraction of light through the atmosphere of a profoundly bizarre Betamax world, it was possible to see the minutest details of what was going on on the surface of Earth. Minerva leaned forward in the Chair and concentrated on a certain spot in the Caucasus mountains.

What she saw was . . .

For the first time in a long time, a very long time, a very long time indeed, Mars was beginning to think that life wasn't such a pain in the neck after all.

Fighting he didn't hold with, but he was a born organiser, in the way that profoundly disorganised people often are. Without pausing to pluck the untidy desk and overflowing cupboard under the stairs out of his own eye, he delighted in sorting out the messes of others. Give him a clipboard, a box file and seven thousand little yellow stickers and he was as happy as a lamb in springtime.

'All right,' he was shouting, 'what's the hold-up? Get that lot unloaded and down to Base Camp 2 and look sharp about it. There's fifteen thousand tons of prefabricated girder bridge trying to get through. . . Oh, for crying out loud, you pillocks, not that way round. And who forgot to bring the butane cylinders?'

The Forms, stripped to their shirt-sleeves and sweating despite the cold, ignored him. In their opinion, in order to lynch one heavily-chained Titan there hadn't really been any need to bring one hundred and five thousand tons of pretzels, eight million forage caps, forty-seven million reams of white A4 duplicating paper, fifty-nine miles of three-core electric flex and seventy thousand soldering-irons. Someone, they felt, had got just the teeniest bit carried away. As for the piano ...

Stupidity, promoted for the day to the rank of Staff Drum Lieutenant, tapped Mars gingerly on the shoulder.

'Sir,' he said, 'excuse me, sir.'

'Yes?'

'What should we do with the piano, sir?'

Mars glowered at him. 'Put it in the mobile officers' club,' he said, 'what do you think?'

'But sir,' said the Form, 'we didn't bring the mobile officers' ...'

'You what?'

'It wasn't on the manifest, sir,' said the Form. 'Look ...'

He thrust a clipboard under Mars's nose. The Widow-Maker groaned.

'Right,' he said. 'In that case, clear out one of those mobile field chiropody units, put in a few chairs and tables, get some bottles and some glassware and a few cut flowers and shove the piano in that. Whatever the hell happened to initiative?'

'Sir!' Stupidity saluted briskly, turned and wandered away, shaking his head sadly. Bloody amateurs.

For his part, Mars sat down on a half-empty packing case that had contained forty-six thousand pairs of tropical weight nylon undersocks, licked the tip of his biro, and started to write.

From: C-in-C, Caucasus Theatre
To: Divisional Commanders
Re: Centralised Stationery Distribution ...

He was just getting nicely into it when a Colonel of Spectral Warriors came and stood over him, casting a shadow over his page.

'All ready to go, sir,' said the Spectral Warrior.

'Sorry?'

'All units deployed, sir,' the Warrior explained. 'Weapons checked, intelligence reports received and analysed, ammunition distributed, sir.'

Mars looked up. 'So?'

'So,' said the Spectral Warrior, 'do we go get the bastard, or what? Sir,' he added.

Mars wobbled nervously. 'Are you sure everything's ready?' he said.

'Positive, sir.'

'Don't you think it would be a good idea to have a final kit inspection and a general stocktaking at brigade level?'

'No, sir.'

'Lines of supply all in place, are they? Pontoon bridges all built?'

'Yes, sir.'

'Everybody returned their pink pension scheme questionnaires?'

'Yes, sir.'

Mars swallowed hard. This was the bit he didn't like.

'So,' he said, 'what you're saying is, there's absolutely nothing to stop us getting on with it.'

'Correct, sir.'

'Ah,' Mars replied. 'Fine. Well done, everybody. Well then, I suppose we'd all better ...'

Just then, a tiny dot appeared in the sky. It was so small and so far away that you'd have thought nobody would have noticed it. Somehow, though, everybody did.

'Hold it a moment, Colonel,' Mars said. 'What do you make of that?'

The Spectral Warrior shaded his eyes with his hands. 'Looks like an eagle to me, sir. And a man. And a dog. Sir.'

Mars suddenly began to feel a very familiar feeling of being about an eighth of an inch away from the smelly stuff. 'Well don't just stand there,' he snapped. 'Get going. Nail the little sod.'

The Colonel saluted, then turned back, perplexed. 'By that, sir, do you mean the Titan or the eagle with the ...?'

By then, of course, it was all too late. The dot had become bigger. It had also become three dots. Three dots streaming through the air. Three dots ...

'Fire!' Mars yelled hysterically. Nothing happened.

Jason, meanwhile, had leapt from the eagle's back and was standing on a mountain-top, brandishing the Sword. At his feet, the Triple-Headed Hell-Hound was baying – with two heads; the third was sniffing something on the ground directly under Jason's left foot – and overhead the eagle circled menacingly.

'This is asinine,' Mars yelled at his huge, silent, foot-shuffling army. 'There's twenty million of us and three of them. Pull your bloody fingers out, the lot of you!'

In the Spectral ranks, nobody moved. As for the Forms, they were all trying to turn back into figures of speech without anybody noticing. Stupidity hid behind the piano and, rather counter-intuitively, began to pray.

Then, from the Divine ranks, a single figure stepped forward.

'Hoo-bloody-ray,' muttered the Widow-Maker. 'Now can we please make a start, before the little jerk dies of old age?'

Nobody paid any attention to him. Forty million eyes were fixed on the one black shape strolling easily up the side of the mountain towards Jason, the eagle and the dog.

In the snooker-room of the Spectral Warriors Social Club and Institute one can, if one has the necessary degree of masochistic nerve, hear all the nastiest, most stomach-churning stories in the world's repertoire. Approximately seventy-two per cent of them share the same central character.

For example, there was the occasion on which Jupiter put out a contract on the King of Trasimene, who had incurred the Sky-Father's unquenchable enmity by wearing lemon socks with an Old Carrhasians tie. Owing to a complicated nexus of oracles, oaths and rainbow-sealed covenants, the gods were forbidden to offer violence in any shape or form to Gorgias II during his lifetime. So they sent for the one being in the whole of Creation capable of dealing with the problem, with the exception of the Air Traffic Controller at Athens Airport unquestionably the most widely feared and hated being in the whole of the Universe. And sure enough, twenty-four hours later, Gorgias II had ceased to exist. Nothing was ever found of him, not so much as a trouser-button or a fire-blackened cufflink. A consignment of two dozen lavender silk cravats ordered by him from Gieves and Hawkes were found on arrival to have dissolved into their component atoms and soaked away into the wrapping-paper.

Some said that he had worked it by travelling back through time, hanging around Gorgias's mother shortly before she met Gorgias's father, and so preventing him from ever being born. Others pointed to the appearance of an unpredicted bifurcation in the fabric of possibility, closely followed by a violent eruption of molten logic in Macedonia measuring 34.76 on the Rictus scale, and the observation of a hitherto unrecorded star in the constellation of the Distributor Cap. Most people, however, just shuddered and tried not to think about it.

There was a silence you could have filled cracks with by the time he reached the top of the mountain, and Jason could hear nothing but the sound of his own heart pounding. It wasn't a very pleasant sensation, since he could tell that this wasn't just ordinary Let's-get-the-blood-moving-along-chaps pounding; this was the heart demanding to be let *out* . . .

'Hi.'

'Er,' Jason replied. Not the snappiest of answers, perhaps, and maybe Boswell wouldn't have jotted it down if Johnson had said it of a Saturday night down the Cheshire Cheese; but it is worth recording as one of the few replies that he has ever received from a potential victim.

'Nice up here, isn't it?'

'Well . . .'

'Good view.'

'I ...'

'Apparently, you can see Stavropol from here,' he said, staring out in entirely the wrong direction. 'On a clear day, of course,' he added.

'Er.'

'Stavropol,' he went on, 'is somewhere I've never been, actually, but they say you can get a really authentic shish kebab at Jagadai's Café, down by the railway arches; I mean, you can really taste the little bits of burnt wool and everything. I forget who told me that.'

'Um.'

He turned round, swung his arms and appeared to do deep breathing exercises. 'Lovely air, too,' he said, and coughed. 'Sort of crisp.'

Jason squeezed a little of this highly recommended air into his chest, past the rather large blockage that had formed in his windpipe, but all he did with it after all that effort was say 'Um' again.

'Sorry?'

'Nothing.'

'Well,' he said, 'this is nice, isn't it?'

A tiny message wriggled up Jason's spine and clambered into his brain. This guy is scared, it said, and was immediately shushed by millions of nervous brain cells. That, presumably, is why it's known as the nervous system.

'Er,' said he.

They looked at each other.

Just as Jason felt his bowel muscles starting to give up – not, of course, that he knew the meaning of fear; it must have been something he ate – he made a slight whimpering noise, put both hands over his ears and started to run back down the mountain, as fast as his legs could carry him or maybe just a little faster. One little brain cell inside Jason's head smirked, said *I told you so,* and then wondered why it found it so hard to make friends. Jason, meanwhile, was dashing off down the mountain after him, and when he tripped over his flowing black robe and sprawled headlong, Jason wasn't far behind.

'Eeek!' he said and curled himself up into a tight, quivering ball, like a bald hedgehog.

'Come on out of it, you,' Jason replied sternly. It's remarkable what an effect the sight of a cowering enemy can have on one's vocabulary; if someone had asked Jason right then for a word meaning 'Painful emotion caused by impending danger or evil', he'd probably have replied 'Seasickness'.

'No.'

'All right then,' said Jason. 'Suits me.'

The ball uncurled itself quickly, and Jason could see two eye-sockets staring up at him from the recesses of his shroudlike hood.

'Please don't say it,' he said.

Jason blinked, but managed to keep his stern, remorseless expression steady and not giggle. 'We'll see about that,' he replied. 'Say what, exactly?'

'The Joke,' he replied. 'Whatever you do, please don't say it. Not that I'm saying you wouldn't do it terribly well, but ...'

Jason remembered. The Joke, of course; Gelos's joke, the great joke, joke of jokes. So that was what they were all afraid of ...

'There was this guy,' he said savagely, 'went into this hardware shop, right, and he said ...'

'Eeeeeeeeeeek!'

'Don't panic. It's all right,' Jason said. 'Just kidding about. But you tell your pals down there that next time ...'

'Yes. Right.'

'Got that?'

He nodded vigorously. If he'd had a tail, he'd have wagged it, and that would have been Jason's stern, remorseless expression gone for good.

'Fine,' said Jason. 'Now push off.'

He scrambled up, gave Jason a look of pure terror, and then bounced away down the slope and into the serried ranks of Spectral Warriors, who retreated slightly. The eagle, who had been circling overhead, swooped down and pitched on Jason's shoulder.

'Ouch,' Jason said.

The eagle ignored him and put its beak next to his ear. Eagles cannot, of course, whisper, because of the bone structure of their beaks.

'Yes,' Jason said. 'Nice one.'

The eagle spread its wings and launched itself into the air. For his part, Jason straightened his spine, put his shoulders back, and faced the Divine Army, ranged below him in the natural amphitheatre formed by the mountain slopes. He took a deep breath and tried to imagine he was wearing a loud check suit and a red nose.

'Ladies and Gentlemen,' Jason shouted, 'a funny thing happened to me on the way to the Caucasus this evening. I was walking along, minding my own business, when this man ...'

He paused and looked down. The Spectral Warriors, Forms and gods had all gone, vanished into thin air, and he was alone. Except for the three-headed dog, of course; and the eagle, who floated over and nodded approvingly.

'It's the way you tell them,' it said.

'Look!' said the eagle.

Jason turned round. 'Where?' he said.

'There,' replied the eagle. Since eagles cannot talk, it naturally follows that they cannot have voices that are resonant with awe and reverence. So it must have been Jason's imagination.

'I can't see anything,' Jason said. 'Are you sure you're ...'

'There, you cretin,' said the eagle. 'Oh, blow you.' It spread its wings and floated off on a gust of warm air that had no meteorological foundation whatsoever. Jason stared hard but couldn't make out anything. It was getting late and cold and he couldn't really see that he was needed here any more; and he was beginning to feel peckish. He thought of Baisbekian's Diner.

Then the mountain behind him cleared its throat.

Readers are asked to pay close attention to what follows, as the author cannot be held responsible for any sensations of disorientation or confusion which may result from careless reading practices.

'Jason,' said the mountain, 'are you busy for a moment?'

Jason thought hard. No, he decided, mountains can't talk, and neither can eagles, for that matter, let alone three-headed dogs. In a world such as this, there is much to be said for staying in bed with your head under the pillows.

'Hello?' he ventured.

'Yes, hello to you too,' said the mountain. 'Are you busy for a moment?'

'That depends,' Jason replied.

'On what?'

'On what you had in mind,' Jason said. 'And if you're a mountain, will you please stop talking to me, because I only have a very tenuous grip on reality at the best of times, and . . .'

'I'm not a mountain.'

'It's all very well you saying that,' Jason said, 'but how can I be sure? You look pretty much like a mountain to me.'

'What you're looking at is indeed a mountain,' said the mountain. 'I happen to be behind the mountain. Does this clarify matters for you?'

'Not really,' Jason replied. 'Who are you?'

'Prometheus.'

Little wheels went round in Jason's mind, and the result was three oranges and a Hold. 'Oh,' he said, 'yes. Right. Where exactly are you, then?'

'Behind the bloody mountain, like I just said.'

'Fine,' said Jason. 'Give me ...' He made a quick estimate. 'Give me half an hour and I'll be with you.'

In fact, it took him just under twenty minutes to get within sight of the Titan, thanks to a short-cut through a narrow ravine, which fortunately didn't say anything to him as he clambered through it.

'What kept you?'

'Look.' Jason had turned his ankle in the ravine and accordingly he wasn't feeling at his most lovable. 'Would you mind just explaining ...?'

'The chains,' said Prometheus.

'Yes,' Jason replied. 'Aren't they?'

'Aren't they what?'

'Chains.'

Prometheus raised his head, uprooting a large tree, and looked at him. 'Just cut them, will you?'

In the back of his mind – the only part still capable of function – the right question drifted to the surface and bobbed uncertainly.

'Why?' Jason asked.

'What do you mean, why?' Prometheus said. 'Because they're stopping me from moving, that's why. Get on with it, please.'

'But,' Jason said, 'what I mean is, why should I? I tried to go into all this before, but things kept happening and I never came to a satisfactory conclusion. Look, will someone please give me some idea of what's happening, because otherwise I'm going on strike.'

As it happens, there have been occasional strikes by Heroes, the most notable being the Withdrawal of the Labours of Hercules; however, they rarely last long and never achieve anything, perhaps because all Heroism is intrinsically unnecessary. When Hercules fell out with Jupiter following a breakdown of negotiations over unsocial hours payments, for example, Jupiter replied by drafting in contingents of Forms who were able to do

Hercules's feats in half the time and without terrorising supernatural wildlife or stopping every twenty minutes to beget children. On the other hand, it is felt that Heroes marching up and down outside temples with placards looks bad, and in any event the demands of the average Hero are so modest that it would be mean minded not to agree to them.*

'You can't,' Prometheus said, however. 'The schedule's too tight.'

'What schedule?'

'Just cut the chains,' Prometheus replied. 'Come *on*, will you?'

'Oh for crying out ...' Jason hefted the Sword of That's A Silly Name For A Sword, Anyway, whirled it round his head, and sliced through the nearest chain. The shock of the metal biting into the adamant jarred every bone in his body. The chain fell in two.

'Ouch!'

'And the next one.'

'All right, keep your hair on.'

'It's not my hair I'm concerned about.'

'If I cut through the next chain, will you tell me what's going on?'

'If you don't cut through the next chain, I won't tell you what's going on.'

'Ouch.'

'Two down, two to go.'

'Look ...'

'You'll find it over there, at the top of that mountain. It won't take you a quarter of an hour if you run.'

'But ...'

---

*It is a little-known fact that all Heroes really want out of life is power, glory, victory, wine, sex, money, respect, adventure and chocolate, not necessarily in that order. The celebrated Bellerophon, who tamed the winged horse Pegasus and killed the murderous, death-dealing Chimera, wanted jam on it as well; but so what, jam's cheap.

*

'I see,' Jupiter said.

Big chief speak with forked tongue. It was obvious, to Mars at least, that Jupiter didn't see, one little bit. Whether in the long run it would be worth making one last effort to enlighten him was something that Mars (who, unlike Apollo, is not a prophetic deity) could only guess at. He guessed safe.

'All those Forms,' Jupiter continued, 'all those Spectral Warriors, all that overtime, and you ran away. Because,' said the Thunderer, his eyebrows coming together, 'one mortal offered – I'm sorry, threatened – to tell you a joke.'

'Well,' said Mars, 'yes.'

'A joke.'

'Exactly.'

Jupiter stroked his beard, and the static electricity thereby generated would have removed the need for nuclear power in the industrialised nations for a century. 'Don't you think you might have been a trifle over-cautious, all things considered? Played it just a little too safe?'

Mars straightened his back and shook his head. 'No,' he said. 'Definitely not.'

Jupiter raised an eyebrow. Nobody ever said *Definitely* to him unless they were absolutely convinced of something or else had a great desire to be a frog. 'Perhaps,' he said, 'we ought to have a board meeting.'

Mars, feeling like a turkey on Christmas Eve who hears that everyone has been converted to Jainism overnight, nodded and hurried out of the Presence.

He found Minerva in the sun-lounge, lying on the sofa with her shoes off reading *Harpers & Goddess*. She looked at him over her spectacles.

'Well?' she said. 'Where's the fire?'

'Board meeting,' Mars replied. 'In ten minutes in the Great Hall.'

'Board meeting?' Minerva swung her legs to the floor and put heel to slingback. 'What's happening, Ma?' she said. 'There hasn't been a board meeting for eleven hundred years. He's not on about privatisation again, is he, because I went through the figures and . . .'

Mars frowned. He had thought it strange that Minerva had been lying around reading at a time like this anyway. 'It's the Prometheus situation,' he said, 'what do you think? Look, I've got to dash. Ask someone else, all right?'

'What Prometheus situation? I thought you'd . . .'

'It was a wash-out,' Mars replied quickly. 'So now . . .'

'You messed it up, you mean?'

'Yes.'

'How?'

'Flair,' Mars replied. 'Either you've got it or you haven't.'

'Right.' Minerva stood up briskly and marched out of the sun-lounge. Oh dear, said Mars to himself, it's going to be one of those meetings.

He found Apollo in the library, Diana in the gym and Neptune beside the swimming-pool, and then rushed off to find Demeter, who wasn't in the kitchen. Instead he found Pluto, making himself a cup of tea.

'Board meeting,' he announced.

'You don't say?' Pluto replied. 'Well, well.' The spoon writhed between his fingers, hissed and slithered away behind the sink.

Demeter turned out to have been in the kitchen garden, weeding the sunflowers. 'What's a board meeting?' was her reaction, and when he explained she asked if this would be a good time to raise the issue of rainfall allowances for the cloud-shepherds. As he chased off to round up the rest of the quorum, Mars found himself speculating as to why he bothered.

'Ye gods!' he muttered under his breath.

*

Clang.

'*Now,*' Jason said, 'Will you explain?'

The Earth shook. Slowly, very slowly, painfully slowly, the Titan flexed muscles that hadn't moved since before the destruction of Atlantis. He wiggled his toes, scattering topsoil in a whirling cloud.

'Only,' Jason went on, 'so many downright weird things have been happening lately, with me all mixed up in them, that unless someone lets me in on it all pretty soon . . .'

Imagine the sound – the last thing we want is endless product liability lawsuits, and so we will only tax one area of sensory perception to its uttermost limits at a time – the sound of a glacier scoring its way across a landscape at forty miles an hour instead of its usual mile every four thousand years. That's Prometheus getting to his knees.

The next sense we will dislocate with sheer vastness is sight. Imagine a mountain rearing up in front of your eyes, stretching, complaining, and then standing upright. That's Prometheus getting to his feet.

And finally, imagine the sort of earthquake you'd get if some gigantic and malevolent deity squeezed the Earth like an enormous spot, sending molten magma spouting out of all its half-healed volcanoes, faults and fissures. That's what it felt like to be standing in the Caucasus when Prometheus landed after he'd jumped up, punched the air and yelled 'Yo!' at the top of his voice.

'When you've quite finished,' Jason said.

The Titan looked down at the tiny dot below him, and grinned. 'Sorry,' he said, 'I'd love to stop and chat for a bit, but I have to get going. Ask the eagle, she'll tell you.'

Then, with a stride that arched over mountains, the Titan walked off. Far away, Jason could hear a sound like someone very tall and strong punching the palm of his hand with his fist and saying 'Right!'

'Be like that,' Jason said, and started to walk down the

mountain. He had gone about thirty yards when a foot the size of York Minster landed beside him.

'Jason Derry?'

Metaphor is tricksy stuff. It is not actually possible to jump out of one's skin, but it is possible to try. Jason tried.

'It is you, isn't it?' The voice was slightly muffled, but that was because the words had to travel through a lot of thick cloud before they reached Jason's ears. 'Has he gone?'

Jason looked up. By craning his neck until he felt something give, he could just see, far up in the sky, a belt buckle. 'Sorry?,' he said. Then, for no reason at all that he could see, his lips arched into a grin and he felt a laugh creep cough-like across his lungs. No need to ask who the tall person was.

'Prometheus,' said the voice of Gelos. 'Has he gone yet?'

'Yes.'

'Which way?'

Jason blinked. 'I'd have thought you'd be able to see him from up there.'

'You know how it is,' said the voice. 'My eyes aren't what they were, I can't pick out little tiny details any more. Look, time's pressing rather; we've only got five minutes before the orbits are lined up, so ...'

Jason may have been small compared to Gelos, but by now he was so fed up that mere size really didn't matter. 'Right, Buster,' he said grimly. 'Tell me what's going on or I'll ...' He stared up at the mountain of toecap that rose high above his head. 'Or I'll give you a chiropody session you'll never forget. You hear me?'

Gelos chuckled. 'I won't tell you,' he said, 'but you can watch.'

A hand – we can tell it was a hand because we're far enough away to see it all in proportion; to Jason it was just a very big pink thing – reached down and very gently flicked Jason up into its own palm. 'Which way?' the voice repeated.

With a monumental effort Jason hauled himself up out
of a ravine that was in fact Gelos's life line. 'Straight
ahead,' he said. 'Head for that tall mountain over there.'

The enormous thing lurched forward. 'Which mountain?'

'The one you just trod on.'

'It's all right,' said Gelos, 'I can see him for myself now.
Hey, Pro!'

Far away, Jason could see the Titan. He seemed to have
grown; so, in fact had Jason. Actually, all that had
happened was that his brain had adjusted the field of view
and proportion registers of his brain to enable him to cope
with the scale on which he was now operating. Under
normal circumstances this would have taken several
million years of evolution, but we can only assume that
Jason was a quick learner. Anyway, he could see Prometheus, and above him he could see Gelos, and below him –
very much below him – he could see the world. There was
just about enough room on it for them both to stand,
although very soon there wouldn't be.

'Hold tight, Jason Derry.' It sounded as if both giants
had said it at the same time; and that wasn't as remarkable as it might have been, since now that Jason could see
them both clearly, he noticed that they looked extremely
alike. Sort of like twins; or reflections in a mirror. No, let's
stop pussyfooting. They are *exactly* alike.

And now there was only one of them.

'Excuse me,' said Jason.

'Yes?' There were two voices; but both speaking in
perfect harmony and coming from one throat. The two
giants had merged.

'Oh,' said Jason. 'Nothing.'

'Excuse us,' said the giant(s), 'but we need our hands
free, so if you wouldn't mind ...'

Jason felt himself travelling through the air at devas-
tating speed; and then what he could now perceive was a
hand put him in what he was able to recognise as a shirt

pocket. The pocket of a very big shirt; so big that the gaps between the weave of the cotton were large enough to fly an airliner through. Fortunately, the fibres of the cotton were as wide as the average motorway, and so there was no danger of falling through; and through the weave, Jason had a splendid view of what happened next.

High above his head he could see the stars; not as little points of light but as huge balls of fiery gas. The planets of the solar system were so big that he felt he could reach out and touch them. But what he mostly noticed was the other Earths.

We know them to be Betamax worlds, but Jason didn't. He just thought they were a lot of identical – fairly identical – copies of the thing he remembered having seen on globes. One of these globes was swinging down through the firmament, dragging a moon behind it like a very fat lady with a very fat dog on a lead. The giant(s) reached out a hand, grabbed hold of it, closed his/their fingers round it and said, 'Gotcha!'

'Excuse me.'

'Yes?'

'What are you doing?'

The giant(s) smiled. 'Saving the world,' he/they said.

'Ah,' Jason said. 'Right.'

'Not this one, of course,' the giant(s) went on. 'The other one.'

'Fine.'

'This one,' said the giant(s), tossing the Betamax world up in the air and catching it, 'is a right little tinker.'

'Really?'

'Here,' said the giant(s), 'look for yourself.'

'No, really,' Jason said. 'I'm quite happy to take your word for it.'

The giant(s) laughed. 'You wanted to know what was going on, you look and see for yourself. Here, catch.' And the giant(s) threw the planet to Jason.

Who, to his everlasting amazement, caught it.

*

According to ancestral belief, Delphi is the dead centre of the world; or, as the ancient Hellenes so quaintly put it, the earth's navel. On a hot day in high season, however, armpit might be a more fitting description.

Betty-Lou Fisichelli plodded from her office across the road from the museum up towards the temple site to post the day's messages in the usual place. Not that there was anything much: *Is this a good time to invest in Far Eastern unit trusts?* and *Congratulations! You have been selected as a lucky finalist in our prize draw* didn't seem to her to be crammed with arcane significance and could probably wait. Nevertheless, a good Pythoness doesn't take it upon herself to edit; only to relay.

When she finally reached the Treasury of the Athenians, she found it deserted except for forty-six French tourists, a three-headed dog and an eagle. Oddly enough, the tourists didn't seem able to see the dog or the eagle, but nothing tourists failed to notice surprised Ms. Fisichelli any more. What did surprise her was that the eagle was there at all.

'You!' she said.

The eagle looked down at its talons and made a very slight but deprecating gesture.

'How you've got the nerve to show your beak here,' Ms. Fisichelli went on, 'after the way you ...' She tailed off. The dog was looking at her.

In fact, there was no anthropomorphic message in the dog's stare; it was just a doggy stare, plain and simple. But Ms. Fisichelli was nervous around dogs at the best of times, and a doggy stare in triplicate was not her idea of good vibes.

'Be that as it may.' She pulled herself together. 'Well, if you've got anything to say, I'd be grateful if you got on with it. My time is not without ...'

The eagle gestured with its head towards the tourists,

who were staring at her. They seemed uneasy, and none of them had asked her to take a photograph of them beside a pile of fallen-down masonry; in Delphi, this is tantamount to ostracism. Ms. Fisichelli sighed, and led the way up the hill.

On top of the hill at Delphi there is a large Roman race-track, trimmed tastefully with bushes. There, Ms. Fisichelli sat down heavily on a stone (did we mention that the hill is steep?) and said, 'Well?'

The eagle looked at the dog, who wagged its tail as if to suggest that it was incapable of speech and none of this had been its idea anyway. It's amazing what can be communicated with a few inches of mobile fur-covered appendix.

'Hi, Betty-Lou,' said the eagle.

'Mary,' replied Ms. Fisichelli, coldly affable. 'How've you been keeping?'

'Oh, fine, fine,' said the eagle. 'Look, I guess I owe you an explanation.'

'I guess you do.'

'Well,' said the eagle. It shifted its grip on the rock and winced. 'Look, would it be easier for you if I became human for a bit?'

'That's entirely up to you,' said Ms. Fisichelli. 'Far be it from me to dictate ...'

'Thanks,' said Mary, shedding her feathers and donning a pale blue sun-dress with small pink flowers. 'My talons were killing me,' she explained.

'So then,' Ms. Fisichelli said. 'You were about to say something.'

'Yes,' Mary replied. 'Look, you've probably guessed or been told, I'm Prometheus's eagle. You know, the one who was given the job of ripping the poor guy's liver out every morning and evening as part of his punishment ...'

'I'm a graduate of six universities,' Ms. Fisichelli interrupted. 'I do know my basic mythology, thank you.'

'Sorry.' Mary repressed an urge to spring into the air,

spread her wings and scream; she picked at her thumbnail instead. 'Well, Pro and I ... When you've known someone as long as that, you can't help sort of getting to understand a guy, and besides, what the gods did to him was wrong. He was only trying to help the mortals, and they stomped him. The gods don't like us, Betty-Lou, they ...'

'By us,' Ms. Fisichelli said, 'do you mean humans, or eagles?'

'Neither,' Mary said, 'only themselves. You know about the First Joke, don't you? And how they want to do away with comedy and take the world over again?' Ms. Fisichelli nodded. 'And you don't think someone ought to stop them? Godsdamnit, Betty-Lou, can you imagine for one moment what that would be like? A world with no laughter in it? We just couldn't survive.'

Mary realised as she said this that Ms. Fisichelli had managed to survive for over thirty-five years in this cold, hard world without having a lot to do with humour; probably she kept out of its way, and if she couldn't do that she sort of stepped over it. But that, Mary felt, proved her point.

'Well,' she went on, '*we* couldn't survive, anyway. So Pro asked me if I'd help him, and I said yes. And so I sort of became his assistant, did all the leg-work for him. It was fun; I enjoyed it. For one thing, he showed me how I could make myself human again; in fact, several humans. That's cool, except there's some of me give me a pain in the butt, but never mind. I don't have to live with me, after all.'

Ms. Fisichelli remained unimpressed. 'So?' she said.

'So,' Mary went on, 'we found this hero, an actual son of Jupiter, someone who'd actually have the nuts to defy the gods and cut the chains at the proper moment and ... pardon me, have you got the right time there, please?'

Ms. Fisichelli showed Mary her watch-face.

'That's good,' Mary said, 'because any minute now, Pro's going to be set loose and he's going to put a stop to this down-with-laughter thing once and for all. And once that happens, Betty-Lou, there's going to be big trouble.'

'So I should think,' said the Pythoness, loyally.

'For the gods, I mean.' Mary shrugged. 'Me,' she said, 'I can't see what Pro's worried about. If you ask me, they've got it coming. But he says no, they're the gods, you've got to have them, so long as they don't interfere too much. Without gods, he says, who could we blame for things? He wants to save them.'

'Save them?' Betty-Lou gasped. 'What from?'

'Themselves, mostly,' Mary said. 'You see, right now, they're having a board meeting. Have you the faintest notion what that means?'

Betty-Lou shook her head.

'Think of the end of the world,' said Mary, 'with added bickering, and you'll get the idea. Once they discover what's happened, Jupiter is going to be very, very angry. He's going to want to start saying it with thunderbolts. Now these days, you can't do that; you start spraying thunderbolts about the place, you're going to set off all the nuclear early-warning systems the superpowers aren't supposed to have any more, and the next thing you know it'll be goodbye, Earth. And the gods will be so busy falling out with each other and accusing each other of cutting bits out of the Sunday papers and leaving the top off the toothpaste that they won't notice what's happening and stop it. And if the Earth ceases to exist, then so do the gods. This is the world they're tied to; when it goes, so do they. Not us,' Mary added, 'them. When all the dust settles, it'll be them who aren't there any more. We'll be all right.'

'Why?'

'Reality bifurcation,' Mary said.

Ms. Fisichelli frowned; for a moment she'd thought Mary had said Reality Bifurcation. 'Pardon me?'

'It says,' Mary replied, 'in Article Seven of the Universal Charter of Possibility that it's impossible for the gods to destroy the Earth – the Number One Earth – except at the ordained time and through the proper channels. There's, oh, forms that've got to be filled in, that sort of thing. Public enquiries. Notices posted up outside town halls. What I mean is, they can't just do it by accident. So what'll happen is that an alternative world will come into being on which they *do* manage to destroy themselves – and the world too, of course; pretty short-lived world, huh? – and then it'll just happen. Only they won't be here any more. The Probability Police will see to that. I'm telling you, those guys are *mean.* You think death's a tough baby, you wait till you meet Sergeant Kawalski.'

Betty-Lou sagged like an Easter egg on a radiator. 'You can't be serious,' she said. 'They're the gods, Mary; nobody can push the gods around.'

'Don't bet on it,' Mary said. 'Just think what happened to Woden.'

Ms. Fisichelli fell silent and gnawed her lip, for Mary undoubtedly had a point. One of the first things young astrotheological students are told is the story of how, shortly after Woden, chief god of the now defunct Nordic pantheon, offended against the Possibility regulations by restoring his dead son Balder to life on a Sunday without a resuscitation certificate in a residential area, he was abducted by three large, anonymous men in a blue and white chariot. His severed head was later found outside the palace of Offa, King of the East Saxons (who shortly afterwards abandoned the beliefs of his forefathers, accepted Christianity and made a pilgrimage to Salt Lake City); the rest of his body was never recovered. The kidnappers were later identified as Possibility Policemen. Although nobody has ever been able satisfactorily to establish what actually happened to Woden, it is thought that they made him an Offa he couldn't refuse.

Ms. Fisichelli thought about it, and shuddered, until she resembled a brightly-dressed blancmange on a speeding trolley. 'But he wasn't a proper god, surely,' she said at last. 'And anyway ...'

She fell silent; somehow or other she had contrived to run out of anyways.

'It's serious,' Mary said. 'That's what Pro thinks, anyway.'

Ms. Fisichelli frowned. 'So just what am I supposed to be able to do about it?' she said.

'Easy,' Mary replied. 'Just get Apollo down here before he has a chance to go to the board meeting.'

'Apollo?' Ms. Fisichelli's eyebrows shot up like share prices in April. 'Why him?'

Mary grinned. 'You'll see,' she said. 'Do you think you can get in touch with him? Quickly, I mean? Without all that fooling around?'

Ms. Fisichelli shook her head. 'No,' she said. 'You know as well as I do how we go about invoking him. If you're right, there just isn't time ...'

Mary looked at her.

'All right then,' Ms. Fisichelli said, 'so there is a way. But it's more than my job's worth ...'

Mary looked at her again. These things are cumulative. 'Betty-Lou,' she said, 'just what do you think your job'll be worth if Apollo ceases to exist?'

'Well ...'

'Betty-Lou.'

The Pythoness hesitated just a moment longer; then she shrugged.

'What the hell,' she said, 'you can only be turned into a weevil once, I guess. You win.'

Mary smiled, as the Pythoness took a step to one side and prepared her mind for what was to follow.

There are many different ways of summoning gods. You can sacrifice goats, or burn incense, or say mantras, or any combination of the three. There are also complex invocation rituals, some of which we have seen; you can leave messages on the architraves of temples, or use the statue.

By and large the gods don't really mind being summoned in any one of these ways, because the summons is not binding, and they can use the divine equivalent of leaving the phone off the hook. But if you use the one method which they have to obey, regardless of where they are and what they might be doing at the time, you are guaranteed to get a god, quite possibly a god in his pants and socks and without his teeth in, and almost certainly a very angry god. Nothing, after all, gets up the nose of an omnipotent being like being told what to do.

What you do is, you put two fingers in your mouth and you whistle.

Largely as a result of the enormous quantum increase in philosophical productivity caused by the introduction of the new technology, many of the fundamental maxims that make up the structure of the modern astrophilosopher's world model have required amendment and expansion. For example, Descartes' immortal conclusion *cogito ergo sum* was recently subjected to destruction testing by a group of graduate researchers at Princeton led by Professors Montjuic and Lauterbrunnen, and now reads, in the revised version to be found in the *Shorter Harvard Orthodoxy*:

(a) I think, therefore I am; or
(b) Perhaps I thought, therefore I was; but
(c) These days, I tend to leave all that side of things to my wife.

Developments such as this have in turn served to make academics working in the divinity subjects more commercially aware, and many of them now retain the services of specialist ecclesiastical lawyers, accountants and, of course, agents. The leading firm of ecclesiastical representatives is, needless to say, Alfred Furbank of New York and London, whose Mr. Kortright represents (among many others) Betty-Lou Fisichelli. Mr. Kortright is, understandably, a very busy man, and when he received two simultaneous calls from clients in mid-flight on his way to the annual Theological Trade Fair in Frankfurt, he wished that he had been able to find a suitable assistant to whom he could delegate. However, the qualities required of a successful ecclesiastical agent are rarely met with.

'Who?' he asked again.

'The Pythoness of Delphi on red,' replied the New York switchboard, 'Aleister Crowley on blue. He's on a pay phone. They're both holding.'

Kortright shuddered slightly. Against his better judgment, the New York office had recently installed one of those gadgets that plays callers piped music while they're holding, and some fool of a managing partner had chosen the *Dies Irae* as a suitable tune. Something to put the fear of God into 'em, he'd said.

He pressed the button. 'Right,' he told New York. 'Put on Fisichelli, tell Aleister no, not till I get the money, and then no more calls until we touch down. If anyone else calls in with a burning bush, tell them to call the fire department.'

Click.

'Betty-Lou, hi there, how's the prediction business?'

'Mr. Kortright?'

'Here.'

'Mr. Kortright, can you get me access to all the major networks, please? There's something very important I have to tell the world. From Apollo.'

I didn't think it could get worse, Kortright thought, but I was wrong. 'Betty-Lou,' he said, 'we've all got something very important we've got to tell the world. Some of us do it by shooting the president, some of us take overdoses, some of us just make do with the phone-ins. The competition for air time is very great at all times.'

'But this is *important*,' Betty-Lou said. 'It's a genuine message from the gods. Or at least one of them,' she remembered. 'He's putting himself in jeopardy speaking out like this; you have no idea how much trouble he'll be in when Jupiter finds out. The least we can do is make sure people hear him.'

'Are you sure about that, Betty-Lou?' said Kortright. 'I mean, it sounds to me like it'd be a very bad idea, from his point of view. And yours,' he added. 'There's this thing called credibility, you know, and I've been working very hard to build yours up. One little slip, like you going on the *Johnny Carson Show* saying you've been hearing voices, and you'll think Joan of Arc had it easy. It won't just be the English who roast you alive, it'll be *Newsweek* and ...'

'Mr. Kortright,' said Betty-Lou firmly. 'You have to arrange for me to broadcast to the world. If not ...'

'Yes?' said Kortright impatiently. 'Go ahead, worry me.'

'Well, I hate to do this, but you have to understand ...'

'What?'

'If you'll just look out of your window, Mr. Kortright.'

Kortright glanced out of the window. In the air just above the wing of the Lear jet, he saw what looked remarkably like an elderly car with a team of four winged horses attached to it by means of a complicated arrangement of transmission parts and drive-chains. In the driver's seat was what Mr. Kortright instinctively recognised as a very angry Sun-God, who was aiming at him with a bow of burning gold.

'Mr. Kortright?'

'Here.'

'What do you think you can do?'

Mr. Kortright looked at his watch. 'Give me fifteen minutes, OK?' he said. 'We can syndicate it through one of the big agencies. They'll send someone over to do the actual interview. Oh and Betty-Lou ...'

'Yes, Mr. Kortright?'

'Do you think you could ask your friend with the bow to back off slightly? Only one of his horses is trying to eat the wing of this jet, and if I crash there won't be any interview at all. You got that?'

'I'll see what I can do, Mr. Kortright.'

Kortright pressed the button, leaned back in his seat, screamed, and then pulled himself back together. When you started seeing god yourself, it was time to move over more towards the administration side of the business.

He called up London office.

'Get me Danny Bennett,' he said.

J ason looked about him.

Far above, he could just make out four enormous pink bars that seemed to be clamping the sky to the Earth. The Caucasus had vanished, and he appeared to be standing in the streets of a city, though not any city that he could recognise. It was snowing bitterly, but for some reason the snow didn't settle on him; in fact, each single snowflake somehow contrived to jink out of his way at the last minute and land somewhere else. He had the strange feeling that wherever this was, he was really somewhere else.

'Where am I?' Jason asked.

'You know,' said a voice beside him, 'I never expected to hear anyone actually say that. It's only people in books ...'

'Yes,' Jason said, 'but where in god's name actually am I, and we'll leave the literary niceties till later. And who are you?'

'Prometheus,' } the voice or voices replied,
'Gelos,' } saying the names together,

'and you're on the world you're holding in your hand. It's hardly an original device, I we know, but there, it's your fault for wanting to know what's going on.'

'Ah,' Jason replied. 'So I now know what's going on, do I? Thank you so much.'

'Jason,' said the voices or voice, 'the world you are standing on is a world which actually exists. Its technical name is Betamax 87659807 and it is the same as your world in most material respects. It is your world; or it could be. Your world could be merged with it, and nobody would know. Now there are some differences, as you will shortly find out, but once the merger had happened nobody would remember them. It would be as if everything had always been like this, and anyone who remembered otherwise would be sent somewhere quiet and restful with high walls until he was well again. Now the gods want your world merged with this one, and they've been trying to bring the merger about for a very long time. I we would like you to have a look at this world and let me us know what you think of it.'

Jason shrugged. It was like, he decided, those offers you get from the timeshare companies where you go along and listen to their spiel, and afterwards they give you a portable television. The only element lacking, so far as he could tell, was anything resembling a portable television.

'Where are we now, then?' he asked. 'I don't recognise this at all.'

'This is the street where you live, or would have lived, or will live, in Anglia, which is, was or will be what they call England,' he/they said. 'And the date is December the twenty-fourth. Sorry if this all seems needlessly Dickensian, but we haven't got much time, so we wanted to get in as much culture shock as possible. This is a world where Prometheus never stole the Joke from Heaven, and where the gods never retired. Right, roll 'em.'

As Jason stood there recovering from the above conversation, which put him in mind of a multiple choice English grammar exam, he looked up and saw a small knot of miserable-looking people trudging up the street. They wore grey homespun overcoats and grey knitted scarves, and they were getting drenched in slush by a passing ox-cart. The leader of the party was carrying a collecting tin,

with *For The Gods; Please Give Fearfully* written on it.
The party stopped outside one of the delapidated thatched
houses that made up the street and started to sing.

> '*We wish you a Saturnalia*,' they sang
> '*We wish you a saturnalia*
> *We wish you a Saturnalia*
> *And a pious New Year.*'

'No Christmas, you see,' he they said in Jason's ear. 'No
Donations of Constantine, no Christianity, ergo no
Christmas.'

'Huh,' Jason replied, and for two pins he'd have added
'Humbug.' Christmas always bored him rigid, partly
because he was a Hero and lived on a higher plane of back-
ground experience, and partly because his family always
gave him socks. Something about the song troubled him,
however. 'Shouldn't it be "We wish you a happy Saturnalia," though?'

'No such thing as a happy Saturnalia.'

The singers had finished their song and the door of the
house opened. A terrified-looking man poked his head
round, thrust two gold coins into the tin, and slammed the
door. The leader ticked a name off a list and they moved
on down the street. Outside the next door they sang;

> '*Bad King Atreus looked out*
> *On the slopes of Pindus.*
> *Lightning came and rubbed him out,*
> *Blowing him to cinders.*
> *Atreus, the silly sod,*
> *Came to Jove's attention.*
> *People who offend a god*
> *Don't collect their pension.*'

There was complete silence for a while, broken only by
the mooing of a distant cow; then the shutter of an
upstairs window opened and a very old woman poked her
head through.

'Piss off,' she said. 'I haven't got any money, do you hear?'

The leader shuffled through the papers on his clipboard. 'According to the priests,' he said, 'you've got two denarii five quadrantes left out of your pension.'

'But that's got to last me till January.'

'Tough,' replied the leader – not unpleasantly; he clearly wasn't enjoying this very much. He was just very, very determined. 'You shouldn't have spent it all on butter then, should you? One denarius you're down for. We haven't got all night.'

'Go *away.*'

'Look, gran,' said another of the group, 'we know it's hard, but we're only doing our job.'

'Is that you, our Timon?'

'Yes, gran.'

'Then you should be ashamed of yourself.'

'Steady on, gran,' said their Timon. 'It is the season of illwill, you know.'

Jason turned. He couldn't see his companion or companions, but he turned nevertheless. In the circles in which he moved, if you wanted to talk to someone without someone else hearing, you turned, and that was that.

'Shouldn't that be the season of . . .?'

'No,' he they replied. 'Shut up and listen.'

'Look,' said the leader of the group, 'it's no skin off our nose if you don't make your voluntary offering, right? If you want to offend the gods and get blown to bits by a thunderbolt and spend the rest of eternity on the wrong side of the Styx just because the thought of going hungry for a few days meant more to you than paying your respects to the everlasting gods . . .'

'All right, all right,' said Gran, and shortly afterwards there was a shooting back of bolts and a slight tinkle, such as might have been caused by a small silver coin dropping into a very full collecting tin.

'Bye, then,' said the leader. 'Have a pious Saturnalia.'

'Bog off.'

The party slouched off down the street, and soon Jason could hear them singing about how, away in a manger with a crib for his bed, the impious Thyestes was found very dead. Snow fell. Jason's sensitive nostrils detected the smell of totally inadequate drains; or more accurately, no drains at all.

'A brief history lesson,' said the voice or voices. 'In our world, the Roman Emperor Constantine declared Christianity to be the State religion, and the worship of the gods was suppressed. In this world, however, Constantine never existed. There was never a Constantinian revolution. Constantine's predecessor, Diocletian, remained in power. Now Diocletian believed in a place for everybody and everybody in his place, and also in the gods. He set up a system of government along those lines and, in this world, the system has worked. One thousand seven hundred years later, things have not changed much, largely because no-one's seen the need. There is still an Emperor in Rome – Severus the Thirty-Third – and the science of urban sanitation died in infancy; you are presently standing in the main sewer of the town. Petrol is still a black messy substance that interferes with well-digging operations in Mesopotamia, penicillin is an unfortunate by-product of inadequate bread management, and electricity is something that comes out of the sky to let you know you've forgotten to sacrifice to Minerva. The only known cure for an abscess under a tooth is death. This is because people never learned to laugh at the gods, and so never realised that it's possible to tell them to get lost. Discontent cannot exist without laughter.'

'Was Diocletian the one who made his horse prime minister?'

'That was Caligula, and not on this world he didn't. It was a joke, you see, and here there are no jokes.'

'None at all?'

'Try for yourself.'

Jason thought about this, and as he was contemplating it a man appeared at the top of the street. Jason had been wondering if he was in fact visible to the people of this world, and asked as much of his companion(s).

'No,' he they said, 'not as such. The Possibility Police wouldn't allow it. However, since this is a controlled environment and we can adjust things later, we can make you visible for a few minutes if you like.'

Once this had been dealt with Jason walked up to the man and stood in front of him.

'Excuse me,' he said, 'but what's brown and lives in the sea and attacks young women?'

The man stopped and thought about it. 'Good question,' he said. 'You've got me there. It could be Neptune, because he lives in the sea and he's a bit, well, like that, His name be praised, but I never heard that he was brown, particularly. There's the Old Man of the Sea, of course, but he just attacks everybody, thanks be to him. Then there's Porphyry, I suppose, except he's ...'

'Actually,' Jason said, 'it's Jack the Kipper.'

'Who?'

'Jack the Kipper.'

'Never heard of him,' said the man, after a moment's thought. 'Is that another name of Scylla the Hundred-Headed Sea-Fiend?'

'No,' Jason replied, 'it's a pun.'

'A what?'

'A pun.'

The man thought again. 'No, sorry,' he said, 'you've lost me there. You sure you're not thinking of the Old Man of the Sea, because ...'

'All right, all right,' Jason said. 'Try this one. Why did the chicken cross the road?'

'Which road?'

'Sorry, forget I said that. How many dentists does it take to change a light bulb.'

'What's a dentist?'

'Ah. Well, thanks for everything, have a nice day.'

'What's nice?'

Jason shivered, not entirely because of the cold. Fortunately his companion or companions chose this moment to wipe the man's memory clean, and he hurried by without saying anything further.

'All right,' Jason said, 'you've proved your point. Can I go and have something to eat now, please?'

But the person or persons he couldn't see shook his or their invisible head or heads. 'Not yet,' he they said. 'You wanted to understand what was going on, didn't you?'

'In a way, yes,' Jason replied. 'Not this way.'

'How, then?'

'More a sort of comfortingly meaningless truism sort of way,' Jason said, 'or, failing that, a detailed exposition over lunch. Do they have food here, by any chance?'

He they considered. 'They eat,' was the reply.

'Whatever it is they eat, could I eat it too?'

'No.'

'Oh.' Jason thought about it, and remembered the story of Persephone in Hell. 'You mean, if I eat any of the food here, I'll have to stay here for ever and ever?'

'No,' said his companion(s), 'but if you eat any of the food here you'll be ill. It's winter, remember. No fresh veg, all the meat is salted, and there's ergotism in the bread. If you're really hungry there's always rats, but ...'

'I think I'll wait, thanks,' Jason said. 'Okay then, so what else have I got to see before I achieve enlightenment and you let me go home, because time's getting on and ...'

'Not here it isn't.'

'Look ...'

'Roll 'em.'

'I shall now,' said Jupiter, 'call this meeting to order.'

He looked around him and frowned. Either all the gods had suddenly gone deaf or else they had forgotten what had happened the last time.

'I shall now,' he repeated, 'call this meeting to order, and anyone who doesn't shut up will spend eternity as a dung-beetle. Thank you.'

In the resulting silence the Great Sky God looked round and counted heads. Someone was missing.

'All right,' Jupiter said, 'where is he?'

Silence.

'I see,' Jupiter went on. 'Solidarity. Right.' Jupiter cast his eye across the assembly, muttering under his breath. By the time he got to Eeny-meeny-miny he was staring straight at Mars.

'He was called away,' Mars whimpered. 'An urgent summons from Delphi. He asked me to make his apologies for him, and ...'

'Called away.'

'Yes,' Mars continued, sounding like a whole Wealdful of sheep bleating simultaneously. It is part of the Divine Code of Ethics that gods stick up for their fellow gods and try to conceal each others' cock-ups from the Great Eye. Other components of the Divine Code are fair dealing, honesty, justice, consistency and kindness to animals. It was last observed on October 16th, 1145. 'At least that's what he told me,' Mars continued. 'I said to him, I said ...'

'Called away.'

'Um,' Mars quipped brilliantly. 'Yes. Exactly what I said to him. I said ...'

Jupiter stroked his beard, producing enough static electricity to power all the food processors in New York. 'In that case,' he said, 'as of now Apollo ceases to be a member of this council. Mercury will convey this news to him after we have taken Any Other Business. In the meantime he shall cease to function as an independent entity. Moved and unanimously carried, I trust.'

The gods looked at each other. On the one hand it was a terrifying precedent. On the other hand it was just plain terrifying. They nodded.

'Moved, then,' Jupiter said smugly, 'and carried unanimously. At this rate, we'll have this lot wrapped up by teatime. Isn't it satisfying when everyone does as they're told? Right, next item on the agenda, the destruction of Earth . . .'

Something hopped into Mars's mouth and bumped up against his clenched teeth. He was horribly afraid it was a protest. 'Um . . .' he said.

'Sorry?'

'Um,' Mars said again. Something told him that his point required a degree of clarification and expansion if it was to have maximum effect. 'Er . . .' he added. Everyone was looking at him, and he suddenly realised how pleasantly restful it was when people were just shooting at him.

'I believe,' Jupiter said – why is there no word meaning 'said' but having lots of harsh, grating consonants in it? – 'that Mars wishes to address the meeting?'

'Well,' Mars said, 'I'm terribly sorry to interrupt, break the flow and so forth, but did Your Um just say something about the destruction of Earth? On a point of order, and so on.'

'Yes.'

'Ah. Thank you.'

'And the transfer,' Jupiter went on, 'of our entire field of operations to Betamax 87659807, ultimately to be renamed –' Jupiter paused melodramatically – 'New Earth. I leave the motion to the floor.'

If the floor had any opinions on the subject, it kept them to itself, as did all the gods sitting on it. The discovery that the Supreme Being has finally flipped his lid is always likely to cause disorientation, even among gods.

'If nobody has any comments to make,' Jupiter said, 'then I shall put the motion to the vote. Seconded and carried . . .'

'No.'

Everyone swivelled round and stared at Mars, Demeter going so far as to count his legs. Jupiter frowned.

'No?'

'No.' Mars was standing up. 'You can't,' he added.

'Oh can't I?'

'No you can't.'

'Yes I can.'

'No you can't.'

'Yes I can.'

'Look,' interrupted Mercury, who was taking the minutes, 'do I have to put all this down, because if it's going to go on much longer I'm going to need a new note-book.'

'It's not going to go on very much longer,' said Jupiter, 'as dung-beetles have no *locus standi* to address a meeting of the gods.'

'You still can't do it,' Mars said. His right hand was creeping upwards towards his mouth, with the general idea of tearing his own tongue out by the roots; but it was naturally cautious and had only reached chest height. In the meantime, Mars carried on. 'Because if you destroy Earth, we all cease to exist. There's no way out of that, and you know it.'

'He's right.' Minerva looked round to see who had spoken and realised it was her.

'Who asked your opinion?' Jupiter snarled.

'You did. You left the motion to the floor, and ...'

'But you're not a floor,' Jupiter replied. 'Though that could be arranged,' he added.

'If you destroy the Earth,' she said, ignoring him – ignoring Jupiter is rather like trying to fly through rather than round a mountain, but to the gods all things are possible – 'then the laws of possibility require that we cease to exist, at least in our present form.'

Jupiter considered this before saying 'Balls,' and the Olympians held their breath. Minerva continued:

'What will happen is that there'll be a reality bifur-cation into a world where you decided to destroy the world – which won't be around for very long – and a world where you changed your mind at the last minute. Since that's impossible, because you never change your mind at the last minute, that world will quickly fizzle out, and all of us with it. On the world where you destroyed the world, we'll all be destroyed with it. Curtains.'

Jupiter scratched the tip of his nose. 'You're right, of course,' he said.

'I'm so glad,' Minerva started to say, 'and please forgive me for having the temerity to remind you of the fact, but ...'

'Nevertheless ...'

Apollo grinned nervously, straightened his laurel wreath and stared at the monitor.

'Six – five – four – three – two – one – on air!'

Danny Bennet switched on a smile that Amundsen could have driven a sled over, and leaned forwards.

'Your Majesty,' he said, 'is it true that the gods are conspiring to bring about the end of the world?'

Apollo opened his mouth to speak, and then something happened to his vocal chords. Difficult to say what, exactly; either they'd all fused together or someone had nipped quietly down his throat in the last five seconds and removed them. Something funny had definitely happened. In any case they weren't there any more. Meanwhile there were ninety billion people or whatever it was, all out there looking at him. Live.

'You know,' Apollo managed to say, 'I'm glad you asked me that question.'

'So what's the answer?' Danny demanded. 'Your Majesty,' he added.

When his agent had told him about this wonderful offer from the satellite TV people, Danny had taken all that stuff about the sky being the limit with a pinch of salt. You know where you are with the BBC, he had told himself, even if it is on the scrapheap. It had only been the promise that if he signed on the dotted line he could at last make the epoch-shattering documentary, based on shocking revelations by a renegade astrotheology don and provisionally entitled *Death of a Carpenter*, that had induced him to turn his back on the Corporation and hoist the Jolly Roger. And now here he was interviewing this strange, distinctly luminous person whom his producer assured him was the god Apollo. For approximately five minutes, he had panicked, before he had remembered the interviewer's golden rule: the bigger they are, the harder you hit 'em.

'The people,' he added, 'have a right to know.'

'No they don't.'

'You're admitting there's been –' Danny's lips caressed the magic words as they passed the gate of his teeth – 'a cover-up?'

'Of course there's been a cover-up,' Apollo replied. 'There's always a cover-up. That's what it's all about. That's not the point. Look, unless you want me to turn you into a frog or something ...'

'Mr. ... Your Majesty,' Danny retorted, 'I think you'll find that threats are rivet rivet rivet rivet.'

Apollo blinked. Did I do that, he asked himself. Must have. Oh well. He unhooked the microphone from its stand and placed it on the chair beside the frog.

'Now I think you've put your finger on what I might call the nub of the problem, Mr. Bennet,' he said smoothly. 'Basically, when it comes down to it, in the final analysis ...'

'Rivet rivet rivet rivet rivet,' said the frog. 'Rivet.'

'Quite so,' Apollo replied. 'Your point is, of course, entirely valid. But the message I'm trying to get across ...'

Apollo fell silent. Hell, it was on the tip of his tongue. Something about something important. At that moment some words drifted down out of the air into his mouth, and he spoke them. They had come a long way, were slightly scorched and tasted disconcertingly of marzipan.

'Oh yes,' he said. 'The world is about to end.'

'Riv ...'

'There is,' Apollo went on, 'absolutely no cause for alarm. The situation is under control, and even as I speak negotiations are in hand to attempt to reach a settlement that will be satisfactory in the eyes of all parties.' Just then, a cloud passed over the sun, and Apollo drew himself up short. Why was it, he wondered, that sitting in this chair being stared at by a camera made you say all sorts of silly things you didn't mean? 'They'll all fail, of course,' he added. 'Absolutely bugger all *you* lot can do about it, anyway. It's all up to the Derry boy and the dog and the eagle. And Prometheus, of course, and Gelos too, if he's turned up yet. But all I can say is they're cutting it a bit fine, because, well, there's a board meeting going on right now up in the sun and pretty soon they're all going to start chucking thunderbolts about and then it'll be you lot for the chop and why have you switched the cameras off, I haven't finished yet.'

'Now look,' said the producer's voice, 'I've had some nut cases on this show in my time but if you think I'm going to put my job on the line letting you say things like that over the ark ark ark ark ...'

Apollo turned slightly in his chair and smiled at the camera, smiling as brightly as the sun (which had just emerged from the clouds overhead). The camera was being operated by a natterjack toad in a leather jacket and designer jeans. Do what you like to him, a television cameraman will always basically remain the same.

'Ladies and gentlemen of humanity,' Apollo said. It was easy once you got the hang of it, which was basically bearing in mind that if you let your brain register the fact that there are *ninety billion people out there staring right at you* then you're inevitably going to dry up, but if you just don't think about it then there's no problem, no problem at all. 'This is the god Apollo speaking. Throughout history it has been my pleasant task to pass on the messages of heaven to mortal men. Well, all good things must come to an end. The world's been a good thing, by and large, hasn't it? Well, it's got to come to an end, too. Now I know that's going to be hard on some of you, perhaps even all of you, but in the final analysis you'll all have the satisfaction of knowing that it's part of a divine plan that stretches back many thousands of years to the time of the creation of mankind itself.'

Apollo paused for a moment, rallied his mental forces, and tilted his head slightly on one side as if he'd been doing this sort of thing all his life. After all, he reasoned, PR is PR, whether it's done by television broadcasts or the entrails of sacrificial animals or posters on the sides of buses.

'Now some of you,' he went on, 'will be saying to your-selves "Now hang on, that's a bit thick, isn't it?" And let me assure you that the Divine community as a whole has a great deal of sympathy with this view. We know only too well how hard it is to make sacrifices – or in our case, how to go without sacrifices. We understand, and we're going to do everything in our power to make what I would call the transitional period as painless as we possibly can. But . . .'

At that moment, a large eagle smashed its way through a skylight and pitched on Danny's chair, with the result that about nine hundred thousand viewers who had just come back from the kitchen with the tea got the impression that it was one of those ventriloquism acts that never quite ring true on television.

Apollo frowned, trying to remember who he'd turned into what, and while his mind was temporarily engaged in this fashion, the eagle spoke to him.

This statement simply cries out for qualification. The eagle didn't speak as much as transmit telepathic messages direct from its brain to his; and the messages were in fact being relayed via the eagle from a huge composite brain presently in possibility orbit round the entire concept of Earth. To complicate matters, there was a mild thunderstorm in the vicinity and the composite voice was transmitting on a rather popular mental frequency, with the result that there was a lot of crackling and a few distant snippets of a conversation between two CB Radio enthusiasts driving Leyland Roadmasters round the M25, but the messages were more or less intelligible.

'What the hell do you think you're playing at?' he they said.

'I beg your pardon?'

'Come on, Pol, pull your finger out. Have you heard what you've just been saying?'

'I . . .'

'Listen.' The entire interview so far was played back through the eagle's brain. Telepathic communication is very rapid indeed; compared with two seasoned telepaths thinking quickly, words are second-class letters to Penzance posted in Dundee on a Sunday. 'Is that what you intended to say?'

'No,' Apollo replied, puzzled. 'Far from it.'

'What were you going to say?'

'I was going to say that the gods were about to betray humanity, and the only way out of it was for everyone to believe in them as quickly and as sincerely as possible. I was going to help by doing a few miracles.'

'Do you know what's happened?'

'I've been got at.'

'Who by?'

'Jupiter.'

'Correct. He's just passed a resolution that you aren't a god any more.'

'He's done what?'

'You heard me. You've been reduced to the ranks. As soon as the meeting's over, they're going to snatch you back to Olympus, and then it'll be a career in the real estate business for you. Meanwhile, he's using you as a mouthpiece, beaming signals down from the sun into your brain. Fortunately, I we have just put a green baize cloth over the sun . . .'

'How ...'

'Don't ask. I we reckon that gives you about three minutes. Whose side are you on, Pol?'

'Reduced to the ranks!' Divine wrath filled Apollo's mind. He fizzed slightly, and the tubular steel arms of his chair were transmuted into pure gold. I'll show that jumped-up son of a concept exactly where he gets off ...'

'That's the ticket, Pol. Now, why don't you tell the folks at home the truth?'

'Roll 'em.'

It seemed to Jason as if he were flying, and also standing still at the same time. Air appeared to be rushing past him, but he wasn't conscious of any movement on his part. He was standing still and the world was turning very fast. You could get travel sick very quickly this way.

There was a click; the world jolted to a halt, paused for a stomach churning fraction of a second, and rushed back in the other direction. Then another click.

'This looks like it,' he they said. 'Right. Watch very carefully.'

The world was moving yet again, but this time at its normal pace; in fact, Jason wouldn't have noticed the motion if he hadn't been aware of the lack of it in between clicks. This was time running on playback speed.

He had apparently moved in space as well as in time, for he was inside a building of some sort now; a dark building, not particularly cheerful. Despite his innate optimism, Jason couldn't quite bring himself to believe that it was a restaurant. Which was not to suggest that it wasn't a place designed at least in part for eating in; it was just that a human being standing there would be justified in wondering on which end of the fork he was ultimately going to wind up.

'The temple of Jupiter in Londinium,' he they whispered. 'Not everybody's cup of tea.'

'Talking of ...'

It was only then that Jason became aware that the place was full of people; thousands of them, but they were so extraordinarily still and quiet that they simply hadn't registered in his mind. They were all dressed alike, in rather threadbare homespun jackets and knee-length kilts. The women had their heads covered. All of them had that air of nervous resignation that you usually only find in doctors' waiting rooms and tax offices. Jason wondered what they were all doing there.

'Having a good time,' he they whispered.

Jason frowned. 'Are you sure?' he asked.

'I we use the term loosely,' he they replied. 'Actually there's no such thing as a good time here; the nearest equivalent is a pious time, and I we suppose you could say they're having that. This is popular entertainment, Betamax style.'

'What is it, exactly?'

'It's a game show,' he they replied. 'Listen.'

Jason was on the point of applying for further and better particulars when two huge curtains parted at the far end of the hall and a procession entered. At the head of it were two enormous men with black masks and very large axes, followed by a third man carrying what looked startlingly like a chopping-block; then came three very sour-faced young women in extremely decorous costumes – in Jason's world they would have been dentists' receptionists – carrying silver vessels of indeterminate use. Finally, there was a tall, white-haired man with a beard like a silver doormat, dressed in the most outlandishly ornate robes Jason had ever seen; the sort of thing Louis XIV would have gone in for if only he'd had the money.

The procession halted in the middle of a sort of raised dais, and the masked men grounded their axes with a crash. The overdressed man stepped forward, stood for a moment and then spoke.

'A pious evening to you all, worshippers and females; my name is Godfearing George Maniakis, and I'm your host for tonight, when we're all going to play God's My Witness. Now before we begin, let me tell you all about a very spiritually uplifting thing which happened to me on the way to the temple tonight ...'

Jason looked round nervously. The building was almost as ornate as Godfearing George's costume; it had butresses, archetraves, roodscreens, pilasters and what Jason failed entirely to recognise as a narthex, but no doors. Pity.

'"Thy Will be done?" I said, well you could have knocked me down with a simpulum, so I turned to him and I said ...' Godfearing George was getting steadily more solemn as his routine continued, and some of the congregation were starting to quiver slightly. Any minute now, Jason felt, some idiot was going to shout "Halle-lujah!" He did his best to ignore the rest of the story, which had something to do with everlasting punishment and the transmigration of the soul. Finally it ground to a halt, and there was a deep, respectful silence.

'And now,' said Godfearing George, 'it only remains for me to welcome tonight's first contestants, who are going to join me in playing God's My Witness. Mr. and Mrs. Constans; many are called but tonight, *you've* been chosen!'

There was a shriek from the second row of the congregation. Not that sort of shriek. A real shriek. For a moment nothing seemed to be happening; then the two axemen sprang forwards and returned shortly afterwards with an elderly couple, who were struggling with them in a spirited but entirely pointless way. At last the remaining dribble of fight evaporated and they stood facing Godfearing George with all the light-hearted exuberance of rabbits caught in the headlamps of a rapidly approaching lorry.

'And your name is?'
'Mmmmmmm.'

'Could you just speak up, Mr. Constans? The gods can hear you, of course, but we can't.'

'Flavius Constans,' the man whimpered.

'And you're a retired executioner?' Mr. Constans nodded feebly. 'That must have been a horrible job, Flavius. Didn't you ever wonder whether the people you executed might actually have been innocent?'

Mr. Constans snivelled. Clearly the thought had occurred to him, once or twice. Godfearing George turned to Mrs. Constans, who was somewhat belatedly trying never to have been born, and gave her a smile that would have stripped paint.

'And how about you – Domitilla, isn't it?' Mrs. Constans made a very small, very shrill noise, like a fieldmouse in a blender. 'How did you feel about all this, Domitilla, sharing your bed with a man who made his living by killing people? Didn't you sometimes wonder, Domitilla? Anyway, worshippers and females, how about a good, fervent prayer for the souls of our two contestants, who are going to play God's My Witness here tonight.'

There was a confused mumbling, like many angry bees. Mr. and Mrs. Constans tried to cling to each other, but the axemen parted them with the shafts of their axes. Godfearing George took a bundle of cards from a cedarwood chest which one of the stern young women had presented to him. Someone somewhere dimmed some lights. There was absolute silence.

'Now,' Godfearing George intoned. 'I'm sure I don't have to remind you of the rules. This first round is all about religious knowledge. For each question you get wrong, you get the opportunity to spend five thousand years in the Bottomless Pit Of Sulphur – that's after you're dead, of course, although I'm sure you don't need me to tell you that life is but a dream. For each correct answer, you get five denarii, which you'll be entitled to offer to the god of your choice when we play Sacrifice of the Century – always supposing you live that long, of course. Right then, Flavius, you have the choice of answering questions on Myths, Orthodoxy or Heresy.'

'Myths, please,' said Mr. Constans.

'You've chosen Myths,' said Godfearing George, 'and you have five seconds in which to answer the following question.'

The lights dimmed ever so slightly. You could have built tower blocks on the silence.

'Tell me, then, Flavius,' said Godfearing George, and Jason could feel the palms of his hands becoming distinctly moist, 'in the legend of the Seven Against Thebes, what were the names of King Adrastus's daughters?'

Mr. Constans seemed to freeze. A great drum somewhere offstage marked the passing of the seconds: one, two, three ...

'Deipyla,' Mr. Constans croaked.

'And?'

'Aegeia.'

'Correct!' The congregation sagged with relief, and someone actually did shout "Hallalujah". 'Heaven be praised, Mr. Constans,' said Godfearing George, 'Deipyla and Aegeia is right. Now, Mr. Constans, your second question is ...'

To his utter astonishment, Jason knew the answer to this one (who removed the bones of Orestes from Tegea?), which was plainly more than could be said for Mr. Constans. On the fifth drumbeat he gasped out 'Mercury,' and the silence in the hall solidified still further. A wild guess. Jason shuddered to think what you got for a wild guess. It almost certainly wasn't a souvenir cheque-book and pen.

'I'm sorry,' said Godfearing George, 'but your sins have found you out, Mr. Constans. The answer is, of course, Lichas. I expect it was on the tip of your tongue, wasn't it? Well, you'll have five thousand years in Tartarus to reflect on that, won't you? Now then, Mrs. Constans, do you want to answer questions on Myths, Orthodoxy or Heresy?'

Mrs. Constans squeaked pitifully.

'Heresy it is, then. Now, in the accursed rituals of the Paphlagonians ...'

Mrs. Constans didn't do terribly well.

'Oh dear,' said Godfearing George, 'that's two incorrect answers, Mrs. Constans, and as I'm sure you're aware that means immediate decapitation. Never mind, let's have a really heartfelt prayer for the soul of Mrs. Constans, worshippers and females. She's been a truly wretched contestant ...'

And that was more or less all that Jason could take for one day. There were some people, he knew, who didn't believe in the gods; not these gods, not any gods. That had always amazed him; it was like not believing in cholera. The two certain things about human life are, first, that there are gods; second, that pretty well all the gods would benefit enormously from a good hard kick in the head. With a yell that should have caused serious damage to the structure of the building, he unsheathed the Sword of Thingummytite and hurled himself at the dais ...

Only to find that it wasn't there. And neither was he.

XIV

'Well, then.'
   Jason considered his options. He had, within the space of a relatively short time, defied the gods, been to Hell, beaten up the Driver of the Spoil and the Grim Reaper, been made to feel about twelve years old by his mother, discovered that he had Free Will, discovered that, on the contrary, his entire life had been planned out for him from the start by the personification of laughter and an eagle, acquired a three-headed dog, mislaid a three-headed dog, been taught most but not all of the funniest joke ever, routed a divine army, spent a long time in his own shirt pocket and tried without success to murder a game show host. More or less the only thing he hadn't done in the last few days, in fact, was have a decent meal.

   But there is that within a man that drives him ever onwards, just as the power of the seasons drives the roots of flowers into the hard earth; and so he decided, against his better judgment, to open his eyes and find out what was going to happen to him next. He was, after all, a Hero whether he liked it or not, and when he had been offered the choice between the path of Luxury and the path of Glory he had chosen the path marked Diversion. Although he was no expert, he had an instinctive feeling that that came under the heading of Asking for Trouble. Anyway, he opened his eyes.
   'So?'

He looked round, and the first thing he saw was sandwiches. Ham, beef, cheese, sardine and prawn sandwiches; also a pork pie, a plate of sausage rolls, two Cornish pasties and an iced bun.

'This,' said the voice above his head, 'is not a bribe.'

'No,' Jason replied, torn with indecision. 'Of course it isn't.' It had been difficult, but he had made up his mind. To start with, the beef.

'And since it's not a bribe,' the voice continued, as the sandwich jacknifed out of his hand and skittered away like a frightened kitten, 'it would be best if you didn't eat any of it until you've decided on your verdict.'

'I just did,' Jason said. 'I thought the beef first, then a bit of that pie, then ...'

'About the future of the human race.'

'Oh, that. Well, I know for a fact that some of them aren't allowed to eat beef, or pork, so they really won't mind if ...'

'About whether the gods should be allowed to destroy laughter.'

Jason remembered. It had been nice when there was just the food to think about, but clearly his destiny, the world's destiny and the destiny of the beef sandwiches were all somehow interlinked; how, he had no idea, but that was all right, he had never claimed he was Marcus Aurelius. Ah yes, the world. He considered the matter with the small area of his brain not mentally eating beef sandwiches, and after a short while he delivered the following judgment.

'Well,' he said, 'if that place, or world, or whatever you want to call it, that I saw just now was what the world would be like if the gods did away with comedy, then I don't think a lot of it and personally I wouldn't like to live there. On the other hand, I wouldn't like to live in Florida, but a lot of people are very taken with Florida, and who am I to say they're wrong? I mean, one man's meat ...'

Meat. Ham. Beef. Pork. Chicken. Turkey. Veal. Lamb.

Sausages. 'One man's meat,' he forced himself – salami! Dear God, was there anything in the whole of creation as wonderful as a salami and mozarella salad, with fresh white bread on the side and – he forced himself to continue, 'is another man's poison and all that. I could just fancy a poison meat casserole, as it happens, but never mind. What I'm getting at is ... Are you still there?'

'Yes.'

'What I'm getting at is ... Will there be any mustard? Eventually, I mean?'

'Quite possibly.'

'What I'm trying to say is that I refuse to make a judgment, one way or another. I know what I want and what I'd do, but I'm blowed if I'm going to lay down the law to anybody else. Please stop me before I finally drift over the edge into complete incoherence, but I don't hold with deciding things for people. My dad does that, and I don't respect him very much for it. I don't think it's right to decide what other people's lives are going to be like. Personally, when I think of the hash browns, corned beef hash, no, the hash, the cock-up I've made of my own life, I can't really say that I'm in any position to shape other people's. By the way, exactly why is all this up to me, anyway?'

'Because.'

'Ah. I might have guessed. Well, if you want me to decide between you and the gods, then, bearing in mind all the experiences I've had over the last few days, what I've seen of you and the various insights I've had into the way the gods go about things, and also bearing in mind the fact that Jupiter has always bossed me about and apparently you've been manipulating me ever since I was born and I always seem to find myself doing what my mother tells me to do, my decision is that I choose whichever side will make it possible for me to eat all this food at the earliest opportunity. Satisfied?'

'No. Like I said, it's not a bribe. More a sort of – what's

the word? Torture, that's it. Until you make up your mind and reach a decision, citing good reasons, you can't have any. Now get on with it.'

Jason scowled and, with the speed of a cat pouncing on a trailing ball of wool, hurled himself at an Eccles cake, which promptly scuttled away down a rabbit-hole.

'Are you Prometheus?' Jason asked.

'I am,' Prometheus replied.

Jason looked around; he had no idea where the voice was coming from. 'Where are you?' he said. 'I can't see you.'

'I'm not surprised.'

'Why's that?'

'You're not looking in the right direction.'

Jason scanned through three hundred and sixty degrees. Nothing; well, lots of sandwiches and pies and pasties and cakes – and, he noticed, a Black Forest Gateau and some cheese straws which he'd previously overlooked. He loved cheese straws. Not that he was averse to cocktail olives, crisps, cashew nuts, Ritz crackers with little bits of fishy carnage on them and baby frankfurters, and right now he could eat the stale bread left out for the birds. Yes, lots of food. But no Titans of any description whatsoever.

'Why me?' he asked. 'Because will not be acceptable as an explanation.'

'Why not?'

'Because it's meaningless and patronising and ...'

'No,' Prometheus replied, 'Why not is the answer to your enquiry. Now, if you don't mind coming to a decision ...'

'No.'

'The pasties are going cold.'

'I'm not hungry.'

'Now look here ...'

'No.' Jason folded his arms, and there was a scream of pain and terror. He looked down and saw Prometheus in his shirt pocket, pinned to the wall of his chest by a gigantic forearm. He quickly removed his arm and apologised. 'What on earth are you doing in there?' he added.

'Damn you, Jason Derry,' said the diminutive giant. 'Why must you always be asking questions?'

Calmly, Jason lifted Prometheus out of his pocket and sat him down on the palm of his hand. 'Because,' he replied. 'Now, either you can tell me what's going on, properly this time, or else you can be put between two slices of bread and eaten. The choice is yours.'

'Where are you going to get two slices of bread from, then?'

'I can do without bread,' Jason replied, 'at a pinch.'

'It would be cannibalism.'

'Very probably.'

'I taste horrible.'

'How would you know?'

'I can't explain what's happening,' Prometheus said furiously, 'until you've made the decision.'

'I can't make the decision,' Jason shouted back, 'until you've explained.'

'What's so difficult, for crying out loud?' Prometheus shrieked. 'It's us or them, don't you understand?'

'Which is which?'

Prometheus didn't reply; instead, he tucked his head between his knees and started to hum at the top of his voice. Jason swore and then put him gently down on a slice of anchovy toast, which immediately lifted into the air like a magic carpet and whisked him away into mid-air.

It was then that Jason came to a decision and the decision was that he'd had enough. He stood up, and as he did so he became aware of something round and hard, like a cricket ball, in his trouser pocket. It was uncomfortable, and so without looking at it he pulled it out and hurled it away with all his strength. Doing that was meant to make him feel better. It did. Much better.

'Oh,' he said, 'I see.'

'I thought you would.'

Prometheus was standing beside him.

'Hello' Prometheus,' he said. 'You've grown a lot since I saw you last.'

And indeed he had. He was now about eight feet tall and still going strong.

'And what do you see?' Prometheus said.

'Hang on,' Jason said. He made a sideways lunge at a cream horn, which stayed very still and let him catch it without a trace of a struggle. He ate it. Served it right.

'Now then,' he said, licking cream off his upper lip. 'What do I see? I see that the thing I just threw away was the world I was just in, the one where there were no jokes and the gods were in control. I see that I threw it so hard that it's shortly going to punch a hole through the wall of the space/time continuum and vanish for ever.'

'Very good,' Prometheus said. He snapped his fingers and a guided eclair hopped up from the ground and piloted itself neatly into Jason's mouth. 'What else?'

'I see that I subconsciously decided to do that because I don't hold with the gods. They exist all right, but there's no point in encouraging them. They're quite big and strong enough to take care of themselves. As it is, they run the world as a huge game, scoring points for all the horrible things they trick us into doing. But it's we who do them, of our own free will (if you'll pardon the expression); they just persuade us into it, like Dad persuaded me into being a Hero. No, stuff the gods. And the only weapon we have against them is laughter, because once there is laughter then nobody, however serious-minded or humourless he may be, will be able to take a bunch of clowns like Jupiter and Minerva and Mars and Neptune seriously for more than five minutes. Am I right?'

By way of affirmation a sausage roll hopped up onto his shoulder and slid down his chest into his hand. A moment later a salt-cellar appeared, running frantically along and puffing. Late as usual.

'On the other hand, laughter itself cannot rule the world because it is a force of anarchy – did I just say that? Where do I pick these expressions up from, I wonder? – it's a force of anarchy and cannot assert itself or exert authority. You can dissuade people from invading the country next door by making jokes, but you can't make them do it. Thus Gelos can never rule.'

'Actually,' said Prometheus, as a doughnut snapped itself into two and one half floated towards Jason's face, 'you've got the right conclusion but for the wrong reason. Hence only half a doughnut. But do please carry on.'

'Finally,' Jason said, 'I make this decision of my own free will, and I'm the only person in the history of the world who can, because ... Hang on, that can't be right.'

'Don't think about it,' Prometheus urged. 'Look, have some profiteroles.' Profiteroles like chocolate-sauce-drenched cannonballs obligingly bobbed in the air in front of Jason's eyes, but he ignored them.

'No, but seriously,' Jason said. 'A couple of pages must have fallen out here or something, because ...'

'Stay with it, Jason,' Prometheus said, 'and don't talk with your mouth empty.' He turned to make impatient gestures at a cheesecake which had overslept and was now dashing towards them, yawning and struggling into its kiwi-fruit as it ran.

'I make this decision of my own free will,' Jason repeated slowly, 'and I'm the only person in the history of the world who can, because ... Look –'

'Just say it.'

'*Because it is fated.* Now just look here, will you?'

'There now,' Prometheus said soothingly, between sighs of relief, 'that wasn't so bad, now was it? Have a peach melba.'

Jason shook his head angrily. 'I don't want a peach melba,' he snapped. 'I want an explanation.'

'Oh don't start all that again.'

'How can I have free will if it was fated all along?'

'It was fated that you should have free will,' Prometheus replied. 'Brandy snap?'

'Bugger brandy snaps.'

'Cream slice?'

'Stop drivelling away about food and tell me what it means. I don't object to revelations as such, but I do insist on them being intelligible. I mean, how would Saint Paul have felt if Someone had popped up on the road to Damascus, thrown him off his horse and then said "The cauliflower is mightier than the hairdryer"?'

'Apple doughnut?'

There was a long silence.

'What did you just say?'

'Would you like an apple doughnut?'

'Look ...'

'Two apple doughnuts?'

'With fresh cream?'

Prometheus shuddered slightly. 'Of course,' he said.

Nature held its breath while Jason thought about it. After all, it wasn't as if it was entirely illogical, was it? Everybody else is predestined, but it is foretold that one day a Hero will arise who is able to choose for himself. *Apple* doughnuts. Oh, sod it, yes, why not?

'Since you're offering,' Jason said, 'yes.'

'Yes what?'

'Yes please?'

'That's better.' Prometheus nodded to a waiting spirit, who hared off to Plato's ideal world to borrow a couple of apple doughnuts. Luckily he got the last two. He returned.

'Not bad,' Jason said, licking his fingers. 'Is that it, then?'

'Not quite,' said Prometheus.

Instinctively, Jason made a grab at the nearest plate, but missed by six inches. The food was playing hard to get again.

'Don't try to fight it,' Prometheus advised him. 'Think how embarrassing it would be going out to dinner and having the prawn cocktail leap out of the glass and hide under the sideboard until you've gone. Everyone else would be wondering which fork to use, and you'd be scooping in yours with a butterfly net.'

'If this is your idea of helping me stay unbiased and impartial ...'

Prometheus laughed. 'Blow that,' he replied. 'You've made the decision. Now we need you on our side for the actual fighting.'

'Ah,' Jason said. 'Fighting.'

'Didn't I mention the fighting?'

'Not in so many words, no.'

'Well,' Prometheus said, 'when the gods find out that the world they had such high hopes for has been kicked into touch and is now entirely beyond their reach, there's a material risk that they might feel rather upset. Particularly,' Prometheus added, 'as they have now sworn to destroy this world so that they can move everything and everybody onto the other one. And you know how it is with gods; once they've sworn to do something, then it's just got to be done ...'

'Balls,' Jason replied.

Prometheus shook his head, startling a flock of lemon meringue pies that had pitched in a nearby tree. 'You're thinking of promises to mortals,' he said. 'That's different.* I'm talking about a promise Jupiter has made to himself. He can't break that.'

'Can't he?'

---

*Promises made by gods to mortals are binding on the gods, but the gods reserve the right to interpret the terms of the promise.

Promises made by gods to other gods are also binding on the parties concerned; but this is effectively a dead letter, since a god can always point to the relevant Betamax world on which the promise actually was fulfilled and thus justifiably claim to have carried out his pledge.

Promises made by gods to themselves actually are binding, partly because the Possibility Police insist, partly because gods, being immortal, have to live with themselves rather longer than the rest of us.

'No. So you see there may actually be quite a bit of fighting in the not too distant future.' Prometheus paused for a moment. 'That'll be nice, won't it?'

'Will it?'

'I'd have thought you'd have been pleased,' the Titan replied. 'You're a Hero. Heroes like fighting. It's what they're good at.'

'That doesn't always follow,' Jason replied. 'My mum's cousin Henry is a dentist, and people are always saying how good he is at it, and he doesn't enjoy it at all. Sometimes I think it's that way with me and Heroism.'

'Nonsense,' Prometheus said firmly. 'You'll enjoy it once it's started, I'm sure. And besides, you aren't supposed to know the meaning of fear.'

'Actually,' Jason confessed, 'I looked it up in the dictionary. Came as quite a surprise, actually. I always thought it was some sort of large bird.'

'All right, all right,' Prometheus said impatiently, 'I should have said you know no fear. Now can we ...?'

'Maybe not fear,' Jason interrupted, 'but acute apprehension and blind panic I can manage quite easily. It's just practice, after all, and these last few days ...'

Just then, Jason felt something cold and wet against the back of his hand. Something cold, wet and tripartite. He looked down.

'Hello, Cerberus, where the hell have you been?' he started to ask, and then he noticed that Prometheus was staring at the dog with a look of combined loathing and horror. Normally Jason wouldn't have thought anything of it, since he knew a lot of people who reacted to dogs in precisely that way; but Prometheus hadn't seemed the type. He looked again. In one of its three mouths, the dog was holding a small blue, green and brown sphere that seemed extremely familiar.

'Oh hell,' Jason said. 'He hasn't, has he?'

Prometheus nodded. 'Looks like it to me,' he replied in a hoarse whisper. 'You threw the Betamax world away;

Fido here has fetched it back for you. Oh *hell!*'

The dog, sensing that man's best friend had cocked it up again, laid his ears back and wandered over to the shade of a boulder, where he proceeded to lodge the Betamax world between his front paws and chew it. Jason and Prometheus looked at each other.

'We'd better get it back from him quick,' Prometheus said.

'By *we* ...'

'Don't stand there arguing the toss. Get the bloody thing.'

Jason shrugged and reached for the surface-to-air scotch egg. It shied away. Jason started to protest, and Prometheus apologised. 'What are you up to, though?' he added.

'Canine psychology,' Jason replied. 'I'll also need a Bakewell tart and some sausages.'

These were provided and Jason wandered over to the boulder, sat down and started to eat. A moment later, the dog was sitting beside him giving him that wistful, pathetic look that all dogs seem to have in common. Then it opened its mouth to make the quintessential doggy hopeful panting noise, and of course the Betamax world rolled out of its jaws and trundled along the ground. Prometheus swooped down, picked it up and shoved it inside the front of his robe. Jason popped a foodstuff into each of the three sets of jaws, collected the Betamax world and let fly.

For the record, the Betamax world didn't leave the space/time continuum at all. The friction it encountered on leaving the Earth's atmosphere set it alight and it soon degenerated into a comet; given its unique genesis, however, it did not behave exactly as other comets do; that is to say, it combined the regularity of trajectory which is a characteristic of comets with the innate cussedness of all divine or semi-divine artefacts. For the rest of time, therefore, it circled through the galaxy, turning up with remorseless regularity exactly when it was least expected.

In any event, it ceased to be a Betamax world, and that was just as well. Because no sooner had it left Jason's hand than the sky darkened and the sun made a dash for the safety of a dense cloudbank, pausing only to glint significantly on the speartips of the vanguard of a huge divine army making its way rapidly towards the surface of the planet.

Religious revivals have been endemic on the Number One World ever since the gods retired and went to live in the sun. Nobody is exactly sure why. One view is that mankind has a desperate need to believe in something, preferably something so blatantly absurd that only blind, unquestioning faith will suffice – for example, the belief which sprang up in the late nineteenth century and was still widely current in Jason Derry's time and which held that human beings were not in fact created at all but were somehow the descendants of bald, mutant monkeys. The other view is that there is never anything much on television during the summer.

Never, though, has there been a religious revival as sudden and as widespread as the one which followed Apollo's first broadcast to the world. Perhaps it was simply his magnetic charisma – Apollo, after all, looked like a young Greek god,* had a particularly appealing smile and a way of looking into the camera as if it had been the camera he had been searching for all these years – or perhaps it was simply the fact that what he was saying happened to be true. In any event, no sooner had he left the studio and wandered out into the carpark to reclaim his chariot than the entire world suddenly decided that it had seen the light. Those who had seen the broadcast immediately went and told those who hadn't and (being human) threatened to burn them alive if they

---

* He was a young Greek god, which helped.

didn't join in. So quickly, in fact, did the revival gather momentum that half an hour after the broadcast not only was there a High Priest of Durham but he was on TV asking for money.

Another aspect of this revival that made it different from most of its predecessors was the fact that although the gods were now universally believed in and revered, they were also intensely unpopular. Apollo had not pulled his punches. He had made it perfectly clear that the gods were not cuddly.

There had, of course, been religious protest groups before – one thinks automatically of the Guild of Merchant Plasterers Against the Crucifixion which enjoyed a brief prominence during the English Civil War – but none of them had expressly set out to believe the gods into oblivion. That, however, was what Apollo had achieved, simply by stating that it was ordained that if Mankind truly had faith, the gods would not be able to achieve their intended purpose. There was an oracle in precisely those terms, he had said. Which was, of course, perfectly true; as the god of prophecies he had seen to it personally.

The eagle came swooping back just as he had got the winged horse back into the traces of the chariot.

'Well?' Apollo asked.

'Absolutely,' the eagle replied. She had been sent to check that the broadcast had achieved the desired effect, and had just flown round the world in thirty-seven seconds. 'It's worked like a charm.'

'Are you sure?'

'No problems,' replied the eagle. 'Everybody singing hymns and sacrificing like it was going out of fashion. If I was a white ram right now, I'd be very scared indeed.'

'Fine.' Apollo replied. 'Look, do you have to do that?'

'Do what?'

'Sharpen your beak against my spoiler. I've only just had this chariot resprayed, and ...'

'Sorry,' said the eagle. 'Would it help if I assumed human form?'

Apollo remembered that he had seen the eagle in human form not long ago. 'Yes,' he said. 'Why not?'

The eagle became Mary, and sat in the passenger seat of the chariot. She adjusted the rear-view mirror and examined herself in it.

'The trouble with being an eagle,' she said at last, 'is, it does terrible things to your skin. Dries it out. It'll take three days in a mud-pack to get rid of these lines.'

'What's going to happen now?' Apollo asked. Mary looked at him and giggled.

'I don't know, do I?' she said. 'Who do you think I am, God almighty?'

Apollo frowned irritably. 'You seemed to have a pretty good idea just now,' he said, 'when you were telling me what to do. If this is some kind of practical joke ...'

Mary assured him that it wasn't. 'If it was a joke,' she said, 'the last thing it would be would be practical. No, I know what should happen now, of course, but there are no guarantees.'

'What should happen, then?'

'Jupiter,' Mary said, 'should set out to destroy the Earth. Halfway down, he will be met with a surge of faith in an essentially non-violent, ecologically aware carbon copy of himself who wouldn't willingly uproot a dandelion if there was any way of avoiding it. All this faith will get right up his spine and he'll be forced to pigeonhole the entire project.'

'Fine.'

'Well, up to a point fine,' said Mary, powdering her nose. 'The difficulty will be that he'll be very much aware that he wants to demolish the earth but can't, and this may make him resentful. And from what I can remember of the faith mechanics I learnt at college, there's nothing to stop him taking it out on someone in a big way, just so long as that person doesn't happen to be a planet. If I were you,' she concluded, closing her powder compact with a snap, 'I'd be distinctly edgy.'

'Me?'

'You,' said Mary. 'I don't want to worry you, but you are directly responsible for thwarting him. He should be arriving any time now.'

Apollo looked up at the sky; there was a thick bank of black cloud moving in from the east, and another from the west. Although he wasn't to know it, there was in fact another contingent trying to get in from the north, but it had got held up in a contraflow system over Finland.

'What can I do?' he said.

'Try and be dignified about it,' Mary replied. 'Well, it's been nice. Ciao.'

'Hold on,' Apollo said, grabbing her by the wrist.

'Oh, don't let's start all that again.'

Apollo blushed furiously. 'I didn't mean that,' he said. 'I mean, you've got me into this, now you'd better ...'

'Nothing to do with me,' Mary said, 'Gods have free will, remember. And now I really do have to be going.'

'Where?'

'To meet the others. Prometheus and Gelos and the Derry kid. So if you'll just stop crushing my wrist for a moment, I'll be getting along.'

'Let me give you a lift,' Apollo said.

Actually, said a tiny voice at the back of Mary's mind, in a part of her brain that she had recently only used for operating some semi-redundant feathers on her left wing, he's quite good-looking, in a way. For a god. Nice smile.

'All right,' she said. 'Head for the Caucasus.'

'Why?'

'That's where the others are. Come on, hurry up.'

'We'll be safe there?'

Mary considered this for a moment. 'I always think safe is such a terribly subjective word, don't you?'

'What word would you choose, then?'

'Conveniently-situated.'

'Oh.' Apollo hesitated, his hand on the ignition key. The starter motor system had been one of the trickiest parts of the whole conversion job, and Vulcan had finally managed it by wiring the starter motor up to an electrode fitted to the lead horse's rump. When you turned the key, it gave the horse a severe electric shock. Being a divine horse, it was supposed to understand by that that the driver wanted to be taken somewhere; but even divine horses can only stand so much of that sort of thing before they start lashing out with their hind legs. Fortunately for his peace of mind, Apollo wasn't mechanically minded and hadn't yet considered how the thing worked. 'Conveniently situated for what?'

'For a good view of the battle of course.'

Apollo was firmly of the opinion that the best view of a battle in which Jupiter was on the opposing or less friendly side was from the other side of space and, if possible, time, and said so. Mary replied by taking what later turned out to be a small sacrificial dagger from her handbag and pressing it, not unkindly, into the small of Apollo's back.

'I'm hijacking this chariot to the Caucasus,' she said. 'You know you're immortal but maybe I'm not convinced. Shall we go now?'

'I . . .' Apollo considered for a moment and then turned the ignition key. 'Are you sure you know what you're doing?' he asked.

'Yes,' Mary replied confidently. She was by inclination a truthful person, so it was for the best, she reckoned, that he hadn't asked her if what she was doing was sensible or not.

One of the leading drawbacks to travelling to battle in the heart of an inky black thundercloud is that you get very wet indeed. If you are carrying an ample supply of lightning bolts, there is also the risk of a serious short-circuit. Jupiter was therefore not at his most affable during the journey from the sun to Earth. The Captain of Spectral

Warriors who had interrupted his light lunch with an enquiry about the possibility of overtime payments for the Forces of Darkness (it being daytime) and who was now buzzing sadly along behind the Host in the shape of a small bee, was generally considered to have got away with it lightly.

Minerva, as Officer i/c Destruction, North-western Sector, was sitting in her winged-dragon-propelled mobile command centre studying a confused bundle of maps and a dog-eared copy of Baedeker when Mars knocked tentatively at the door and stepped in.

'Well, Ma, what is it now?' Minerva took off her glasses and looked at him sourly. She tended to be impatient with failures, and the fact that after the previous debacle Mars had been temporarily suspended from his duties at War and put in charge of Troop Welfare and Entertainment made her less ready to waste valuable time on him than she would otherwise have been, which was not very. 'If you want me to sing in the Camp Concert, I'm afraid I'm far too busy.'

Mars, who had heard Minerva sing, assured her that he quite understood. 'No,' he said, 'what I really wanted was a quiet word about what's going to happen when we destroy the world.'

'We've been into that already,' Minerva said. 'And I do take your point, but there it is. You can't make omelettes without breaking eggs.'

'I don't want a bloody omelette, Min.' Mars gave her a despairing look. 'For crying out loud, we're all going to die in about twenty minutes and nobody seems to care a damn. What's got into you all?'

'We're trying not to think about it,' Minerva replied, putting her spectacles back on and returning to her paperwork. 'I can only recommend that you try to do the same. Close the door after you, please.'

On his way back to the Welfare Office, Mars met Diana. She had been given the post of Annihilation Liaison

Officer, and she had been going round the army trying to
find out what it meant.

'I don't know,' Mars replied when she asked him. 'I
don't particularly want to find out, either. The whole point
about knowledge, I always thought, was that you find
something out and then you remember it for the rest of
your life. In the circumstances it all seems rather pointless,
don't you think?'

Diana ignored him. 'I'm a bit worried about Pol,' she
said.

'Pol?' Mars stared. 'You're worried about Apollo?'

'Well, he is my brother,' Diana replied defensively. 'I'm
just hoping he's going to be all right.'

'How can he be all right?' Mars shouted. 'He's going to
die in just under fifteen minutes, according to the
schedule. So are the rest of us.'

'All right, yes, you needn't go on about it,' Diana
replied. 'What I mean is, is he going to be all right till
then?'

Mars left her and wandered off in search of the Officers'
Mess. In his opinion, the description fitted the entire
enterprise, but the part of it he was interested in was the
small, tastefully furnished area selling intoxicants.

He finally tracked it down at the south-eastern corner of
the cloud and went in. The only other customer was
Neptune, who was sitting at the bar trying to drown his
sorrows – a difficult undertaking for a sea-god.

'Siddown, Ma,' he said. 'Have a li'l drink. Think we just
got time for a quick one.'

'What are you having?'

'Think I'll have a Gorgon's Revenge.'

Mars looked at him. 'Are you sure?'

Neptune hiccuped and grinned. 'Course I'm sure,' he
replied. 'It's the only time in the history of the world a
man can have five Gorgon's Revenges on an empty
stomach and not have to worry about the morning after.
Gesundheit.'

'You have a point there, Uncle Nep,' said Mars. 'Make mine the same.'

Soon afterwards the barman brought the drinks, and Neptune, by way of experiment, picked out a diamond from his dress crown and dropped it into the glass. It dissolved.

'I've always wondered what they put in these things,' he remarked, staring into the glass. The fumes blinded him for a moment.

'Best not to ask, so they say,' replied Mars. 'Well, here's health.'

Neptune looked round. 'Where?'

'No,' Mars said, 'it's a toast. Cheers.'

'Mud in your eye,' Neptune answered. They drank deeply and for a long time were silent.

'I think I'll have another one of those,' said Neptune.

'Why not?' Mars replied. 'That way, things can only get better.'

The cloud, meanwhile, had smashed its way through a very confused stratosphere and was rushing down towards the surface of the planet. It was just gathering momentum nicely when the prayers hit it.

Being hit by a prayer is no joke. The first thing that happened was that all the lights went out. When the back-up power supply came on, Neptune and Mars found themselves looking at something quite unexpected.

'Here,' Neptune demanded querulously, 'what do they put in these things?'

A shaft of golden light had impaled the cloud like a skewer through a veal *souvlaki*. There were a lot of – well, it went against the grain to say this, but there was no avoiding the fact that they were angels. They were also holding flaming swords.

'How do they do that?' asked Mars.

'I dunno,' Neptune replied. 'Oven-gloves, maybe.'

As if the sunbeam and the angels weren't bad enough, there were other indications that something quite out of

the ordinary was happening. There were a lot of quite
unsolicited flowers, for example, and the air was heavy
with strong, sweet, cheap perfume. Both Mars and
Neptune suddenly felt an overwhelming urge to grant
requests.

'I don't know about you,' Neptune said, 'but right now
I'm feeling a bit funny. I think I'll just go and lie down for
a minute.'

Mars nodded carefully. 'Good idea,' he said. 'Which
way is the door?'

Outside they stopped again and stared. Peculiar though
the other manifestations had been, this was something
else.

It was Jupiter. Jupiter standing in the middle of the
cloud's parade ground. Jupiter smiling.

You could see at once that he was fighting it, with every
fibre of his supreme being. And the harder he tried, it
seemed, the harder it was to resist. The golden sunbeam
had got him right in the navel.

'Do you think we ought to ...' Mars's voice drained
away.

'Help, you mean?'

'Well, yes.'

Neptune shook his head. 'Wouldn't do that,' he said.

'You wouldn't?'

'Certainly not,' he said. Twenty thousand years of
sibling rivalry blossomed on his face into a grin the size of
California. 'That'd be blasphemy.'

'Blasphemy?'

'Absolutely,' Neptune replied. 'To attempt to assist
Jupiter would be implicitly to deny his omnipotence. No,
let the old bastard sort it out for himself. I'm going back to
the bar.'

'But ...'

'My shout.'

Mars shot another glance at the Father of Gods and
Men and headed back to the Mess tent.

'What's going on, Nep?' he asked.

'It's a prayer,' Neptune replied, hopping up onto a bar stool and eating olives. 'A biggy, too. In fact, that's the biggest prayer I've ever seen in the whole of my life. And Jupe's got it right through his guts. Champagne!' he called to the barman.

Apollo and Mary arrived in the Caucasus just in time to see the cloud grind to a halt, waver and slowly start to retreat back into the sun. The golden shaft gradually faded, until there was nothing left but a little sprinkling of silver filings, the residue of a few inappropriate prayers contributed by members of the Tokyo Stock Exchange.

'Thanks for the lift,' Mary said. 'Now, are you going to hang around and catch the fun?'

'Do I have a choice?'

'Of course you have a choice,' Mary replied, pressing very gently with the small knife. 'Weren't you listening to what I was saying about gods having free will?'

'I don't mean a choice between staying and getting knifed,' Apollo said. 'I don't really call that a choice, do you?'

'It's what you expect the mortals to put up with most of the time,' Mary started to say; but then she remembered what her mother had told her about not talking politics on a first date. Her mother hadn't mentioned the social effects of digging a small knife in the guy's back, so presumably that was OK.

'All right then,' Apollo was saying, 'so what's happening?'

'So far as I can see,' Mary replied, 'the gods have just tried to land and blow the Earth away, but all the prayers and faith you managed to whip up have forced them back again. That's it so far as destroying the Earth goes, at least for now. In about five minutes, I expect Jupiter will be back to kill somebody.'

'Fine.'

'Oh look,' Mary interrupted, 'there's Pro and Gel and the Derry kid. I think we should go over and have a word with them, don't you? They might be able to think of something to stop Jupiter killing us all. That'd be nice, wouldn't it?'

'Absolutely.'

Mary bit her lip indecisively. On the one hand, she knew it was totally counterproductive to go around throwing yourself at people; on the other hand, she had the feeling that unless she gave some sort of hint or indication at this stage, a promising relationship might simply fade away and die.

'I don't know if you were wondering,' she said, 'but there isn't anything between me and the Derry kid.'

'No?'

'No.'

'Well, there we go,' Apollo said. 'Do you think you might take that knife out of my back now?'

'There should be,' Mary went on. 'I mean, it was fated and so forth. But what the hell, just because a thing's fated doesn't mean to say you're stuck with it, does it?'

'Doesn't it?'

'And as for Pro and me,' Mary went on, finding it all rather harder work than she had originally anticipated but staying with it nevertheless, 'we really are just good friends. I mean, what there is between me and Pro is very special, don't get me wrong, but really, there's the age difference, the size difference, the species difference. You've got to be realistic about things like that, haven't you?'

'Ouch,' Apollo replied.

'Oh hell, *sorry*,' Mary replied. 'I'm just so clumsy sometimes you wouldn't believe it. My mother used to say to me ...'

Prometheus had seen them and was hurrying over. He looked the same, but there was somehow something different about him; if he had been a tune he'd be in stereo instead of mono.

'Pol, my boy,' he shouted, 'good of you to come. Just in time, too.'

'Hello, Uncle Pro,' replied Apollo resignedly. 'Look, if I'd known it was all going to get as messy as this ...'

'Don't be silly,' Prometheus said. 'And anyway, everything is going to be fine. We've got the eagle, the dog and the Derry boy ...'

'Hello,' said Jason, sheepishly. Meeting new gods for the first time always made him a little bit bashful.

Apollo nodded briefly and smiled a tight-lipped smile and then resumed his search for knowledge. 'Look, Uncle Pro,' he started to say; but Prometheus silenced him with a gesture of his hand.

'I know,' he said. 'But there's nothing to worry about. If Jupiter starts getting violent, Jason here will threaten to tell him the Joke.'

'What joke?'

'The Joke, idiot.'

Apollo's eyes widened like balloons in the course of being inflated. 'You mean to say *he* knows the Joke?'

'Most of it,' Prometheus replied. 'All of it except the punch line.'

'Ah. But even so ...'

'It's all right, don't worry,' Prometheus replied. 'I made sure that neither part of the Joke would be volatile without the other.'

Apollo thought of something. 'How come you know the Joke, Uncle Pro?'

'Uncle Pro doesn't know the Joke,' said Prometheus, 'but I do.'

Apollo didn't understand at first; then the truth dawned on him. He backed away. 'You mean you're ...'

'Thing.'

'Yes.' Apollo said, 'Begins with a G ... On the tip of my tongue ...'

'No, you fool, that's my name,' Prometheus snapped. 'It has pleased me to call myself Gelos and play at being a mere Form for a number of years, but in fact I'm your great-uncle, brother of Cronus and Rhea. Do you believe me?'

'Yes.'

'Well,' said Prometheus, 'just in case you don't ...'

He narrowed his eyes and gave Apollo a good long stare. Suddenly Apollo started to laugh, until he could feel his lungs straining to bursting point. In fact he was just about to black out when the laughter stopped as suddenly as it had begun.

'Again for the sake of convenience,' Prometheus continued, 'I'm sharing bodies with my old friend Prometheus at the moment. Minds, too. We've always had similar tastes in minds, Pro and I, haven't we, Pro? Yes, ever since I can remember, except I like mine a bit less cluttered. Well, we won't go into that now; it takes all sorts. I was only going to say. Later, Pro, all right? Please yourself, then. Sorry, Pol, as I was saying ...'

But before he could continue, his head snapped upwards. Apollo followed his gaze and saw something high up by the sun. He recognised it.

'What is it?' Mary said.

'Jupiter's coming back,' Prometheus replied. 'Right, everyone – action stations.'

'What might those be, exactly?'

'Er, you know, get ready and everything.'

'I take it,' Apollo said, 'that you do have a plan.'

'A plan, yes.'

'A plan of battle,' Apollo said. 'Stratagems and so forth.'

'Sort of.'

'And are you going to let us into the secret, or are we – ouch! For pity's sake, woman, mind what you're doing with that knife. You could do someone an injury.'

'It's all right, Mary,' Prometheus said, 'you can put it away now. Apollo won't desert us at a time like this.'

'Won't he though!' Apollo turned to make a dash for his chariot, only to feel the beginnings of another big laugh clogging his windpipe. 'All right,' he sighed, 'you win.'

'Let's hope so, anyway,' Prometheus replied. 'Now then, Pol, you and I and Mary and the dog will form the rearguard, and the rest of us ...'

'That only leaves me,' said Jason.

'The rest of us will form the front line contingents. Ready, Jason?'

'No.'

'Here they come.'

Strictly speaking, of course, it wasn't necessary for Jupiter to come at all. But if there was one thing the Sky-Father loved it was melodrama, and if there was going to be a big fight, he wanted to be there in person, pitching in and watching the bodies go splat. Sitting in the sun hurling thunderbolts was a poor substitute, he always felt, for actually getting to grips with an enemy's intestines.

His list of priorities was quite clear in his mind. Family first; Apollo and that ungrateful little git Jason Derry – he had something really hot in mind for him. Then, once the first flush of exuberance had worn off and been replaced with nice, grim resentment, he'd sort out Prometheus and that damn eagle. That would leave the highlight of the proceedings, his Uncle Thing, till last. Uncle Thing was the part he was looking forward to most.

As he roared through the air like a vindictive meteor, he quickly ran through the fundamentals of anatomy in his mind. A mental picture of his antagonists with little dotted lines and pairs of scissors drawn all over them draped itself across the retina of his inner eye and he made no effort to get rid of it.

Behind him streamed the selected elite of the divine special services unit. There was no point in cluttering the place up with rookies and idiots, not now that the demolition programme had been shelved indefinitely. For killing bolshy immortals you need quality, not quantity; and the Forms hurtling Earthwards in Jupiter's wake were the sort of abstraction that only a very powerful and extremely unbalanced mind could conceive of. Even he got the creeps just thinking about them, and yet they were merely personifications of the contents of his own head. Now that was scary.

Was he mad, Jupiter asked himself, as he zoomed through the Earth's atmosphere in a cloud of blue flames. He thought it over and decided that yes, he quite probably was. He only needed to look over his shoulder to know that his mind was so unhinged it was a miracle it didn't fall out of his ear.

Ah well. Too late to do anything about that now.

'And what,' Jason was asking, 'will the rest of you be doing while I'm ...?'

And then he saw the flames, and Jupiter at the head of his unspeakable squadron, and realised that he was on his own. Only he could do anything about all this, fix things so that never again would Jupiter be able to command that the world be destroyed. And why? Nobody seemed to know. Because it was fated. Brilliant.

There was a screaming sound – it was just the air being torn apart by the violence of their passing, but it sounded much worse. Jason squared his shoulders, drew the Sword of – I couldn't give a toss what it's supposed to be called, he said to himself, I shall call it Freckles – and took one step forward. He wouldn't mind doing this sort of thing if only people would tell him what was going on.

'Hiya, Dad,' he said.

Jupiter stopped in mid-air, and the shock-waves caused by his sudden loss of momentum sent clouds scudding across the skies of four continents.

'Hi there, Son,' Jupiter replied. 'You're for it this time.'

'Am I?'

'Oh yes,' replied Jupiter. 'I mean, this isn't your parking in a no-parking zone. This is where you and life part company. Sorry, lad, but there it is.'

'Oh well,' Jason said. 'In that case, knock knock.'

'You what, Son?'

'Knock knock,' Jason repeated. 'You're meant to say "Who's there?"'

Jupiter felt as if the air had given way under his feet. 'Now steady on, lad,' he said. 'Let's neither of us get carried away and say things we might regret later.'

'Say "Who's there?"'

'Certainly not,' Jupiter replied. 'Got you now, haven't I?'

'Who's there?' Jason said. 'Cassivelaunus. Cassivelaunus who?'

And then he dried.

Any stand-up comedian will tell you it's a horrible feeling, and when your audience is a Sky-God with an army of very bad ideas at his back, it can get really hairy. Jason opened his mouth and nothing came out of it.

'Go on, then,' Jupiter said, folding his arms and tapping his toe on a wisp of water vapour. 'Cassivelaunus who?'

'Er . . .'

'Cassivelaunus who?'

'Do you know the one about the travelling salesman who goes into this, um . . .'

'I asked you a question,' said Jupiter. 'Cassivelaunus who?'

And then Jason remembered. He couldn't say the punch line because he didn't know it. The dog did. He turned, whistled, and called, 'Here, boy!' as loudly as he could. The dog stayed exactly where he was.

'Is that it?' Jupiter asked. 'Cassivelaunus Here-Boy? I've found funnier things in Christmas crackers.'

'Here, boy!' Jason yelled. 'Cerberus! *Bad* dog!' The dog stood there and wagged his tail at him. Then, very slowly, it faded away.

Jason turned round and looked at his father. He smiled, and while he did so his brain was improvising furiously.

'Well?'

'Er,' said Jason, 'Cassie, the lawn is badly in need of mowing. Um ...'

'What?'

'You heard.'

'Cassie, the lawn is badly in need of mowing,' said Jupiter slowly, relishing every word. 'That's it, is it?'

'And let it be a lesson to you,' said Jason. 'Now, if you've quite finished ...'

'Oh no,' Jupiter said. 'I haven't even started yet.'

The Sky-God grinned, and for some reason that was the final straw. All the aggravation that had been building up inside Jason ever since this whole tiresome business had started suddenly came to the surface and exploded. There was something about Jupiter just then, Jason decided, that didn't only get up his nose, it went right the way through and half way down his throat. With a yell so blood-curdling you could have made black puddings with it, he swung the Sword Freckles round his head and charged.

Jupiter didn't stand a chance. The Forms standing behind him recognised this before he did, and before Jupiter had so much as raised his arm in a fruitless attempt to shield his face, the slowest of them was ploughing through the cumulo-nimbus and motoring nicely. As it rushed sunwards it could just hear the sound of somebody very large a long way away saying 'Ouch!' It didn't stop to find out who.

Jason, meanwhile, was getting nicely into his rhythm. He had split the Helmet of Authority, sliced the thunder-bolts into mortadella, shattered the Breastplate of Power and was just about to make an end of it when ...

'Jason!' said a voice behind him. 'You stop that immediately, you hear me?'

Jason sighed very, very deeply and lowered his sword.

'Yes, mum,' he said.

'So now you see.'

Jason nodded. He supposed that it made sense, after a

fashion. Or at least, if it didn't absolutely make sense, it was at least less glaringly nonsensical than a lot of things which passed for components of that great pile of unwashed laundry known for convenience as The Truth. Perhaps a better way of looking at it was that if it wasn't true it was at least what all the protagonists believed to be true. In such circumstances as these, Jason was beginning to realise, an untruth tends to become indistinguishable from the real thing, simply through the action of protective mimicry.

'Well then,' he said. 'Did you get all that, Mum?'

'No,' said Mrs. Derry.

Jason sighed. He would have to explain.

'Look,' he said, 'what Prometheus was saying was that the reason why it was –' Language, Jason realised, was a large part of the problem, because words say what they want to say, not what you want them to say – 'why it was fated from the start that I'd be the only one who could, like, stand up to Dad and sort all this lot out ...' He paused; somewhere his sentence had wrapped itself round his legs, like a fast-moving dog on a long lead. 'The reason why it had to be me,' he ventured, 'is that ... Well, in the beginning, there was this word, right ...'

'I think what Jason's trying to say,' Prometheus interrupted, 'is that Jason is unique in history because he has more of one particular quality than anyone else who's ever been, and it was this quality, this power, that was required in order to make the whole thing work.'

'Oh yes?' said Mrs. Derry politely. She had only the vaguest notion who this tall man was, and she wasn't sure she liked him. But he seemed to be saying that her son was a very special and important person, and she agreed with that. Like all mothers, she had known that from the very beginning, but it was nice to find someone who agreed with her.

'Let me put it this way,' Prometheus said. 'Some people say that love is the most powerful force in the Universe.

Well, you can take it from me that it isn't. Others say, rather more plausibly, that it's fear, greed, hope or faith that makes the world go round. They're wrong, too. As for those who say that what fuels and drives the Universe is the laws of physics, all I can say is that they're living in a world of their own. No, the most powerful and significant force in the Universe, the one thing that gets things done and makes things happen, is aggravation.'

'Aggravation?'

'Aggravation. Why is it, do you think, that all the little atoms move about within their molecules, bashing into each other like so many Christmas shoppers and creating the effect known to scientists as Brownian motion? Is it love, do you think, or fear, or belief in the Supreme Being? Like hell it is. The plain truth of the matter is that if you put more than two or three atoms together in a confined space for any length of time, sooner or later they're going to get on each other's wick, and then they start hurling themselves about and colliding with each other. They also shout a lot, but since the science of physics is in its infancy, nobody has yet constructed an instrument sensitive enough to monitor the voices of millions of tiny atoms debating with each other whose turn it is to do the washing up. Probably just as well, if you ask me.'

'I see,' lied Mrs. Derry. 'But what's that got to do with ...?'

'When Gelos and I,' Prometheus went on, 'came to the conclusion that something was going to have to be done about Jupiter if he wasn't going to get completely out of hand, we realised that the only thing powerful enough to stand up to him was a really massive dose of raw aggravation. Faith wasn't enough. It would just about be possible, if the world was allowed to lie fallow, if you like, for a thousand odd years so that it could build its faith reserves up to the maximum, to generate a faith field strong enough to repel Jupiter once, but it could only be once; after that, he would be able to come back once he'd licked his wounds and found another Betamax world to replace the one Jason disposed of for us, and have another go. No, somebody was going to have to sort out Jupiter himself, and for that purpose, only aggravation would do. So we set about creating the perfect aggravation conductor. We designed Jason.'

'Well,' said Mrs. Derry, 'that's fascinating. And now Jason and I must be getting along. Come on, Jason ...'

'The specifications,' Prometheus continued, 'were for a Hero who was at least as big and as strong and as brave as one of the old-time Big Three, Hercules, Theseus and Achilles – in other words, a son of Jupiter – but who had spent his entire life being put upon, shoved about and generally pushed around. That way, we could build up the necessary reservoir of aggravation, and then when the time was right we could prime it, so to speak, by letting him know just to what extent he'd been pushed around all these years, and further by giving him the impression that not just his mother and his father but everyone, on all sides, had been using him as a sort of human combination hammer, tin-opener and mole wrench. Finally we would put him in a position of enormous stress and fail him. That was what all that nonsense with the dog was for. There's no way we would have dared entrust the Joke or any part of it to him, let alone to a three-headed dog. We just let him think we had. We set him up good and proper. Sorry about that, Jason.'

'That's all right,' Jason said automatically. He had in fact been intending to pull Prometheus's head off and use it as a football ever since the truth of the matter had dawned on him, at that crucial moment when Cerberus had disappeared. Somehow, though, now that it came to it, he wasn't in the mood. So what?

'Anyway,' Prometheus said, 'we all saw what happened. Jupiter never knew what hit him. The combination of Jason's irritation and his own massive aggravation build-up, caused by the failure of his attack on Earth, led to the

most almighty outburst of pure, undiluted aggro, and
Jupiter just fused out. It was like putting a vastly exces-
sive current through a five-amp plug. Jason, of course, is a
superb natural conductor of aggravation, and so it just
went through him like water through a pipe.'

There was a long silence.

'What you mean is,' Mrs. Derry said at last, 'our Jason
saved the world.'

'Exactly,' Prometheus said. 'He lost his cool and
thereby saved the world.'

'And what about Dad?' Jason asked. 'Not that I'm all
that bothered, not after what he was going to do to me –
well, to all of us, really, but . . .'

'You mustn't blame him,' Prometheus said. 'The sad
truth is that Jupiter's been more or less off his rocker for a
very long time now, pretty well ever since I stole the first
Joke from heaven all those years ago. You see, unlike most
of the gods he actually did care about the world, and –
misguidedly, in my opinion – he felt very strongly that in
order to survive, mortals need an unshakable faith in the
gods. When I snookered him on that score, there was a
huge build-up of aggro inside him, and as we've seen he
just can't handle it. Something gave way inside his head,
and he's been missing on at least two cylinders ever since.
What's happened today has, I'm afraid, finally done for
the poor old devil. His supreme being days are well and
truly over, I fear.'

'Then what's going to happen?' Jason asked. 'Does that
mean that Thing is going to take over?'

'Perish the thought!' Prometheus replied. 'That would
be a very serious mistake, and Thing knows it. He's going
back into retirement, where he belongs. Going to write a
novel, he tells me, and I wish him the very best of luck.
No, what we've decided on is that Jupiter will carry on as
Supreme Being in name only, with Apollo as a sort of
Prince Regent. That way, Pol being Pol, the gods will
spend all their time bickering with each other and they'll

leave the mortals in peace. It'll mean the end of the Game, for one thing, and that can't be bad.'

'What Game?' Jason asked.

'And if Apollo ever does show any signs of getting above himself,' Prometheus went on, 'then we'll have Mrs. Apollo to keep him under control.'

'Mrs. Apollo?'

'Mary,' Prometheus explained. 'As you know better than anyone, the only thing capable of dominating a male with unlimited physical strength is a female with a comparable amount of mental strength. I don't think it'll take Mary very long to get Apollo properly trained, do you?'

'Oh,' said Jason. 'So Mary's ...'

'Yes,' Prometheus replied. 'It's not what was fated, I know, but you take it from me, you've had a very lucky escape there. Bear in mind that Mary is also your Sharon.'

'Ah yes,' said Jason. 'That's a very good point. Thank you.'

'Well, then.' Prometheus yawned and stretched. The sun was starting to sink behind the Caucasus mountains. In the distance, Apollo and Mary were going for a quiet stroll, talking pleasantly of this and that. A couple of Forms in white coats were trying their best to persuade Jupiter that it was safe to come down from his tree. 'That more or less wraps it up, then,' Prometheus said. 'Thanks for everything, Jason. We couldn't have done it without you. Or rather, you couldn't have done it without us.'

'Will the world be a better place?' Jason asked.

Prometheus shook his head. 'I doubt it,' he said. 'It always amazes me, the way the old place quickly gets back to normal no matter what you do to try and improve it. No, you can make it worse, no problem, but it's virtually impossible to improve it. I tried, remember. I gave them fire, and yet millions of people are still cold. I taught them agriculture, and millions of them are still starving. I gave them laughter, and yet the majority of them are still as miserable as income tax. I can only imagine it's how they like it, deep down.'

'And what are you going to do?' Jason asked.

'Me?' Prometheus grinned. 'I'm going to have a holiday, what the hell do you think? After that, I don't know. I might have a shot at sorting out the gods a bit more, but I doubt it. Anyway, I mustn't keep you any longer. Thanks again.'

He smiled and then grew, until they lost sight of his head, then his body, and then finally his kneecaps in the clouds. And then he simply wasn't there any more, and Jason and Mrs. Derry discovered that what they were actually looking at was a mountain.

'Right,' said Mrs. Derry. 'Let's be getting home. I could do with a cup of tea, and you could do with a bath.'

'Mum ...'

'A bath,' Mrs. Derry repeated, 'and no arguments.'

'But Mum, I had one this morning ...'

'Jason,' said Mrs. Derry.

Just then, a helicopter appeared in the sky. In it were Betty-Lou Fisichelli and her agent, a camera crew, and a glass tank containing a frog. The frog seemed agitated, and Ms. Fisichelli was doing her best to comfort it by saying that it was all going to be all right, that Apollo would soon turn him back into human shape and then give him the most incredibly historic interview of all time, just so long as he minded his manners and promised never to coin the phrase Olympusgate as long as he lived. The frog lashed out at the glass wall of its prison once or twice with its hind legs, said 'Rivet' bitterly, and then nodded its head.

'It's been a long day,' said Mrs. Derry. 'Did you understand what that man was saying about aggravation and your Dad and all that?'

Jason considered for a moment. For the first time in his life he had a vague, shadowy idea of what was going on. It was the beginning of wisdom.

'No,' he said. 'Good, here's George with the cart. Come on, Mum, in you get.'

*

In his Lear jet, thirty thousand feet above Nebraska, Mr. Kortright was speaking to Nostradamus on Blue.

'It's a neat idea, sure,' he said, 'and I like it in principle. But you've got to ask yourself, maybe you're aiming your stuff at the wrong slice of the market, okay? I mean, do the people really want to know about Napoleon? Do they really give a two-cent fuck about the advent of nuclear war? That sort of thing just kind of depresses people, Nos, you know? Why do you always have to be so goddam *gloomy*?'

There was an agitated buzzing from the end of the wire. Kortright sighed, murmured something about maybe having lunch Thursday, and replaced the receiver. He ate a pickled onion.

'Odin for you on Red, Mr. Kortright.'

Kortright swallowed a few shreds of peel and picked up the phone. 'Odin,' he said, 'how's tricks? Afraid you missed the boat again this time, but we'll keep trying for you, you know that.'

The receiver turned into a serpent in his hand and Kortright put a broad, friendly smile on his face. Nobody likes having a disgruntled client.

'Look, I've been thinking,' he said. 'What we need for you is a brand new vehicle. You know, launch you from an entirely different angle. I mean, we've tried blood and human sacrifice and all that; how about making you, well, cuddlier? You know,' said Kortright, keeping a straight face in spite of himself, 'lovable. We could say you originally came here from another planet and you got stranded, and we're trying to fix it so's you can go home ...'

The serpent glowed blue and sprouted another head. Kortright made a comforting gesture with his hands.

'Okay,' he said soothingly. 'We'll put that one on ice for now. What you really need,' he went on, 'is a Gospel.'

There was an interested hiss from the serpent.

Kortright thought for a moment, and then smiled.

'With a good Gospel,' he said, 'we could go places with you. We could get sponsorship, you know? Commercial backing. We could make the big time.'

The serpent coiled itself round Kortright's ankle and started to eat his shoelaces. This was, the agent told himself, a good sign.

'How about something like this?' he said. '*In the beginning was the Word, and the Word was Kawaguchi Integrated Circuits, and all rights in the Word were reserved, so that unauthorised publication thereof in any form of cover or binding or electronic data retrieval system other than that supplied by the publisher rendered the user liable to civil and criminal prosecution . . .*'

The serpent bit him.

Jason Derry leaned back, wiped the soap suds out of his eyes and reached for the rubber duck.

On the one hand, he said to himself.